E.1

W9-CFV-173

ECHOES OF BETRAYAL

ECHOES OF BETRAYAL

Una-Mary Parker

This first world edition published 2009
in Great Britain and in the USA by
SEVERN HOUSE PUBLISHERS LTD of
9–15 High Street, Sutton, Surrey, England, SM1 1DF.
Trade paperback edition published
in Great Britain only 2010 by
SEVERN HOUSE PUBLISHERS LTD

British Library Cataloguing in Publication Data

Parker, Una-Mary.
   Echoes of Betrayal.
   1. Aristocracy (Social class) – England – Fiction. 2. Murder –
   Investigation – Fiction. 3. Family – Fiction.
   I. Title
   823.9'14–dc22

ISBN-13: 978-0-7278-6818-3   (cased)
ISBN-13: 978-1-84751-180-5   (trade paper)

Except where actual historical events and characters are being
described for the storyline of this novel, all situations in this
publication are fictitious and any resemblance to living persons
is purely coincidental.

All Severn House titles are printed on acid-free paper.

Typeset by Palimpsest Book Production Ltd.,
Grangemouth, Stirlingshire, Scotland.
Printed and bound in Great Britain by
MPG Books Ltd., Bodmin, Cornwall.

Acknowledgements

I would like to thank Maighread Simmonds for bidding at a charity auction to become one of the characters in this book, thus benefiting the Breast Cancer Haven.

I would also like to thank Alexia Dwarka for her researching expertise and Manuel Pereira Fernandez for his legal knowledge and advice.

Prologue

Buckland Place, Kent, December, 1941

Even after all these years Cathryn could not bear to walk through a certain part of the woods where the fast rushing stream curved sharply back on itself, swirling around a boggy piece of land that protruded from the far bank like a small island. This had long since been cleared of brambles and nettles and the ivy-throttled pine trees which had fallen into sodden decay and become entangled with scattered branches of hornbeams and poplars. Still a torpor of despair, malevolent and dank, hung over the spot, clinging to it like a mantle.

Even the surrounding oaks and elms bowed their branches broodingly as if they too mourned, while the water bubbled and gurgled softly over the stones with a rushing sound, but who could hush the wind whispering in the long grasses? Telling a tale of something terrible that had happened here.

She turned away and although she tried to blot the horror from her mind as she walked towards the open fields with the dogs, she couldn't help remembering the suspicions, the accusations and the ramifications that had followed, tearing apart both the family and the local community. And if there were others who chose to forget the events of that autumn in 1930 when she'd come here as a bride, she would never be one of them, because for her nothing had ever been the same again.

One

DEBUTANTE TO WED DIVORCED PEER

There are shock waves in Society circles as rumours have surfaced of an impending marriage between eighteen-year-old Cathryn Brocklehurst and the thirty-five-year-old Marquess of Abingdon, who figured in a scandalous divorce two years ago. This has set tongues wagging . . .
The Daily Express, Friday 6th June, 1930

THE COURT CIRCULAR

The engagement has been announced between Nicolas James Hillier, 7th Marquess of Abingdon, eldest son of the late 6th Marquess of Abingdon and Conceptia, Dowager Marchioness of Abingdon, of Buckland Place, Kent, Tyndrum Castle, Argyllshire and Eaton Square, London, and Miss Cathryn Honour Brocklehurst, only daughter of Sir Roland Brocklehurst, Bart, and Lady Brocklehurst, of Wilton Crescent, London, and The Elms, Berkshire.
The Times, Monday 9th June, 1930

Cathryn stared at the newspapers, feeling as if it were someone else she was reading about. The facts were right, and she was definitely the young lady whose photograph was plastered on the front page of every newspaper, in her white court dress with the Prince of Wales feathers and short veil on the back of her head, but she couldn't relate it having anything to do with her and Nicolas. They'd met at a cocktail party three months ago, and when their hostess introduced them they'd both felt an instant attraction, a feeling so powerful she knew in her bones they were destined to be together.

'How do you do,' he said, shaking her hand politely.

She looked up at him, taking in his attractive face and quirky smile.

'How do you do?' He held her hand a fraction longer than was necessary.

'So you're coming out this year?' he asked. 'Are you enjoying yourself?'

'Very much. It's all much more fun than I expected,' she replied, suddenly feeling rather immature and silly. The men she'd met during the season were much younger and very boyish compared to this man, who she guessed was in his thirties. As they talked she became aware of the sheer vitality of his presence as he stood looking at her, and she loved the laughter lines that fanned out around his dark eyes, but most of all she loved his voice. It was deep and rich and quietly powerful.

When, after a few minutes of light conversation, he asked her out to dinner, she'd accepted without a second thought as if being taken to the Savoy Grill by a complete stranger was the most natural thing to do. It never even crossed her mind that her mother would be appalled if she knew she was unchaperoned.

It quickly became obvious that Nicolas felt the same way about her. He swept her off her feet with his warmth and charm, taking her everywhere and wining and dining her in all the best restaurants. Everyone knew he was one of the richest men in England but they were also aware he came with a past. While her friends looked on with fascination mixed with apprehension, Cathryn remained oblivious to the drawbacks of forging what could be a dangerous relationship.

Carried away by the excitement of falling in love with this charismatic man, Cathryn revelled in his sophistication and the fact that he was much travelled and worldly in a way she'd never known existed. She'd had to tell someone of her joy or she'd explode, and instinct warned her it shouldn't be her parents. Not yet, anyway.

Within a month of meeting Nicolas Abingdon she'd decided on impulse to call on her friend, Maighread Simmonds, the society hostess who had first introduced them. This feisty Irish redhead who lived with her husband, Vere, in a grand house in Knightsbridge, was someone she could trust and a woman of the world who could give her sound advice.

'You're just in time for tea, my dear,' she welcomed Cathryn, as she led her into a drawing room crammed with an eclectic mix of beautiful antique furniture, paintings, ornaments and books, set against a background of rich fabrics in vibrant colours.

Maighread didn't believe in formality or in following the dreary style of decor that had become so fashionable following the extravaganza of the Edwardian era. Popular, witty and outspoken, she loved to boast that she'd been expelled from her school in County Limerick because the nuns had described her as 'the boldest girl in the convent'. Demure and acquiescent she was not.

'Sit down and tell me all your news. I can't wait to hear what you're up to, Cathryn,' she said with exuberance. They settled themselves on either end of an immense sofa upholstered in emerald green damask.

'I've fallen in love,' Cathryn blurted out. 'You remember you introduced me to . . .'

'Nicolas Abingdon,' Maighread cut in triumphantly. 'How could I forget? His eyes were out on stalks when he saw you, and I could tell you weren't backward in coming forward!'

Both women laughed.

'I've seen him every day since,' Cathryn admitted. 'He's so divine.'

Maighread's blue eyes twinkled naughtily. 'You're very brave to take him on. What do your parents think?'

There was a pause. 'They don't know about him yet. I've managed to keep it from them but I suppose I'll have to tell them sooner or later.'

'They won't let you marry him, you know. Not under the circumstances. It's not that long since he got divorced.' Her tone was flat, dismissive.

'I'm sure they would if they got to know him.'

'My dear, you must be mad!' Maighread said incredulously. 'He's certainly a catch, I'll say that for him, but you'd have an awful price to pay if you married him. You do realize there's a terrible stigma to divorce?'

'I don't care, Maighread. I've never felt like this about anyone before—'

'You're so young, that's why.'

'—and all I want is to be with him, forever.'

Suddenly Maighread clapped her hands delightedly, her large amethyst and diamond ring flashing on her finger. 'Good for you! That's the most romantic thing I've heard since a friend of mine ran away from a convent to get married to a monk who had escaped from a monastery. To hell with the consequences! Sex won in the end! Is that how it is between you and Nicolas?'

Cathryn flushed scarlet. 'Really! I mean, we haven't!'

'Mother of Mary, the child's blushing.' Maighread jumped to her feet and pressed the bell by the side of the fireplace. 'Forget about tea. What we need is a stiff drink.'

Two months later Nicolas Abingdon went to see Cathryn's father, to ask for her hand in marriage. He and Sir Roland remained closeted in the study for a long time, while Cathryn stayed in her room, too nervous to come downstairs.

An hour later she heard the front door being closed. Slowly, with her heart hammering, she crept down the stairs, wondering what had happened. At that moment her father came slowly out of the study and looking up, gave her a sad smile.

'I'm afraid it's out of the question, dearest. I can't give my consent, under the circumstances.'

Cathryn had braced herself, fearing this would happen, but hearing his words made her feel cold and sick with misery.

'Daddy, I want to marry him more than anything else on earth. We love each other. He's a really nice kind man who would make me happy '

'But he's been married before. He's *divorced*!' her mother wailed, coming out of the drawing room. 'As soon as I heard he wanted to meet your father I feared the worst. How long have you known him? What do you know about him? How could you even *contemplate* marrying a divorced man!'

'But we're in love, Mummy.' She was feeling panic-stricken now. What was she going to do if they forbade her ever to see him again?

Lady Brocklehurst spoke quite harshly, for her. 'Love has got nothing to do with marriage except for the lower classes, because they've got nothing to lose. If you were married to this man you'd be ostracized! Hostesses would strike you off their guest lists. You'd never be allowed into the Royal Enclosure at Ascot again! You've got to remember that affairs of the heart are overlooked, but divorce is not.'

Cathryn retorted angrily, 'Nicolas hasn't been shunned by anyone. He's invited everywhere.'

'That's because he's a man, and a man with a powerful position,' Sir Roland explained. 'He's titled and immensely rich. He owns vast properties in England and Scotland. He's a man's man and a nice enough fellow. Men can still get away with things a woman can't. You'd suffer socially if you became the second wife, and people would wonder if you might not be succeeded by a third or fourth wife, like the much married Duke of Westminster. We can't let that happen to you.'

'Papa, I don't care,' she said stubbornly. She knew she might be committing social suicide but Nicolas meant more to her than anything else.

That evening she tried to talk to her elder brother Charles, who was a solicitor and worked in his father's chambers, but he sided with their parents.

'It would cause a terrific rift in the family, Cath,' he warned her. 'The Brocklehursts have never been associated with a divorce.'

Cathryn knew what he said was true, and she did feel heartbroken at upsetting her parents, but there was no way she could resist Nicolas.

'I can't bear the thought of being without him, 'she told her mother tearfully the next day. 'I don't want to hurt you and Daddy, but please don't make me choose between you and Nicolas. I know you'll like him once you get to know him.'

'That's not the point, Cath. Do you really want to marry someone with such a *past*?'

'Nicolas can't help his past. It's not his fault that Miranda ran away. Why should he be punished for it?'

Lilian Brocklehurst spoke fretfully. 'It's what people will say that matters; about him and about you for marrying him. I do wish you'd marry a nice young man, who has a good reputation and a thoroughly respectable background. Like Edward Willoughby or Archie Carnegy. I'd rather you settled for a steady man than someone who is rich and titled but notorious.'

The argument went on for days between Cathryn and her family, and torn between her love for Nicolas and duty towards her family, she was unable to sleep at night.

One of the things her mother had taught her was that it was unseemly for a girl to telephone a young man. It looked too keen, too pushy, she explained. Men didn't like to be chased.

Up to now Nicolas had always been the one to contact her to make the arrangements for their next meeting. Now, however, desperate to speak to him, she made the bold step of going to a call box in the street and dialling the number of his Eaton Square house. The butler answered, and informed her politely that he'd see if his lordship was at home.

Standing in the chilly box, her hands shook and her voice wobbled dangerously when she heard his voice. 'Darling, is that you?' he asked.

'I wondered if I could see you,' she said, tears springing to her eyes, her voice wobbling dangerously.

'Of course, sweetheart! Where are you?'

'I'm in a call box at Hyde Park Corner. Nicolas, I know what my father said to you, and I'm so unhappy . . .' Her voice caught on a sob and she couldn't continue.

'Oh, my darling one . . . !' He spoke tenderly. 'Don't give up hope, because I haven't. Listen, jump into a taxi and come straight here. I'll be waiting for you.'

Crying openly now, she hailed the first cab she saw. By the time she arrived at his magnificent white stucco-fronted house, she felt a wreck. Her nose was pink and her eyes red-rimmed as she hurriedly tried to powder her face. Clutching a damp hand-kerchief in one hand, she handed the driver a shilling with the other, and then hurried up the front steps. The door opened immediately and there was Nicolas. He held out his arms and as his butler diplomatically averted his face, he pulled Cathryn and held her tightly and reassuringly for a moment, as she stood with her face buried in his shoulder.

'Come into my study, sweetheart,' he whispered, taking her hand and leading the way, as if she'd been a child.

'I want us to be married,' she said impulsively, knowing her mother would be horrified by her forwardness. 'You don't need my father's permission, Nicolas. I'll be twenty-one in two-and-a-half years' time, and then they can't stop me.'

He wrapped his arms around her before sitting in an upright chair and pulling her gently down on to his lap. Then he kissed her urgently as if he never wanted to stop.

'I don't think I can wait that long,' he whispered. 'I want you now, darling. I've never felt like this about anyone and I promise you, nothing is going to part us.' His voice was rough with passion. 'We're meant to be together, my darling, and by hook or by crook I'll make sure we are.'

Cathryn wound her arms around his neck, feeling safe and much loved again. 'I was afraid Daddy might have put you off,' she said earnestly. 'I simply couldn't have borne that. What are we going to do? Run away together to Gretna Green?'

He laughed and pulled her close again, kissing her neck and stroking her hair. 'I'll do anything you want, just to be with you. Let me talk to your father again, sweetheart.'

'My mother's the one who needs talking to,' she observed, regaining her normally feisty spirits.

'Then let me take your mother out to luncheon so I can exercise my powers of persuasion,' he retorted, chuckling. Looking tenderly into her tear-blotched face, he raised his hand to stroke her washed-out cheek. 'My darling one, always remember that no matter what happens, I love you more than anyone else on earth and I always will,' he added, before bringing his mouth down hard on hers.

That evening, empowered by the realization of the passion that linked her to Nicolas, she bravely issued her parents with an ultimatum.

'If you don't give your consent to my getting married then we'll elope,' she said fiercely.

'Oh, my God!' wailed her mother. 'Do you *have* to marry him? Are you . . . ?'

Cathryn turned scarlet with rage. 'Of course I'm not! How could you think such a thing? Nicolas is an honourable man and he would never . . .'

Sir Roland his wife looked at each other. The fight went out of them at that moment. Cathryn had always been stubborn and headstrong. Maybe they should be thankful for small mercies, including the fact that at least Nicolas Abingdon hadn't taken advantage of their daughter.

The next day Sir Roland gave his consent to their marriage, and Nicolas, overwhelmed with happiness, presented Cathryn with a magnificent emerald and diamond ring, promising her she'd never regret her brave decision.

'But what will be expected of me as your wife?' she asked,

suddenly nervous when she saw the formal announcement of their engagement in *The Times*.

'I just want you to be yourself, darling,' he assured her tenderly. 'Once we're married we'll stay in our Eaton Square house during the week, then we'll go to Buckland Place at the weekends, and I thought I'd take you to Scotland for our honeymoon; would you like that?'

'As long as I'm with you, I don't care where I am.'

Hugh Verney had been the estate manager of Buckland Place for the past fifteen years and he enjoyed a close working relationship with his boss, Lord Abingdon. They made joint decisions on the running of the house, the 1000-acre home farm, the nineteen cottages which were let out to tenants, and the extensive woodland and gardens, which included large glasshouses that grew both fruit and vegetables out of season, and also flowers for the vast house which had more than seventy rooms.

In principle, Hugh had to make sure the work was carried out to their agreed specifications and he had a team which included maintenance men, farmers, gardeners, foresters, stable hands, drivers, domestic staff and even experienced restorers of antiques and ancient fabrics, to carry out the work. It should have been a straightforward job. Unfortunately, he was stymied at every stage by the interference of the Dowager Lady Abingdon, who insisted on remaining in Buckland Place with her younger son, Lord Ewan Hillier, although there was a delightful Dower House in the grounds, which was kept in hopeful readiness for immediate occupation.

'Don't worry,' Nicolas had told Hugh when he first got the job. 'Pretend to agree with my mother but go ahead and do as we've discussed. It's easier to allow her to think she's still in charge than to argue. She got used to running the place when my father died and I was only a child, but things have changed and if Buckland is going to survive in the twentieth century, and they're saying there's going to be a bad Depression that will wipe out a lot of the stately homes, we've got to implement modern methods and make cuts where necessary.'

Their *modus operandi* worked beautifully and the two men soon became firm friends, and Hugh was delighted when Nicolas announced his engagement to Cathryn. He'd never got on particularly well with the first wife, mainly because she seemed terrified of everything and everybody, but on meeting Cathryn when she came to visit Buckland he saw a young woman of purpose and strength who was obviously going to be a delight to have around.

One morning Nicolas came to his office, which was situated at the end of a long corridor on the ground floor of Buckland, with a list of things he wanted done.

'I'm going to be in Scotland for a while, on honeymoon you know,' he announced, grinning, 'and while we're away can you get them to do some clearing in the woods? There are a lot of rotten trees that have blown down and brambles and bracken cluttering up the place, especially around the stream on the western side. We need to draw up a schedule for replanting so it's not so dense. At the moment it reminds me of one of Arthur Rackham's spooky illustrations,' he added, laughing. 'I expect to be pounced on by a pixie or a wicked witch at any moment!'

The only wicked witch around here, Hugh reflected privately, is the Dowager Lady Abingdon, but he remained resolutely silent. One could only push one's boss's sense of humour so far.

Three months later, on Wednesday 10th of November, 1930, Cathryn and Nicolas were married in the Caxton Hall Registry Office, and according to the newspapers she wore a pale blue dress and coat trimmed with blue fox fur cuffs and collar and a small blue hat. There was no great ceremony, no big reception afterwards, and her mother wept throughout the short civil proceedings.

In the end only half a dozen close friends, including Maighread and Vere Simmonds, attended, while Nicolas's family stayed away altogether, his mother declaring that she and Ewan 'didn't want to be part of a vulgar circus'.

In contrast to the quietness of the panelled room in the Registry Office, they were shocked by the great roar of 'Hurrah!' from the crowds when they emerged. It hit them like an incoming tidal wave, as people shouted and waved and flashbulbs popped all around them. The traffic was at a standstill and the police were frantically trying to move on the dozens of photographers who had gathered, some standing with their tripods on the roofs of vans and cars, others jostling and shoving amid the mass of curious passers-by.

Cathryn felt as if her senses were being roughly pounded. They were showered by confetti and rice and there was a chorus of 'good luck' mingled with the photographers' aggressive demands to 'look this way', along with 'over here!' and 'just one more'.

'Get into the car,' Nicolas urged, pushing her forward. More cheers surrounded them as they clambered into the Rolls and then the chauffeur edged his way through the clamouring throng. As she looked out of the back window she caught a glimpse of her parents as they emerged from the building to a barrage of flashing lights. Her father looked old and her mother distressed. For a moment she felt dreadful. They'd never really wanted to give their consent and although her mother admitted she was making 'a brilliant marriage' as far as money and position were concerned, she warned that it would come at a dreadful price. Nicolas was much older than her, and he had the reputation of a boulevardier. At that moment Cathryn felt him clutching her hand under the fur rug that lay over their knees, and a wave of breathless excitement swept through her.

They were actually married! By this time tomorrow they'd be in Scotland and her life as Nicolas's wife would have begun.

Cathryn fell in love with Tyndrum Castle the moment she set eyes on it. Originally built in the thirteenth century as a medieval fortress, it stood on high ground overlooking Loch Linnhe, on the western coast of Argyllshire. As was popular in the reign of Henry III, it was a small circular castle, set within a quadrangle of high stone walls, topped by ramparts. When she realized one could only enter by crossing the wooden drawbridge, which was suspended thirty feet above the grass slopes that had replaced a moat many years before, she turned to Nicolas, her face alight with excitement.

'You never told me it was like this. I feel as if I'm walking into a fairy tale,' she exclaimed.

He grinned. 'The happiest days of my childhood were spent here. My father used to let us run wild, much to my mother's fury. She thought Ewan and I should be brought up like Little

Lord Fauntleroys, not crofters' kids living in kilts and thick dark blue jerseys. I had the run of the place,' he added wistfully. Then he paused, his arm around her waist as they stood on the drawbridge, his other arm flung out towards the loch and the surrounding heather-clad mountains. 'I'd explore the rocky beach and caves from morning till night or I'd climb upstream to where I discovered brown trout lurking in the pools! I had such a happy childhood.'

She pressed herself close to his side. 'And that came to an end when your father died, when you were only six?' she asked softly.

He nodded. 'Everything changed from then on.' Then he looked lovingly into her eyes. 'We'll let our children run wild here one day, won't we? They can go fishing on the loch, learn to shoot rabbits and hares. We'll have lots of dogs. Oh, I wish we could live here permanently. Coming here helps keep me sane.'

'Why don't you stay here all the time? I'd love it, you know. I really would.'

Nicolas planted a swift kiss on her temple. 'Running Buckland takes too much time for me to make this my permanent home. And maybe,' he continued thoughtfully, 'this place is special because I am only here occasionally. Come on now. Let's get inside so I can show you around your new Scottish home.'

He led her through the front entrance into a great lofty hall, with its oak staircase at the far end, and a large fireplace where logs crackled and blazed. The instant impression she had was of dark panelling, reflecting the flickering of gas lamps, rich tapestries, Jacobean carved furniture and red velvet curtains. Pewter tankards and plates glinted from the shelves of a sideboard and in the centre a round table was heaped with leather-bound books.

'It's so cosy,' she exclaimed in surprise. 'I expected it to be all suits of armour and bowls of dusty heather.'

Nicolas laughed. 'My mother hates this place but even she wouldn't stand for it being formal and uncomfortable.' Then he led her to the dining room, which was furnished with a long polished refectory table and carved chairs. The dark green walls were hung with fine landscapes and there were golden-coloured brocade curtains on the windows.

Beyond it, through double doors, was a snug drawing room, warm and welcoming with deep sofas and armchairs, and she noticed a card table topped with green felt, beside which were shelves filled with jigsaw puzzles, playing cards, a set of chess men, glass marbles for playing solitaire and other games.

'This is a real holiday home, isn't it?' she remarked appreciatively as she looked around.

When they reached their bedroom, she drew in her breath sharply when she saw the view from the windows, which were on two sides of the room. For as far as she could see, majestic blue mountains rose from a glittering loch where fishing boats bobbed gently, while seagulls swooped fitfully in the hope of stealing a catch from their nets.

'Paradise, isn't it?' Nicolas whispered, joining her and putting his arms around her.

To Cathryn it was more than paradise. She'd never imagined how wonderful it would be to be staying in this beautiful place and married to a man she loved more than anyone on earth. And this, she reflected with euphoria, is only the first day of the rest of my new life. From now on, they had so much to look forward to, and everything, she was sure, could only get better and better.

It was a week later that Nicolas received a telegram as they were having breakfast.

'When did this arrive, Craigie?' he asked the butler as he snatched the buff envelope from the silver salver and ripped it open.

'A few minutes ago, m'lord.'

Cathryn watched him as he read it. The past seven days had been the happiest she'd ever had in her life. She and Nicolas had become even closer and more compatible than she thought possible. Surely nothing was going to disturb the perfection of their honeymoon?

'What is it, darling?' she asked anxiously, as she saw his expression harden.

Nicolas sighed deeply and his mouth tightened. '"A crisis has arisen. Stop."' He read aloud. '"Return to Buckland immediately. Stop."'

'Oh, no!' Startled, she put down her cup of coffee, spilling some in the saucer. 'Who is it from?'

There was the slightest pause before he answered. 'My mother.'

'Oh!' The mother-in-law from hell. The mother-in-law who

had refused to come to their wedding, or even meet her family. 'Why? What's happened?'

'I've no idea.' Nicolas spoke impatiently. 'I suppose I'd better put a call through to find out what it's about, but I'm damned if we're returning home unless it's a real emergency.'

Cathryn watched him stride purposefully out of the room, tall and handsome in his kilt and tweed jacket. A feeling of desire flickered through her and she wished there weren't so many servants around, invading their privacy. He was her first lover and he would be her last. He'd taught her that making love was wonderful, fulfilling and an almost sacred act of true belonging in a way she'd never realized existed before.

'Hell and damnation!' he muttered a few minutes later as he came storming back into the room, scowling at the telegram in his hand.

'Nicolas . . . !' She jumped up from the table. 'What's happened?'

'I'm most terribly sorry, darling, but we've going to have to go south. I've spoken to the estate manager, and there's an emergency to do with the estate. I've got to be there to deal with it.'

'What sort of emergency? Is someone ill?'

'Worse than that, but don't worry. It's got nothing to do with us personally but I need to be there.'

'But we've only just arrived.' She failed to keep the disappointment out of her voice.

'I know, sweetheart. It's a great shame.'

'I'm so happy here. Just the two of us . . .' She fought back childish tears.

He turned to look at her, suddenly smiling tenderly. 'It is great here, isn't it? I'm so glad you love it as much as I do and I wouldn't have had this happen for the world, but we really do have to go. I promise I'll make it up to you. Of course, if you'd rather, you can stay on here while I nip down to Buckland. The staff will look after you . . .'

'Wherever you go, I go too,' she said with firm resolve. 'Now that we're married I never want to be apart from you for a single moment.'

He raised one of her hands and kissed it gently. Then he looked directly into her eyes. 'I'll make sure you keep that promise.'

★   ★   ★

Lying on the top bunk of their luxurious first class sleeper that night as the Flying Scotsman thundered through the darkness to London, Cathryn remained awake and alert. Tomorrow she and Nicolas would be at Buckland Place for the first time as a married couple and she wondered which of the thirty bedrooms would be theirs. No doubt it would have a four-poster bed and overlook the gardens, but would it be the master bedroom? Or would Nicolas's mother have kept that for herself in perpetuity? Then there was Ewan, whom she hardly knew, except that the two brothers could not have been more different: the eldest so dashing and charismatic, full of self-confidence and *bonhomie*; the younger one quiet and sulky, behaving all the time as if the world owed him a living.

Who exactly was now going to be mistress of Buckland Place? In all the excitement of getting married she hadn't considered the future domestic arrangements, but the more she thought about it now, the more apprehensive she became. As she lay, unable to sleep, she recalled her previous visit to his home.

Nicolas had invited her to spend a weekend at Buckland shortly after they'd announced their engagement. Cathryn had accepted with alacrity but it hadn't been helpful that her mother had chosen to warn her just before she went about Nicolas's mother, the Dowager Marchioness, who apparently was 'an American'.

'Mummy, how do you know?'

Lilian Brocklehurst gave a defiant shrug. 'I looked them up in *Burke's Peerage*, of course. She was Conceptia Calkin, and she holds the purse strings. Her father was Herbert Lindell Calkin of Chicago. It's said he made millions building railroads. I've since heard the sixth Marquess of Abingdon married her for her money and she married him for the title and position. A real Yankee adventuress she was. The poor man died when Nicolas was six. That's when he inherited everything. His brother, Lord Ewan Hillier, was two at the time. No doubt she drove her husband to his death. Someone with a name like Conceptia is highly suspicious.'

Cathryn cast her eyes to heaven. 'Really, Mummy! Nicolas told me his father was killed in a motoring accident and his mother was heartbroken. He says she's never got over it. It must have very been hard bringing up two small boys on her own.'

'No doubt she had nannies and a vast staff,' Lilian scoffed, a tinge of jealousy in her voice. 'I see she's never remarried. Well, she wouldn't want to give up that title, would she?'

Expecting Nicolas's mother to be sweet and motherly, Cathryn had been shocked to find herself face to face with a tall thin woman, with black hair cut fashionably short and permed, and her face a mask of heavy white make-up, with scarlet lips and rouged cheeks. Stony-black eyes had looked piercingly at Cathryn and her American accent and voice had been as dry as dusty autumn leaves.

'So you're Cathryn Brocklehurst,' she'd rasped, extending a cold bejewelled hand. 'I'm glad Nicolas has chosen to marry you instead of another simpering little fool like last time.'

The two women – one blonde and fair-skinned, with high cheekbones and a warm smile, the other dark, bitter and pinched looking – sized each other up as if wondering how they were going to handle this new relationship.

Cathryn took a deep breath. 'Nicolas has told me so much about you and I've been longing to meet you,' she said, which wasn't exactly true because Nicolas never mentioned his family, but it sounded polite.

'Has he indeed?' Conceptia drawled lazily. 'You must make yourself at home here, honey. Get Nicolas to show you around – although Ewan, who has an eye for art, knows more about the house than anyone else.' Then she turned to Nicolas. 'Are you going to make yourself useful by mixing us some cocktails before luncheon? I like a Manhattan at noon.'

Over the next twenty-four hours Cathryn came to realize that the historic seventeenth century country seat of the Abingdon family was breathtakingly beautiful, yet the atmosphere was far from friendly.

Everywhere Cathryn looked she saw carved doors and damask-covered walls, gilt framed family portraits, ornate marble fireplaces and crystal chandeliers. Each room in the vast house, which was run by an enormous staff, was also furnished with the finest collection of antiques in England.

It was a house in good taste, she reflected, rich in heritage with contents worth millions of pounds, which Nicolas took for granted because he'd known nothing else.

One thing was certain, though. Her mother was going to adore it. It might even persuade her that Cathryn had done the right thing by marrying Nicolas.

It was morning when the train steamed into St Pancras Station, and exhausted after her sleepless night, Cathryn was thankful to sink back into the soft grey leather interior of the waiting Rolls Royce, in which they would be driven by their chauffeur down to Kent.

When they neared the village of Appledore she could see Buckland in the distance, gleaming like a large precious stone set amid the lush countryside. Nicolas was frowning and looking preoccupied as he stared out of the window.

The glass screen between them and the chauffeur was closed, but she still kept her voice low. 'Do you think there's something seriously wrong on the estate, darling?' she questioned.

Nicolas shrugged and glanced at her quickly, before resuming his brooding gaze at the swiftly passing landscape. 'Serious enough for Hugh Verney to think I should return.'

She slid her hand under the car rug and rested it on his thigh. A moment later he placed his hand on top of hers, gripping it fiercely. It was obvious he didn't want to talk.

Cathryn's imagination, already in full flow during the long hours of the night, now went into overdrive. For some reason she had a feeling it was to do with Nicolas's previous wife.

As it happened, the truth was far more horrifying than anything she could have imagined.

Two

KING GEORGE V DISSOLVES PARLIAMENT

The House of Lords last night voted against the People's Budget. As a result Prime Minister Herbert Asquith faced a constitutional crisis as miners threatened to strike unless a deal can be struck with the Unions. Fears that a General Strike over pay could lead to a revolution in the country has forced the King, the first Monarch since 1640, to dissolve parliament . . .

The Morning Post, Monday 21ˢᵗ November,1909

Buckland Place, 24ᵗʰ November, 1909

The laundry room at Buckland Place was hot and steamy and great cauldrons of boiling water, provided by a steam engine, bubbled and frothed, as sheets and pillowcases were lowered into them before being stirred and beaten with wooden paddles. The humidity was so dense the white tiled walls dripped with condensation and the stone floor was always wet with puddles, slopped from buckets and sinks. Two dozen washerwomen, sweating and red-faced, with their sleeves rolled up, busily soaped shirts and linens before scrubbing them against corrugated washboards with a brush. With only two windows at one end of the room which were never opened, the overpowering smell of soap and the pungent sharpness of bleach stung their throats as it permeated the clouds of mist that hovered over their heads. Bags of soda stood in one corner, below shelves of bottles of blue. Exhausted by the stifling heat the women worked for twelve hours a day, six days a week.

On the floor above, where the air was allowed to circulate freely through slatted shutters, the laundry was hung out to dry each day on brass wire lines before being taken to where it would be ironed in another room which was arid with heat, the air parchment dry, as rows of irons were heated on large coal stoves.

Above the noise of the engine spitting jets of steam and the clank of metal buckets, the women had to shout to make themselves heard as they stood before a line of sinks, rubbing and squeezing the smaller items of laundry with their strong hands, before passing them through heavy mangles, requiring one person to turn the handle while another fed the washing through the rubber rollers. The talk was of the plight of the miners – the King appearing to sympathize with them – and their own low wages. 'Bleedin' unfair it is!' yelled one of the women. 'Trust the politicians . . . ! I wish we belonged to a ruddy union!'

Poverty, bad conditions and discontent was the lot for casual workers and that's what most of the washerwomen were. Whilst the rest of the servants lived in and were well fed and looked after, those who were casual labourers and lived in rented cottages in the nearby village were grateful to be getting sixpence for a ten hour day.

Posy's mother, Ida Burgess, was one of them. She brought her only child with her as there was no one to leave her with, because Frank Burgess looked after the cattle on the home farm.

Posy knew how to amuse herself, for she was a bright child with a heart-shaped face, big intelligent eyes and dark curling hair, and she had a sense of curiosity about this enormous place where her mother worked. She sat quietly in a corner, playing with stones she'd collected in the garden, watching the women as they slaved over their sinks, and listening to the coarse banter as they exchanged bits of gossip amid raucous laughter.

When they tired of talking about what was happening to the miners and instead chatted about the goings-on 'upstairs' of the Abingdon family, Posy was especially interested. She was fascinated to hear about the two boys whose mother owned Buckland. The eldest, Nicolas, was fourteen now, and Ewan ten. She loved to hear about the ponies they rode, the expensive toys they had, and the delicious food that was served on silver platters up in the day nursery by three footmen in livery. She watched with envy as her mother washed their exquisite shirts, their soft-looking striped pyjamas and their pure woollen socks.

Posy longed with all her heart to be a part of this fairyland of plenty. She'd once had a peep into the state dining room before a banquet and had been transfixed by the grandeur of the table that seated forty-eight, laden with a king's ransom of sparkling gold, silver and crystal. There were magnificent displays of flowers and candles down the centre and the plates were edged with deep crimson and gilt. Compared to the damp thatched cottage with a privy in the back yard in which she lived with her Ma and Da, this was indeed a glimpse of paradise.

Posy had a dream. One day she'd be a grand lady like the Marchioness of Abingdon, living in a big house with cupboards full of beautiful clothes and drawers crammed with jewels. She'd have wonderful food to eat, several times a day instead of only once, and there'd be cups of hot chocolate to drink. She'd also give the washerwomen a shilling a day and send them home with hot pies and puddings for their children.

Sometimes she followed Nicolas and Ewan as they played in the garden or in the nearby woods, dodging behind trees or bushes so they wouldn't see her. They were sporting little boys, like their late father, and she admired them from afar, pretending to herself that she was their friend, and that they were really playing hide-and-seek.

They never realized she stalked them, of course. They were so intent on what they were doing. And why should they? With her grubby little face and skimpy cotton frock barely covering her thin body, she knew she wasn't pretty or smart.

Her mother never knew she followed the 'Abingdon boys' as the washerwomen called them, but when she climbed into her little truckle bed at night she lay staring up at the sagging ceiling, imagining herself lying in a big bed with a canopy, wearing a white lawn nightdress edged with lace. There'd be servants to wait on her hand and foot and bring her a boiled egg and toast in bed, every morning.

On this particular day, when the wash house was at its busiest and Ida Burgess and the other women were in heated discussion as they plunged the paddles into the bubbling cauldrons, wondering what would happen if they all went on strike over poor pay, Posy went up to her mother and said she was going to go into the garden to look for more stones. She knew it was half-term and she hoped to catch sight of the Abingdon boys, but she didn't tell her mother that bit.

Ida Burgess nodded absently. 'Don't be long, mind you! It'll be dark soon!'

Promising she'd be back shortly, Posy turned and stepped out into the garden to meet her destiny.

Three

POLICE RE-OPEN CASE AT BUCKLAND PLACE

Police are carrying out an investigation at the home of the Marquess of Abingdon who recently married the former debutante Miss Cathryn Brocklehurst in a Registry Office ceremony in London. The couple are understood to be returning earlier than expected from their honeymoon. His mother, Conceptia, Dowager Marchioness of Abingdon, remained out of sight at Buckland Place yesterday and his former wife, Miranda, Lady Abingdon, who now lives in London, was unavailable for comment last night . . .

The Kent Messenger, Wednesday 17th November, 1930

Raised voices in the baronial hall echoed under the lofty carved ceiling and reverberated across the stone floor. In the centre, a group of people were clustered around a shabbily dressed woman in her sixties, who was tearing at her grey unkempt hair with puffy red hands, her face haggard and contorted with anguish.

'I'll get you for this!' she howled. 'I'll make you pay!' Then she spat at Conceptia Abingdon, who stood rigidly with Ewan by her side, as if immobilized by shock.

Two men in dark suits grabbed the woman's arms on either side and tried to pull her away from the group. 'That's enough!' one of them said gruffly.

The butler and the under-butler stepped forward as if to protect her ladyship from the appalling conduct of this lowly washer-woman who lived in the village, but she was not to be silenced.

'I'll see you all rot in hell! He promised me he'd look after her . . .' she sobbed hysterically.

Aghast, Cathryn turned to look at Nicolas. His profile was grim as he marched up to his mother.

'What the devil's going on?' he demanded, glancing around at the group, which included several footmen, three of his foresters and two uniformed policemen. 'I understood they'd found the body of a poacher in the woods? What is Mrs Burgess talking about?'

Conceptia's voice rang out with harsh authority. 'This woman is hysterical. She doesn't know what she's saying.'

One of the men in dark suits dropped his hold of Mrs Burgess, who was weeping bitterly and shaking her head like a wounded beast. He drew Nicolas to one side.

'Lord Abingdon, if I might explain the situation to you? I'm Detective Inspector John Harding. The reason for Mrs Ida Burgess being here is that the skeleton of a child has been discovered buried in your woods and there's a possibility it is the remains of her daughter, Posy, who vanished in 1909. Your foresters made the discovery the day before yesterday, when they were clearing down by the stream that runs through the western area of your estate.'

Nicolas blanched white. 'What? Little Posy Burgess?' he exclaimed incredulously. 'Dear God, she went missing over twenty years ago!'

'Yes indeed, Lord Abingdon. The conclusion at the time, following extensive searches, was that she'd been abducted by gypsies who were camping around this area.'

'Oh my God!' Nicolas rubbed his forehead and his shoulders sagged as if he'd been punched. 'Oh, my God.' Then he turned and went up to Mrs Burgess.

'I'm so, so sorry.' He spoke with compassion. 'This must be a tremendous shock for you. You have my deepest sympathy . . .' His voice faltered for a moment. 'What a dreadful thing! And after all these years. What on earth can have happened?'

She shook her head and, swaying, dabbed her face with a grubby piece of cloth.

'Fetch Mrs Burgess a chair and some brandy,' he commanded.

'That woman has been very rude to me.' Conceptia spoke loudly. 'I don't know why you're making such a fuss of her. It's got nothing to do with us.'

Nicolas threw his mother a filthy look, then remembering they were surrounded by people, he turned back to Mrs Burgess once again.

'What can I do to help?' he asked earnestly. 'I realize nothing will bring Posy back, but I can make sure she's given a proper funeral, with a headstone where, God willing, both you and she will find some peace after all these years.'

Her tearful eyes, buried in the red swollen skin of her face, looked at him in utter despair. 'Now I know it wasn't the gypsies what took her away, I believe she was murdered.'

Nicolas flinched at the word and looked at the Detective Inspector. 'Have you any idea what happened?'

'At present we—' Harding began, but Mrs Burgess interrupted him.

'I want to know who killed m' little girl,' she whimpered, tears rolling down her cheeks again. 'She was murdered, an' that's for sure.'

Instinctively Nicolas drew back, shocked, his face deathly white.

At that moment, Cathryn realized this was just the beginning of something truly dreadful.

'The woman's off her head,' Conceptia cut in angrily. 'Get her out of here, Constable. She'd no right to come barging into my house in the first place.' She turned fretfully to her younger son who was watching the proceedings, his face pale and his mouth slack with shock. 'Come along, Ewan. All this fuss has given me a terrible headache. I must go and lie down.'

Cathryn watched, stunned, as her mother-in-law tucked her arm through Ewan's and they mounted the staircase together, without a backward glance.

'Was she really murdered?' Nicolas asked DI Harding in a low voice.

'All we are certain of at the moment,' Harding replied, before dropping his voice to spare the dead child's mother, 'is that we've found the skeleton of a child. After all these years the remains are in bad condition. We've put up a tent and roped of that area of the woods, while our forensic team examine the bones *in situ*, and the surrounding ground. It's painstaking work and may take a while. At the moment we're in no position to ascertain the cause of death. Obviously, we'll find out more when the remains have been fully examined.'

Nicolas nodded. 'You'll keep me informed?'

'Of course, Lord Abingdon. Whatever the findings, we'll need to take statements from everyone who worked or lived here on

the estate at the time.' Then he averted his gaze, as if embarrassed.
'I should explain that at this stage we haven't yet started our
official enquiries. We are here today because your mother, the
Marchioness, called us to report an intruder. She requested we . . .
ummm,' he paused, embarrassed, '. . . we remove Mrs Burgess
from the premises, telling us she had mental problems and should
be locked away in an asylum.'

Nicolas's mouth tightened. 'Mrs Burgess isn't mad. I've known
her all my life; she's just understandably distressed. She worked
here until the day Posy vanished . . .' he drew his brow together
and closed his eyes for a moment, as if trying to remember something. 'Why on earth would anyone want to harm that little girl?'

'I'll be talking to Mrs Burgess when she's less upset to see if
she can throw any light on the case. Meanwhile, we'll take her
back to her cottage in the village.'

'Let me know if I can do anything.'

'We'll be in touch, Lord Abingdon.' He gave Nicolas a searching
look before adding, 'I can promise you that.'

Conceptia remained in her private sitting room that evening,
sending Ewan down with the message that she was unwell and
would have her supper on a tray.

'I'll stay with her to make sure she's all right,' Ewan said. 'She's
had an almighty shock today, with that wretched maniac from
the village turning up here like that.'

'The poor woman was terribly upset,' Cathryn pointed out.
'She's probably spent the last twenty years praying her daughter
would turn up one day.'

'Well, she *has* turned up, hasn't she?' Ewan retorted brutally.
'And damned inconvenient for all of us it is.'

Nicolas looked at him sternly. 'That's enough, Ewan. Have
a little respect for Mrs Burgess. It's a dreadful situation. I
remember the day Posy went missing. I was on an exeat from
my first term at Eton and we went riding in the morning. It
was the day before the gypsies left the area and moved on, and
I suppose that's why everyone jumped to the conclusion they'd
abducted her.'

'I don't remember.'

'Oh come on, Ewan! You must remember. There was a terrific
hue and cry.'

Ewan eyes widened. 'I was only ten! How the hell am I supposed to remember something that happened all those years ago?'

'One doesn't forget a thing like that, especially when it happens on one's own front doorstep. I can remember the day our father was killed and I was only six.'

Ewan sat in brooding silence, gazing out of the window at the garden.

'Did you all play together, you and this little girl, when you were small?' Cathryn asked, hoping to defuse what looked a pending row between the brothers.

'Play together!' Ewan exclaimed scornfully. 'Don't be stupid. We weren't allowed to play with the village children. My mother said if we did, we'd catch dreadful diseases.'

The next morning, while Nicolas had a meeting with the estate manager, Cathryn took the short walk down to the village, carrying a basket of apples and a bunch of chrysanthemums for Mrs Burgess. She felt compelled to offer her sympathy and give what comfort she could to the distressed woman, for whom she felt profound pity.

Posy, Nicolas had told her, had been an only child and her parents had waited a long time before she was born, so her arrival after ten years must have seemed like a miracle to them.

As Cathryn walked down the main street of the picturesque village, with its thatched cottages with small square windows and little smoking chimneys, she saw an elderly lady, well-dressed in a dark blue coat and hat, coming out of the local post office. Going up to her, she asked, 'Excuse me, but could you be kind enough to tell me which is Mrs Burgess's cottage?'

The lady eyed her up and down, taking in Cathryn's burgundy tweed coat trimmed with mink and her small burgundy velvet hat. Then she smiled in a friendly fashion.

'You must be the new Lady Abingdon?' she asked, in a well-spoken voice.

'That's right.' Cathryn smiled back. 'We only got back from our honeymoon yesterday. Your name is . . . ?'

The blue eyes in the wrinkled face were gentle and motherly. 'I'm Mrs Pilkington,' she announced. 'I've lived at Ivy Lodge all my life and I can tell you anything you want to know about the village and who lives here. You obviously heard they've found poor Posy Burgess's body? Isn't it a tragedy? I'm so sorry for her mother.'

Cathryn nodded. 'Yes. I don't know what I can do, but I'm on my way to see her.'

Mrs Pilkington spoke sadly. 'The poor little mite. I can't bear to think of her buried in those dark woods for all these years. That child didn't deserve what happened to her.'

Cathryn felt taken aback and didn't quite know how to respond. 'I'm sure she didn't,' she replied lamely, 'but what do you mean?'

'You look like a nice young woman,' Mrs Pilkington continued, ignoring the question. 'I hope you and Nicolas will be very happy, in spite of this terrible start coming so soon after your marriage.'

'Thank you. I'm sure we're going to be very happy together. I'm so lucky to have found someone so marvellous.'

'Good luck to you, then!' Mrs Pilkington waved her gloved hand, pointing to a row of rundown little houses. 'Ida Burgess lives in the third one along. I bet she's thinking, "The Lord gaveth, and the Lord hath taken away," and she'd be right.' Then she looked into Cathryn's eyes as if trying to convey something, before turning and walking off in the opposite direction without another word.

Wondering what she meant, Cathryn watched her go. Then she hurried down the lane and a minute later was walking up the narrow cinder path to knock on the Burgess's door.

A weedy little man with sideburns and a tweed cap opened it and stared at her with startled eyes.

'Yes?' he asked sharply.

Cathryn had a sudden and awful vision of herself, all dressed up in expensive clothes and jewels, like a Lady Bountiful, visiting 'the poor'.

She flushed with embarrassment. 'I'm Cathryn Abingdon, I've come to see Mrs Burgess; is she in?'

'Ida!' he called over his shoulder into the dark gloomy interior. He too looked awkward and, whipping off his cap, shuffled his farmer's boots and muttered, 'You'd best come in, m'lady. The missus ain't too good today.'

Cathryn entered, and instantly smelt the stench of poverty and despair that hung like a miasma over the low-ceilinged room. The small fire in the grate gave out more smoke than heat and what furniture there was looked battered. Ida Burgess sat in a deep chair, her legs covered by a stained patchwork blanket made of knitted squares of different colours stitched together. Beside her on the floor was an empty mug. Looking around, Cathryn instantly realized her offerings were unsuitable and inadequate. What this couple needed was hot soup, a meat pie, eggs, butter, bread, cheese. Hastily putting the apples and flowers on one side as if wanting to get rid of them, she perched herself on the edge of an old kitchen chair with a wonky leg and spoke firmly, although inwardly she quaked; what if this decent hardworking couple were offended and thought her behaviour patronizing?

'Mrs Burgess, I want to help,' she began tentatively. 'I'm so terribly sorry about Posy, as is my husband, and there must be something we can do to make life a bit easier for you? I will see that a hamper of food is brought to you this afternoon, but what else can we do?'

Ida gazed at her with red-rimmed eyes, almost blinded by grief. 'A bucket of coal would be nice. It's ever so cold in this cottage,' she said and there was the pain of the squalor and deprivation of the gutter in her voice.

Cathryn felt her heart constrict. Human beings shouldn't be living in these terrible conditions. Even the horses at Buckland had luxurious stables by comparison and the dog kennels were warm and comfortable.

'I'll also arrange that today,' she promised, determined to add to the list blankets and bedding, clothes, hot water bottles and candles, because the only means of lighting appeared to be an ancient oil lamp. 'Have you heard any more from the police?'

Ida shook her head, and produced the same grubby piece of cloth she'd had the previous day with which to wipe her nose. 'I don't know when they'll let us have Posy back, so as we can bury her.' She sounded disconsolate, as if overtaken by a sense of helplessness. 'What are we going to do now? I'd always hoped she'd find her way home one day and come back to us, right as rain.' A sob broke from her throat. 'And now I know that's never going to 'appen and my baby's gone for ever.'

Frank Burgess had shuffled out to the back yard and through the dingy little window Cathryn could see him now, head bent

low as he tenderly patted a mangy goat that was tethered to the
fence, his head bowed as if the pain was too much to bear.

Cathryn rose swiftly, eyes stinging. Their agony was becoming
her agony. 'I'll go now, Mrs Burgess, and I'll see you get everything you need.' Then she hurried out of the cottage and walked
back to Buckland, unable to get the scene of hardship and suffering
she'd just witnessed out of her mind.

When she entered the hall she heard raised voices. Hurrying
into the library, she found Nicolas in a state of confrontation
with his mother and brother. The atmosphere was tense and filled
with hostility as they faced each other, unaware of Cathryn
standing in the doorway.

'This is all your fault, Nicolas,' Conceptia shouted from where
she stood with her back to the fireplace, a skeletal figure in dark
blue, her face bleached white and her eyes blazing in their
sockets. 'If you hadn't given orders for that part of the wood
to be cleared so you could do some more of your damned
replanting, none of this would have happened. Why can't you
leave things alone? You're always meddling. Always wanting to
change things.'

'Mother, Buckand belongs to me. I give the orders here,' he
retorted hotly.

Cathryn had never seen him look so angry and she was startled by the fervency of his feelings. Since she'd known him he'd
always seemed relaxed and easy going but now she saw another
side to him; a determination and strength that she couldn't help
admiring.

'You're never *here*!' Ewan chipped in pettishly. 'How can you
expect to run the estate properly if you're up in London all the
time, chasing after women!'

At that moment they all noticed Cathryn's presence.

'Darling!' Nicolas strode over to her.

She gave him a quick intimate smile before turning to Ewan.
'Not women, just one woman: *me*,' she said lightly, but there was
a steely look in her blue eyes that dared him to say anything
more.

Ewan shrugged and turned to look knowingly at his mother
as if to say *I told you she'd be trouble*.

'Ewan's right,' Conceptia said, agreeing with her younger son as usual. 'Nicolas is always gallivanting off somewhere, so it's left to me to keep the place running smoothly.'

Nicolas looked at her squarely. 'No, Mother. It's up to me and Hugh Verney. He's the estate manager and we make joint decisions.' More gently he added, 'I relieved you of the burden of running Buckland when I came of age. Remember?'

'And a fine mess you make of everything, including your first marriage,' Conceptia snapped, hurrying out of the room and slamming the door behind her. Ewan followed her like a lap dog, the epitome of a mother's boy who has been over-nannied and over-indulged all his life.

'What did your mother mean by that?' Cathryn asked. 'I thought your first marriage ended because your wife wanted to go back to her previous boyfriend?'

'That's what Miranda said at the time, but I have a feeling it was just an excuse because she wasn't happy here. In fact, she wasn't happy anywhere. She hated the London house, too. Said it was too big. Then she complained that Tyndrum was too cold. The truth is we simply weren't suited and it's my fault for having asked her to marry me in the first place,' he admitted.

'That's quite sad.'

Nicolas shrugged. 'I'm sorry about that scene just now, darling. Mother's inclined to forget she's no longer the chatelaine here. She still thinks it's 1893, when she married my father and we had ninety-two indoor servants and over a hundred gardeners and foresters working in the grounds. My father always let her do whatever she wanted, and as she had the wherewithal to pay for everything, she rather got used to getting her own way.' He gave a wry smile. 'D'you know she was the only person in the whole house who had a bathroom with a flushing loo in those days? We all had to use chamber pots or commodes, and the watermen had to carry our hot bathwater upstairs in great buckets. We didn't even have electricity until the turn of the century.'

'Talking of hardship . . .' Cathryn began.

'Oh, there was no hardship,' Nicolas pointed out. 'We had a wonderful life until 1914, when the Great War started. It's really been downhill all the way ever since. We don't have more than around thirty living-in staff nowadays . . .'

'Nicolas,' she cut in, 'I've just seen a case of extreme hardship

that I didn't know existed outside a Charles Dickens novel, and
we must do something about it.' Then she told him about her
visit to Frank and Ida Burgess.

'I don't want to get on the wrong side of your mother,' she
added, 'so who shall I get to deliver the things they need so
badly?'

'Give a list of the things you want sent to them to Mrs Temple,
our housekeeper. She'll arrange it all it for you. I'd no idea they
lived in conditions like that,' he added, thoughtfully. 'They're not
one of our tenants; if they had been, Hugh Verney would have
done something about their cottage years ago.'

'So do all the staff who work here live in?' she asked in amazement. 'How many bedrooms have you got, for heaven's sake?'

Nicolas laughed, his anger with his mother forgotten. 'Never
counted!' he retorted cheerfully. 'I must show you all over the
house some time. It's another world on the other side of the
green baize door. Why don't we walk over to the home farm
now? It's too good a day to stay indoors.'

'Frank Burgess works there, doesn't he?'

Nicolas looked surprised, as if he'd forgotten. 'That's right. I
believe he does.'

'How much does he earn?'

'God, sweetheart, I've no idea. The estate office does all the
wages.' He grinned, squeezing her hand. 'You're going to be a
proper little charity worker, aren't you?' he teased, 'fussing round
to see that everyone's looked after.'

'One can't let people on one's own doorstep *starve*,' she said,
feeling slightly hurt at what she took for criticism, 'and believe
me, Mr and Mrs Burgess are starving. Maybe you should tell your
estate manager to raise Mr Burgess's wages?'

'And have everyone on the estate demand higher salaries, too?
That would be a nightmare,' he added, raising his eyebrows at
the thought.

Cathryn looked at him and realized he wasn't joking.

'But you're so *rich*!' she blurted out.

His expression was pained. 'We used to be broke. My grandfather nearly went bust as the result of some bad investments. It
was touch and go. He even contemplated selling up, but then he
died and my father married my mother, and she's been the one

who has restored our wealth. She brought with her an enormous dowry from America that meant my father didn't have to sell Buckland or Tyndrum. Otherwise we'd only have been left with Eaton Square, which we've always rented from the Duke of Westminster anyway.'

Cathryn reflected that her mother had been right. It had been a marriage of convenience. And whichever way you looked at it, Nicolas was indebted to his mother for his inheritance. No wonder she still lived at Buckland; how could he possibly turn her out? In fact, both sons were under a huge obligation to Conceptia and it was obvious she intended to force them to remember that.

Cathryn went over to a big oak desk in the window, where there was some crested writing paper, a brass inkstand and some pens on a brass tray.

'I'll make the list and give it to Mrs Temple now,' she remarked amicably, 'and I'll impress on her that the things must be delivered to Mrs Burgess this afternoon, as I promised.'

It was, she knew, a tiny step in asserting herself as the rightful chatelaine of Buckland. She would go slowly, but in time it was her place, as Nicolas's wife, to make these sort of domestic decisions, and make them she would, whether Conceptia liked it or not.

When Nicolas and Cathryn returned from looking around the farm a couple of hours later, he went straight to the estate office to have a word with Hugh Verney, while Cathryn decided to go to their private suite to change. She was crossing the hall when Conceptia came marching out of the library, almost as if she'd been lying in wait.

'What are you trying to do, Cathryn? Undermine my authority?' she demanded loudly. 'How dare you tell Mrs Temple to take food and bedding to that imbecile in the village? It will look as if we're bribing them at a time like this.'

Cathryn looked at her in blank astonishment. 'What on earth do you mean?'

'You're a bigger fool than I thought! Posy's body has been found on our land and in their ignorance and stupidity, they may try to hold us responsible. If we suddenly ply them with food and fuel and home comforts, it could look as if we're trying to buy their silence.'

'But why would they think we had anything to do with their child's death?'

'You know what these ordinary peasants are like,' Conceptia snapped back. 'They'll try and get blood out of a stone, and if we pander to their wishes, they'll just demand more and more.'

'But Mrs Burgess didn't ask for anything. I offered to help because I couldn't bear to see the miserable conditions they are living in. Nicolas approved of what I was doing. Now I've got to go to find Mrs Temple to say we've decided to send them what they need, after all.'

Conceptia eyes widened as if she couldn't believe her ears. For nearly forty years she'd reigned supreme at Buckland and she didn't intend to let go the reins to a mere girl of eighteen, who was only the daughter of a Baronet anyway. This was war, and her eyes narrowed to dark slits in her white face.

'Don't think young lady for one moment that I'm going to let a jumped-up little debutante tell me how to run this place. Mark my words, Nicolas will tire of you as he's tired of dozens of girls in the past, including his first wife. He's like his father, you see. A charming philanderer, an adulterer, a womanizer. Only stupid little girls like you and Miranda get taken in by his flirtatious manner; the others are happy to leave with a nice piece of jewellery. You'll soon learn you're yesterday's favourite! He'll be finding excuses to go up to London while you stay down here.'

Stung by the venom of her mother-in-law's outburst, Cathryn looked at her steadily and spoke in even tones. 'I think you'll find I'm not like "the others". I'm here to stay, as Nicolas's wife. And I intend to do my duty as his wife no matter what anyone else says.' Then she turned and walked calmly away, up the stairs to her own quarters.

Once inside, behind closed doors, she found she was shaking. Of course Nicolas had had girlfriends before and after his first marriage. He was a sophisticated man in his mid-thirties and it would have been strange if he hadn't had various flirtations, but surely he wasn't a *womanizer*?

Sitting down at her dressing table she gazed at her reflection as if hoping to find the answers. Was she just one of Nicolas's many conquests? Would she be succeeded by a third or even a fourth wife? Her parents' warnings came flooding back. 'He's got a bad reputation.' 'He can have any girl he wants.' 'He's too charming to be trustworthy.'

She studied her face with care. Was she strong enough to cope with a philandering husband, if what his mother had said was true? Steady blue eyes looked back at her. She had a generous mouth and a firm jaw line in a face that was openly honest and serene. Hers was not the vampish little face of Miranda, with the cupid's bow mouth and blank, intrinsically stupid expression that she'd seen in the newspaper photographs. In her heart she did not doubt his fidelity, but his mother's words were nevertheless upsetting.

It struck Cathryn with uncomfortable force that Conceptia was a dangerous woman who did not want her here in the first place. She was obviously going to take every opportunity to make mischief, to try to drive her away as she'd probably driven the first wife away.

Filled with resolution, she decided she would not let that happen. She might only be eighteen but she knew how to look after herself and with Nicolas beside her, she was unafraid. To tell him what his mother had said would be pointless and only make things worse, but in future when she gave orders to the staff she'd make it clear that they were her orders, regardless of what the Dowager Lady Abingdon said.

Four

ARMISTICE SIGNED BETWEEN BRITAIN AND GERMANY

After four years, the Great War came to an end yesterday, on the eleventh day of the eleventh month at the eleventh hour, when Britain and Germany signed an Armistice Treaty . . .
                              The Daily Telegraph, 12th November, 1918

Kent, 25th November, 1918

Hilary Pilkington dressed with care in her bedroom at Ivy Lodge as she got ready to go to the party Nicolas Abingdon was holding at Buckland Place to celebrate his twenty-third birthday. Wounded in Northern France, he'd been granted leave on his return to England and had asked his estate manager to issue invitations to over a hundred of his closest friends and neighbours. From her window the previous day she'd already had a glimpse of him as he drove through the village in his open Peugeot 5HP, looking handsome and dashing in his uniform. No one knew, not even her widowed mother, how much she'd longed for this night. Nicolas was back from the war, safe and sound, though thousands hadn't been so lucky. The insanity of the conflict had practically wiped out a generation of young men and she thanked God that at least the man she loved had been spared. Nicolas, whom she'd adored since they'd both been small children; Nicolas, with whom she played in the garden of Buckland – they had ridden their bicycles side by side when they were ten and twelve years old. Nicolas, for whom she'd wept when he was sent away to Eton but who came back in the holidays with the healthy bloom of ripening adolescence in his cheeks, yet a look of innocence still in his dark eyes. Then finally Nicolas when he grew into the prime of his manhood with athletic grace, a ready laugh and enormous charm. There'd been a farewell dinner party at Buckland the night before he joined his regiment to go to fight for his country and he'd kissed her when they'd said goodbye.

The memory of that kiss, so warm and firm and impulsive, had remained with her ever since. He'd pressed his lips to the corner of her mouth, pulling her close in his arms, and whispered, 'I'll be back soon.'

She looked at her reflection in the long mirror in her bedroom now. She'd grown into a pretty young woman, with curves and long chestnut hair piled up into a chignon, since he'd last seen her. Would he remember their kiss? Would he be filled with desire when he saw her again? Would he whisk her into another room and hold her close and kiss her again, and say he'd promised to return, hadn't he? Were all her daydreams about to come true?

Full of excited anticipation yet sick with nervous longing, she fastened the clasp of a small string of pearls around her neck, picked up her evening bag and carrying her dark blue velvet cloak over her arm, hurried down to the drawing room, where her mother was sitting, reading.

Anne Pilkington appraised her daughter's appearance with her gentle blue eyes.

'You look very nice, dear. That dress suits you; pink is such a pretty colour. Samuel's waiting in the car to take you up to Buckland, and he'll collect you just before midnight.'

'So early, Mummy?'

'I don't think the party will go on until late, you know. Anyway, it's never a good thing to be the last to leave.'

Hilary wished she could stay at Buckland forever. All she wanted was to curl up in a large bed with Nicolas, and spend the rest of her life by his side.

'I'll be off then,' she said, giving her mother a quick kiss.

'Come and see me when you get back and tell me how you got on. I'll still be awake.'

'I will!' With shaking hands she let herself out of the front door and stepped into her mother's ancient car, with their gardener acting as a chauffeur for the evening.

When she arrived at Buckland, the party seemed to be already in full swing. She could hear dance music coming from one of the salons, and there were footmen standing holding trays of champagne. Young men in uniform were mingling with beautiful girls wearing clinging silk and chiffon dresses in strong vibrant colours, their skirts falling in deep folds from low on the hips, their satin evening shoes dyed to match. Loud chatter punctuated by bursts of laughter came from the big dining room, where she could see a buffet supper had been laid out.

Suddenly feeling rather washed out in her old-fashioned pink frock and not recognizing anyone she knew, she took a glass of champagne from a silver tray and started searching for Nicolas. She'd expected him to be in the hall, receiving his guests with his mother, but there was no sign of Lady Abingdon and no sign of him either.

'Hello there!' said a man's voice. She spun round, but her disappointment was clear to see when she realized it wasn't Nicolas.

'Hello,' she replied distractedly. 'I was looking for Nicolas . . . ?'

'Ah-h-h!' The handsome young captain looked knowing. 'The last time I saw him he was in the library with his girlfriend.'

Blindly, dizzily, her heart frozen in her chest with dread, she scurried down the corridor just in time to see Nicolas leaning forward in the library doorway. He was putting his arms around a slim girl with short blonde hair, who had her arms linked around his neck as he pulled her close. They were kissing and kissing and her head was tilted back and then she placed her long slender fingers on either side of his face as if to bring him closer still.

'Is that you, Hilary? Good gracious, girl, what's happened?' Mrs Pilkington rose from her chair in concern as Hilary staggered into the room, bedraggled and tear-stained, with her new pink shoes ruined with mud.

'I had to get away,' she sobbed. 'I've walked home. I couldn't stay another minute. It was too dreadful for words.' She collapsed into a chair, unable to speak for crying.

Her mother frowned. 'I don't understand. You've only been gone half an hour. The party is being held tonight, isn't it? We didn't get the date wrong?'

'He's . . . he's got a girlfriend.'

Mrs Pilkington watched her daughter with a detached curiosity. 'You mean,' she asked carefully, 'you'd hoped you'd be able to pick up where you left off nearly four years ago? That you'd still be chums?'

'Not just chums . . . ! I've always been in love with him,' Hilary blurted out. 'I thought . . . the last time we said goodbye . . . that he was in love with me, too. He promised me he'd be back.' She doubled over in the chair, as if in physical pain. 'I've prayed every night that he'd survive the war and come back to me, and I was so sure he'd . . . he'd . . .' but she couldn't finish the sentence.

With dawning realization, Mrs Pilkington patted her daughter's shoulder. 'Yes. I see,' she said thoughtfully. Young girls often imagined themselves in love, especially with someone who wasn't around to disprove the situation. 'Did he ever tell you he loved you?' she asked tentatively.

Hilary's head shot up defiantly. 'He didn't have to. He kissed me.'

Her mother sighed. That was the trouble with living in a village where there weren't any suitable young people for Hilary to meet. The girl was naïve and inexperienced. She'd blown up what had probably been no more than a friendly gesture from Nicolas into a Romeo and Juliet fantasy.

'Did anyone see you leave?'

'I don't know. There were so many people there and I didn't know anyone . . .' She covered her face with her hands and rocked back and forth. Then she jumped to her feet and threw her evening bag into the smouldering fire.

'I'll never forgive him for this!' she burst out passionately. 'He's ruined my life. After all my prayers . . . I wish he'd died. I wish he'd been killed . . . !'

'Hilary! Control yourself at once. You're hysterical!'

Hilary wasn't listening. Taking off her spoiled shoes she threw them one by one into the fire as well. 'I don't care how long it takes, I'll get even one day!'

Five

CHILD'S BODY FOUND AT PEER'S HOME

Following the discovery of the remains of a child, thought to be that of nine-year-old Posy Burgess, in the wooded area of the Marquess of Abingdon's family seat, many of the locals in the adjacent village of Appledore are finding it hard to remember the details of the day she vanished in 1909.

'It's so long ago,' said a close friend of Nicolas Abingdon, who spent yesterday with his solicitors. 'A lot of the people in the village weren't even born then. What we know is mostly hearsay from our parents and grandparents.'

The second Lady Abingdon, eighteen-year-old Cathryn, a debutante the Marquess married only a few weeks ago, also remained out of sight at the family home. A member of their staff told us they wished to make no comment at this time . . .

Daily Mail, Friday 19th November, 1930

'It's a nightmare,' Cathryn told her mother, as they talked on the telephone. She was sitting in the library and being careful what she said, because she couldn't help feeling that Conceptia might be listening in on an extension.

In the past few days the two women had been careful to avoid each other, except when Nicolas was in the room, and then his mother was sweetness itself, purring that it was lovely to have them both around at this terrible time and she hoped they wouldn't be rushing back to London.

The atmosphere in the house was tense and the gossip in the village feverish.

Everyone had a theory about Posy's disappearance – from the women who had been working alongside Ida in the wash house on the day she'd vanished, to the local gentry who talked darkly about the child's background.

Newspapermen were camping on the grass verges outside the

main wrought iron gates of Buckland, and Nicolas had ordered several male members of staff to go to the assistance of Jack Stevens, the gatekeeper, who was feeling the strain of having to deal with endless requests for information from reporters and photographers.

Gardeners and foresters had also been posted around the perimeter of the estate to prevent anyone sneaking into the grounds.

'It's like being under siege, Mummy,' Cathryn continued. 'I can't even go out for a walk, except on to the terrace where I can't be seen.'

'Why don't you come and stay in town with us?' Lady Brocklehurst coaxed. 'Your father and I would love to see you.'

'Mummy, I can't leave Nicolas.'

'Oh darling! This is turning into an absolute disaster. Even worse than we'd thought. It was such a mistake to marry Nicolas, you know.'

'Mummy, there's no point going over all that again. We're married and we're blissfully happy, apart from this dreadful upset. There's no turning back now.'

'But you're all over the newspapers these days, like some Hollywood actress. Daddy can't bear going to his club because everyone's ribbing him about your notoriety.'

'This has nothing to do with Nicolas, though. It's not his fault that this child's remains have been found. He's as shocked as everyone else.'

Lilian Brocklehurst was not to be comforted. 'Yes, but because of his divorce and reputation as a socialite, and because the little girl was found in the grounds of *his* estate, Daddy says he's news-worthy, whatever that means. *Everything* you and he do for the rest of your lives is going to be written about. It's so terribly vulgar, darling.'

'That's something we're going to have to get used to,' Cathryn pointed out. 'Lots of people get written about and they're totally respectable.'

'Yes, for entertaining royalty, like the Duke of Devonshire, for example. The Prince of Wales spent last weekend at Chatsworth; that's quite different to Nicolas being connected with a scandal, yet *again*! How much worse can it get, Cath?'

'But it's got nothing to do with him.' Cathryn was getting very angry at her mother's attitude. 'Do stop making such a fuss, Mama.'

'But can't you see how bad it *looks* . . . !' Lady Brocklehurst bleated frantically.

'I'm sorry but I've got to go now,' Cathryn said impatiently, as Conceptia came into the library at that moment. 'I'll telephone you again soon.'

'Don't bother,' her mother snapped pettishly. 'I'm sure to be able to read all about you in the newspapers.' There was a click as she hung up.

Conceptia, looking distracted, went and sat at the desk in the window. Shocked, Cathryn realized she was crying.

'Are you all right?' she asked automatically.

'I'm just . . . exhausted,' Conceptia murmured slowly. She drew a lace-edged handkerchief from her pocket and blew her nose daintily. Her dark eyes were mournful. 'I've given my whole life for the good of this family: my youth, the country of my birth, my father's fortune, my energy and my heart and soul to bring up two sons on my own. I was once a great beauty, you know.' Her voice dropped to a croak. 'Great artists used to pester me, wanted to paint me. Now I ask myself: what was it all for?' A tear trickled down her sculpted cheekbone and her scarlet mouth trembled.

Cathryn sat down on the other side of the desk, watching her mother-in-law warily.

The older woman did seem genuinely distressed, but was it an act to gain her sympathy? A trick to get Cathryn on her side for some Machiavellian reason? The icy aura that surrounded her mother-in-law was still intact, forbidding comforting contact, but had she glimpsed a chink of vulnerability in Conceptia's steely armour?

'You have two wonderful sons,' she ventured encouragingly, 'and the most beautiful home in England.'

'And a husband who never loved me.'

Cathryn remained silent, certain now she was going to hear another tirade against Nicolas.

'All William wanted was my money. When I was a girl, the English aristocracy were desperate to find rich American wives for their heirs. Droves of us came over and we all married peers of the realm, and thought ourselves lucky at the time.' She looked down at the blank sheet of writing paper she'd placed on the blotter. 'I was in love with William but he was never in love with me. He continued to have affairs throughout our marriage. A brood mare, that's all I was, someone to produce an heir who would grow up to ruin someone else's life.' She pounded the desk with her fist, in a burst of passionate rage. 'That's all he wanted from me. My money and an heir.'

Cathryn blinked, inwardly recoiling. Any woman would be hurt under those circumstances, and she quickly comforted herself with the thought that Nicolas had no motive for marrying her, except for love. But why was Conceptia telling her all this?

'William was rotten to the core,' she continued, leaning back in her chair as if tired. 'I hope to God the business about this child is over soon. It happened over twenty years ago. Why are they making such a fuss about it now? The past is best forgotten.'

Cathryn looked closely at her mother-in-law and wondered where this diatribe was leading.

'That Burgess woman is ignorant and unbalanced,' Conceptia continued, beginning to sound more like herself now. 'She was always a bit irresponsible and she should never have had a child. Now, I must get on and write some letters.'

Cathryn rose. She'd been dismissed from the regal presence. 'I'll see you later, then,' she said coolly, but Conceptia, dipping her pen into the brass inkwell, didn't answer.

Going in search of Nicolas, she found he was talking to Hugh Verney in the estate office in the west wing.

'Hello darling,' he said, jumping to his feet when he saw her. Hugh also rose and pulled up a chair for her.

'What have you been up to?' Nicolas asked.

'Telephoning my mother and then talking to your mother, mostly about the tragedy of Posy Burgess. Isn't there anything I can *do*? I'm feeling a bit useless.'

'It's the waiting that's the worst,' Nicolas agreed. 'I hope they'll be able to move her remains soon, and then we can organize a suitable funeral for her. I can't even bear to look in the direction of the woods without thinking about her being buried there all these years.'

'It's surprising her body wasn't discovered sooner,' Hugh observed.

'It was so overgrown with fallen trees and brambles that it was impassable. That's why I ordered the area to be cleared. Little did I know what would be discovered.'

'Why is everyone suggesting she was murdered?' Cathryn asked. 'She could have fallen and hurt herself so badly she couldn't get home. Then she might have frozen to death, because it was winter when she vanished, wasn't it? '

Hugh looked doubtful. 'Yes, I believe she went missing in November 1909, but I believe a full search was carried out, so she'd have been found if she'd just had a fall.'

Nicolas's voice was hollow. 'I remember everyone on the estate searching for her but it was already dark when her mother realized she was missing so that made it very difficult. I heard people say they were afraid she'd either fallen into the river and drowned or got locked accidentally in one of the outhouses. I can remember them calling her name all through the night. I lay awake, hearing their voices.'

The silence in the room hung heavy as they all sat, visualizing the plight of a nine-year-old child, lost perhaps and frightened, in the dark and densely grown woods.

Cathryn's eyes filled with tears. 'I can't imagine how her mother must have felt when she went missing and how she must be feeling now.'

Nicolas sighed deeply and reached for her hand. 'We're going to do all we can for them. We're increasing Frank Burgess's wages, and we're going to do up their cottage. It belonged to Frank's grandfather and I don't think they've been able to do anything to it for the past hundred years.'

'I'll call on Mrs Burgess tomorrow to see how she's doing,' Cathryn promised.

'Meanwhile, why don't I show you around the nether regions of this house?' Nicolas suggested. 'You haven't been below stairs yet, have you?'

'Not so far.'

Verney smiled at her. He was in his forties, a young-looking jovial man who had managed the Buckland estate for the past fifteen years, and who lived with his wife and three children in one of the houses on the property. 'It's another world, Lady Abingdon,' he assured her cheerfully. 'There are four staff dining rooms, you know, because the hierarchy is taken more seriously downstairs than upstairs. There's also a wine cellar the size of a tennis court, a walk-in safe for the silver, and whole rooms given over to storing nothing but china and crystal glasses.'

Cathryn found it was everything Hugh Verney had said and more. Having shaken hands with over fifty servants of varying importance, and having seen the domestic operation that was carried out on a daily basis, it seemed to her as if Buckland could be a five star hotel, except that Conceptia and Ewan were the only people who actually lived there all the time.

'We used to entertain a lot before the war,' Nicolas explained when she queried the number of staff they employed. 'Hopefully, now we're married, we can entertain again, though perhaps not on quite such a grand scale as my parents and grandparents. It's the building, not the people, that needs so much care and attention. These old houses start to crumble away unless they're properly maintained, and that's why we have to have such a large staff that includes builders, decorators, electricians and plumbers.'

He led her into the laundry room. 'We modernized this after the war. It used to be a hellhole.'

White tiles still covered the walls, and the floor was still made of flagstone, but there were large modern basins and tubs along the wall down one side, with taps supplying hot and cold water, and the eight washerwomen were standing on slatted wooden decking to keep their feet dry. It was still a hot and steamy place though, and the workers were still having to wash and scrub everything by hand, but it was quieter now and more clinical.

Nicolas stood looking thoughtfully around. Then he walked over to the open door that led into the kitchen garden. He paused, and the washerwomen all stopped scrubbing to look at him, their expressions curious.

'What is it?' Cathryn asked .

'It was here that Posy Burgess was seen for the last time. She went out through this door and seemed to vanish into thin air.'

Shaken, Cathryn drew in an emotional breath. 'How do you know?'

'Everyone knows,' he replied, his eyes sombre as they swept

along the watchful line of washerwomen. 'Everyone who was working here that day saw her go.'

Conceptia clutched the telephone receiver and spoke in a deep throaty voice. 'I need you here, David. I don't like what's going on. You don't think . . . ?'

'Calm yourself, my dear. After all these years there's nothing to fear.' The manner of the middle-aged solicitor she was speaking to was silkily smooth. 'Of course I'll come if you really want me to.'

'I do, David. I shan't have a moment's peace until . . . you know . . .,' she paused, hearing footsteps outside the library. 'I can't talk now but come and stay. Just until it's all over.' Her tone was coaxing now, less commanding.

'Very well, my dear. When would you like me to arrive?'

'Today. Come in time for dinner. I'm having to cope with so much here, including the presence of the new wife. You won't like her. She's far too uppity.'

David Partridge chuckled, amused. 'I'm sure you'll keep her in her place, Conceptia.'

'She's not at all *sympathique*. I don't think she realizes how much Buckland means to me, although I told her it was my money that had saved it from ruin,' she grumbled, 'and now with this new worry . . . !'

'Please don't get yourself upset, my dear. It'll be all right, I promise you.'

The next day, as Cathryn was sitting at her dressing table getting ready to go down to breakfast, Nicolas received a telephone call from Detective Inspector Harding, confirming that the skeleton was definitely that of a child between the ages of eight and ten and that the remains were about to be taken to the mortuary.

'That was a foregone conclusion, wasn't it?' Cathryn asked, puzzled.

'I don't think there was ever any doubt about it being Posy's body,' Nicolas replied, looking troubled.

She looked at him closely. 'What's the matter?'

'They've found pellets in the ground around where they found her skeleton. Including some in her skull.'

'What? Rat poison?' She looked horrified. 'I remember when my father had to put pellets in the barn at our place in Berkshire to get rid of them and he told us not to let the dogs go in there. My God, does that mean she was accidentally *poisoned*?'

'No, darling. Not that sort of pellets. What they've found are lead pellets. From an air rifle.'

The shock at the police findings flowed through Buckland like a tidal wave, immersing everyone in horror and causing wild speculation in the servant's hall.

Conceptia, feverish with anguish at the family's good name being 'dragged through the sewers' as she described it, sat huddled in her private quarters with David Partridge, endlessly asking him what was going to happen next. Meanwhile, Nicolas calmly continued to liaise with Hugh Verney on matters relating to the estate, while Ewan pursued his latest fad, which was to write and publish a book listing all the trees of Britain, much to the amusement of the foresters, who said he didn't know his ash from his elder, so how could he possibly write a book?

Cathryn, suffering from insomnia because she was unable to get the thought of a small terrified child being fired at in the darkness of the woods, stayed awake long after Nicolas had fallen asleep. Had Posy died of her wounds? Or had she been killed instantly?

Curled up beside Nicolas in the large carved bed hung with oyster cream damask, she tried to pinpoint various remarks she'd heard made in the past week, hoping that strung together they might form a whole picture that would provide clues about Posy Burgess's death.

What, for instance, had Ida Burgess meant when she'd screamed at Conceptia that first day, sobbing, 'He promised me he'd look after her!'

Who had promised? And what had Mrs Pilkington meant when she'd quoted: '*The Lord gaveth and the Lord hath taken away*'? Had the person who'd given Posy life robbed her of it, too?

Then there was Conceptia. Why had she told DI Harding angrily that Ida Burgess had 'mental problems and should be locked away'? When it was plain the poor woman was suffering from shock and grief?

Cathryn lay in the darkness, racking her brains. Nothing fitted.

She felt as if she was trying to do a jigsaw but was working with pieces from different puzzles. Even Nicolas's reaction to pellets having been found in the ground by Posy's body was puzzling. He'd refused to enlarge on it, telling her curtly 'it didn't matter', but judging by his worried expression it clearly did.

Then she thought about Ewan, still a spoilt child at thirty, who would always be remembered as the man who 'nearly did everything'. He was always dreaming up new schemes, which his mother endlessly financed. He lost interest in every new project, though, and it fizzled out as it was 'not worth doing' according to him.

Even in the short time she'd known the family Ewan had decided he would become an archaeologist and take a trip to Greece 'to dig'. When that lost its appeal, he fancied the idea of writing a biography of Admiral Nelson. 'Such a brave romantic figure,' he enthused, as he bought every book that had ever been published on the subject in order to 'do research' on his hero. Now it was trees.

'He's always been like this,' Nicolas observed, so used to his brother's ways that he no longer noticed. 'He can never stick at anything for long.'

'He's obviously quite clever,' Cathryn pointed out, 'and he's in such a privileged position he could really achieve a lot. Maybe he needs to get married and be settled, and then he'd have a purpose in life.'

'He'll never change.'

'Why don't we introduce him to some nice girls?'

'He'd hate that, darling.' Nicolas smiled warmly at her, as if he was amused by the suggestion.

'But why? He's nice looking and eligible.' she said, mystified. 'I know lots of girls who would go after him.'

'You've got to remember,' Nicolas began slowly and carefully, 'that he was only two when our father was killed, and he's never had a male role model in his life, and so I suppose Mother has kept him too close to her, although I know she thinks it's for his own good. But then she needs him too, now. When Father died she did spoil Ewan dreadfully and let him have anything he wanted. He even slept in her room for years. When he went to Eton he was so unhappy he became quite ill. In the end he was allowed to stay at home with a tutor.'

Cathryn admired his staunch loyalty to his brother and she could just imagine how things had changed after their father died. Nicolas had grown into a strong, handsome and athletic young man while Ewan, being an over-mothered weakling, had clung to Conceptia's skirts for dear life; the mother who was still grieving for the husband she'd loved but who had never loved her.

'That's really sad,' Cathryn said thoughtfully. 'Don't you think it would do him good to get a nice wife?'

Nicolas shook his head, and studied the carpet at his feet. 'He'll never marry,' he replied with finality.

On the outskirts of the village, Ivy Lodge stood by itself in a shady bleak garden of trees and shrubs, where flowers never seemed to bloom and birds never sang.

Mrs Pilkington and her daughter Hilary sat as usual in their shabby drawing room, listening to a wireless. The sound was getting fainter, as the accumulator needed recharging but neither could be bothered to get up and fetch the spare one. Faded cretonne chair covers and curtains patterned with pink and red roses were the only splashes of faded brightness in a room otherwise drained of colour.

Mrs Pilkington looked up from the list she was making. Christmas was only three weeks away and whilst she and Hilary would spend it quietly on their own, she liked to send cards to various distant relatives and friends, 'to keep in touch'.

'Hilary?' she observed. 'Shall we drive into Canterbury tomorrow? I'm going to need over twenty cards and the village shop doesn't have any decent ones. We might have a little lunch at the Anchor afterwards. What do you say?'

Hilary continued to flip listlessly through the pages of the December issue of *Home Chat*.

'Whatever you like, Mother.' Her face had formed itself into planes of discontent over the past twelve years. Her brow was lined and her mouth drooped in a perpetual sulk. Unseeing grey eyes scanned the pages revealing 'Top Tips for the Dining Table' without interest. When was she likely to preside over an elegant dining table entertaining flocks of amusing friends? Stuck here with her widowed mother, her future was about as exciting as that of the inmate of a gaol staring at a blank wall.

Envy dug deep into her heart as she thought of that new bitch-of-a-wife up at Buckland Place. Why was it always someone else and never her who attracted Nicolas?

When Miranda had left Nicolas, for a while Hilary's spirits had soared with renewed hope and expectation. It must mean that Nicolas had got tired of his silly little wife and had asked her to go, for surely no sane woman would actually want to leave *him*?

Hilary told herself he must have realized he didn't love someone as shallow as Miranda. What intelligent man would? A man like Nicolas needed a woman of quality, someone who would help him run Buckland. A friend and companion as well as a lover. Someone like her, in fact.

Hilary chose to ignore the fact that Nicolas had had a stream of girlfriends both before and after his first marriage, because not to do so would be to admit that the only man she'd ever loved was a philanderer. As the years passed they'd seen each other around the neighbourhood and he'd always been charmingly friendly and asked her how she was, but his kindness was like a knife through her heart when she realized he was just as sweet to the eighty-year-old biddies he bumped into in the village.

'Well, shall we go into Canterbury tomorrow?' her mother persisted.

'Yes, all right.'

Mrs Pilkington looked at her quizzically. 'You've seen the local newspaper today, haven't you?'

'Why? What's in it?'

'The police have discovered some lead pellets in the earth where they found the remains of that little girl, up at Buckland. Pellets from an air rifle. They think she might have been shot.'

Hilary gazed out of the leaded glass window, eyebrows drawn together. A flicker of memory . . . or was it a dream? passed through her mind. A distant fragmented recollection . . . boys laughing, running footsteps, passing shadows . . . Then the *pop* of an air rifle being fired that echoed in the chilly mist of a November day when she'd been twelve.

'I'll read it later,' she said slowly. 'So what time do you want to set off for Canterbury in the morning?'

For the next few days, like the refrain of a recurring melody, the vague recollections of a forgotten time kept coming back to Hilary. Sometimes there was a momentary splinter of recall in the dim recesses of her mind . . . but of what? In a fraction of a second it had slipped away again, leaving her floundering in darkness. Something told her she *must* recapture that first flashback. She'd been scared . . . and cold. Had she run home . . . ?

Until . . . until . . . Then it occurred to her that maybe the details didn't matter. As if awaking from a dream, she could always burnish and polish that distant hazy memory to fit whatever way she liked. Make it as bright as the day it happened, in fact.

Six

MURDER ENQUIRY
MARQUESS OF ABINGDON QUESTIONED
BY POLICE

The newly married Lord Abingdon has been arrested and taken to Canterbury police station to be questioned in connection with the skeleton of a child found buried on his Kent estate. A member of the public has come forward and made a statement, the details of which have not yet been released, which led to his arrest. His young wife, Cathryn, is said to be distraught.

The Sunday Dispatch, November 25th, 1930

'Who has made such a statement?' Cathryn demanded frantically. It was a question she'd been asking everyone for the past twenty-four hours.

The shock of Nicolas's arrest and of seeing him being driven away in a police car like a common criminal still caused her heart to pound and her brain to reel with incredulity whenever she thought of it.

'No one in their right mind could possibly think Nicolas guilty of such a thing. It's sheer madness! Why won't they tell us who this 'witness' is?'

'It's known as witness confidentiality,' David Partridge informed her in a serious voice. 'This is very upsetting for your mother-in-law, you know,' he added severely.

'Upsetting for her?' Cathryn retorted. 'What about for Nicolas? And me?'

He gazed at her from under lidded eyes, reminding her of a lazy lizard. When he spoke it was gently and smarmily. 'I'm sure Nicolas will sort it out. Before he can be charged the police have to find some evidence.'

'But there's none to find.'

'Then why are you so worried?'

There was something so loathsome about this older man she could barely stand being near him. He was creepy, with a menacing charm that repulsed her and worried her too. Why was he staying with them, except to pander to Conceptia's whims?

'I'm not worried,' she retorted sturdily, 'but I do have a feeling someone is out to get him.'

'Out to get him?' he repeated softly. 'What a strange observation. What makes you think anyone is out to get Nicolas?'

'Miscarriages of justice do happen. My father knows of many cases when the prosecution has produced twisted statements that have resulted in a jury bringing in a guilty verdict.'

A sly shaft of light flickered in his grey eyes and his loose lips tightened. 'What a fine little advocate you'd make! Quite worthy of the Old Bailey!' he mocked in amusement, while his eyes remained cold.

'Will you kindly keep your voice down,' Conceptia said, storming into the room. 'I don't want the servants to overhear us talking.'

'Neither do I,' Cathryn retorted, flushing with anger, 'but I'm Nicolas's wife, and I have to know what's going on.'

Conceptia and David Partridge exchanged looks. There was a long pause, making Cathryn feel like a child who was too young to be told what the grown-ups were talking about.

'I have a right to be in on every discussion concerning Nicolas,' she reminded them.

'Of course you do, my dear,' the solicitor said soothingly, 'and we have no intention whatsoever of talking behind your back. Why should we? We all want what is best for him.'

The three of them regarded each other coldly, as they seated themselves on chairs in a triangle of hostility.

'Nicolas should sue for defamation of character,' Cathryn said forcefully. 'At the moment his reputation is in shreds.'

'We have to wait and see what happens first.' David leaned back in his chair, his short stout body encased in a dark blue suit, reminding her of an overstuffed bolster. 'You seem to know a lot about the law.'

'My father and brother are both solicitors.'

He opened his arms wide and spread out his fat little fingers. 'There you are, then! You have no need of me!'

'Don't be stupid,' Conceptia snapped. 'You've looked after the affairs of this family since William died and I don't know what we'd have done without you.'

He grinned widely, showing a row of tiny shark-like teeth, and clapped his hands gleefully. 'See? See how popular I am? Oh, my dear Conceptia, you have made my day! But I fear your dear daughter-in-law might not agree. Umm?' He raised dark eyebrows and looked at Cathryn enquiringly.

'All I want is for Nicolas to be allowed to come home, and have his name cleared,' Cathryn said unbendingly. She did not trust him. And listening to Conceptia in the ensuing half hour talk to David about what had happened to Posy, in a strange and guarded way as if she were skirting around the most important part of all, Cathryn began to wonder if there wasn't a darker side to their relationship.

'I'm sure Nicolas can take care of himself,' he said smoothly when Conceptia had finished talking. 'Unless, of course, he has something to hide?'

Cathryn stiffened, a cold wave sweeping over her. 'How can you suggest such a thing?'

'I'm not suggesting anything.'

'He's not suggesting anything,' Conceptia repeated swiftly. Then she changed tack, like a yachtsman suddenly dropping the mainsail to lower his speed. She smiled sweetly. 'We're just so sorry this has happened, Cathryn, especially so soon after your marriage. It's not a very nice start for you, is it? We can depend on David, though, if need be.'

'I just want to see Nicolas's good name restored,' Cathryn said coldly.

David's smile was sardonic. 'I can see you'll defend him to the death.'

'And beyond,' she replied, her blue eyes looking steadily into his.

Conceptia moved restlessly on the sofa, her right hand searching the pocket of her jacket. 'All this is very upsetting for *me* too, you know. The good name of the family, which I have given my life to preserve, is at stake. Nicolas has already cast a shadow over us by marrying that halfwit, Miranda. Then there was the divorce. And then the marriage to you and now this! I can't stand much more of it.'

Cathryn let it pass. There was no point in being drawn into

a row with Conceptia, who was trembling now and seemed agitated. Instead she said, 'Do you think it's possible that Miranda is behind all this? Wanting to get Nicolas into trouble as some sort of revenge because their marriage didn't work?'

David Partridge looked startled. 'Miranda?' he asked incredulously.

'God only knows!' Conceptia replied theatrically, leaning back in her armchair, a lace-edged handkerchief pressed to her temple. 'But that little trollop was capable of anything!'

Cathryn spent another sleepless night desperately missing Nicolas and feeling so alone in the great empty bed as she lay in the darkness thinking of him being held in a cell. She felt helpless, too. The whole situation was bizarre and she had no control over what was happening, and that was the worst feeling of all.

When the first grey streaks of a winter dawn filtered through her windows she got up, desperate to have something to do. There were too many servants in this house, she reflected, as she got dressed into warm clothes, and not enough privacy. She felt inhibited by the staff indoors and imprisoned by the press camped out by the main gates. If she'd been at her parents' home she'd have felt free to go to the kitchen and make herself a cup of tea and then sit by the old stove to get warm. The thought made her nostalgic for the days before her marriage. Now she felt trapped. Then she'd been able to do as she liked. Now she was bumping into servants wherever she went.

Letting herself out of the main door, she began walking around the perimeter of the house, where the photographers couldn't see her. It was freezing and her breath curled smokily into the air, her eyes stinging from the sharp wind which whipped around the building.

All around her the gardens of Buckland lay shrouded in the early morning mist, the grand vista that led to an ornamental lily pond with a fountain, resembling a stage set in an opera.

She thought about her parents' home in Berkshire, where she'd spent so much of her childhood in the garden. It was always a riot of colours and scents, with everything growing in careless profusion.

Now, as she regarded the forbidding grandeur of Buckland, a terrible moment of doubt swept through her. Had she made an irretrievable mistake? It wasn't Nicolas who made her unhappy

– it was this place. There was something about Buckland that
seemed tainted with tragedy. It was as if the very soul of this
great old family who had reigned supreme for 400 years was now
facing disaster and trying to take Nicolas down with it.

With her hands dug deeply into the pockets of her tweed coat
and her head bent against the cutting wind, she made another
turn around the building, keeping close to the walls. Then she
heard the sound of a car coming up the drive. A moment later
it swerved and drew up at the front entrance. Looking tired and
crumpled, Nicolas climbed out of the passenger seat. As soon as
he saw her he walked quickly towards her, arms outstretched.

'Nicolas!' she exclaimed in relief, running towards him and
flinging her arms around his neck and pressing her cold cheek
against his. 'Are you all right, darling?'

'Yes, but what a bloody waste of time,' he growled, kissing her
briefly. 'Hours and hours of idiotic questioning!'

She nodded, her arm linked with his as they entered the hall.

'Let's go upstairs,' he said, ordering the under butler to bring
hot coffee and toast right away to their private quarters.

'David Partridge is staying, by the way,' she whispered.

Nicolas stopped and looked at her. 'Here? What the hell's he
doing here?'

'Your mother invited him.'

'Oh God! '

'I think she hoped he'd act for you if need be.'

'Good Grief!' Nicolas rubbed his face with both hands. 'As if
I didn't have enough on my plate without that old codger poking
his nose in.'

'So tell me what happened,' she said, as soon as they were alone
at a table in front of the fire in their private sitting room. 'Who
made a statement suggesting you were involved in Posy's death?'

His eyebrows shot up and he looked grim. 'Involved is an
understatement and I wish I knew the bastard who started all
this, but the police wouldn't tell me. They've no evidence against
me but that's the only reason I've been released, for the time
being anyway.'

'What do you mean?' Her voice rose with alarm.

Nicolas took a deep breath as if trying to unburden himself.
'The gist of it is that someone has come forward, after twenty

years, mind you, *twenty years*, to say they *saw* me shoot Posy Burgess in the woods on the day she went missing.'

Cathryn stared at him, too stunned to speak.

'It's an eyewitness statement according to the police,' he continued flatly.

'Who could have dreamed up a lie like that?' she gasped, horrified.

Nicolas looked at her, touched by her ebullient defence of him.

'Maybe someone who has got their dates mixed,' he said slowly.

'I don't understand.'

'When I was eleven I was given an air rifle, so I could practise target shooting. I was often in the woods having a bit of harmless fun, aiming at a cardboard target nailed to trees, that sort of thing.'

Cathryn looked horrified. 'You were given a rifle when you were eleven?'

Nicolas smiled for the first time. 'An air rifle, darling. Not the sort of gun I have now for shooting. Didn't your brother have an air rifle when he was a little boy?'

'Absolutely not! Daddy didn't let him shoot until he was about seventeen and then always under strict supervision with a gamekeeper. Who gave it to you?'

Nicolas sensed the criticism in her tone. 'It's a family tradition. My father had an air rifle when he was about ten. You use pellets, you know. Not bullets.'

'Even so,' she replied, unconvinced. She felt deeply shocked. This made a frightening difference to the situation. Even if someone had got the dates mixed, how was Nicolas going to prove he wasn't in the woods on the day Posy went missing?

'There is no evidence,' Nicolas repeated. 'There is no way it can be proved that I shot Posy.'

'And there's no way, after all this time, to prove that you didn't,' she countered, suddenly sick with fear.

'Exactly.'

'So what happens now?'

'I'll have a talk with my solicitor, Anthony Warner. This is a trumped-up statement. Totally without foundation, but it puts me in a very bad light.'

'Oh, God, Nicolas. Who could have done such a thing?'

They stopped talking at that moment as a footman walked in

with their breakfast, followed by the butler, checking that every-thing was in order.

'Wills, have the newspapers been delivered yet?' Nicolas asked.

'I believe they're being ironed at the moment, m'lord. I'll fetch them right away.'

'I want them all, even the rags, Wills.'

'Very well, m'lord.' His eyes were downcast as he left the room.

''ave you ever?' Ida Burgess said in a low voice. 'It's in all the newspapers that 'is lordship bin questioned but that ain't goin' to bring m'little girl back, is it?'

In spite of the improvements to their cottage, plus a cellar full of coal and a kitchen stocked with food, Ida could not come to terms with the terrible reality that Posy was dead. All along, at the back of her mind, there'd been the hope that one day her little princess would come back to them, a grown woman now, but safe and sound because the gypsies had looked after her well enough.

Frank grunted. He was a man of few words but in his heart of hearts he was sure Lord Nicolas, as he always called him, was not involved in Posy's death. He'd known his master since he'd been a small child, and in his opinion there wasn't a bad bone in his body. He'd been an honest kid, right from the beginning, and if he'd hurt Posy accidentally he'd have admitted it at once. As for Lord Ewan, he was such a sissy he wouldn't have known one end of an air rifle from the other. A real mother's boy, he was, even to this day. Not that his stuck-up mother knew what he got up to after she'd gone to bed.

Frank crossed his arms as he sat in the chair opposite Ida, and stretched his legs, warming his feet by the fire. Many was the night, he reflected, when he'd been tending a cow who was in calf up at the home farm, when he'd see Lord Ewan walking up the lane to the local inn, which he'd enter by the back door. Not for a pint of ale but to see the landlord's nineteen-year-old son. The next day the boy would be seen flaunting an expensive wrist-watch, or a nice pair of cufflinks, as he worked in the bar. Frank pursed his mouth in disapproval. He never mentioned it to Ida, though. He wasn't even sure she'd understand, but he'd been in the army in the Boer War and had learned a lot about people's behaviour that had shocked him profoundly. And to think a fine upstanding man like Lord Nicolas had a brother who was a pansy!

At that moment, there was a knock on their cottage door. When Frank opened it he found himself staring at two policemen.

'Sorry to disturb you, Mr Burgess, but may we come in?' one of them asked.

They were fresh-faced lads and seemed uncomfortable with what they had to do.

'We've come to ask you and Mrs Burgess a few questions about the day your daughter vanished,' explained the other.

'You'd better come in then,' Frank said sourly. Hadn't they suffered enough already? 'We don't know no more than we did when she went missing. We made statements then.'

'This is a fresh investigation, Mr Burgess,' the older of the two pointed out politely. 'Then we were merely trying to find a missing child. This is now a murder investigation. We'd like to know if either you or Mrs Burgess suspect anyone in particular who could have shot your daughter?'

'Well, it ain't Lord Nicolas and that's for sure,' Frank remarked flatly, resuming his seat beside the fire.

'He's right. It ain't his lordship. Wasting your time, you were, asking him questions yesterday,' Ida chipped in. 'He's a gentleman, he is. Wouldn't hurt a fly.'

For an hour the police persisted in their questioning, but to no avail. Ida and Frank said stubbornly that they had told them everything twenty years ago and they had nothing further to add to the fact that Posy had gone into the garden to play and that was the last time anyone had seen her.

When the police finally left, Ida rose to make a cup of tea. 'We didn't have to say no more, did we?'

'Nah!' Looking glum, Frank put some more coal on the fire. 'None of their business.'

'It wouldn't alter things neither, would it?' She put three spoons of tea into the pot and waited for the kettle to boil.

'Best left unsaid,' Frank agreed. 'You know what this village is like.'

At dawn the next day Appledore was bustling with life in spite of the early hour.

The newspaper boy had been out on his bicycle doing his delivery round, this having the effect of a tornado sweeping recklessly through every household, causing a mixture of salacious excitement and shock amongst the inhabitants. The vicar in the rectory cast his eyes to heaven, the headmaster of the local school braced himself for awkward questions from the pupils, and Mrs Evans, who ran the local general store, knew she would be facing the busiest day of the year, because people always popped in for something in the hope of meeting someone they knew when there was a bit of juicy scandal afoot.

Opening her shutters and unlocking the entrance door, she didn't have long to wait. As she served customers for a packet of tea or a pound of sugar, the babble of voices drowned out the *ping* of the cash till.

'I wouldn't have believed it of her, would you?'

'Oh, I always thought she was a little minx!'

'Serves him right though, don't it?'

'Her ladyship ain't 'alf going to go mad!'

'Wot? The new one? Or the old bitch?'

'The new one don't know wot she'd let 'erself in for, if you ask me.'

On and on it went, and if people weren't gossiping in the general store, they were in the post office, the butcher, the fishmonger or the baker. They clustered on street corners and were grouped in doorways. The newsagent even had to send to Canterbury for more supplies of what Nicolas referred to as 'the rags'.

There was nothing like a really good story of someone else's disgrace to draw the community together, and this was the biggest shock to hit the people of Appledore since the conquering Romans had landed on the Kent coast.

The atmosphere at Ivy Lodge, however, was calm. Anne Pilkington, who only took *The Times*, sat at the breakfast table with Hilary. The newspaper, which lay to one side, merely reported in a two-inch column on the second page that: *After being questioned at Canterbury police station regarding the remains of a child found buried in the grounds of his estate, the Marquess of Abingdon was released and has not been charged with any offence.*

It was a different story in the tabloids.

Seven

EX-LADY ABINGDON TELLS OF HER AGONY

Miranda, the ex-Marchioness of Abingdon, yesterday spoke of her heartbreak when she realized her marriage to one of the richest men in England was over two years ago. 'I'd found out certain things about his family,' she said when she was interviewed at her London house, which was part of her divorce settlement. 'Nicolas didn't like that. He's very secretive. I was kept in the dark about so many things. I loved him so much but he made my life tortured.'

The pretty twenty-five-year-old socialite, formerly Miss Miranda Metcalfe, daughter of Colonel Neville Metcalfe, was tearful as she spoke about her former husband. Asked if she knew anything about his involvement in the death of nine-year-old Posy Burgess, whose remains were recently found buried on his estate, she replied, 'I believe he did have something to do with her disappearance. Someone in the village told me about it when we were first married and that was a terrible shock, but now it's all come out in the open I have to say I think Nicolas probably was involved . . .'

The Mirror, November 27th, 1930

'What the hell are you trying to do to me, Miranda?' Nicolas blazed furiously as he gripped the telephone. 'Why are you telling all these lies? Have you gone mad?' His face was flushed, and sitting a few yards away from him, Cathryn could see the tension in his tightly fisted hands and rigid shoulders. 'Are you trying to ruin me? How could you even think I had anything to do with this terrible business?'

'Don't talk to me like that!'

Cathryn could hear her sobbing down the line.

'They asked me so many questions!' Miranda continued. 'And you did keep secrets from me! So did your mother, who was always horrid to me!'

Nicolas was clearly struggling to contain his anger. 'Miranda,' he began with forced patience. 'Who put you up to this? The disappearance of that little girl was never even mentioned in the three years we knew each other. How is it you suddenly have all this farcical information involving me now?'

'I did know about it! After we got married I heard how she'd disappeared. Stop being so nasty to me, Nicolas. You've no idea how unhappy I was at Buckland. You were always off doing your own thing, leaving me alone with your mother . . .'

'But who told you all this garbage? Posy vanished twenty years ago. I think we'd all forgotten about it until recently. Who's been raking it up after all this time?'

'The people in the village didn't forget. Now leave me alone. I don't want to have anything more to do with you.'

'Then stop talking to the damned newspapers,' Nicolas countered, slamming down the receiver. Then he sank slowly on to a nearby chair and looked at Cathryn. 'Did you hear all that?'

Cathryn nodded.

'It's obvious she wants to ruin my reputation. How could she have talked to the press like that? Now all the other newspapers will pick it up and run with it. God, what a mess.' He rose and came and stood before her. 'I'm so sorry you're in the middle of this dreadful nightmare, darling,' he said regretfully. 'You do believe I had nothing to do with Posy Burgess's death, don't you?'

Cathryn stood up quickly and slipped her arms around his neck. 'Of course I know you didn't.' But she couldn't help a little voice at the back of her mind asking, *Why are you so sure? You've only known this man for seven months. What do you really know about him? And his first marriage?* 'I'm in love with you, darling,' she breathed, burying her face in his shoulder. 'No matter what, I'll always stand by you.'

'How do you mean? No matter what?' he asked sharply, pulling away from her. 'Do you believe there's anything in what Miranda said?'

'No, of course not. Absolutely not.'

He wandered moodily to the bay window, which overlooked the magnificent vista and the trees in the far distance. 'I must talk to my solicitor,' he said suddenly. 'Miranda has got to be stopped spreading lies about me and my family.' He turned abruptly to leave the room.

'Nicolas?'

He stopped in his tracks. 'What is it?'

'It's just . . .' she hesitated, seeing he was still angry. 'Have you any enemies? Maybe Miranda was telling the truth when she said someone in the village had told her about Posy?'

'Don't talk rubbish,' he snapped, walking out of the room.

This was the first time Nicolas had spoken to her so harshly and her eyes widened with hurt. She only wanted to protect him from mischief-makers, but she could see her observation had only annoyed him all the more.

'There's no need to snap my head off,' she said coldly to his retreating back view.

Later that morning it occurred to Cathryn that no one in the family was thinking about the feelings of Mr and Mrs Burgess as the story of their daughter's death was splashed on the front pages of the popular newspapers. She would pay them a visit to make sure they were all right.

As soon as she entered the outskirts of the village and sensed the electrifying atmosphere she realized it had been a mistake to come. The moment she'd been spotted, walking briskly down the lane from Buckland, a slim well-dressed young woman in a perky red felt hat and a mink coat, a signal seemed to spread like wildfire.

'She's here!'

'The wife!'

'As bold as brass!'

'What does she want?'

'What has she got to say for herself?'

People came out of their front doors and peered out of windows. Groups whispered feverishly. One woman pointed, and there was a yelp of raucous laughter.

Cathryn composed her features into an expression of calm compassion, and raising her chin and looking straight ahead, strode up the cinder path of the Burgess's cottage and tapped on the front door.

'She never . . . !' someone exclaimed loudly. Another gave a nervous snigger.

The door opened slowly and Ida Burgess stood looking stonily at her.

'How are you and your husband?' Cathryn said gently. 'Have you got everything you need?' She looked beyond the stout woman and saw that the walls of the tiny living room had been whitewashed, and that there was a new rug on the floor and new armchairs on either side of the grate, in which blazed a coal fire.

Ida's expression was implacable, and there were heavy bags under her eyes.

'I won't ask you in,' she whispered. 'People are saying you and Lord Nicolas have bribed us by doing up our cottage and giving us things, and it's all getting more than I can bear. The police were here yesterday. There's nothing more we can tell them, but no one believes that. They think you've given us hush money. It looks bad you even being here now, m'lady.'

Cathryn looked at her, stunned. 'But that's ridiculous,' she exclaimed. 'None of us have anything to hide.'

'This lot don't believe that. We told the police yesterday that Lord Nicolas had nothing to do with Posy's death, but now his first wife like . . .' she paused, embarrassed.

'I know. My husband and I have seen the article. It's all lies. Terrible lies.'

'I'm sorry, but this is hard for us. I think you'd better leave, m'lady. We don't want no more trouble.'

'I understand.' Cathryn spoke hurriedly. 'I'll get the estate office to issue a statement saying you were only helped financially as part of Frank's job at the home farm.' She turned to go and there was the sound of tittering from a few women who were leaning over a nearby garden wall.

Appalled, Cathryn turned away to walk briskly back to Buckland; her face was pale with anxiety and she was aware that people were nudging each other and whispering.

A neatly dressed woman in her early thirties, with bland features and mousy brown hair, walked past at that moment, and after looking enquiringly at Cathryn, she smiled shyly.

'I believe you're Lady Abingdon?' she enquired in a light floating voice. 'I think you met my mother the other day? Mrs Pilkington? We live at Ivy Lodge.'

Cathryn smiled back, relieved at finding someone friendly amid the animosity that was shattering the usual tranquillity of the village.

'Yes, of course I remember your mother. I believe you've always lived here?'

'That's right! Poor you, you've really arrived at a very bad moment, haven't you? I was only saying to Mother this morning that I felt terribly sorry for you. It must be a nightmare and you're newly married, too.' Her voice dripped with sympathy. 'I heard you even had to cut your honeymoon short. Such a shame.' She glanced around at the gawping faces and curious eyes and her voice dropped a level. 'Look, why don't you come back to Ivy Lodge for a cup of coffee? I know Mother would love to see you again.'

Cathryn spoke gratefully, anxious to escape the prying eyes. 'That's very kind. I'd like that very much.'

'Wonderful! Come along then and we can get acquainted. My name's Hilary, by the way.'

Nicolas knocked on Conceptia's bedroom door. His voice was stern. 'Mother, I'd like a word with you.'

'What do you want?'

He entered the room and as he'd expected she was sitting up in bed against a mound of pillows, having her breakfast on a tray. Beside her lay *The Times* and the *Telegraph*.

'You obviously haven't seen the rags this morning?'

'I never look at the rags,' she replied disdainfully.

'Well, you should. Miranda has spun a whole lot of lies about me to the *Daily Mirror*. The story's all over the front page. I'm trying to get Anthony Warner to put an injunction preventing any of the other papers following it up.'

'Why didn't you ask David to do it? He's right here in the house and he's very good at that sort of thing.'

'Because Anthony is my solicitor.'

'So what exactly has she said? No doubt she's trying to get back at you for not giving her the divorce settlement she demanded, the greedy little slut.'

'Mother, Miranda was never money-grubbing. She's saying that people in the village told her I was involved in Posy's disappearance. Do you know who could have said such a thing?'

Conceptia averted her gaze and her hand shook as she poured herself another cup of tea. 'Why are you asking me? I never listen

to village gossip, and only a little fool like Miranda would be
swayed by idle talk. If you will get involved with these stupid
young women it's your own fault if they spread lies.'

'I trust you're not referring to Cathryn?'

His mother shrugged. 'She's very pushy. You'd better watch
out or she'll be calling all the shots and making you look like
a ninny. Then she'll push off too, because she's not getting
enough attention.'

Nicolas looked at her squarely. 'I know you hate me because
you think I'm like my father, but I'm not like him at all except
in appearance. You've spent your life trying to drive a wedge
between me and the people I like, but there's no need to take it
out on whoever I'm married to. I'm beginning to suspect it's
what you did with Miranda . . .'

Conceptia pushed the tray violently to one side and some of
the fine china crashed to the floor, smashing loudly.

'Damn you!' she shouted, as she rose up in her bed. 'God damn
you! Get out of here at once. How dare you talk to me like that.'
She stared at him, her face ugly with hate. Then she reached
imperiously for the bell by her bed.

'I'll have you thrown out if you don't leave now.'

He gave her a mocking look of pity. 'Don't be absurd, Mother.
You can't have me removed from my own house.'

'And whose money was it that saved the place?' she raged, as
he calmly turned to leave the room. 'Where would you be if I
hadn't . . .'

'You've played that old tune once too often,' he cut in. 'I'm
warning you, don't make Cathryn's life the hell you obviously
seem to have made Miranda's.'

'Miranda is virtually saying she thinks Nicolas killed Posy,' Cathryn
observed as she sat in Hugh Verney's office. He'd become her
confidant in the past week, and she felt she could say anything
to him and that he could be trusted.

'You knew Miranda. What was she like?' As she spoke she
glanced at the newspaper again. From the photograph Miranda
looked like a very prim debutante with a painted mouth and
tight blonde curls. Vapid too, Cathryn reflected with a flash of
insight. *I wonder what Nicolas saw in her?* Then she pushed the

thought away. It was none of her business and dangerous territory. She was married to him now and she intended for it to stay that way.

'Miranda was unable to stand up to the dowager,' Hugh said frankly. 'Lady Abingdon bullied her and she just buckled. She was too scared to complain to Nicolas in case it caused more trouble, so she used to come to me, weeping and wondering what to do.'

'So she ran away?'

'Everything got on top of her. She wasn't a strong character like you, Cathryn. She failed to get pregnant and that depressed her, too. Nicolas did his best but in front of him his mother was warm and sweet to Miranda, so he failed to realize what was going on behind his back.'

Cathryn's brow furrowed. 'Did you never tell him what his mother was doing?'

'I did, and he spoke to her about it and told her to leave Miranda alone and stop criticizing everything she did, but Lady Abingdon got in a huff and said she was only helping the girl to settle in.' Hugh's voice ended in a tone of disgust. Then he continued in a low voice, 'The truth of the matter was Nicolas should never have married her. They were utterly incompatible and he realized it shortly after they were married. He did his utmost though to make her happy, giving her everything she wanted, and he would have stuck by her through thick and thin, but, wisely, I believe, she decided to cut her losses and leave. He gave her a most generous settlement and bought her a house of her choice in London, so I can't imagine why she's done this to him now,' he added grimly.

'Perhaps someone else has put her up to it?'

Hugh splayed his hands in a helpless gesture. 'But why, for God's sake? She doesn't need the money. And it was Miranda who decided to leave him, not the other way around.' He looked thoughtful. 'On the other hand, she is a weak character and if someone had pressurized her . . .' His words hung in the air.

'Someone who has a grudge against him?' Cathryn suggested. 'Maybe the person who has made this false statement to the police?'

Hugh shrugged. 'Who knows? All I can say is thank God he's married to you now. You're the right wife for him, Cathryn. I don't know what he'd do without you right now.'

As Cathryn entered the hall at Buckland later that day, having managed to take a walk up to the folly and back without being spotted by the loitering photographers, Wills appeared.

'There was a telephone call for you, m'lady. From Mr Charles Brocklehurst. He left a message to say he'll be arriving tomorrow morning and hopes to stay for a couple of days. I have informed the housekeeper, m'lady, and she's having the blue suite prepared for him.'

A look of delight spread across Cathryn's face at the thought of her brother's visit.

'Thank you, Wills. Is my husband around?'

'I believe he's with Mr Verney, m'lady.'

When she entered the estate office, both men looked up and smiled in welcome. To her relief, Nicolas seemed less harassed.

'Hello, darling. You're looking pleased with yourself,' he observed.

'Charles is coming to stay for a couple of days. Isn't that marvellous?'

Nicolas nodded. 'Wills told me. It will be nice to see him again.' The brothers-in-law had become friends in the run-up to the wedding and Nicolas had been grateful for Charles's support in the face of Sir Roland and Lady Brocklehurst's undisguised disapproval.

At that moment Ewan came bounding into the office to ask Hugh if he knew any newspaper editors. All thin gangling legs and floppy hair, he dropped into a nearby chair, completely ignoring Cathryn and Nicolas.

'I think I have a talent for writing,' he announced importantly. 'I've decided to postpone publishing my book on trees because what I really want to do is to become a journalist. Doing interviews and all that. Especially on a gossip column like William Hickey. With our social contacts I could get some good stories, couldn't I?' he added, triumphantly, waving his white bony hands around.

Nicolas looked stunned, then burst out laughing. 'You? A journalist? What's brought this on? Miranda's short career as a storyteller?'

Ewan frowned, annoyed. 'I'm serious! Why are you always such a wet blanket?'

'Because you decide on a new career as often as I change my socks.'

'Absolute rubbish. Writing is writing! Journalism is just a more immediate form of writing than publishing a serious book or a novel. I like the idea of getting a scoop. Working in Fleet Street. Having a byline.'

'You really have been immersing yourself in the rags, haven't you?' Suddenly Nicolas looked grim-faced. 'If you so much as put pen to paper about this family I shall personally make sure your allowance is cancelled. Is that clear?'

Conceptia marched into the estate office. 'What's going on?'

Ewan's Adam's apple bobbed wildly in his pale throat. 'Nicolas is threatening me. I only said I wanted to take up journalism instead of writing books . . .'

'You'll never be a writer,' Nicolas fumed. 'This is just another of your pie-in-the-sky fantasies! You've become so titillated by the stuff in the rags recently that what you'd really like to be is a stringer: someone who phones up the editor with nasty little bits of gossip about people you know so that you can sit back and feel good about yourself.'

Conceptia cut in. 'Why do you always try to put your brother down, Nicolas? The moment he really wants to do something, you're disapproving and you throw cold water over it.'

'Then that's something I must have learned from you, Mother,' Nicolas retorted coldly. 'You criticize everything I do; you even criticize me for things I *haven't* done.'

'Apologize to Mummy at once!' Ewan bleated.

Cathryn listened as words were being exchanged, flying through the air like poison darts, and she wondered what on earth had made Conceptia pander to one son with an almost feverish adoration, while so obviously detesting the other.

Charles's arrival the next day was like a breath of fresh air in a house that had become claustrophobic with an atmosphere of malevolence, so that at times Cathryn felt she could hardly breathe.

Conceptia was now refusing to talk to Nicolas at all, to the point of ignoring his presence in the room, while David Partridge still hung around the place like the smell of stale cooking, making sneering remarks at every opportunity. Ewan was sulking and scowling and only Nicolas was bravely trying to keep up a feeling of normality.

As soon as she heard a car coming up the drive, Cathryn rushed to the front door to greet her brother by flinging her arms around him as if she hadn't seen him for months.

'What ho, old thing!' Charles said, hugging her back. 'You're looking top hole in spite of all the drama!'

She cast her eyes to heaven and made a little grimace. 'It's so good of you to come and see us. Nicolas is in the library. Come and have a drink before lunch.'

Conceptia and Ewan were sipping sherry in front of the log fire with David Partridge when they entered the room, and all three of them studiously ignored Charles's arrival.

Only Nicolas came forward to greet him, shaking his hand warmly.

'Good to see you and thanks for coming. Can I get you a drink?'

'That's very decent of you. I'd love a pink gin.' With great politeness Charles walked over to the others, saying, 'How do you do,' and shaking hands with Conceptia first, then Ewan, and lastly David, who eyed him with cold gravity.

'So what brings you here, Mr Brocklehurst?' Conceptia enquired, as if he were a servant applying for a job.

'To offer succour to my dear sister,' Charles retorted, with a cocky smile to hide the fact he found the dowager marchioness terrifying. 'Not to mention legal advice if necessary, free of charge, if your son requires it.'

Conceptia looked at him with narrowed eyes and he reflected that if she'd been a cat she'd have been swishing her tail from side to side at that moment. 'We already have a solicitor in Mr Partridge. We have no need for further legal advice,' she rasped, waving a bejewelled hand in David's direction.

Charles blinked at the snub before turning to Nicolas with a cheeky grin. 'Oh well! Then I'll just drink your gin instead!'

Nicolas laughed. 'Steady on, isn't gin a bit girlie? I had you down as a brandy and soda man.'

'No, it's Mother's ruin for me, thanks.'

Cathryn smiled, delighted by their banter but at the same time willing her brother to be less crass. Conceptia was not known for her sense of humour.

'Which legal firm are you with?' David asked in a patronizing tone.

Charles looked at him levelly. 'The family firm of course. Brocklehurst, Milne and Chilcott of Chancery Lane. And you are with . . . ?'

David raised his chin, offended. 'Bruce and Hutton.'

'Still practising then?'

David gave a brief nod and sipped his drink in a silence so disapproving it could have been sliced by an ice pick.

Charles turned to Nicolas. 'How are things?' he asked quietly as they moved away from the group by the fireplace to sit by the window. Cathryn joined them.

Nicolas shrugged, keeping his voice low. 'Pretty rotten, really. I don't know where we go from here. It's become a murder hunt and for a moment I seemed to be suspect number one, but I gather they are questioning a lot of people now. As soon as the police release the remains of the child, there'll be the funeral, of course. I just pray the newspapers don't hound us on that day.'

'Is it wise for us to go?' Cathryn queried. 'Wouldn't it be better if we let them have a private service?'

'If we don't go there will be people who'll say we're too guilty to show our faces,' Nicolas retorted bitterly, 'and if we do go, others will say we're showing no remorse and what bare-faced cheek we have, to flaunt ourselves in public.'

'You're in a no-win situation, aren't you?' Charles agreed sympathetically. 'I gather there have been no charges, as far as you're concerned, though?'

'They have no evidence against me,' Nicolas agreed, 'but mud sticks. When you've got someone who claims to have been an eye witness . . . well, how do you disprove that?'

'It's your word against theirs,' Charles agreed, 'but it's damned messy! Can't you find out who made this claim?'

'I haven't been able to so far, and my ex-wife's agreement that I must have had something to do with the child's death hasn't helped. I'd really like to return to town, but that's not a good idea either. So poor Cathryn is stuck down here with just me for company, and not a decent shop for miles around,' Nicolas added, attempting to sound light-hearted.

Charles's eyebrows shot up. 'Never mind! This is a spiffing place you've got here! I wouldn't mind being incarcerated in a house like this for a while.' He gazed around the imposing room, with its oak shelves lined with books, a fine painting over the mantle shelf and comfortable sofas and armchairs. 'You'll obviously stay down here for Christmas?'

'Yes. I'm afraid it's not going to be much fun this year.' Then Nicolas's expression brightened. 'Why don't you come and stay with us? In fact, why don't your parents come too, unless they've got other plans?'

Cathryn longed to suggest they stay with her family in Berkshire, which would be relaxed and cosy and away from the current nightmare, but she knew it was her duty to be with Nicolas in his own home at this time.

'That's a nice idea!' she said instead. 'Charles, do come! And get Mummy and Pa to come, too. This is my first Christmas away from home,' she added poignantly, 'and it would be lovely if you were here, too.'

'I'm game! And I'm sure they will be too,' Charles replied enthusiastically.

Nicolas looked pleased. 'Then that's settled. We usually give a big supper party on Christmas Eve for all the tenants and staff and most of the village but I don't know this year whether . . .' his voice faltered and he looked at Cathryn. 'Will they want to have anything to do with us, under the circumstances?'

She gripped his hand tightly. 'No one thinks . . .'

'But they do,' he cut in, his voice suddenly sharp. 'I know they do, darling. Hugh Verney has told me exactly how they've reacted and it was very brave of you to go into the village yesterday. It can't have been much fun,' he added drily.

Her eyes smarted with emotion. 'I don't think they believe you did anything, Nicolas. I think they're just feverish with curiosity at having something like this happen on their own front doorstep.'

'The gory way the newspapers have handled it won't have helped,' Charles observed. 'As they say, there are no bad situations that a few banner headlines from Fleet Street can't make worse.'

From across the lofty library Conceptia's acid tones came wafting. 'Are you discussing Christmas? I've already decided we should go up to Tyndrum, away from everyone here. That's what you'd like, Ewan, isn't it?'

'Yes. Definitely,' he agreed eagerly.

'Then why don't you and Ewan go, Mother? Cathryn and I will stay here and entertain her family.'

There was a stunned silence. Conceptia, Ewan and David Partridge glared at Nicolas with hostile eyes, as if he'd betrayed them all.

'I'd love to stay here,' Cathryn said boldly.

'Then that's what we'll do.' Nicolas spoke with satisfaction, as he put his arm around her waist. For the first time in days he sounded light-hearted and more like his usual self. 'It will be a quiet Christmas but a very peaceful one, and I'll give most of the staff the week off. How about that?'

'Perfect,' she said softly.

'Well, we'll have to see about that.' Conceptia spoke querulously. 'I've too much on my mind to make snap decisions about things like Christmas. I have a lot of responsibility here, and the servants can't be given time off, just like that.'

'Poor Mama,' Ewan sympathized. 'Never mind, I'll do anything you want; unlike some people I can mention,' he added, glancing at Nicolas venomously.

Charles watched this altercation with bafflement. He'd only met the dowager marchioness once before, very briefly, and he was horrified that Cathryn's in-laws bickered in this unpleasant way. He tried to catch her eye several times but she studiously avoided looking in his direction and seemed intent on studying the pattern of the Persian rug at her feet.

It was only after a rather awkward luncheon, when the social niceties were observed for the benefit of the servants and the weather seemed to be discussed for ages, that he finally found himself alone with Cathryn, in her private sitting room.

'I'd no idea things were as bad as this, Cath,' he said, making himself comfortable on the brightly patterned chintz-covered sofa that stood facing a crackling fire. 'How can you stand it?'

'You mean the terrible disaster of the little girl's body being found?'

'I mean the terrible disaster of having to live with such dreadful people,' he retorted bluntly. 'What the hell have you got yourself into?'

'Nicolas is wonderful,' she said, hurt. 'We're so happy together and . . .'

'He may be Mr Wonderful but his family are ghastly! Do they quarrel all the time? And what's that creepy old lawyer doing? Is he a part of the household?'

Cathryn found herself rising angrily to the defence of both Nicolas and his family. 'He's a friend of Conceptia, and her sort of advisor, I think. I know she's tricky but . . .'

'And as for that nancy boy? Why didn't someone cut the umbilical cord, for God's sake?'

'Charles, you're being really rude. And what do you mean by a "nancy boy"?'

He looked stunned. 'You don't know?'

'Know what? I agree he's a mother's boy and a bit feeble but I blame Conceptia for that.'

'Oh, Cath, you're more naïve than I realized. A nancy boy is a man who prefers men to women. Do you understand?' He looked at her searchingly and she frowned, unsure.

'They never want to sleep with women,' he continued.

'Oh!' She looked stunned. 'So that's why Nicolas said Ewan would never get married.'

'Did he say that? Well, it's true.'

'Oh, My God. I hadn't realized.'

They sat in silence. The only noise in the room was the gentle crackle of the fire and the ticking of the clock on the mantel shelf. It was getting dark although it was only half past three, and through the window they could see the bleakness of a grey landscape shrouded in dense clouds.

Charles moved restlessly. 'How do you stick it here? When you got married I thought you'd be living in Belgravia, entertaining in a swish manner, and going to balls and parties every night. I thought I'd see a lot of you, and you and Nicolas would come to dinner with Ma and Pa and we'd hear all about the glamorous life you were leading, the marvellous clothes and furs you'd bought, and the trunks full of jewellery Nicolas had showered on you and instead . . .' he paused, appalled, 'instead I find you living with the family from hell, looking thoroughly unhappy.'

Her eyes brimmed, hurt by his criticism. 'I'm not unhappy, I'm just dreadfully worried and anxious. This terribly tragic case has knocked everyone sideways and the newspapers really seem to have it in for us. It's bad enough having to deal with the village being up in arms without the press adding to our troubles. Someone has been spreading lies about Nicolas and has apparently made a statement saying they saw him shoot Posy.'

'What sort of a person would do that?'

'Someone with a grudge against him, though Nicolas thinks it is someone who saw him target shooting but on another day, and they've got their dates mixed.'

Charles nodded. 'There are probably some very elderly people in the village, aren't there? And memory can play funny tricks, especially with old people. It did happen a long time ago.'

'I know. My heart breaks for Nicolas. He doesn't deserve all this vilification. Even when his name has been cleared, it's going to take years, if ever, for him to live down the scandal.' Tears trickled down her cheeks. 'He's such a good man,' she wept, 'and so kind and I love him so much.' She pulled a handkerchief out of her pocket and blew her nose. 'I don't know how his first wife could have talked publicly about him like that.'

'Have the police examined the air rifle he had as a boy? Surely that would show whether it was the weapon that was used?'

She shook her head, still sniffing. 'No one knows what happened to it.'

'Someone must know. An air rifle isn't a toy, Cath, like a bike or a tennis racket.'

'I know, but the police have searched the gun room, which is the only place it would have been kept, and it's not there. Nicolas has no idea where it is. He can't even remember when he last used it.'

Charles pursed his lips. 'It might be a good idea if it could be found, because then that might eliminate Nicolas from their enquiries.'

'I know.' She spoke with utter despair. 'I think someone must have taken it, shot Posy and then got rid of it.'

'Then it could be anywhere? Chucked in the river or buried in the grounds?'

'Quite. It would be like looking for a needle in a haystack.'

'Did anyone else shoot with it?'

She shook her head. 'Ewan has never learned to shoot, he's far too mollycoddled by Conceptia. And the gamekeepers have shotguns so they'd have no use for it.'

Charles frowned. 'It's a mess, isn't it?'

'It's a nightmare,' she said, trying to regain her composure. Then she gave him a watery smile. 'It's so good to have you here, Charles, and thank you for coming. I'm sorry I'm such a misery guts but I've no one, apart from Hugh Verney, to talk to. I don't want to add to Nicolas's troubles by letting him see how worried I am.'

'I'm glad to be here, Cath. Why don't you come back with me? Mother would love to look after you for a while and it would give you a break.'

'I can't possibly leave Nicolas. He needs me.' There was a touch of pride in her voice.

Eight

MARQUESS ATTENDS CHILD'S FUNERAL

The Marquess of Abingdon, who was recently questioned about the body of a child found buried on his estate, attended the funeral of nine-year-old Posy Burgess yesterday, accompanied by his second wife. The grieving parents, Mr and Mrs Frank Burgess, led the mourners at a service held at St Mary's Church, Appledore. It has been confirmed that Posy was shot by an air rifle but so far the weapon has not been found. Last month Lord Abingdon was questioned by police but no charges were brought, pending further inquiries . . .

The Daily News, December 7th, 1930

Cathryn thought she would never again see such a pitiful sight as the small pine coffin carried by the four farmhands who had worked with Frank Burgess for the past thirty-five years. On the lid lay a bunch of Winter Aconite, the simple yellow flowers as delicate and pretty as a little girl's party frock.

Sitting beside Nicolas in the family pew, Cathryn struggled to keep her composure as she reflected that Posy had never had a party frock, or anything else very much either, in her short life. Posy had been born into poverty and hunger. Not many toys would have lain scattered around their tumbledown cottage, and Father Christmas had probably only left meagre gifts carved by Frank from bits of wood.

Tears sprang to Cathryn's eyes and she bit the inside of her cheek in an effort to quell them. The village people were watching her, the new chatelaine of Buckland Place, and to break down in public would have been to commit a social *faux pas*. Everyone was thinking the same thing though: what had happened to Posy when she'd stepped out of the laundry room to go and play in the garden on that fateful day? She'd have been wide-eyed and curious, a lively child who'd become bored by having nothing to do while her mother worked. Was she looking for adventure?

Had she wandered near the gypsy encampment? Had someone followed her into the woods? Watched her as she played before taking aim . . . ?

To her fury neither Conceptia nor Ewan had come today in a show of family loyalty.

'We should present a united front,' Nicolas had pointed out the previous evening as they'd dined formally, with David Partridge still in attendance. 'Everyone on the estate will be there, and people from the village and all around the neighbourhood.'

'So will all the reporters and photographers,' Conceptia pointed out acidly.

Nicolas protested, 'It will look awful if we don't support Frank and his wife.'

'What rot!' Ewan declared, taking a gulp of his wine.

'It isn't rot,' Cathryn protested. 'We should all go. They'll expect us to.'

Conceptia raised her chin and glanced at her younger son's sulky face. 'Neither Ewan nor I need to be told how to behave by the likes of you, Cathryn. We're not going and that's an end to it.'

Nicolas shrugged, but there was an expression of deep hurt in his eyes and he looked tired and weary.

When the service came to an end, they walked back down the aisle together and she saw Hilary Pilkington waiting just inside the church door. Her nose was pink and her eyes were awash with tears. Cathryn smiled sympathetically and Hilary, seeing her, smiled back with lips that trembled. Then she shook her head slowly, as if the funeral was almost more than she too could bear.

Cathryn gave an imperceptible nod of agreement. 'How nice to see you,' she whispered when they reached her.

'It's too sad for words, isn't it?' Hilary replied. 'Hello, Nicolas,' she continued, turning to him with a look of compassion. 'This must be a very difficult day for you.'

He looked mildly surprised. 'It's a difficult day for everyone, especially Frank and Ida.'

'I know.' She nodded, her plain face looking drawn and washed out against the severe black of her coat and hat. 'Absolutely dreadful. But you're having a terrible time too, aren't you? I think the press are behaving in the most appalling way. Why can't they leave you alone?'

Nicolas remained silent, ignoring her question.

Hilary spoke again, this time in an almost exhilarated fashion. 'Don't you think it was wicked of Miranda to give that interview? We don't take the *Mirror*, of course, but our cook does, and I was horrified to see she'd sold her story like that! Have you heard from her recently? She's probably livid you've remarried, and if I may say so, to someone so sweet.' She smiled at Cathryn, as if they shared a special secret.

'I've no idea,' he said tersely. 'Will you excuse us, Hilary?' He moved swiftly away, to join the group of other mourners outside the church.

Hilary grabbed Cathryn's arm, holding her back for a moment. 'Do drop in to see me for a cup of coffee, next time you're in the village.'

'Thanks, but why don't you come to tea one day soon? I'll telephone you and we'll make a date.' Following Nicolas, Cathryn thought how nice it was to have met someone who lived so near and who was becoming such a good friend.

Later that day Nicolas announced he intended going up to London on business. 'I'll leave early in the morning. I should be back by the end of the week.'

Cathryn stared at him. 'Can't I come with you?' she asked, shocked.

His tone was dismissive. 'It's better you stay here. There are people I have to see.'

'But I thought . . . ?'

He looked up sharply. 'What did you think? Cathryn, I've been forced into a terribly difficult situation and I need advice on how to handle it. Just because the police haven't charged me doesn't mean it's all blown over. They're going to go on worrying at the situation like a dog with a bone.'

'But why should they? There's not a shred of evidence against you.'

'That's not the point.' He sounded bitter. 'Thanks to my mother's arrogant attitude towards the village, we're not the most popular family around here. There are some people who would love to see us brought down and disgraced.'

'Can't I go to London with you? Now that we're married I thought we were going to do everything together,' she asked, hurt.

'Not this time, Cathryn.' He started pacing up and down the room, his hands dug deeply into the pockets of his trousers. 'I shall be very busy. I've got to find a way to stop the newspapers speculating in this disgraceful fashion. It was bad enough when I was divorced but now they seem intent on completely ruining my reputation.'

Nicolas left before breakfast the next morning and his departure left Cathryn feeling very vulnerable and at a loose end in the great unfriendly house. There was no one she could talk to. Hugh Verney was cooped up with the estate's book-keeper, and there was no way she could enter into private discussions with Miss Lewis; her mother had told her you should never become too familiar with a servant, so whilst her lady's maid knew the colour of her underclothes, it would be unseemly to talk to her about her private worries. In the end she decided to telephone Hilary Pilkington and invite her to morning coffee.

'I'd love that,' Hilary replied. 'I'd invite you here but the atmosphere in the village is still a bit hostile, I'm afraid.' She sighed deeply. 'People can be so jealous and vindictive, can't they? It's such a shame.'

'So it seems.'

'Is there anything I can bring you from the village shops?' Then she giggled. 'Silly question, you've probably got everything you'll ever need at Buckland.'

'Everything – and nothing,' Cathryn said, overwhelmed with a sudden need to confide in someone. 'Nicolas has had to go up to London for a few days and the house is bleak and empty without him.'

'Oh, I'm sure it is! Poor you. Never mind, we can have a good chat and I'll do my best to cheer you up.'

When she arrived an hour later she presented Cathryn with a bag of homemade fudge and the latest edition of *Vogue* magazine.

'That's so kind and thoughtful of you,' Cathryn exclaimed, feeling quite touched by this show of friendship.

'Mere trifles, my dear, to amuse you,' Hilary replied lightly, as she took off her coat and hat and they settled before the fire in Cathryn's private sitting room. 'So, tell me what's happening? It must be awful for you being incarcerated because of those dreadful

Fleet Street hacks hanging around the place. How long is Nicolas away for?'

'Several days. He's in talks with his solicitor to try to bring injunctions against various newspapers.'

'Why didn't you go with him?'

'He thought it would be better if I stayed here, as he'll be so busy.'

Hilary raised her dark eyebrows and remained silent, watching Cathryn pour the coffee that a footman had just brought up to her quarters.

'He's under enormous strain,' Cathryn continued. 'Well, we both are, really. It will be such a relief when it's all over. At least my parents and brother are spending Christmas here, which will be lovely.'

'What about Nicolas's family? Are they going to be staying here, too?'

'They're going up to Tyndrum. At least I think they are.' Conceptia hadn't mentioned it again and she dreaded the thought of having to spend the festive season with her in-laws and David Partridge. 'However, we'll see,' she said with forced brightness. 'It's not really up to me.'

Hilary gazed at her sympathetically. 'He's very lucky to have you, especially at a time like this.' She leaned forward, dropping her voice confidentially so the departing footman wouldn't catch what she was saying. 'He's a very sweet man and you're so suited to each other.' Then she gave a little tinkling laugh. 'He wasn't for me, though. I was too young when he asked me to marry him . . . Oh, years ago now! I made the right decision, too. You're the type of wife he really needs.'

Cathryn blinked, taken aback. She'd always presumed Nicolas had had lots of girlfriends, but apart from Miranda she didn't realize he'd actually proposed to anyone else.

'I hope I am,' she said in a small voice. 'We're certainly very happy together.'

Hilary beamed at her. 'Then if you're happy under these terrible circumstances, you're certainly suited,' she said sweetly.

She left not long after that, telling Cathryn she must come and have tea with them, 'as soon as the newspapers leave you alone'.

'Thank you,' Cathryn replied walking with her to the front door. 'I hope that will be soon.'

'You seem to be getting on very well with her,' Anne Pilkington observed, when Hilary recounted their meeting as they sat down to a luncheon of cold ham and salad followed by stewed rhubarb and custard. 'I'm glad you're getting in with the Abingdons again. They used to give such lovely parties, and maybe they will again now Nicolas has remarried. Cathryn seems like a nice young woman.'

Hilary shrugged. 'I suppose she means well.' She cut into her slice of ham with precision, like a vet operating on a small animal. Then she popped it into her mouth. 'She's living in cloud cuckoo land though. Sooner or later the police are going to find out who killed that child, and the shame will ruin the family.'

'It's merely making them notorious; it won't ruin them,' Mrs Pilkington protested. 'It's nonsense for the newspapers to suggest Nicolas had anything to do with it.'

'Why are you so sure of that?'

'Nicolas guilty of shooting a child? Don't be silly, dear. He's always been a fine upstanding young man and now he's married Cathryn I think he'll be very happy.'

'They've only been married a few weeks. Give it a few months and he'll grow tired of her, the way he always tires of people,' Hilary added bitterly as she dissected another piece of ham.

'Oh, don't say that. It was very unfortunate his first marriage ended in divorce but he and Miranda weren't suited. Right from the beginning it was a mismatch because she was so highly strung. You said so yourself at the time.'

'I never said there was anything wrong with Miranda,' Hilary retorted with a touch of arrogance. 'He only married her to get an heir. She was like a lamb to the slaughter. He's married Cathryn for the same reason and if she doesn't produce a son within eighteen months he'll get rid of her, too.'

Mrs Pilkington looked pained. 'I think you're being rather fanciful, Hilary.'

'I'm not! Miranda was terribly unhappy when she was with Nicolas. He never loved her. Cathryn's already lonely and unhappy, that's why she was so glad to see me. Nicolas is up in London, doing God knows what, and he's left her alone at Buckland.'

'I sincerely hope you didn't express your feelings to Cathryn?'

'She'll find out for herself in good time, like all the other women in his life have done.'

'You make him sound like Casanova!' her mother mocked, amused.

'No, I don't. Casanova *loved* women.'

After Hilary had left Cathryn phoned Maighread Simmonds for a chat. As usual her friend was fizzing with vivacity.

'My dear Cathryn! How divine to hear from you. My God! you and Nicolas are never out of the newspapers these days ... unfortunately for all the wrong reasons, but never mind, I'm simply dying to hear all about it! How about meeting for lunch? Are you free today?'

'I'm stuck down at Buckland. Nicolas is in town but ...'

'What do you mean, you're stuck down at Buckland?' Maighread sounded quite indignant. 'Why are you still there if he's in town?'

'He's gone up on business and he wanted me to hold the fort here,' Cathryn replied defensively. Then she heard Maighread's sardonic laughter.

'Don't be absurd,' her friend chided. 'The only person who has ever held the fort there is the dreaded Conceptia! Come up on your own, for God's sake! You're not a child, Cathryn! Get someone to drive you up to London. It will only take you forty-five minutes and I'll take you to lunch at Claridge's and we'll have a good old chinwag.'

'I don't think ...' Cathryn began doubtfully, but Maighread interrupted her robustly.

'Why are you letting yourself be treated like a four-year-old? Tell them you're going to do some shopping if you're afraid of the old witch. Just get in a car and *go*! I'll meet you in the bar at one o'clock. I've got some interesting information for you, by the way.'

Cathryn found herself grinning. Her friend always fizzed with vivacity and energy and talking to her was like a tonic. She made a swift resolve. 'I'll be there,' she promised.

Maighread's throaty voice was filled with enthusiasm. 'Good. Order the Dry Martinis if you get there first. See you later, darling.'

As Cathryn changed hurriedly into a dark green woollen dress to wear under her mink coat, and a chic little hat trimmed with green feathers, she realized how much she missed Maighread and how much she longed to get back to spending time in London again. Nicolas's detached manner the previous day had left her badly shaken, making her feel isolated and removed from her friends and family and everything that was familiar to her. It was also as if he were trying to shut her out of his affairs, just when she wanted to be most involved. Maighread was an experienced woman of the world; perhaps she'd be able to help her understand what was going on.

Cathryn was the first to arrive at the hotel, where the string quartet played Viennese waltzes in a corner of the lounge, and the waiters skimmed around serving drinks. As she entered the high-ceilinged, elegant room she became aware of a ripple of interest, of whispered conversations and discreet glances, of knowing looks and gentle nudging.

It was an altogether more refined coterie of gossipmongers than those she'd had to face in the village but nevertheless it was an ordeal to be carefully ignored, no matter how unpleasant.

She chose a table under a palm tree in a discreet alcove where they would not be overheard. A few minutes later Maighread swept into the room, immaculate in a dress and coat of deep amethyst trimmed with black fox fur and a cloche covered in purple violets. With her red hair, the result was sensational, and another flurry of whispering and turned heads rippled across the assembled company like an incoming wave on a beach.

'Well, look at you!' Maighread exclaimed enthusiastically, raising black-gloved hands when she saw Cathryn. 'Draped in mink, my dear, and no doubt dripping in diamonds?'

They exchanged social niceties for a few minutes while Maighread studied Cathryn with her sharp blue eyes. Then she spoke. 'What's wrong? I mean apart from the fact you married a divorced man who has since been arrested and accused of murdering a little girl?'

'I need your advice,' Cathryn said simply, ignoring her friend's joking manner.

Maighread feigned umbrage. 'You've got me here under false pretences! I thought you were going to force caviar and champagne down my throat instead of which…!'

'Stop it,' Çathryn said with a thin smile. 'This is really important, Maighread.'

'Good grief! The child thinks I'm not taking her seriously.' Then she smiled warmly and laid her manicured hand on Cathryn's arm. 'Of course I'll do anything you want, my dear. What's it all about?'

Over a luncheon of *foie gras* followed by lamb cutlets, Cathryn described life at Buckland Place. Maighread sat listening, nodding her head from time to time, as serious now as a judge listening to a barrister outlining his case.

'Why don't you both come up to London?' she asked at last. 'Why are you staying at the scene of the crime? It happened over twenty years ago. It must be as depressing as hell. Apart from which that old bitch is there all the time, not to mention Nicolas's batty younger brother. You've got a huge house in Eaton Square; why aren't you living in it, at least during the week?'

'Nicolas doesn't want to appear to be running away from what happened.'

'Over *twenty* years ago?' Maighread repeated forcefully. 'Tell me honestly, do you think he had anything at all to do with that child's death? Even accidentally?'

Shocked, Cathryn turned pale. 'I know he had nothing to do with it. Absolutely nothing.'

'How can you be so sure?' Maighread's eyes narrowed. 'You've only known him a few months. You know nothing about his past, or his childhood. His father died when he was six and his mother's a witch and . . .'

Cathryn interrupted her. 'Why did you describe Ewan as "batty" a few minutes ago?'

'Would you call him normal? Aged thirty-one and still clinging to his mother? Never had a girlfriend? Never done anything, in fact, except sit around all day like an old woman? If that's normal I'm the Queen of Sheba!' She downed her Dry Martini and signalled for the waiter to bring more drinks.

'How do you know so much about him, Maighread?'

Her friend gave a mischievous smile, scarlet lips framing her even white teeth. 'I told you I had some interesting information for you, didn't I?'

'Yes.'

'Right, then.' She leaned closer and spoke confidentially. 'I've made a new friend. I met her at a cocktail party and I pretended I didn't know who she was. She still doesn't know that I'm a friend of yours.' Then she leaned back with a satisfied sigh. 'So far it's been a *most* enlightening relationship.'

'Who is she?'

There was triumph in her voice. 'Your predecessor, my dear! Miranda, Marchioness of Abingdon.'

'Her?' Cathryn gasped. 'My God, what's she like?'

'As dim as a spent battery torch.'

'I suppose you read her kiss-and-tell article in the *Mirror*?'

'Yes, I did. She really hates the Abingdons.'

Cathryn frowned. 'What's she got against Nicolas? He was very angry about that article but also hurt that she could stoop so low.'

Maighread shrugged. 'I think she had her reasons for leaving,' she observed carefully.

'What reasons? Apart from wanting to return to her previous boyfriend?'

'There's no "previous boyfriend".'

'What are you saying?' No doubt Miranda harboured bad feelings about Nicolas and wanted to justify why she had left him, but right now Cathryn didn't want to hear what those reasons were. At the same time she felt driven by a sense of curiosity. Miranda had been married to Nicolas for several years; time enough to find his flaws and failings. She'd only been married to him for two months.

Maighread continued, 'I'm saying she ran away because she was bitterly unhappy.'

'I've heard the marriage was a mistake,' Cathryn agreed. 'What's she doing now?'

'She's getting on with her life, working in the Red Cross Hospital library, and I think she'd like to marry again one day.'

'She sounded very vengeful in that article.'

'That's the way it was written, my dear. You know what the newspapers are like only too well. Everything has to be sensationalized. If Nicolas's ex-wife had said nice things about him it wouldn't have been a story.'

'I hate the press,' Cathryn exclaimed bitterly. 'They ruin people's lives!'

Maighread gave a worldly smile. 'Some people do that all by themselves,' she retorted lightly. Then her face lit up. 'I've just had a wonderful idea. Why don't we call on Miranda this afternoon? It would give you two a chance to talk and . . .'

'Are you mad?' Cathryn said incredulously. 'Why would I want to meet her?'

'To tell her not to talk to the newspapers again? To tell her to withdraw her accusations against him because he deserves better from an ex-wife? You could be doing him a really good turn. Honestly, my dear, it's always better to face your enemies and have it out with them.' Maighread paused. 'You realize she may tell you things you'd rather not know?'

'Nothing could make me love Nicolas less,' Cathryn said sharply. 'I know him through and through and he has already told me all about himself.'

'Mother of Mary!' Maighread cast her eyes up. 'Show me a man who tells you all about himself and I'll show you a damned liar!'

They finished their lunch in silence. Then Cathryn gathered up her gloves and handbag.

'I'm not going to go and see Miranda,' she said with finality. 'Nicolas would never forgive me and he'd be right. This woman has already damaged him and hurt him, and I don't want to have anything to do with her.'

Maighread looked disappointed. 'Are you sure? You don't think you could persuade her to retract her remarks?'

Cathryn shook her head. 'I think it could make things worse. Anyway, I have a feeling she's got nothing to do with what's happening now. I think someone local has got a grudge against Nicolas and I want to find out who that person is.'

'All right, darling,' Maighread agreed. 'If I hear anything of interest, or if I bump into Miranda again, I'll let you know. Now take care of yourself and come back to London soon, for God's sake! At this rate you're in serious danger of turning into a country bumpkin!'

'I will, but now I've got to get back to Buckland,' Cathryn replied smiling as she hurried to her car, which was waiting for her outside the hotel. Maighread waved, watching her leave, noting she hadn't said she had to get back 'home'.

★ ★ ★

'Where have you been?' Conceptia demanded loudly as Cathryn entered the hall and hurried towards the staircase to get to her own rooms. 'I've been looking everywhere for you but no one seemed to know where you'd gone.' She was standing on the first floor landing looking down imperially on her daughter-in-law, her arms folded forbiddingly across her chest.

Cathryn glanced up at her. 'I've been having luncheon with a friend, and I was not aware I had to ask permission to go out,' she retorted coldly.

'There's no need to be rude. You're not living in a hotel, where you can come and go as you like. Cook has to know how many to expect for meals.'

'Then next time I shall make a special point of informing cook.'

'Did Nicolas know you were going out today?'

Cathryn stopped in her tracks. 'He's not my keeper, why should he know?' she asked with asperity. If Conceptia thought she could be browbeaten, like Miranda, then it was time she realized her new daughter-in-law was different.

'Wouldn't you like to know what *he's* doing, all on his own, in London?'

Cathryn had reached the landing and she faced the older woman with a level gaze. 'I do know what he's doing in London and he has my full approval. He's fighting to try and save his reputation and it would be nice to think that you were helping him to do just that, instead of trying to make mischief between us.'

'He lost his reputation the day he announced his engagement to you.' The dowager's black eyes sparked vindictively and she almost spat out the words.

Cathryn's cheeks flushed with anger. This was open warfare. If she didn't make a stand now Conceptia would walk all over her and the battle would be lost. 'I make him happy, which is more than you have ever done,' she said, forcing herself to sound calm and dignified. 'And make no mistake, I'm here to stay.'

Nine

LORD ABINGDON RETURNS TO LONDON ALONE

The Marquess of Abingdon, who was recently questioned by police in connection with the disappearance twenty-one years ago of a nine-year-old girl whose remains were recently found buried in the grounds of his country estate, returned to London alone yesterday to take up residence at his Belgravia house. Cathryn, his second wife, arrived in London separately and went straight to Claridge's Hotel, before returning to Kent a few hours later. A close friend of the family confirmed that their recent marriage is already under strain . . .

Daily Mail, December 9th, 1930

'This is all rubbish!' Cathryn exclaimed furiously as Ewan handed her the newspaper the next morning, having first read the piece aloud to her in a sneering voice. 'I've a good mind to telephone the editor and tell him . . .'

'I don't think that would help. Nick's going to be livid!' He grinned with delight at the prospect. 'Who were you meeting?'

'How dare they print these lies, insinuating that our marriage is in trouble,' she continued, ignoring his nosiness.

'It's not a lie if you were in London, and if Nick was also in town and you didn't see each other then that's not a lie either, and you haven't got a leg to stand on.'

'Stop being so pedantic, Ewan,' she said irritably.

'I bet he's having a whale of a time on his own, too,' Ewan sniggered mischievously.

The butler came into the room at that moment. He walked over to Cathryn and spoke in a quiet discreet way.

'M'lady, there's a telephone call for you. It's his lordship.'

'Thank you, Wills.' Jumping to her feet, she hurried across the hall to the study, where she seated herself at Nicolas's desk and picked up the receiver.

'Hello darling, is that you?'

'What the hell are you playing at, Cathryn?' Nicolas thundered furiously down the line. 'I can't believe you've been so stupid. What were you doing in London? Why didn't you let me know you'd decided to come up, after all?'

'What do you mean – "after all"?' she retorted, shocked by the intensity of his anger. 'I wanted to go up to town with you all along! Then when I telephoned Maighread she suggested I drive up and meet her for luncheon, which I thought would be fun.'

'I told you to stay at Buckland.' He sounded exasperated. 'This really puts the cat among the pigeons! They'll have us in the divorce courts next! What were you thinking of?'

'This is ridiculous, Nicolas,' she burst out, upset now. 'It's not like I was having lunch with a man. You were busy seeing your solicitor and I desperately needed a break. I feel like a prisoner in this house.'

'But why didn't you tell me you were coming to town? Can't you see how the papers want to make something out of nothing? And having come up, why did you slink back to the country again without saying a word?'

'You didn't want me to be with you,' she shot back, clutching the receiver with one hand, and wiping the tears streaming down her cheeks with the other.

'I wanted you to stay at Buckland to protect you from all this nastiness.' His voice rose, rough with emotion.

'Nicolas, we can't talk like this on the telephone. I want to be with you and I want to support you. I'm going to leave here now and I'll stay with you until we both come back here at the end of the week. That will put a stop to rumours that our marriage is in trouble.'

He sighed deeply. 'I think it may be too late.' There was a click and she realized he'd hung up.

Distraught, she ran up to her bedroom, praying Conceptia wouldn't be lurking in the corridor, spying on her, trying to catch her unawares.

Once in her room she composed herself with an effort and rang for her lady's maid.

'Will you pack enough clothes for me to take to London, right away please?' she asked when Miss Lewis appeared. 'I'm joining my husband for three or four days and I'll just need the bare necessities.'

'Yes, m'lady. Would you like me to ask Rogers to drive you up to town again?'

'Yes please. As soon as possible.'

Cathryn arrived at 15, Eaton Square shortly after eleven thirty, and found Nicolas had already gone to the city to have 'meetings'. Having planned what she was going to say to him on her way up to town, this was deeply disappointing and made her feel he obviously didn't want to see her.

Standing in the middle of the white marble hall she gazed despondently at the housekeeper, Mrs Peters, who showed not a flicker of surprise at her arrival.

'The master bedroom is all ready, m'lady, and I'll send up Doris the head parlour maid to unpack your case,' she said smoothly.

'Thank you, Mrs Peters.'

'Can I get you something to drink? A cup of coffee? Or tea, m'lady?'

'Coffee, please.'

Cathryn had been several times to this palatial house when they'd been engaged but now she realized the white stucco-fronted building, originally favoured by Nicolas's father, was enormous and in its own way almost as imposing as Buckland Place.

There were five large reception rooms, ornately decorated and furnished in Edwardian style, and she guessed there must be ten or fifteen bedrooms. Nicolas had told her that the staff of ten had worked for the Abingdon family for many years. She knew the place would continue to work like clockwork without any intervention from her, but that gave her no sense of belonging. She was beginning to feel like a constant visitor in someone else's house.

Although her family had always had servants, her mother had remained very much in charge of everything. When they'd first been married her parents had bought the Wilton Crescent house and had chosen all the furnishings together, making the place cosy and warm and welcoming. Now, as Cathryn glanced around the ground floor rooms of this formal residence, she realized there was nothing remotely welcoming about it, or even friendly.

When Mrs Peters came with her coffee she also brought

suggested menus from cook for that evening's dinner. 'Will you be having any guests, m'lady?'

'I think we'll be dining on our own.' Cathryn studied the carefully handwritten menu and she suddenly felt very grown up as she made a swift selection of the dishes she knew Nicolas liked best.

'We'll start with a fillet of sole followed by veal with a parsley sauce. Then gooseberry trifle, and as a savoury we'll have the anchovy rissolettes,' she said unhesitatingly. 'I imagine my husband will choose the wines?'

'Lord Abingdon usually does,' Mrs Peters agreed, smilingly. 'What would you like cook to prepare for your luncheon today, m'lady?'

'I think I'll probably go and see my mother and have lunch with her; did my husband say what time he'd be back?' She tried to keep her voice steady. No doubt the speculation in the servants' hall was rife, and Mrs Peters may even have overheard Nicolas shouting down the phone at her that morning, so it was important she keep her dignity and act as normally as possible.

Mrs Peters averted her eyes. 'As far as I know he's returning late in the afternoon, m'lady, but he didn't actually say when.'

'Very well. If he should contact you during the day will you tell him I'm at my mother's house? And that I've arranged for us to dine in? And will you tell Rogers that I'll need him in fifteen minutes to drive me to Wilton Crescent?'

'Certainly m'lady. Rogers is in the kitchen having a cup of tea and I'll tell him right away.'

As soon as Cathryn was alone again, she telephoned her mother.

'Oh, Cath!' Lilian Brocklehurst wailed. 'Are you all right? Where are you – down at Buckland?'

'No, Mother, I'm in London. I was wondering if I could pop over to have luncheon with you?'

'No! No, that's a bad idea,' she said firmly. 'There are newspapermen *everywhere* these days. It's too dreadful for words! I feel quite stifled. It will look bad if you come here. They might think you've come running home to your parents.'

Cathryn sighed with frustration. She could just see the headline: 'Young bride deserts marquess and returns home'.

'Oh my God, you're right! Then can you come over here? Shall I send the car to fetch you?'

'I'd better get a taxi and only tell the driver where I'm going when I'm out of earshot of those dreadful little men with their notepads.'

Half an hour later a taxi juddered up to number fifteen. Martin, the butler, had been instructed by Cathryn to watch out for her mother's arrival, and to have the front door slightly open in readiness so she could dodge the waiting press men.

A moment later Lilian Brocklehurst rushed up the front steps in a flurry of furs and a veiled hat.

'Oh, Cath! What a to-do this is!' she gasped as soon as she got inside the building and saw her daughter waiting in the study doorway. 'I've never known anything like this in my life! I feel positively *hounded*.' As she spoke, all fluttery and breathless, she followed Cathryn up the wide curved staircase to the drawing room. 'You look ghastly, darling.'

'I'm harassed to death,' Cathryn confessed. 'Would you like a glass of sherry? I've ordered luncheon for twelve thirty in case Nicolas comes home early.'

Lilian stopped and turned to look askance at her. 'Isn't he here? Where is he?' she added in alarm.

Pride forbade her to admit she and Nicolas were having problems, because wasn't that what her mother had prophesied? 'He's at a meeting with his solicitor,' she replied lightly. 'He'll be back later.'

'I sincerely hope he will; it will look terrible if he doesn't, especially after that piece in the *Daily Mail* this morning. What *is* going on, Cath? My friends have been telephoning me asking if you and Nicolas have split up.'

Cathryn realized that if the village at Buckland was a hotbed of tittle-tattle, London, by comparison, was a frightening whirlwind of rumour and speculation which showed no signs of abating and could destroy them.

'Of course we haven't split up!' Cathryn retorted stoutly. 'Whatever will people say next? The whole thing is ridiculous and that's what Nicolas is doing: trying to find a way of stopping these wild stories being printed.'

Fortified by a drink, Lilian sipped away and chatted on heedlessly. 'We're going to have to move down to The Elms for a while, you know. I feel quite ill with worry.'

'Oh, Mama, I'm so sorry.'

'What have you *done* by marrying Nicolas? Have you any idea what we're all going through?'

Cathryn threw up her hands in exasperation. 'It's not his fault. He's done nothing wrong.'

'There's no smoke without fire, Cath. With a mother like Conceptia, nothing would surprise me about that family.'

'You mustn't say that!' Cathryn exclaimed in alarm. 'If you were overheard . . . ? Oh, my God!' She covered her face with her hands for a moment. 'Please be careful. If the servants were to hear you, those sorts of remarks will get around and be terribly damaging. I promise you Nicolas had nothing to do with this child and it's far worse for him than it is for any of us. He's doing everything he can to prove he's innocent.'

But Lilian wasn't listening, 'It's bad enough that when you married him he had already been married and divorced. But now he's being questioned about the murder of a little girl! That's the most terrible thing I've ever heard. This scandal is ruining all our lives. Your father's reputation as well as Charles's is being tarnished, by association.'

'Mama, what can I say?' Cathryn asked in desperation. 'I know it's terrible and absolutely unjust but I love him and he's my husband—'

'More's the pity!'

'—and he's not to blame for what's happened. In the first place, would he have asked the foresters to clear that bit of land for replanting if he'd known the little girl lay buried there? She'd been missing for twenty years and until now no one has even suggested he was involved in her disappearance,' Cathryn continued heatedly. 'Now, all of a sudden, you'd think he was Jack the Ripper. Someone is using this tragedy as a means of ruining him and I intend to find out who it is.'

'There were so many nice young men you could have married,' Lilian murmured regretfully.

'But Nicolas is the one I fell in love with and apart from this ghastly situation we're divinely happy.' She blotted out the way he'd spoken to her on the phone that morning and her real reason for coming up to London. Certain that their love was strong enough to get them through this ordeal, she reminded herself that Nicolas was under enormous pressure. It was no wonder he'd snapped.

Cathryn was waiting in the drawing room when Nicolas returned at five o'clock, looking gaunt and tired. He stood in the doorway looking straight at her, his dark eyes boring into hers, his arms folded defensively across his chest.

'Nicolas . . . !' She jumped to her feet, her arms outstretched as she flung herself at him, holding him close, pressing herself against his body as she gazed up at him. 'I'm so sorry I upset you by coming up to London yesterday. I really didn't mean any harm.'

He remained standing, silent and unresponsive.

'Please say you'll forgive me? I wouldn't do anything to hurt you and I can't tell you how sorry I am,' she whispered, tears gathering in her eyes.

Gently but firmly he disentangled himself from her embrace and walked over to the drinks tray. 'Let's put it behind us, shall we?' he said coldly. 'If we start fighting with each other we really will be in a pickle.' Then he picked up a bottle of gin and poured a measure into two cocktail glasses.

In miserable silence she watched as he added ice cubes and then a splash of Dubonnet before handing one of the glasses to her.

'I've spent two days trying to bring an injunction against the various newspapers who are out to destroy my reputation,' he continued in a flat voice, as if he were addressing an audience.

'Have you succeeded?' she asked hopefully, as she dabbed her eyes and sat down on the hard upright sofa, hoping he'd come and sit beside her.

Instead he walked pointedly over to an elegant chair on the opposite side of the fireplace. 'I don't know yet. It's going to cost a small fortune, but anything to stop this relentless scurrilous reporting is cheap at the price. Through Anthony Warner, my solicitor, I've appointed Sir Oscar Neville as my QC. He doesn't hold out much hope of stopping the newspapers but he'll certainly do his best.' Again his manner was remote, as if he hardly knew her.

'You must be exhausted,' Cathryn said sympathetically. 'I've ordered dinner for us, but perhaps we can have an early night?'

Nicolas frowned. 'I've got a lot of paperwork to catch up on,' he said.

Cathryn got up and walked over to him, looking at him earnestly. 'Nicolas, please don't shut me out. I made a mistake and I'm really sorry but now is not the time to cold-shoulder me. We need to stick together to get through this. I love you and I'm your wife. Don't treat me like a stranger.'

'As I said, let's just forget it. What's done is done. Just don't talk to *anyone* about this affair, Cathryn. Someone is tipping off the press about our movements. That's why there are photographers waiting for us wherever we go.'

'Do you mean we're being watched? What, now?' she added, horrified.

Nicolas stepped nearer the window and peered down to the lamp-lit street below.

Then he stepped back sharply. 'Bastards!' he swore angrily. 'There are four of them waiting like vermin, huddled against the railings of the garden square. They're out to hang, draw and quarter me if they get the chance!'

'Don't say things like that!' she said, distressed. 'We'll get through this, Nicolas. You're an innocent man.'

He ignored her. 'Don't go out, Cathryn. I have to see a few people tomorrow in the city and we'll return to Buckland the next day. And be careful who you talk to on the telephone and what you say,' he added. Then he strode over to the door without a backward glance. 'I'm going to have a bath before dinner.'

Left alone in the grand cream and gilt room with its shimmering mirrors and glittering chandeliers, Cathryn felt a wave of deep sadness sweep over her. Their beautiful life together and their boundless happiness seemed to have faded, leaving her wondering what lay ahead. Who was she really married to? A cold man whose previous wife had run away because she'd been so unhappy?

In spite of being the wife of one of the richest man in England, she felt like a prisoner in her own house. Had Miranda ever felt like this, she wondered? When things had gone wrong, had Nicolas shut her out, too?

Two days later, they returned to Buckland Place and for once, to her surprise, Cathryn was happy to be back. She noticed fresh flowers had been arranged in her bedroom and sitting room, logs were crackling cheerily in the fireplaces and in her dressing room Miss Lewis had laid out country tweeds for her to change into.

She rested on the *chaise longue* for a while as if she'd just returned from an arduous journey. All day yesterday Nicolas had absented himself 'to have meetings', so she'd been alone at Eaton Square, passing the time by acquainting herself with the staff and planning in her head the parties she'd like to give once this dreadful ordeal was over. If it ever did come to an end, that is, she reflected gloomily. Supposing the police never found out what had happened to Posy? Supposing the false rumours continued about Nicolas's involvement? How were they going to continue living under such a cloud of suspicion and scandal?

Nicolas had hardly said a word to her on the drive down, and as soon as they'd entered the house he'd disappeared in the direction of Hugh Verney's office. This wasn't a marriage, she reflected. It seemed more like a battlefield and in spite of her robust dismissal to her mother that they were happy, it was beginning to strike her that just maybe their marriage was coming to an end before it had really begun.

The thought was too dreadful to contemplate. She jumped up and started busying herself by changing into the warm clothes laid out on the bed. This would never do. She must make an effort to get on with things, and what she needed most of all was to get out into the open. Days spent indoors in London had made her feel claustrophobic, and press or no press, she needed to get out. Stretch her legs. Breathe deeply the cold clean country air and get a grip on herself.

The wind was freezing, slicing across the countryside like sharp knives, stabbing the branches of the trees and lashing out at the hedges. Pulling down her felt hat she started walking down the Long Walk, head bent and her hands dug deeply into the pockets of her overcoat, while her eyes watered and fierce gusts almost took her breath away. If only Nicolas were striding along beside her now, she thought sadly, with the vapour of their breaths mingling as they laughed and talked together. The last time they'd been this way they'd walked arm in arm, without a care in the world and with their perfect future all mapped out before them.

Suddenly she had a sense she was being followed. Turning quickly, she saw David Partridge lurking by one of the trees. When he realized he'd been spotted he stepped out from the shadows, raising his hat in bland greeting.

'Good morning, my dear!'

'Good morning,' she said, startled, her heart hammering uncomfortably. 'I didn't know you were staying.'

He gazed at her from under his heavy lidded eyes. 'Conceptia told me you were up in London with Nicolas.' He spoke gently and smarmily. 'Then, lo and behold! I see you walking briskly on this chilly morning.' He fell into step beside her. 'You're looking radiant, my dear. But how are you bearing up under the strain of this most unpleasant situation?'

'I'm fine,' she said shortly, gritting her teeth. There was something so abhorrent about this old man, she could barely stand his presence.

'But it must be so unpleasant for you?' he persisted. 'People are saying such dreadful things about your husband.' He looked at her pityingly. 'I really do admire your courage, Cathryn.'

She turned to face him, her eyes flashing. 'I have nothing to be afraid of,' she said firmly. 'Nobody who knows Nicolas thinks he had anything to do with that child's death, so I'm not being brave in ignoring the gossip, because I know he's absolutely innocent. I'd just like to find out who believes otherwise! Spreading these vile lies is slanderous.'

David Partridge gave an exaggerated shrug. 'That's what comes from living in a small village.'

'I don't think it's the village people who are running to the newspapers,' she retorted sharply. 'I still don't know who went to the police with their accusations either, but I intend to find out. It's that person who started this witch hunt and I won't rest until I know who he or she is.'

'You're unlikely to find out, I'm afraid. This is a very closed community and the police aren't allowed to break the law of confidentiality.'

'As my grandmother used to say, "There are more ways of killing a cat than choking it with butter." I'll find out if it's the last thing I do and believe me, whoever it is will wish they'd never been born. Now, if you'll excuse me, Mr Partridge, I'm going to walk over to the home farm.' She turned away without a backward glance, heading west, knowing he was unlikely to follow her across the frozen ground.

Frank Burgess was mucking out one of the cow sheds when Cathryn entered the cobbled farm yard twenty minutes later.

He looked up, startled, touched his cloth cap and then went on sweeping as if he didn't expect her to stop and talk to him.

'Good morning, Frank. Cold morning, isn't it? How are you and Ida getting on?' she asked gently.

'Not too badly, m'lady,' he mumbled. She wasn't sure whether it was the sharp wind or tears that were making his pale blue eyes water. 'Our 'ouse is a lot warmer now, thanks to you.'

'Is there anything else you need, Frank? I'll be sending over a Christmas hamper in a few days, but in the meantime, what can I do to help?'

He wiped his nose with the back of his hand. 'Nothing goin' to mend a broken 'eart.'

There was an embarrassed silence and he shuffled his feet as if he'd said too much.

'I know,' Cathryn said softly. 'That was a beautiful funeral for Posy. Everyone in the village was there, weren't they? I know she'll never be forgotten.'

'Aye. The missus was pleased an' all and we're very grateful to his lordship for payin' for it. We've chosen a lovely headstone too. It's being engraved right now.' He sighed deeply and looked at her again, the pain etched deeply into the lines of his thin face. 'No one knows how much we miss Posy, even after all these years,' he said gruffly. 'She'd have been thirty now! A grown woman with children of her own. She was the bonniest wee girl you've ever seen. We was that delighted with 'er when she was born, we christened 'er after a bunch of flowers.' He paused, staring at the ground around his feet, biting his lower lip. Then he looked up, straight into Cathryn's face again. 'An' then we lost 'er! That was the worst day of me life.'

'Oh, Frank, I'm so sorry.' She blinked fiercely, trying to quell her own tears. 'I've not had a child yet and I cannot begin to imagine how terrible it must be, and not knowing what had happened to Posy must have been the worst time of all.'

'Aye. For a long time we thought it were the gypsies what took 'er. Me wife used to sit in the winder, lookin' out, watching the lane, praying our Posy would come runnin' back one day, or someone would come and tell us they knew where she was . . .' His voice drifted off thinly. 'It never 'appened though.'

'She is at rest now,' Cathryn said softly.

He nodded. 'Aye, but it were like the end of the world when she went. And I loved that child as if she was me own.'

Then he started sweeping energetically again, turning his back on her and moving away to indicate their conversation was at an end.

The full meaning of his words sank in, sending a ripple of shock through her veins as she walked slowly back to the house. *As if she was me own.* What had he meant? Was that what he'd actually said? Or had she misheard him? Surely Nicolas had said Ida and Frank had tried to have a baby for ten years before they'd succeeded, so there was no question of Posy being Ida's child by a previous marriage.

Stunned, she quickened her pace, feeling sure this had put a new slant on everything. Whose child had Posy been? Was she even Ida's little girl? Or had she been adopted by the barren couple who'd been unable to have their own child?

Anxious to talk to Nicolas, she hoped she'd find him in Hugh Verney's office.

'I'm afraid he's not here,' Hugh told her cheerily, looking up from his desk as she barged into his room. Piled up in front of him were invoices and statements and quotes for new fencing around the boundary of the estate. 'Actually he said he was going out to look for you,' he added

'Do you know which way he went?'

'I guess towards the gardens on the south side of the house, so he is out of the range of photographers. That's one of his favourite walks anyway and he probably thinks that's where you're most likely to have gone.'

'Thanks, Hugh. I'll go and find him. This is like being under house arrest, isn't it? God, I wonder how long it's going to last?'

'The press will get tired of the story sooner or later, unless of course there are any dramatic turns that will put Nicolas in the spotlight again.'

She spun round to look at him, her expression horrified. 'What do you mean? What dramatic turns?'

He gathered his brow apologetically, feeling he'd said too much. 'Oh, I don't know.' His tone was vague. 'Like you, I'm hoping their enquiries are at an end and we can all get back to normal.'

She placed her hands on his desk and, leaning forward,

lowered her voice. 'You don't for an instant imagine Nicolas was involved, do you?' Her tone was challenging and she searched his mild face with sharp eyes. For a moment she'd nearly told him about Frank's remark but now she held back, unsure of his loyalty.

He spoke openly and frankly. 'No, of course I don't, but what worries me is that the only air rifle on the estate at that time, as far as I know, was the one belonging to Nicolas. The police are still looking for it, and if they find it and can prove the pellets found with Posy came from that rifle . . . well, there could be a problem, couldn't there?'

Cathryn nodded slowly. 'And obviously everywhere it might be has been thoroughly searched?'

'Absolutely, and so have the cellars, barns, outhouses and every other likely place where it might have been hidden.'

Hidden . . . ? The word jarred. It wasn't the same as lost. Or mislaid. Hidden meant someone had purposely put it in a place where it couldn't be found.

'Yes, I see. Have you any theories, Hugh?' she asked outright.

He shook his head but inwardly he was worried. Nicolas was known to have gone into the woods for target practice when he'd been a boy. Everyone knew he was a keen shot and a good shot, longing for the day when he would be old enough to join the shoot with a proper gun. Was it possible that he'd inadvertently shot Posy Burgess without realizing it? It got dark quite early in November. He might not have seen her in the dense woods, might not have realized she'd been there, which in any case she should not have been, as he aimed and fired at a cardboard target nailed to a tree.

Then he'd have gone home for tea, leaving his air rifle in the gun room as usual. Perhaps someone had known he'd shot Posy and had hidden the rifle to protect him?

Hugh Verney tried to banish the thought, because he had a high regard for Nicolas, who'd become his friend as well as his employer. It would be a tragedy if it were discovered he'd killed Posy by accident and the consequences would be devastating.

Cathryn would suffer, the Abingdon family and all it stood for would be destroyed, and, thinking selfishly, he'd probably lose his wonderful job as Estate Manager.

Sighing deeply, he rose from his desk and started pacing around his office, regretting now he'd said so much to Cathryn. Nicolas needed her to be staunch and supportive, not filled with doubt and negative thoughts.

'No, I've no theories at all,' he replied, trying to sound reassuring. 'I wouldn't worry too much, Cathryn. We have the best legal system in the world. No one is going to believe Nicolas did anything wrong.'

'I hope you're right. I'll go and find him now.' It didn't take her long to find Nicolas, striding through the knot garden.

'Hugh said I'd find you here,' she said, smiling.

'Where have you been? I've been looking for you.' He looked flushed from the strong icy wind that was whipping across the lawn, but he seemed to be in a better mood.

She slipped her arm through his and they started walking slowly together. 'Did you know that David Partridge was staying?' she asked. 'I met him in the Long Walk but I managed to get rid of him. I really don't like him and I don't trust him.'

Nicolas smiled down at her. 'I don't trust him either but he's someone for my mother to talk to, which keeps her off my back, so I try to pretend he's not around.'

'I wish I could. For some reason he's desperate to be friends with me. But that's not why I came looking for you. I need to tell you something.'

'What is it?' he asked cautiously.

'I walked over to the home farm and talked to Frank Burgess and he said something that staggered me.'

They stopped walking and Nicolas looked down into her face. 'What did he say?'

She repeated Frank's remark. 'Why would he say that if it wasn't true? Did they adopt Posy? I thought perhaps . . .'

'Oh, God!' he groaned before she could finish her sentence. 'I feared as much.'

'What do you mean?'

'Oh, I believed Frank was her father, as did everyone else, when she vanished and we thought the gypsies had abducted her. But when her body was found I realized that someone local was responsible for her death. Someone who wanted revenge.'

She looked bewildered. 'I don't understand. What are you talking about?'

There was a pause and Nicolas looked away, his face troubled as he gazed unseeingly at the landscape. 'Sometimes things are not as they seem, darling. There are several children around this area who are illegitimate. I'm almost sure Posy was one of them. After being supposedly barren for ten years, Ida suddenly has a baby. Everyone in the village was surprised. Maybe someone wanted to get rid of Posy in case she became an embarrassment as she grew older.'

Cathryn looked bewildered, only half understanding. 'So who could her father have been?'

'*My* father.'

'Your . . . ?' Her hand flew to her mouth and her blue eyes were wide with shock. 'That explains a lot,' she said slowly, as the realization sank in. 'So your father . . .' Her voice trailed off. Was that why Conceptia hated Nicolas's father? And why Conceptia had been hostile towards Ida Burgess when she'd come to Buckland just after they'd found Posy's remains, calling her 'hysterical' and 'off her head'?

It also explained Ida's remark when she'd sobbed, 'He promised me he'd look after her.'

William Abingdon had been killed in a motor accident, though, leaving a son and heir of six, another son of two, and an illegitimate daughter who would have been one year old at the time, a baby too small to know what was happening, but who, by the time she was nine years old, might have become aware of her potential position as the child of one of the richest men in the country.

'Who else knows this?' Cathryn asked quickly.

'Probably everyone in the village,' Nicolas replied wearily. 'My father favoured seducing hired help from the village rather than live-in servants. He could meet them secretly while their husbands were at work and if they got pregnant, everyone would assume the baby was the husband's child.'

'That must have been awful for your mother?'

Nicolas turned and looked at her squarely. 'I'm afraid I have a feeling she may have driven him to it.'

'What do you mean?'

'My mother was always a very difficult woman. She's mellowed over the years compared to the way she was when I was a child.

She drove him crazy with her demands, and all the time she was taunting him that it was her money that was paying for everything.' He paused, remembering how as a child he'd heard them quarrelling, their voices raised, his loud and angry, hers shrill and high-pitched. 'Their fights were monumental,' he continued, 'and although I was small my mother never failed to tell me what he was up to with the local women, as she tried to poison my mind against him.'

Cathryn's face softened and she gazed at him with compassion. 'That must have been very hard for you.'

'I worshipped him and when he died it was the end of my small world. There was no one left to protect me from her wrath.' He gave a little twisted smile. 'She punished me every day by saying I was just like him . . . and she still does in her own way.'

'That's the cruellest thing I've ever heard.' She reached for his hand and held it tightly. 'Parents must always show a united front to the children. Did she say horrid things about your father to Ewan, too?'

He nodded. 'She made sure of that and that's why she's determined to hang on to him with all her might. I'm the bad boy of the family and he's the good one who will always be by her side.'

'Nicolas, there's nothing bad about you and you must know that,' she exclaimed fervently. 'I wouldn't have married you if I'd thought there was. Can't we go back to Tyndrum? Can't we get away from here? The villagers are up in arms and I'm sure they're whispering dreadful things about us. We were so happy in Scotland where no one disturbed us and you showed me all the places you'd loved when you'd been a boy.'

His eyes still had a strained look, but his smile was warm now. 'I promise you we'll go back the minute this ghastly business is over, though God knows when that will be. Then we'll have a long honeymoon and let the rest of the world go hang.'

She pressed herself to his side, wanting to block out everything except the depths of their love for each other. 'I can hardly wait,' she whispered. 'All I want is to be alone with you again, away from all this.'

Ten

PEER SENT POISON PEN LETTERS

The Marquess of Abingdon has reportedly received a string of anonymous letters at his family seat in Kent. The first, thought to be a Christmas greetings card, arrived on 23rd December, accusing him of the murder of nine-year-old Posy Burgess . . .

News of the World, January 7th, 1931

'I can't tell you how terrible it is down here,' Cathryn told Maighread, who, having read the newspapers, had telephoned to find out what was going on. 'My family left here two days ago after a fairly bleak Christmas, and now Nicolas is going out of his mind over these terrible letters!'

'Have you any idea who sent them?'

'No. They're not handwritten. They're pasted-up letters made into letters cut from newspapers and magazines. It gives one a really horrible feeling to read them and realize someone hates us so much. We've given them to the police but they say it's going to be difficult to trace who sent them.'

Maighread's voice was sharp with concern. 'Surely the post-mark says where they've come from?'

Cathryn sighed with frustration. 'They've been posted all over the place. London. Cardiff. Guildford. Even Brighton! The envelopes have been typed, but that's not much good! It only shows that perhaps the person works in an office and not from home.'

'Unless it's a journalist?'

'That's always a possibility I suppose.'

'My dear girl!' Maighread sounded sympathetic. 'You are being put through the mill, aren't you? How many letters have there been?'

'Five so far. One of them even accuses him of being a paedophile.' Her voice rose, shrill with pain. 'I'd like to *kill* whoever is sending this filth! It's ruining our lives! I just want to get away from this place before we're all driven mad.'

'Was Christmas absolutely ghastly? I'd hoped you'd be in town for the divine party we gave on Christmas Eve.'

'I wish we had been. It was lovely seeing my parents and Charles and I think they enjoyed themselves, but on the other hand,' she continued, dropping her voice so she wouldn't be overheard, 'Conceptia and Ewan decided to stay instead of going to Tyndrum so it was all very tense.'

'That sounds like the understatement of the decade!' Maighread retorted. 'Mother of mercy! I can't think of anything worse than having to spend Christmas with *her*!'

'Never again! Nicolas has promised me we'll go back to Tyndrum as soon as we can, but he says we can't leave here just yet. Not with all this going on.'

'He's right, Cathryn. Running away now would be fatal. Why don't I come down and see you, my dear ? Maybe we can rack our brains and try to work out who is behind it all. They always say "an outsider sees all the game" and maybe I can bring a fresh eye to the situation.'

'Oh, Maighread, would you really? Can you bear it? We're all creeping around treading on eggshells and it's not exactly fun down here at the moment.'

'Maybe we can shake things up,' her friend retorted spiritedly. 'I'm itching to take on the old dowager, for a start.'

Cathryn couldn't help chuckling. 'Then please come and stay – if Vere can spare you for a few days?'

'My dear, he's so busy he won't even notice I'm away. He's planning to build a hotel near Victoria Station and he's hardly ever home these days, not that I mind because he's making millions by the minute.' Her warm laughter was cheerful and her manner positive. 'I found emerald and diamond earrings under the Christmas tree this year, not to mention a sable wrap and an exquisite pearl bracelet. Isn't he an absolute darling? Cathy, I'll be with you tomorrow afternoon, how about that?'

'That,' Cathryn replied gratefully, 'would be absolutely marvellous.' Then she went to see Mrs Temple the housekeeper, to inform her that Mrs Vere Simmonds would be staying and to prepare a suite of rooms for her. Apart from her family, it was the first time she'd had a friend to stay and she felt childishly excited by the thought.

'Very well, m'lady,' Mrs Temple replied smilingly. 'Shall I put Mrs Simmonds in the Peacock Suite, next to your private quarters?'

'Thank you. That would be perfect.'

At that moment Conceptia appeared, looking rake thin and harassed, her face paler than ever against the severity of her black dress. 'Who have you invited to stay?' she asked querulously.

'My friend, Maighread Simmonds. She's a very intelligent woman, and we're going to try and work out who is responsible for these letters.'

'What is she? A private detective?' Conceptia scoffed harshly. 'It's better to leave these things to the police. We don't want interference from total strangers.'

'Maighread is my best friend, not a stranger,' Cathryn retorted hotly. 'All the police seem to be doing is trying to pin something on to Nicolas when he's utterly innocent.'

'Humph! Nicolas has caused me problems from the beginning, and the older he gets the worse it seems to be.'

Cathryn stared at her mother-in-law. 'How can you say that? What sort of problems has he had, apart from being divorced? Don't you care that he's being put through hell?'

'The police say the child was shot by an air rifle and the only air rifle on the estate was the one owned by Nicolas, who was at home at the time.' Conceptia raised her chin and her expression was stubborn. 'If you've any brains, work it out for yourself.'

Shards of ice particles seemed to dart through Cathryn's veins and pierce her heart. 'You surely can't believe it was him who killed Posy?' she asked incredulously.

'According to a statement made to the police, someone *saw* him shoot that child.' Conceptia's black eyes bored deeply into Cathryn's, as if willing her to believe Nicolas was guilty.

'But the police haven't brought charges against him,' Cathryn protested. Her mind was spinning wildly. How could a mother feel like this towards her son? For a moment she even wondered if Conceptia was responsible for sending the poison pen letters herself, but then she dismissed the notion as ridiculous. 'You're so wrong!' she burst out, enraged. 'I refuse to believe he had anything to do with Posy's death. I just know he wasn't involved,' she added vehemently.

Conceptia's tone was cold and level. 'They didn't charge him because they had no evidence, not because they believe he's innocent. You're very young, Cathryn, and very naïve. Just because Nicolas is rich and titled you see him as some sort of god, a perfect man who would never do anything wrong.' She sighed theatrically. 'One day you'll wake up to the fact that most men are rotten to the core, one way or another!'

'You're standing there telling me you actually believe your son, my husband, killed that child when he was fourteen?' Cathryn demanded.

'He was always a good shot. He inherited that from his father, too.' There was disgust and spite in the older woman's voice.

'Dear God!' Reeling with shock and anger that her mother-in-law could really believe Nicolas was guilty, she lashed out in sudden fury. 'What sort of a mother are you? My mother would defend Charles and me to the end of time if anyone accused us of doing something dreadful. Yet here you are, pointing at Nicolas as if he were to blame for this whole disaster. What is the *matter* with you?'

Conceptia stiffened, her thin frame shaking. 'Don't you dare talk to me like that! Who do you think you are? A jumped-up little debutante who thought she'd struck lucky by marrying one of the richest men in the country; rich, may I remind you, because of *my* money! You'll find out soon enough, as Miranda did, that Nicolas is not all he seems to be.' Then she turned abruptly and stalked off at a brisk pace, her dark head held high, her shoulders hunched with righteous indignation.

Cathryn watched the receding figure with a tinge of fear. Her first thought was that Conceptia was deranged. Barking mad. She actually seemed to want Nicolas to be found guilty. Her second thought was that she must protect Nicolas from his crazy mother. It would add to his worry and hurt if he realized she was talking as if she were certain he'd killed Posy. Then she was hit by another truly hideous thought. Supposing Conceptia told the police she *knew* Nicolas was guilty? I wouldn't put it past her, Cathryn reflected with something akin to panic. Maybe she would also disinherit Nicolas, and make her beloved Ewan the next owner of Buckland Place?

Nicolas was out, riding around the estate, so she rushed over to his desk, grabbed the telephone and dialled her father's office number.

An impersonal woman's voice answered. 'Good morning. Brocklehurst, Milne and Chilcott. Can I help you?'

'I'd like to speak to Sir Roland, please.'

'I'm afraid he's with a client at the moment. Can I ask him to return your call?'

'Yes please. This is Lady Abingdon. Can you tell my father it's rather urgent?'

'Certainly, Lady Abingdon. I don't think he'll be long.'

Cathryn replaced the receiver, her hand shaking. She decided to stay in the study and wait for the call, afraid that if Conceptia were around she might pick up the receiver and prevent her talking to her father. Disconcerted, she watched as Ewan strolled into the room at that moment, cigarette in one hand and a newspaper in the other.

'What are you doing?' he asked suspiciously.

'What are *you* doing?' she snapped irritably. 'Why are you always hanging about? Don't you ever go out of doors? Surely the horses need exercising or something?'

'It's beastly cold outside,' he retorted, settling himself like an old woman by the fire.

Ewan was someone she found difficult to have a conversation with. Lacking verbal gifts, he questioned everything that was going on, but was then unable to respond further except for querying everything she said.

'I'm waiting for a private telephone call,' she said pointedly.

'Who from?'

'Actually it's no business of yours, Ewan.'

'What goes on here is my business. This is as much my house as yours,' he added pettishly.

'It doesn't belong to either of us and you know it.'

'You're not even an Abingdon; you've just married into the family.'

'Yes, and I'm Nicolas's wife. Now if you'd like to go and sit somewhere else, I wish to talk to my father in private when he calls me back.' She gazed at his pale weak face and loose mouth. He was so different to Nicolas it was hard to believe they were brothers.

He opened his copy of *The Times* and settled himself more comfortably in the armchair. 'Well, I'm not moving. This is the warmest room in the house.'

Cathryn rose, flushed with anger. Striding out of the library, she slammed the door loudly before sprinting across the hall and along the corridor that led to Hugh Verney's office, where there was an extension of the house telephone.

'Can I seek sanctuary for a few minutes in here?' she asked Hugh breathlessly as she rushed through his door. 'I'm waiting for a call from my father. I need his advice, but I don't want to talk in front of the family and that idiot boy Ewan won't budge out of the library to give me a moment's privacy.'

Hugh jumped to his feet, his face filled with amusement at the way she'd spoken.

'Of course you can, Cathryn. I'm on my way to the home farm, so you can have my office to yourself. I must say, I like your description of Ewan,' he added laughingly.

'Thanks.' She grinned, recovering her good humour. 'Is Nicolas still out?'

'He's ridden over to inspect the replanting programme. We're putting in a lot of elm and oak trees, as well as silver birch and ash.'

'Where they found...?'

Hugh nodded. 'Nearby. The place will soon be unrecognizable. Much lighter and more airy.'

'But they're not diverting the stream? I mean there'll still be that jutting-out bit of land on the far side, like a little island?' Her voice quavered. She'd gone to see where they'd found Posy's remains and had been deeply affected by the atmosphere of tragedy coupled with a malevolence that shrouded the dark area by the water's edge, under the overhanging branches of ancient oaks.

'The stream's still there,' Hugh replied in a quiet voice.

'I don't think I can bear it.' She stood by his desk, one hand covering her mouth, the other supporting herself.

'Are you all right, Cathryn?'

She turned to look at him, her blue eyes awash with tears. 'Did you know Nicolas's mother thinks he killed Posy?'

Hugh started, then blinked. 'What*?*'

'She's just told me that Nicolas was a good shot and that he was at home the day Posy vanished, and that the only reason the police didn't bring charges was because they didn't have enough evidence.'

'We all know Nicolas is a good shot but for her to say that . . .' Hugh broke off, looking deeply concerned.

'Conceptia has really got it in for Nicolas. Supposing she tells the police he shot Posy? That's why I want to speak urgently to my father. I want to know if that would be sufficient evidence for them to charge him – his own mother saying he's guilty?' She covered her face with her hands for a moment. 'I'm going out of my mind, Hugh. She's the most evil woman I've ever heard of. She seems intent on making all our lives a misery, and I believe she'd like to see Nicolas disgraced so she can disinherit him and make Ewan her heir.'

Hugh stared at her in alarm. It wasn't supposed to be his business to get involved and comment on the private lives of his employers, but something was going to have to be done to stop the dowager bringing the whole family down.

Cathryn understood his predicament but she trusted him now and he'd become her only friend at Buckland. 'It's because Nicolas reminds her of his father, isn't it?' she prompted. 'He was very unfaithful to her.'

'So I believe.'

She was about to ask him if Conceptia realized that Posy was her husband's child but at that moment the telephone rang and he hurriedly picked up the receiver. 'It's for you,' he told Cathryn, handing it to her. 'I'll leave you in peace,' he added tactfully, as he slipped out of his office.

'Daddy? Thank you for ringing back. Listen, I need to ask you about something.'

She outlined what Conceptia had said. 'Could the police arrest Nicolas if she were to go to them to confirm their earlier suspicions?'

There was a long pause as Sir Roland took in this new turn of events. 'Well, they didn't charge him when someone else made a statement the other day saying they'd seen him shoot the child, did they?' he said slowly and thoughtfully. 'We don't know who made that statement but it's true the police might take the word of his own mother more seriously, but listen Cath, it's a complicated situation. It comes under *Article 50 – The Age of Criminal Responsibility*. Nicolas was fourteen at the time, wasn't he?'

'Yes.'

'Ummm.' Sir Roland paused, deep in thought. 'If he'd been under the age of ten, he could not be charged with any wrongdoing. The law originally set the ages between seven and eight but changed it to ten because a child of that age does not necessarily have a sense of responsibility.'

Cath spoke apprehensively. 'And at fourteen?'

'Children from the age of ten to fourteen can only be convicted of the offence if the prosecution can show that the child was aware that he was doing something wrong.'

'I see. So if it could be proved it was an accident and harm was not intended, it would be all right?'

'If it could proved, beyond a shadow of doubt, that Nicolas was merely target practising, in the growing darkness of the woods on a late November afternoon, and he failed to see a child, who shouldn't have been there in any case, and shot her by accident, then there is no case against him.'

'You're absolutely sure?' she asked, desperate to believe that what he was saying was true.

'Absolutely sure. It comes under the Children's Act, 1908–1929.'

'But we're now in 1931?' she asked nervously. 'Has it changed at all?'

'No, my dear. There might be a slight change in the law in a couple of years' time, but so far this stands.'

Cathryn led out a long sigh of relief. 'Thank you, Daddy. I know Nicolas didn't shoot her, but it's such a relief to know that if he's being framed he can't be charged with murder or manslaughter.'

'Try not to worry so, Cath. It's not the thought of Posy's shooting you have to worry about, but the dreadful way it's being reported in all the newspapers. The press coverage is committing him to a life time of notoriety and it seems nothing can be done to stop it. As far as Conceptia is concerned I'm sure he can look after himself—'

'But he doesn't know what his mother is saying,' she cut in. 'And who else is she saying it to? At the same time I don't want him to know because he'll be so dreadfully hurt.'

Sir Roland spoke forcefully. 'You must tell him, Cath. The last thing he needs is to be kept in the dark. He needs to be prepared for every eventuality. Tell him at once.'

'All right.' She spoke reluctantly. How do you tell someone that their mother believes they were once capable of killing another child?

'Let me know how you get on,' Sir Roland continued. 'If there's anything I can do, you know you've only got to ask.'

'I know, Daddy. Thank you. I'll talk to you soon.'

With a heavy heart she went up to her dressing room and put on some warm outdoor clothes and strong lace-up shoes. She'd go and find Nicolas in the woods and God knows how she'd tell him but her father was right. He had to know what was going on behind his back.

As she made her way across the lawn, past the tennis courts and to the woods beyond, a sense of dread settled on her like a sickness. Her legs felt weighed down, her hands were trembling and the blood was pulsing through her body, making her short of breath. Then she heard voices. Nicolas and the foresters were discussing the layout of the replanting and they stopped when they saw her coming.

Nicolas had dismounted and was standing beside his horse, absently stroking her neck.

'Hello, darling? What brings you here?'

'I came to see how you were getting on,' she lied, purpose-fully avoiding looking at the bend in the stream and the jutting little island with its newly disturbed earth.

He took one look at her pale face and anxious eyes and knew that wasn't the real reason. 'Right,' he said easily, turning back to the workers. 'Well, I think that's about it for today?'

'Yes, m'lord,' they replied in unison.

'Good. Then I'll leave you to get on, and you'll order another dozen hornbeams to plant near the East Avenue, McKay?' he asked the head forester.

'I will, m'lord. They should be here in about two weeks.'

'Thanks.' Holding the reins in one hand Nicolas turned his

horse around and, linking his other arm through Cathryn's, strolled away at a leisurely pace until they were out of sight. Then he stopped and looked at her anxiously.

'What's happened?'

She told him, as lightly as she could, what his mother had said, as if repeating the absurd ramblings of a demented woman. 'I've spoken to my father,' she continued, 'and he said I should tell you so you wouldn't get a shock if it got back to you.'

Nicolas looked grim. 'He was right. I wonder who else she's imparted this choice piece of information to?'

Then she repeated all the information her father had given her.

'That's much what my QC told me,' he assured her. 'He quoted me chapter and verse of the Children's Act.'

'And you remember the day Posy vanished?'

'Oh yes. How could one forget? I was at home trying to catch up on my studies. I'd been lazy all term and I'd got behind. I worked in the library, just joining my mother and Ewan for luncheon. Then the balloon went up at about five o'clock. Ida Burgess had suddenly realized Posy had gone missing. Christ! I can remember the hue and cry and it actually crossed my mind that if I *had* been shooting in the woods that day it would never have happened. I'd have told her to go back to the house and keep out of the way of anyone with a gun.'

'Ida must have been frantic?'

'Everyone was! She was a popular little soul. Bright and intelligent. All the servants were searching the grounds and the barns and the stable. They even searched the cellars and every room of the house. I remember Ida the next morning, sobbing her heart out in the kitchen, frantic with fear and worry. Everyone concluded Posy had been abducted by the gypsies because by dawn they'd abandoned their camp on the other side of the woods and gone.'

He stopped and stood still, his eyes roaming the countryside of undulating hills that stretched into the distance on this grey and bleak winter morning. It all belonged to him but at this moment he'd have happily exchanged it for a quiet and trouble-free existence as a farmer.

Cathryn stood watching him closely. 'How did your mother react to Posy's disappearance that day?'

He frowned. 'I don't remember seeing much of her. Ewan had come down with a bilious attack after luncheon and I think she spent most of her time looking after him. I know she sent me to bed quite early and I wasn't allowed to join in the search. I don't really know what happened after that. I seem to remember David Partridge arriving during the evening, but I think he'd left by the next day.'

'I suppose the search continued for days?'

'I suppose it must have done, though I have a feeling that once everyone realized the gypsies had gone it was all rather hopeless. They could have been hundreds of miles away by then, taking Posy with them. Little did I know she'd been killed and buried less than a mile away from the house. I think someone knew, though,' he added slowly, 'and for some reason that person is now trying to destroy me.'

Cathryn shivered and rested her cheek against his shoulder. Then she straightened up and turned to face him, her expression determined. 'I don't think this adds up,' she said firmly. 'Posy's remains would never have been found if you hadn't ordered that part of the woods to be cleared, right?'

'That's correct.'

'And you wouldn't have asked for that to be done if you'd known she'd been buried there?'

'Obviously not.'

'Quite.' Her blue eyes shone with eagerness. 'I think someone, who is not necessarily connected to Posy's death, is using the discovery that she was shot as an opportunity to try and ruin you now. Someone who is out for vengeance at any price.'

His brow cleared in understanding. 'You mean someone has just jumped on this bandwagon as a vehicle for revenge?'

'That's exactly what I mean. If they knew it was you who'd shot Posy why didn't they tell anyone about it twenty years ago, when it happened? Or before her body, which could have lain undiscovered for another twenty years, was found a few weeks ago?'

'But who hates me that much? My mother?' He looked aghast. 'To use this as an opportunity to bring me down, knowing I'm innocent? She must hate me to the point of madness.'

'She's certainly obsessed to the point of madness in her possessive adoration of Ewan,' Cathryn said quietly.

Nicolas turned to look at her again. 'She's not alone in this though, is she? Who is sending the anonymous letters, posted all around the country? Who is stirring up trouble in the village?'

'Oh, my God!' Cathryn dropped the sheet of writing paper as if it had stung her, as they were having breakfast the next morning.

Nicolas glanced up quickly. 'You haven't received one too, have you?'

'Yes! Oh, it's too horrid for words. Look!' She passed it across the table to him. Then she picked up the plain white envelope. 'It's handwritten,' she exclaimed. 'That's why I opened it, thinking it was from a friend.'

Maighread had arrived the previous afternoon, and picking up the envelope, examined it closely. 'That's the writing of an educated person,' she observed.

Nicolas scanned the note, which was made up of cut-out letters pasted to a plain sheet of paper.

> *Dear Lady Abingdon,*
> *The Abingdons are rotten to the core, as his first wife found out. Do not be deceived. He has the blood of a little girl on his hands. He should rot in hell. Get out while you can. Signed: One Who Knows*

He threw it down with a groan of disgust. 'What sort of person writes a letter like this?'

Maighread raised her eyebrows and looked knowing. 'A bitter twisted woman who hates the very guts of the Abingdon family, but who comes from a well-to-do background herself; the quality of the writing paper is good.'

Cathryn looked astonished. 'How can you tell all that?'

'It's simple. No man would go to all the trouble of pasting these letters together, and no man would bitch about a first wife,' she said, adding, 'It's also from a woman who reads cheap novels.'

Cathryn looked at Nicolas but his expression was blank. He flipped the letter back to her. 'What's the postmark?'

'It's smudged,' Maighread complained. 'What a pity. Where are all the other letters you've received?'

'We've given them to the police.'

She looked thoughtful. 'I'd guess it's someone local who is desperate to keep their identity a secret, but who wants to frighten you. They've certainly got a grudge against you, Nicolas.'

'I know, Maighread.' He got up and went over to the sideboard to help himself to more coffee. 'Personally I think we should ignore them. This is a war of nerves. Whoever is sending them wants to shake my confidence, though God knows what good it will do them.'

'They also know these letters will hurt you or they wouldn't be informing the newspapers that you're receiving them. That's a really crafty way of getting it over to the press that you're guilty without coming out and saying so in person,' she said, studying the letter again.

'Perhaps there won't be any more,' Cathryn said hopefully.

'There'll be more,' Maighread retorted. 'You can bet your life on it. Something very evil is going on here.' Like a deadly drip . . . drip . . . drip of pure poison, the letters were infiltrating the atmosphere with suspicion and distrust.

Luncheon was a strained affair that day, with a mix of people who would not normally have chosen to be together.

Conceptia sat at one end of the mahogany table, which was set with glittering glass and silver and bowls of flowers from the glasshouse. Her face was looking more skeletal than usual, supported by a thin neck encased in a wide tight choker of pearls, which disguised her sagging jaw line. On her right was David Partridge, pandering to her every wish, his voice soft and whispery, his heavy lidded eyes gazing at her solicitously, as if she were a semi-invalid.

At the other end of the table Nicolas, as always warm and charming in spite of his state of anxiety, was telling Maighread the history of Buckland Place and how it had been in the family since 1672.

'I'd love a house like this,' she exclaimed enthusiastically, waving her be-ringed hands about, 'but my husband would want to turn it into a country hotel with a golf club and God knows what else.'

Nicolas gave a faint smile. 'The day will come when the likes of us will be forced to make properties like this pay for themselves. The current depression has been a shock to us all and the country is facing great changes. In a few years there won't be many estates like this left in private ownership.'

'Utter nonsense!' Conceptia's harsh tones came ringing down the table, still with the *twang* of her American accent. 'I would rather see this house burned to the ground than have it turned into a common commercial enterprise.'

Cathryn blushed at her mother-in-law's rudeness, but Maighread was swift with her own put-down.

'But I applaud the way the United States is a world leader in commercial enterprise. Every bit of land you can lay hands on you develop into cities and towns with the most modern hotels in the world! Surely you don't disapprove? Where, for instance, would America be without its railroads?' she said blithely, patting her halo of red curls.

Conceptia's eyes became slits of dark fire and her gash of a scarlet mouth tightened.

David Partridge smiled his toothy ingratiating smile. 'You're so right, my dear Mrs Simmonds, but to *touch* Buckland Place would be like destroying a part of our history and our heritage, both of which are sacrosanct. Creating public transport is a service to the community and quite a different matter.'

Ewan, sitting opposite Cathryn, suddenly spoke rapidly, his voice high-pitched. 'Mummy has been the making of Buckland. She's cared for it for years and years and done so much good. It would be a ruin by now, without her.' Then he cast a withering glance in Nicolas's direction. 'And it should have gone to someone who really deserves it.'

Maighread smiled mischievously. 'And luckily it *did*! Who is more deserving than Nicolas? But supposing, Lady Abingdon,' she continued, turning to Conceptia as if to seek the wisdom of her advice, 'you'd had no sons and only daughters? What would have happened then?'

'The title would have died out,' Conceptia snapped with acerbity.

'And this estate?'

Conceptia rose majestically from the table, throwing down her white damask table napkin. 'This is all pure supposition. I *did* have two sons and it's a great pity that Ewan wasn't the eldest. Then at least we wouldn't all be immersed in this terrible *cause célèbre* that endangers everything I've worked for.'

There was a stunned silence, broken only by the clip-clip of her high heels on the parquet floor as she stormed out of the room.

David Partridge looked shifty and Ewan smirked in amusement, but Cathryn's eyes stung as she looked at the shocked hurt on Nicolas's face as he watched his mother's retreating figure.

'Holy Mother of God!' Maighread burst out loudly, her Irish accent suddenly very pronounced. 'What a way to talk about your eldest son! You should be proud of him. Look how hard he works to run the place! I know women who would be grateful to have a son like Nicolas.'

But Conceptia had gone, leaving only the sickeningly sweet scent of essence of roses in the air.

'Well, now we really know where Mother's loyalties lie,' Nicolas said calmly and resignedly. 'I'm sorry, Ewan, if what you wanted was to be the eldest, but think yourself lucky in that you can have the pleasure of living here but with none of the responsibility.'

Ewan shrugged. 'You've never understood Mummy as I have. You've never tried to get on with her.'

David Partridge looked at Nicolas as if he'd awoken from a reverie about times past. 'You have to realize your mother was the greatest beauty of her age,' he said severely. 'None of the other American millionairesses who came to this country could hold a candle to her. London society turned her into their heroine. She was painted by Giovanni Boldini in 1903—'

'I remember that painting!' Ewan cut in eagerly, his face alight. 'I was in the painting with her, wasn't I? When I was four, and I was dressed in a white sailor suit.'

David nodded. 'You were indeed, and although tragically a widow she was still at the height of her exquisiteness.' He sighed and his eyes were misty. 'The most terrible thing that can happen to a woman who has been fêted as an international beauty, is to grow old. To lose that incredible allure. To—'

Maighread interrupted this time. 'I thought you were going to say the greatest tragedy that can happen to a woman with young children is to lose her husband? We all grow old. Beauty is the most ephemeral gift of all. Any intelligent woman knows that and comes to terms with it,' she added flatly.

David ignored her. 'Conceptia was always defined by her beauty.

Her husband brought her no happiness, only heartbreak.' He stared at Nicolas. 'Unfortunately, Nicolas, you remind her of your late father so there's not much you can do about that.'

'Except to be a loyal and loving son, which he is,' Cathryn burst out angrily. 'He's never said a word against Conceptia. And although he inherited this place he allows her to remain as the chatelaine and she can still do as she likes.'

'Jealous, are we, Cathryn?' Ewan sneered. 'You could never fill Mummy's shoes. She made this place the way it is today. Everything would fall apart without her!'

'Especially you,' Maighread muttered under her breath.

'This is not getting us anywhere,' Nicolas said firmly, getting up from the table. 'I've got work to do. I'll see you all later,' he continued, but his smile was directed at Cathryn. He touched her shoulder briefly as he passed her to leave the dining room.

As soon as they were on their own, Maighread turned to Cathryn, her blue eyes shrewd. 'I can see what you're up against, my dear,' she said in a low voice as they went to sit by the log fire in the leathery comfort of the library. 'Was I terribly rude? I do apologize but that woman is a nightmare! How do you put up with her? I'd march her to the nearest cottage on the estate and lock her in for the duration if she were my mother-in-law!' She took a cigarette from her gold cigarette case and placed it in a long jade holder. 'Where's this Boldini painting they were talking about? I adore his work. Have you seen his portrait of the Duchess of Marlborough? It was done about twenty-five years ago, with her son, Ivor Spencer-Churchill, when he was a little boy.'

'I don't think I've seen any of his portraits.'

'Oh, my dear, they're totally divine. The one of the Marchesa Luisa Casati, wearing furs and a big hat, with her greyhound, who's sporting the most magnificent diamond dog collar, was exhibited at the Royal Academy in 1908 and it caused a sensation. How I wish I'd been painted by him; it's one of my greatest regrets. He's old and frail now. I heard the other day he's not expected to live much longer.'

Cathryn put her head on one side, her eyebrows raised. 'So that's why Conceptia has greyhounds!' she observed knowingly, 'Not that she pays much attention to them.'

'So where is this painting?'

'I've no idea. It's obviously not on display anywhere, because Ewan seemed to have forgotten all about it.'

Maighread drew on her cigarette and then exhaled slowly and thoughtfully. 'This Mr Partridge is in love with her, isn't he?'

'Do you think so? I can't bear the man; he creeps around the place doing her bidding all the time, and sucking up to her.'

'I told you, he's mad for her. He'd do *anything* for her.'

'What are you saying, Maighread? That they're lovers?'

Her friend laughed. 'No, and I'm not suggesting he's either Nicolas's or Ewan's father either. She probably doesn't let him touch her with a barge pole, and that's obviously why he's stayed around for years, clutching at crumbs and a wild sense of hope. Poor man,' she added patronizingly.

Cathryn grinned. 'Do you want to have a search for this Boldini, as you're obviously enraptured by his work?'

'Oh, my dear! There's nothing I'd like more! And if we're caught snooping around, I'll say you're giving me a conducted tour of your beautiful new home.'

The two women set off, walking through each of the ground floor reception rooms before mounting the grand staircase to the first floor bedrooms. Through one of the windows in the picture gallery they spied Conceptia, followed by her dogs, striding towards the park beyond the formal gardens.

'Quick! Let's have a look in her room while she's out,' Maighread insisted.

'I don't think . . .' Cathryn hesitated. She'd never been invited into her mother-in-law's private quarters and she viewed the prospect with deep trepidation.

'Nonsense! This is your house now, and anyway, she'll never know. Come on, which way is it?'

Cathryn turned and led the way along the wide gallery, which was hung with portraits by Holbein, Rubens, Millais and Reynolds, until they came to double mahogany doors. She knocked, waited a moment, and then opened them. 'Quick, before anyone comes,' she whispered, glancing nervously around.

'*Well . . . !*' Maighread said in a stage whisper, as she gazed around in astonishment at Conceptia's bedroom. It was all purple velvet and smoked mirrors, black satin sheets and white orchids.

'What a scream!' she exclaimed in amusement. 'Have you ever seen anything like it?'

The sickly aroma of rose perfume permeated the adjoining sitting room, dressing room and black marble bathroom. Maighread was laughing so much she had her hand clasped over her mouth. 'Darling, isn't it hysterical?'

There was no sign of the Boldini portrait, though, and a few minutes later they were safely back in the portrait gallery and inspecting the other bedroom suites that were kept for guests.

'No sign of the painting anywhere,' Cathryn concluded over an hour later, when they'd looked in every likely place.

Maighread folded her arms and looked amused. 'Then it'll be in the attic,' she said solemnly.

Cathryn laughed. 'Like in *The Picture of Dorian Gray*, except she'll still be young and beautiful in the painting? I hardly think so, Maighread.'

'I'm serious, my dear. Conceptia is exactly the type to hide her portrait so she's not reminded of how she used to look.'

The door to the large attic, which ran across two thirds of the building directly under the flat roof, was locked, so Cathryn had to get the keys from Wills, who was very reluctant to hand them over.

'Her ladyship has forbidden anyone to go into the attic without her permission,' he warned nervously.

'I understand, Wills, but this is my husband's and my house and I want to acquaint myself with all of it. Don't worry, if Lady Abingdon finds out I shall tell her I insisted on having the keys. You will not be blamed, I can assure you.'

'If you say so, m'lady.' The elderly man looked sour and unhappy.

'We'll give them straight back to you when we've had a peep,' Maighread promised.

Then they hurried up the stairs again, anxious to explore the nether regions before Conceptia returned.

It didn't take them long. Through the gloom of centuries they flashed their hand torches around, seeing stored furniture and trunks, suitcases and rolled up rugs under fragile canopies of spiders' webs. There were stacks of books tied up with strings, ancient kitchen equipment, garden ornaments, dressmaker's dummies from the Victorian and Edwardian era, and boxes of old-fashioned shoes, some still unworn.

'What a historical treasure trove,' Maighread murmured, opening a large trunk and fingering a lace-edged silk crinoline. 'Some of these old costumes should be given to the Victoria and Albert Museum.'

Suddenly Cathryn exclaimed, 'Look! Over there!'

'What is it?'

Propped up against a low beam they saw a dust sheet draped over a six foot high frame. Cathryn pulled the sheet to one side.

'Oh, dear Mother of God. There it is!' Maighread exclaimed, awestruck.

They found themselves staring at a portrait of the young, fresh-faced Conceptia, standing before a grey panelled background, wearing an ivory chiffon and satin dress to the ground in the style of the 1900s, with a froth of chiffon frills at the elbows and a black satin sash around her tiny waist. The neckline was high, with black satin ribbons ruched elegantly at her throat.

There she was, the young Marchioness of Abingdon, revealed by Giovanni Boldini as a ravishing beauty with large, dark doe-like eyes, a small soft mouth and skin as flawless as a gardenia petal. A profusion of dark curls framed her exquisite features, with the rest of her hair, which was long, wound up into a loose bun on the top of her head.

Glistening pearl drops hung from her earlobes, and a tangle of long ropes of pearls cascaded down her front. Clinging to her skirts was Ewan, a small boy in a white sailor suit and little black patent leather shoes, pressing himself against her thighs, while one of her hands was placed on his small chest, holding him close, making him still a part of her.

'Every picture tells a story,' Maighread breathed softly, 'and what a story this is!'

'And twenty-eight years later nothing has changed, except their ages,' Cathryn agreed.

The two women stood in silence, spellbound, seeing into another age of elegance and art and the privilege of the upper classes.

'I'd say this is one of Boldini's best works,' Maighread observed. She moved closer, lifting away more of the dust sheet until it fell to the ground in heavy folds, bringing something clattering with it.

'What was that?' Cathryn asked in alarm.

Her friend reached down and felt something cold and metallic. 'Oh, my God!'

'What is it, Maighread? What have you found?'

Maighread stood upright, her hands held out as if she was fearful of touching something. 'No wonder your mother-in-law doesn't allow anyone up here.'

'Why?' Cathryn shone her torch to where Maighread's was pointing.

Lying at their feet was an air rifle.

Eleven

NEW DEVELOPMENTS IN CHILD MURDER INQUIRY

New evidence has been found which may lead the police to the killer of Posy Burgess twenty years ago at Buckland Place in Kent, the home of the Marquess of Abingdon. He is expected to be questioned further, having been previously released by the police through lack of evidence . . .

The Daily Sketch, January 10th, 1931

'It was the right thing to do,' Nicolas had argued fiercely the previous day, as he'd glared at his mother when she'd criticized him for telephoning DI Harding to tell him of their find. 'Why are you in such a state? I've got nothing to hide. But how the hell did my air rifle get there in the first place?'

Conceptia was shaking all over, almost deranged with rage. 'Your damned wife and her friend had no business to go snooping around the attic. I could kill Wills for letting her have the key. I gave strict instructions that no one was to go there without my permission.'

Cathryn spoke firmly and boldly. 'It wasn't Wills's fault and I take full responsibility. I do live here too, you know, and this is also Nicolas's and my house. Whoever hid the air rifle must have had a reason and it certainly wasn't Nicolas who hid it there.'

He was pacing up and down the library, where they were all grouped, late that afternoon. 'Cathryn's right,' he said, 'and it would have been quite wrong to have kept it hidden under the circumstances. How long has it been there, for God's sake? I can't even recall when I last saw it.'

'Where was it normally kept?' Maighread asked. She had her own theories about her find, but she was keeping them to herself for the time being.

'In the gun room.'

'So anyone could have had access to it at any time?' she persisted.

'Yes, but who would want to?' Nicolas queried. 'It was a serious toy and useless for bringing down pheasants or partridges. I was given it for my tenth birthday by the tenants on the estate, so I could learn how to get my eye in.'

'How charming!' Maighread turned smilingly to Ewan. 'And did they give you one too? When you were ten?'

'No fear! I hate blood sports of all kinds: hunting, shooting and fishing. I don't believe in killing things,' he added, with an air of superiority.

'Ewan takes after me,' Conceptia pointed out, grim-faced.

Nicolas ignored her. 'No doubt the police will be examining the rifle for fingerprints, so I hope you're all prepared to have yours taken, with the exception of Cathryn and Maighread of course.' He knew they'd been careful to leave the rifle where they'd found it, so the police could move it from the attic themselves, carefully wrapped in a cloth to take back to the police station.

David Partridge gave a wintry smile. 'There's little point in them taking mine. Like Ewan, I've never touched a weapon in my life.'

Cathryn looked at him with distaste.

'It's a beautiful portrait of you we found, Lady Abingdon,' Maighread intervened brightly. 'Quite one of Boldini's best works.'

Conceptia scowled furiously. 'You had no damned business to go poking your nose where it wasn't wanted. And as for *you*,' she said, turning to Cathryn. Her bony hands were shaking as she clutched her lace-edged handkerchief. 'I wish Nicolas had never met you. I wish to God you'd never come here. You're even worse than Miranda.'

Nicolas turned sharply on her. 'Mother, I will not let you talk to Cathryn like that. Apologize to her at once, and to our guest.'

His mother stared at him, stony-eyed and white-faced. 'Go to hell!' she snarled, fists clenched. 'God damn you all! Ewan, help me to my room. My head is splitting.'

Ewan jumped to his feet, pale and nervous looking as he took her arm. She seemed to have aged twenty years in the past few hours; tottering and stumbling she headed for the door, clinging to him like a frail old lady.

There was an uneasy silence in the room. David Partridge looked tired and sad, the bags under his eyes pronounced, while Maighread gazed out of the window, deep in thought.

Then Nicolas spoke. 'I must apologize for my mother's behaviour,' he said haltingly. 'There's really no excuse, but I think she's as upset about her portrait being seen as she is about the discovery of the rifle. She hates people to see how she's lost her looks.'

Cathryn smiled wanly at him, touched by his sense of loyalty. 'It's understandable, darling,' she said softly, 'and it's not your fault. She was certainly a great beauty when she was young and it obviously meant a lot to her.'

'It is a divine portrait, Nicolas,' Maighread agreed, 'but I was in the wrong for making Cathryn show it to me. I apologize for that. It was none of my business and I'm so sorry it's opened up old wounds.'

'The painting should never have been hidden in the first place,' he said regretfully. 'I'd forgotten that it used to hang in the drawing room when I was a boy.'

'How many years ago did she have it put in the attic?'

He shrugged. 'Ten, maybe fifteen years ago. I can't remember exactly. I was probably away at school at the time.'

Maighread spoke carefully. 'Then it was still in the drawing room when Posy vanished?'

He stopped and looked at her, his brow puckered as if he were trying to work out a puzzle. 'No, I don't think so. I think my mother had already hung the Rembrandt in its place.'

'So the rifle could have been hidden under the dust sheet directly after Posy went missing?'

Nicolas nodded slowly. 'I suppose so.'

The next morning, Conceptia stayed in her room, suffering from a severe migraine according to Ewan, who himself only made a brief appearance at breakfast, looking wan and tired.

'She's too ill to get her post so I'll take it up and read it to her,' he announced, gathering up the mail by her side plate.

'Is that wise?' Nicolas asked. 'If it's anything like my post, she won't want to see it.'

'What . . . more poison pen letters?' Ewan's eyes widened, popping in his thin face.

'I've had another one too,' Cathryn said sombrely. 'Accusing Nicolas of "interfering" with Posy and then shooting her afterwards in case she told anyone.'

'I think you've received one yourself, Ewan,' Maighread pointed out, indicating a typed envelope by his place at the table.

Ewan snatched it up and ripping open the envelope, pulled out a familiar sheet of plain white paper and scanned it briefly. 'Mine says the same, describing you as a child molester, Nicolas.'

'This is unbelievable,' his brother groaned despairingly. 'Who in God's name is doing this to us?'

'The police *must* be able to put a stop to it,' Cathryn implored anyone who was listening. 'It's too wicked for words!' It flashed through her mind that perhaps she ought to inform the police of her suspicions about Conceptia, but supposing she'd got it wrong?

Unless her mother-in-law had an accomplice, how were these letters postmarked from various places around the country? Conceptia never left Buckland, not even to do a little shopping.

'Where were today's letters all posted from?' Maighread asked at that moment, as if she knew what Cathryn was thinking.

Nicolas and Cathryn looked at their envelopes. 'Bristol,' they said in unison.

'So is the one addressed to Mummy,' Ewan added.

Later that morning Wills bustled into the library where Cathryn and Maighread were sitting with the newspapers.

'Miss Hilary Pilkington has called to see you, m'lady. Shall I show her in?'

Cathryn got to her feet, surprised. 'Yes, of course, Wills. And we'd like some coffee, please.'

Hilary came trotting into the room a minute later looking windblown and shabby in an old tweed coat and a brown felt hat pulled down over her straggling hair.

'I'm sorry to descend on you like this, Cathryn,' she said breathlessly, her cheeks flushed and her manner strangely excited, 'but I really wanted to see you.'

'It's nice of you to come,' Cathryn replied warmly, before introducing her to Maighread.

The two women shook hands and Cathryn could tell that Maighread was mystified by their unexpected visitor who appeared desperate to impart something of importance to them.

'Come and sit down, Hilary.' Cathryn indicated the sofa beside her. 'How are you?'

Hilary ignored the question. 'Have you heard?' she demanded, dazzle-eyed. 'Everyone in the village, but *everyone,* has received a dreadful anonymous letter this morning, accusing Nicolas of the most ghastly things!'

Cathryn stiffened and Maighread's fine eyebrows shot up.

'So our neighbours are receiving them too?'

'Don't tell me you've had one, Cathryn!' Hilary clapped her hand over her mouth.

'We've all had several, in fact,' Cathryn replied.

Hilary's hands flew to her cheeks in horror. 'Oh, my dear! How truly ghastly! What are you going to do?'

'We're passing them to the police and when they find the person responsible I hope they're sent to prison for a very long time.' Cathryn spoke with passion.

A footman arrived with their coffee and set the silver tray down on a table in the centre of the room. They remained silent while he served them but as soon as he'd withdrawn Hilary burst out in distress, 'Who can be doing this to Nicolas? He doesn't deserve to be humiliated in this ghastly way. Poor man, he must be so upset.' Her eyes were red, brimming with tears.

Cathryn looked at her in surprise. 'He's a strong man, Hilary. He's determined not to let these filthy letters get him down, and of course we're all being as supportive as we can,' she added. 'He's taking very good advice. He's innocent so he's really got nothing to fear.'

'How is the dowager taking it? And Ewan?' she asked. 'Nicolas has never really got on with—'

'They're both concerned,' Cathryn cut in, determined to show loyalty to the family, 'but it's obvious that the person behind this is mentally ill and should be put away.'

Hilary bit her lower lip and pushed her straggling hair back from her face. 'I wish there was something I could do but I've been rushed off my feet by Mother. Her sister's ill and I'm having to drive her all over the place to collect things for Aunt Adela, who insists on being nursed at home. It's a real trial.'

'Where does your aunt live?'

'Ross-on-Wye.'

'Nice place, Hereford,' Maighread observed, sipping her coffee.

But Hilary wasn't listening. 'What is going to happen next? I hear the air rifle has been found in the attic?'

'Goodness, news does travel fast in a small village.'

Hilary nodded like a puppet on a loose string. 'What do the police say?'

'Nothing so far. They have to test it for fingerprints.'

Hilary was determined to wallow in the gossip of it all. 'I see Miranda hasn't given any more interviews. Do you think she could be the one sending these letters? I wouldn't put anything past her. She's out for vengeance; always has been ever since her marriage to Nicolas broke up.'

'Oh, I doubt it,' Cathryn protested, feeling uneasy. Were her words going to be flashed around the village within hours? 'I don't think she'd stoop that low,' she said carefully.

Hilary swooped down on her remark like a hungry bird catching a worm. 'You don't know her like I do. I never trusted her and Nicolas should never have married her. I told him so at the time, but would he listen? Men never do, do they?'

Cathryn sat very still, wondering now if Hilary had told Nicolas that she was the wrong wife for him too? She caught Maighread's eye and knew her friend was thinking the same thing.

It was another twenty minutes before Hilary finally left, reluctantly dragging on her unfashionable hat and gathering up her handbag, gloves and long woollen scarf. 'I'd better get back to Mother and see what she wants,' she grumbled. 'It's been so nice seeing you, Cathryn, and I'm sorry I missed Nicolas, but you will give him my love, won't you? And tell him I'm thinking of him and wish him well?'

'Of course I will,' Cathryn promised automatically, but she felt uneasy at the intensity of Hilary's manner. Walking to the front door, she watched the young woman clamber into her shabby old Austin Seven. At first she'd liked Hilary and welcomed the idea of having a friend living nearby, but now she found her attitude towards Nicolas faintly disturbing.

Maighread was lighting another cigarette when Cathryn returned to the library. 'That young woman's got it badly for Nicolas, hasn't she?' she said immediately.

'I think you're right. She told me when I first knew her that Nicolas had proposed to her years ago and that she'd turned him down.'

'Turned him down my foot!' Maighread scoffed. 'Did you ask

Nicolas about her? Did he really propose? Looking at her, it seems most unlikely to me.'

'I never mentioned it. I don't think men like wives delving into their past, do you? After all, he is thirty-five. He may have proposed to a dozen women for all I know, but I agree with you about Hilary; she isn't his type.'

'So you've only got her word for it? My dear, I wouldn't trust that woman an inch. And what about her Aunt in Ross-on-Wye?'

Cathryn looked blank. 'What about her?'

'Ross-on-Wye, my dear? A mere stone's throw from Cardiff and Bristol?'

'You can't mean . . . ? No, surely it's not possible? If she's mad about Nicolas why would she want to hurt him by sending poison pen letters?'

'Revenge because he married you and Miranda and not her? There's nothing as twisted as unrequited love. I imagine she's not married. Has she got a boyfriend?'

'No. She lives with her mother.'

They sat staring at each other as if they'd come to an impasse and didn't know which route to take next.

'I think you should make Nicolas aware of her feelings,' Maighread said carefully. 'Maybe he had a boyish crush on her when they were very young and as a result she expected to become his wife?'

Such a possibility had never occurred to Cathryn, and her cheeks flushed now with unaccountable jealousy. 'I don't think so!' she exclaimed, appalled.

'Why not, dear girl? Nicolas and Ewan must have known the children of the local county families around here when they were young. Went to each other's birthday parties? Played tennis or went riding together? Had Christmas parties and kissed under the mistletoe? Was she a debutante?'

'I shouldn't think so. Her mother's been a widow since Hilary was small and they're very poor.' Suddenly she realized she shared no history with Nicolas, as Hilary obviously must do. No memories of picnics on a summer's day or games of hide-and-seek or croquet. No reminiscences of shared jokes or amusing experiences. Was it possible they also shared recollections of furtive touching and tingling youthful skin, exchanged looks and suppressed desire? She sat very upright. 'He's never given any indication they were ever interested in each other,' she added falteringly.

'How old is she?'

'I believe she's thirty-three.'

Maighread shrugged. 'Whether they had a little juvenile fling or not, I'd list her among your suspects for causing all this trouble if I were you. She obviously tries to come over as a sweet little-girl-lost, wanting to be friendly and helpful, but don't trust her, Cathryn. The quiet ones are always the most dangerous.'

'I don't think Conceptia likes her either. Whenever I mention Hilary she sneers and describes her as "that dreary old maid who wears dreadful clothes".'

Maighread laughed outright. 'Think what her life would have been like if she'd married Nicolas. I feel quite sorry for the "dreary old maid" at the thought of it!'

Later that day Maighread returned to London, promising to keep in touch. 'Let me know what's happening, my dear,' she said, arranging her sables around her shoulders as she stepped into the new chauffeur-driven silver Bugatti Royale her husband had given her, 'although no doubt I'll be reading about it in the newspapers first.'

'Thank you for coming, and I apologize for my mother-in-law's rudeness.'

'Don't worry about it, but mind your back and don't forget to ask Nicolas about Hilary. Take care, dear girl.' She waved her gloved hand out of the window as the car swept down the drive towards the main gates. Cathryn waved back. Her world was closing in around her. She now had to guard against Hilary and Conceptia and there was no one she could talk freely to, except for Hugh Verney.

Tonight she was going to have to ask Nicolas outright about Hilary and she dreaded the thought of delving into his past. She really didn't want to hear that he'd loved other women. It was bad enough that Miranda would always be there in the background. The First Wife. But if she was going to have to dig deeper the thought made her fear that one day she might find out he really was a philanderer who might fall in love with someone new and she'd be left behind, no longer desired.

Oppressed by sudden feelings of insecurity, she turned back into the house and it seemed the weight of centuries was dragging her down into a dark place.

As she walked slowly across the Great Hall the Abingdon ancestors, in their heavy gilt frames, glared forbiddingly down at her while the dark Grinling Gibbons carvings of juicy pears and peaches, grapes and pomegranates had a sinister gleam, watched over by mischievous fat-cheeked cherubs, whispering secrets only they knew.

I hate this place, she thought with sudden passion. I hate the atmosphere of malevolence created by Conceptia and her useless and weak younger son. I hate the fact this is not our own home, where Nicolas and I could be by ourselves.

The next morning the household awoke to find the front door of Buckland Place had been smeared with blood in the night and a dead hare was hanging from the large iron knocker.

The police left, having tested for fingerprints and made a thorough search around the entrance to the building and the drive. Everyone in the house had been questioned, as had all the estate workers, but the police had drawn a blank.

'So who's your enemy?' Detective Inspector John Harding had asked Nicolas. 'There's obviously someone around here who doesn't like you,' he added, his voice as dry as tinder.

Nicolas frowned. 'I didn't realize until recently that I had any enemies. Now they seem to be crawling out of the woodwork.'

'I'd say this is a vendetta of a personal nature,' the DI continued. 'We think these are the actions of one person. The poison pen letters, the bloodied hare on your front door, the way the newspapers seem to be made aware in advance of your movements. They're giving us a picture of someone who is very disturbed.'

Nicolas looked at him blankly. 'A man or a woman?'

'We can't be certain yet but we will continue with our enquiries and I'll let you know if we have any results.'

When they were alone again, Nicolas looked at Cathryn and there was anxiety in his eyes. 'I hate to say this and that's why I didn't mention it to the police, but do you think Frank Burgess could have had anything to do with it?'

'I wouldn't have thought so,' she replied, surprised.

'If there's anyone who has a grudge against this family it could be him, but I hate to think he felt as bitter as this. I've always liked old Frank.'

'He's not educated enough to have sent those letters.'

'That's true, but he could have killed that hare and tied it to our door knocker. It's a very countryside gesture of grievance; unsophisticated and brutal.'

'Not poor Frank,' Cathryn said, distressed. 'He's far too timid a man to do something like this. Oh, I hate what is being done to you,' she added in anguish, seeing the pain behind Nicolas's eyes. 'It's so unfair.' She hadn't had a chance to talk to him the previous evening because they'd been entertaining the Lord Lieutenant and his wife, but now she knew she had to take the plunge.

She took a deep breath like someone about to jump from the high diving board into shallow waters. 'Nicolas, I need to talk to you about something. Hilary was here yesterday.'

'Hilary?' he looked puzzled for a moment. 'Why was she here?'

'She dropped in during the morning to commiserate. Apparently everyone in the village has been receiving poison pen letters and she was terribly upset that you were being put through the mill in this dreadful way. She sent you her love.'

Nicolas sounded surprised. 'Really? She was upset at Posy's funeral, wasn't she? The tragedy of that little girl's death has got to everyone, I think.'

Cathryn tried to keep her voice level. 'I didn't realize you'd proposed to her.'

'What?' He looked at her, stunned. 'Hilary?'

Cathryn nodded. 'She told me that you'd proposed to her ages ago but that she'd turned you down. It's clear though that she still has deep feelings for you and I wondered if you'd realized that?'

'Propose to Hilary Pilkington?' he repeated incredulously. 'Are you joking? She is about the last woman on earth I'd ever want to marry!'

Cathryn felt an unexpected pang of sympathy for Hilary. How dreadful to love someone only to realize they'd never felt the same.

'From what she said she implied it was when you were both

very young,' Cathryn pointed out. 'Did you ever suggest jokingly that you and she ought to get married when you grew up?' She tried to picture them out walking and laughing about something when they'd been in their teens, and then Nicolas making this amusing throwaway line as a humorous quip.

'I never even went out with Hilary,' he said slowly. 'There was never anything between us, and I certainly never asked her to marry me.'

'Maighread met her when she was here yesterday and she warned me not to trust her. She'd told us she'd been visiting her aunt in Ross-on-Wye, and as Maighread pointed out, that's quite near where two of the anonymous letters was posted. Do you think she could have anything to do with this hate campaign?'

Nicolas shook his head. 'This is the most extraordinary thing I've ever heard.'

'Then it's not true you asked Hilary to marry you?' Cathryn persisted.

'Come on, darling!' he was smiling now but his tone edged on impatience. 'Nice she may be, but Hilary is one of the plainest women I've ever seen, and quite the dullest! We've known each other since we were small, but we didn't even have a brother and sister sort of friendship. She's living in cloud cuckoo land if she thinks I was ever interested in her. Surely you believe me?'

'Of course I do,' Cathryn responded quickly. 'I wonder why she made up such a story? I must say I was a bit surprised.'

'Surprised? I wonder it didn't shock you into next week! Marry Hilary?' He closed his eyes in mock horror. Then he said, 'The poor girl. I hope I never did anything to lead her on – but I *know* I didn't. It must all be in her imagination.'

In bed that night, after they'd made love, Nicolas and Cathryn lay close together, talking quietly.

'You know I have to remain down here for the time being,' he told her, knowing she hated being stuck at Buckland in what felt like being under house arrest, 'but you could stay in London if you'd rather, darling? Or I could arrange for you to go back to Scotland until the dust settles?'

'On my own?' she asked, appalled. Then she slid her arms around his neck, kissing him again. 'I told you that now we're married I'd never leave your side, and I meant it with all my heart. I'm not going anywhere, Nicolas. We'll see this through to the bitter end.'

'I don't know what I'd do without you,' he whispered, his voice thick with desire again.

'You'll never know how much I love you and I'll never leave you, not in a million years,' she promised, covering his face in butterfly kisses.

Later, much later, she spoke tentatively. 'I wish we could be on our own all the time. Will your mother and Ewan always live here?'

'Their presence is getting you down, isn't it?'

'Only because we're stuck here and can't nip up to London when we feel like it.'

'This won't last for ever, sweetheart. Once the newspapers get bored with us and find another story to sensationalize, we can spend all the time we like in town, although I do have to attend to matters here at the weekend. There's nothing I can do about my mother, staying on here, though.'

'Is it still her money that keeps this place going?' she asked carefully.

'Not any more. It's true her initial investment restored the place but I owe her a moral obligation because without her my father would have been forced to sell the estate before I was even born. I suggested she move into the Dower House when I married Miranda but she absolutely refused. I think this house means a lot to her.'

This was not what Cathryn wanted to hear and the prospect of having to share Buckland with Conceptia filled her with depression. Especially as Ewan seemed part of the baggage, too. If he hadn't left home by the age of thirty-one, it was unlikely he ever would.

'Will Ewan ever have anyone in his life?' she whispered awkwardly.

'Mother will never allow it. She's terrified of gossip. He once brought home a young chap he'd met in Canterbury and she went mad. Insisted the chap leave immediately. I think that's why she's so worried about there being so many police around at the moment, taking such an interest in us all. She's terrified they'll guess he's a pansy.'

'Did Miranda know?'

'She guessed the first time she met him.'

'God, I must be naïve!'

Nicolas kissed her tenderly. 'But not too naïve,' he whispered, as he closed his eyes and placed his arm protectively around her, ready for sleep.

The next morning Wills announced that Detective Inspector Harding was on the telephone and would like to speak to Lord Abingdon.

Nicolas and Cathryn looked at each other with apprehension.

'Thank you, Wills. I'll take it in the estate office.' Bending to give Cathryn a quick kiss, he said, 'Wish me luck!' before hurrying from the dining room.

The DI spoke clearly, not mincing his words. 'Lord Abingdon, we've had the forensic results from the lab where the air rifle has been examined, and now we'd like to question you further. Could you come to the station right away?'

'Very well.' Nicolas replaced the receiver slowly.

Watching him from behind his desk, Hugh Verney spoke sympathetically. 'Bad news?'

Briefly he repeated what the DI had said.

'Christ, what the hell's going on?' Hugh demanded.

'They're bound to have found my fingerprints, even after all these years,' Nicolas pointed out reasonably. 'No one else used that rifle apart from me as far as I know. That doesn't prove I shot Posy, though.'

Cathryn had followed him, desperate to know what the police wanted. 'What's happened?' she asked, as she entered the office.

'I've got to go to the police station for more questioning.'

'Oh God, why can't they leave you alone?'

Nicolas shrugged. 'They're only doing their duty.'

'Then I'm coming with you. You're not going on your own.'

His eyes softened as he looked at her and he reached for her hand.

'There's no need for that, darling.'

'Yes, there is. I insist on going with you.'

'Let's go then,' he replied grimly.

With Nicolas at the wheel of their Rolls Royce, they turned out of the drive of Buckland Place, past a flurry of press photographers who shouted for them to slow down. Then they headed along the winding country lane towards the police station, which was some ten miles beyond Appledore.

As they approached the village, Cathryn leaned forward to pick up her handbag from the footwell and at that moment she heard Nicolas exclaim in horror as he slammed on the brakes.

'What the hell . . . ?' he shouted.

She looked up and saw an angry crowd blocking the road, yelling and waving their fists, and surging towards them, forcing Nicolas to brake sharply. Then, as if a war cry had been sounded, more people came pouring out of the cottages and village shops and down the footpaths onto the narrow pavements.

'Murdering bastard!' a woman screeched.

'Filthy child molester!' yelled a man.

A moment later the crowd had exploded into a vandalizing mob, hurling stones and bricks at the car, denting the bonnet and wings and smashing the windscreen, covering Cathryn and Nicolas with broken glass. Baying like wild animals attacking their prey, they spat and screamed abuse, kicking the side doors and rocking the car violently. Then a stone was flung through a side window, splintering the glass and hitting Cathryn on the cheek.

'Rot in hell, you monster!' a voice roared.

'Scumbag! Pervert!' screamed another.

The voices were rough, shrill, ugly. Terrifying in their intense hatred.

'Keep your head down, Cath!' Nicolas yelled, putting his hand on the horn as he revved the engine until it whined, and he tried to inch his way forward through the crowds who were pounding the car with their fists and feet now they'd run out of missiles.

With the horn blaring Nicolas suddenly accelerated, sending the screaming rabble scattering angrily. Some tried to chase after the car, yelling obscenities, but Nicolas wasn't slowing down. With a quick horrified glance at the blood streaming from Cathryn's face, he put his foot down hard and headed for the local hospital.

Twelve

MARQUESS AND HIS WIFE VICTIMS OF ATTACK

Lady Abingdon required hospital treatment after their Rolls Royce, driven by Lord Abingdon, was pelted by stones when a mob of angry village people attacked them as they drove to the police station where he was due to be questioned for the second time in connection with the death of Posy Burgess . . .

Daily Mail, January 15th, 1931

'You shouldn't have come with me to the police station, darling.' Nicolas looked deeply distressed as he gazed at her black eye and the bruise and cut on her cheek, which had required several stitches.

Cathryn was sitting up in their bed, having been discharged that morning from the local hospital, who had insisted she stay in overnight as she'd also suffered from concussion.

'It could have been much worse and at least my cheekbone isn't broken,' she said, wincing with pain as she spoke.

The brutal attack the previous day had left her more deeply shaken than she'd realized. She'd had a bad night in the impersonal private hospital room she'd been assigned, waking with sudden terrifying flashbacks and wondering where she was. For a while she'd lain on the narrow iron bed, trembling and weeping until a nurse had given her a sedative.

The ugly scene of vengeful men and women screaming abuse, on the brink of turning into a lynch mob, so intent were they on trying to punish Nicolas for something he hadn't done, was something that would haunt her for a long time.

Being driven home from the hospital, Cathryn had sensed the hostility that seemed to seep from behind every closed door and tightly shut window. The narrow streets were strangely deserted except for a couple of police cars.

As they passed Ivy Cottage she thought she saw Hilary looking out of the window but almost immediately the net curtains twitched as if someone had suddenly stepped back into the room, not wanting to be seen.

'What happened at the police station, after you'd taken me to the hospital?' she asked, as they drove through the gates of Buckland, where there were more photographers gathered than ever.

'They questioned me endlessly about the air rifle but it was all so inconclusive they said I could go home,' he said shortly.

She looked at him anxiously, fearing he was hiding something.

'What about the forensic tests? Weren't they looking for finger-prints that would incriminate whoever had fired the rifle?'

His jaw tightened. 'There were no fingerprints. Whoever hid the rifle had wiped every inch of it clean first.'

'That's good, isn't it?'

'It's not good at all,' he retorted with sudden harshness, drawing up at the front entrance of the house. 'Whoever wiped it clean did so for a reason.'

She remained in the passenger seat, frowning. 'We've got to think this through, Nicolas. Maybe whoever hid the rifle believed you *had* shot Posy and so they wiped away the fingerprints to protect you?'

'Or set me up? It was my air rifle and even after all these years you'd naturally expect to find my prints on it, wouldn't you? The police can't prove it, but they probably think I panicked when it was realized Posy had been killed by lead pellets from an air rifle, so I wiped away all traces of having handled it, and then hid it in an attic hoping no one would ever discover it.'

'Oh God . . . !' Her face was hurting and she felt helpless and useless at this moment.

Nicolas spoke decisively as he thumped the steering wheel with the heel of his hand.

'Something sinister is going on. Who, for example, told the people in the village we would be driving through a few minutes later on our way to the police station? Didn't you think it strange they appeared to be expecting us? All ready armed with sticks and stones?' He got out of the car. 'Now let's get you into the house and up to your bed. The doctor said you must rest for several days.'

'I'm fine, really,' Cathryn protested. 'There's nothing wrong with my legs.' Nevertheless she was weaker than she'd realized and she was thankful to get up to their bedroom.

'What else did the police ask you yesterday?' she wanted to know once she was settled, propped up against a mound of feather pillows.

'They went over all the questions they'd asked me the first time, but I'm beginning to think they don't believe a word I say.'

'Did you tell them you think someone is trying to deliberately ruin you?'

He shrugged. 'It sounds so melodramatic, like a Wilkie Collins novel. You know, the young lord up at the big house shoots his father's love child to save the family name, then buries the body in the woods where it lies hidden for twenty years, and when it's discovered he refuses to confess and pretends some unknown enemy is determined to pin the blame on him.' He shook his head dismissively. 'No wonder the newspapers are having a field day,' he added bitterly.

'It's so unfair you're being treated in this way,' she said with sudden passion, her eyes blazing with angry tears.

Downstairs in the study, Conceptia looked across at David Partridge as they sat having a mid-morning cup of coffee. Her eyes were flashing black jet buttons in her mask-like face.

'How dare the police demand to question me again,' she raged. 'Why should I have to see them? Don't they know who I am? David, you must tell them that I absolutely refuse to be treated like a common servant. I'm the chatelaine here and they should remember that.'

David Partridge had already spent half an hour trying to explain the police merely wanted Conceptia and Ewan to make a further statement, recalling what they remembered of the day Posy Burgess had gone missing.

'It's just routine, for their paperwork,' he stressed.

'I've already told them I spent the whole afternoon looking after Ewan who was ill in bed with a bilious attack. Why don't they trace the nanny and the nursemaid we had at the time? They could corroborate what I said. Why should I have to repeat myself again and again?' she added heatedly.

'Conceptia, it will look very odd if you refuse,' he warned.

'They're questioning every single person who was here that day in order to get a general picture. Not just you and Ewan, but all the servants, the gardeners, the foresters, the woodsmen, not to mention people in the village who were living around here in 1909.'

'They can interrogate whoever they like as far as I'm concerned but I will not be treated like this. I've said my piece. What more do they want?' she added arrogantly, but there was a note of fear in her voice. 'Why can't you see them for me, David?'

His grey eyes slid like a lizard's under his heavy lids. 'I wasn't here that day, my dear. Remember?'

She looked away. The sinews in her neck strained like strands of white cord above her pearl choker, giving away her age. There was a long pause. Her voice was low and almost inaudible. 'I remember I was all alone here that day.'

'I came as quickly as I could, Conceptia.'

'I know.' There was a grudging gratitude in her voice. She looked at him anxiously, and her hands were shaking as she fumbled with her gold cigarette case. 'But what more can I tell them, David?'

'Tell them what you've said all along, my dear.' His voice was hushed and soothing as if he were talking to a small scared child. 'You were indoors looking after Ewan, who was in bed, having one of his regular bilious attacks. It was November, during the afternoon, when you were informed that the servants were searching for the child of one of the washerwomen, who'd gone missing.'

She nodded. A pale blue vein throbbed through the alabaster skin at her temple. 'The woman was only a casual labourer, not one of our regular laundresses.'

'That's right. You were not responsible because she was not on your staff. Nevertheless you encouraged your servants to help search for her little girl.'

Conceptia looked uncertain. 'I want you to be present.'

'I promise you I will, Conceptia. I'll suggest to Detective Inspector Harding that he talks to you and Ewan first, while his officers question those members of staff who were here at the time.'

'Yes.'

He licked his thick lips. 'You've nothing to worry about, you know.'

Then she turned to him, her expression bleak. 'If only I could turn back the clock forty years, to when I was a beautiful young woman with the world at my feet. I had a dozen proposals, you know, and I could have had any man I wanted. Life was so sweet then and so much fun.' Her voice became dreamy. 'When I came to England I was the toast of the town. Artists begged to paint me, great designers offered to dress me, I was invited everywhere. Then I met William.'

'And of course he fell in love with you,' David spoke encouragingly although he knew the story by heart.

'He was handsome and debonair, a marquess with a grand estate, and I fell in love with him the moment I saw him. I thought he'd fallen in love with me too. I was invited to a house party here given by his mother, and one day he opened the safe and showed me the family's jewels!' Her scarlet painted lips gave a bitter sweet smile. 'He draped my neck and bosom with diamonds and emeralds. He placed a tiara on my head, and a dozen diamond bracelets on my wrists. Then he showed me a magnificent diamond ring . . .' She broke off and looked down at her bony wrinkled hands as if trying to recapture that magical moment. Her voice dropped to a whisper.

'He said it was all mine: Buckland Place, the works of art, all the jewels. Everything. As long as I married him.'

There was a painful pause and David knew her next words by heart.

'It was only after we were married that I realized the Abingdons were on the verge of bankruptcy, and if I hadn't married him, everything would have had to be sold. So in the end I paid a very high price for this place, and for the jewels. Within three months, once more solvent thanks to me, he'd acquired a new mistress. The first of many.'

Her mouth tugged down at the corners with raw pain. 'When I saw the Boldini the other day it broke my heart. Who wants to be reminded of how beautiful one looked when one was young?' Her hand brushed across her eyes. 'I wish I'd died before I grew old,' she murmured brokenly.

'And deprived me of the solace of your friendship?' David

asked tenderly. 'I'm very glad you didn't, my dear Conceptia, because what would I do without you?'

Rallying, she shot him a deadly look. 'You've never *had* me, David, and that's why you still stick around.' Her American accent had a scornful rasp to it now, and he flushed at the truth of her words. His love for her was unrequited and he'd often wished he could walk away, turn his back on a woman he knew didn't deserve his devotion, and instead find himself a nice wife. But every time they fell out Conceptia managed to reel him in as if he were a floundering salmon, and he was hooked once more, a willing victim of her magnetic allure.

'No one understands that I still have the feelings of a young woman,' she continued querulously, pressing her hand to her heart. 'The trouble is I'm lumbered with the body of a sixty-year-old woman and what man wants to make love to a dried-up old stick? No man will ever desire me again.'

'I desire you,' he mumbled thickly.

Conceptia turned on him, striking with the venom of a viper. 'I mean no *young* man!'

Mrs Pilkington put down her knitting and glanced at Hilary, who was sitting at her desk, writing letters. 'Do you think it's safe to leave the house empty when we go back to Ross-on-Wye tomorrow?'

'Why wouldn't it be?' Hilary asked, without looking up.

'We don't want that marauding crowd swarming all over the place and maybe attacking this house because they know we are friends of the Abingdons. I've never seen anything as fearsome as that riot yesterday and I always thought this was such a quiet and peaceful village.'

'There is justification for their anger,' Hilary pointed out quietly. 'The Burgess child is said to have been shot while on the Buckland Place estate and that does make the family responsible.'

'Embarrassed maybe, but not responsible. I don't for one moment believe Nicolas or his family had anything to do with it or any of the servants either. People seem to have forgotten the gypsies were camping up there at the time, poaching and stealing everything they could lay their hands on. I remember the police had been trying to get them to move on for weeks but they paid no attention. When they were finally faced with criminal charges for trespassing and were threatened with forced eviction it's my belief they killed Posy out of revenge!'

She started knitting furiously again, her needles clicking like angry crickets in the quietness of the room. 'Why aren't the police trying to trace those gypsies now instead of hounding poor Nicolas? That's what I'd like to know!'

'Because they're untraceable,' Hilary said. 'They could be anywhere. After all, they came over from Ireland in the first place. They're probably back there now.' She gazed out of the living room window, remembering catching sight of Cathryn's injured face yesterday as she'd sped through the village in Nicolas's car on her way back to Buckland from the hospital. How long would it be before she threw in the sponge and fled back to her parents? How shocked she must be at the way her marriage had turned out. How hollow her victory at having married the immensely wealthy Nicolas Abingdon, only to find he was suspected of molesting and killing a child and that his reputation now lay in tatters?

A secret smile stole across Hilary's face. It wasn't her fault that Posy's remains had been discovered while Nicolas and his new wife were on honeymoon. It was fate, pure and simple. And how was she to know that a little hint here and a pointed suggestion there would lead to an out-of-control wildfire, which was conspiring to point the finger of guilt at Nicolas?

She drew in a deep breath and put down her fountain pen. Whatever happened now, whether he was found guilty of shooting Posy or not, the strain would wreck his marriage. Cathryn would leave him, broken-hearted and sickened to death at being associated with a man who would never be accepted in high society again. In fact, everyone would turn against him and he'd be friendless and isolated from the world he was used to.

But not entirely. She would stand by him, and be his comforter and supporter. She'd devote her time and energy to making him feel loved and wanted again. And one day, one glorious day, he'd know that she'd always been the real love of his life. It was just that he hadn't realized it before. She'd forgive him, of course, for his silly marriages to Miranda and Cathryn, and then she'd show him how wonderful it was to be married to the right woman at last . . .

'So do you think it's all right to leave the house empty, Hilary?'

Startled, Hilary jerked her head up and glared at her mother, angry that her reverie had been broken.

'Of course it will be all right,' she snapped back.

Lilian Brocklehurst was beside herself with anxiety. 'We've got to get Cath to come here,' she said, putting down the *Daily Mail* with a despairing gesture. 'She could have been killed yesterday. As it is, her beautiful face is probably going to be scarred for life.'

Sir Roland nodded. 'It must have been a terrifying experience.'

'Why don't you drive over to Buckland and force her to return here, Roland? Take Charles with you. It's not safe for her to stay with that wretched man any longer.'

'I don't think she'll come, she won't want to leave Nicolas,' he replied wearily. 'The last time I spoke to her she was adamant about sticking by Nicolas whatever happened.'

Lilian shook her head dismissively. 'That's all very well but the situation has now become dangerous. They were *hounded* yesterday.'

An hour later, dressed in a neat coat with a beaver collar and a pale grey toque trimmed with feathers, Lilian stepped into their Bentley, as upright and as dignified-looking as Queen Mary, whom she copied in all things, including covering her bosom in multiple rows of pearls.

'Where to, m'lady?' Dixon enquired politely.

'I'd like you to take me to Buckland Place. It's in Kent, not far from Canterbury. You'll find it quite easily on the map. I shall require you to wait for me and then we'll be returning to The Elms.'

Dixon switched on the engine and put the car into gear. 'I do have to meet Sir Roland at the station at seven o'clock,' he ventured cautiously. Never before had he seen Lady Brocklehurst so commanding and determined. She was one of those ladies, he reflected as he headed towards the main road, who let her husband rule the roost and deferred to him for everything.

'If we're likely to be delayed, you can telephone him at his office, Dixon. Then he can get a taxi from the station,' she said firmly.

★ ★ ★

Wills opened the imposing entrance doors of Buckland Place and his implacable expression broke for a moment as a quiver of surprise passed over his features. Quickly he readjusted his face to its normal blandness.

'M'lady,' he said in an even voice, recognizing Lilian from her photograph in the newspapers. He opened the door wider.

'Good morning. I've come to see Lady Abingdon. My *daughter* Lady Abingdon,' she corrected herself quickly.

'I'll inform her ladyship right away that you're here. Would you like to wait in the drawing room?' He led the way across the Great Hall and opened the double doors on the far side. To Lilian's relief there was no one in the room, but it was freezing cold and unwelcoming. She would never have allowed a guest to wait in such an uncomfortable room, and she was shocked by the unfriendly atmosphere.

As if Wills had read her thoughts he spoke. 'M'lady, may I offer you a cup of coffee or tea? Or something stronger, perhaps?'

Lilian pulled off her beige suede gloves as she walked over to a sofa by the empty fireplace. 'Nothing, thank you. I'm just here to fetch my daughter.'

Again a quiver of emotion crossed his face, but vanished again a second later. Bowing, he turned and left the room, closing the door quietly behind him.

'What's she doing here?' a voice hissed from the shadows. Conceptia stepped from the open study door and confronted him.

Wills, accustomed to the way his employer slunk around the house like a black cat spying on them all as if they were mice ready to be pounced on, paused and gave a slight bow.

'M'lady, Lady Brocklehurst has come to pay a visit, to see Lady Abingdon,' he replied carefully.

Conceptia gave a little grunt, then marched over to the drawing room doors and flung them open with a theatrical flourish. Lilian looked up, startled by the sudden entry of this thin black-garbed creature. No one who was anyone wore *black* in the country, she reflected disapprovingly.

'Good morning,' Conceptia rasped without preamble. 'I was sure you would come to collect Cathryn, sooner or later.' There was unchecked triumph in her voice.

Lilian rose and extended her hand politely. 'Good morning, Lady Abingdon.'

They shook hands formally. Conceptia's fingers were icy, and so were her black eyes.

'I'm worried about Cath,' Lilian said. 'Is her face badly damaged?'

Conceptia shrugged. 'Even great beauties have to realize that looks don't last forever,' she remarked crisply, striding over to a drinks tray which a footman had just placed on a side table. 'Would you like a glass of sherry?'

'But Cath is only eighteen!' Lilian exclaimed, ignoring her offer. 'Is Nicolas in? I'd like to talk to him.'

'I never know where he is. Out on his horse somewhere, I suppose.' She poured herself a drink. 'What on earth have you got to talk to him about? I would have imagined he'd be the last person on earth you'd ever want to see again.'

Lilian was determined to stand her ground. 'There are things we must discuss.'

'Like a divorce settlement, you mean?'

'I mean nothing of the kind, Lady Abingdon.'

'Well, the marriage is finished and that's for certain after yesterday. Nicolas has brought nothing but trouble and disgrace on us all, including your daughter. I don't know how I ever came to have a child like him,' she added, banging the cut glass sherry decanter back down on the silver tray.

It was too much for Lilian. 'But he's your *son!*' she protested. 'Our children may get into awful scrapes but they're our children and you go on loving them, no matter what.'

'Speak for yourself, Lady Brocklehurst! Your daughter's a nice enough girl but don't tell me you wanted her to marry Nicolas. You were opposed to the marriage from day one.'

Lilian hesitated, wrong-footed. 'One wants one's child to be happy.'

Conceptia took a sip of her sherry. 'Quite.' Suddenly her manner changed and grew softer as she leaned towards Lilian and spoke confidentially. 'I hate to see your daughter being made so miserable. It's terrible for any young woman to have to go through the abuse she's suffered in the past few weeks. And to have her husband accused of killing that child has been agonizing for her! It's made me utterly miserable to see her so unhappy. You must get her to return home with you, Lady Brocklehurst. I fear for her if she stays here much longer.'

The drawing room door burst open and Nicolas came hurrying into the room, having been informed by Wills that his mother-in-law had arrived.

'What's going on?' he demanded looking at them both.

'Nothing,' Conceptia snapped defensively. 'I was just about to ask Lady Brocklehurst to stay for luncheon. I suppose Cathryn isn't well enough to join us?'

'Have you asked her?' He turned to his mother-in-law. 'Good morning, Lady Brocklehurst. Does Cathryn know you're here?'

Lilian shook her head. 'I don't know. I didn't tell her I was coming but I plan to take her home with me. She needs to get away from all this unpleasantness and have a rest, after her terrible experience yesterday.'

'Take her home with you?' Nicolas repeated. 'I don't think she'll want to do that and she can rest here as much as she likes.'

'You mustn't be selfish, Nicolas,' Conceptia said, her tone unusually benign. 'The poor girl needs her own mother at a time like this and Lady Brocklehurst has come all this way, so we mustn't disappoint her.' She rose and reached for the bell by the fireplace. 'I'll get Wills to lay another place for luncheon, and he can ask Cathryn's lady's maid to pack a few things she might need.' She turned to Lilian. 'You're returning to Berkshire, I presume?'

'Yes, I am.'

'Good! Now do change you mind and have some sherry.'

Lilian realized she needed fortifying. 'Thank you.' Then she started to relax. This was so much easier than she'd expected. In fact, Conceptia was being sympathetic and understanding and making it quite simple for her to take Cath home. She'd expected a fight, and here she was being plied with sherry followed by luncheon by a woman she'd previously loathed but now felt quite warm towards.

Nicolas stood watching this polite drawing room conversation with incredulity.

'Don't you think Cathryn should be consulted about these plans?' he asked sarcastically. 'You seem to have made up your minds, between you, that this is not a fit place for her to be.

Speaking as her husband, I believe she should be allowed to decide for herself what she wants to do.'

Conceptia raised her eyebrows. 'It's what her mother thinks is best and I happen to agree with her,' she retorted. 'She's imprisoned in this house, as are all of us because of the press, and God knows when, if ever, it will be safe for her to go down to the village again. How can she possibly stay here? It wouldn't be fair to expect her to.'

There was a swish of satin and silk and at that moment Cathryn swept into the drawing room, looking dishevelled in a nightdress and negligee edged with lace, the black eye and bruises and the stitched cut on her left cheek vivid against the paleness of her skin.

Lilian jumped to her feet, horrified. 'Oh, Cath! My darling, you look dreadful!'

'Mother, please don't fuss!' She hurried to Nicolas's side and linked her arm through his. She looked at the two older women squarely. 'If you think I'm leaving Nicolas and returning home you're mistaken. I couldn't believe it when I found Miss Lewis packing a case. I'm not a quitter and I'm staying here, no matter what,' she added defiantly.

'But Cath . . .' Lilian pleaded.

'Mother, Nicolas has done nothing wrong and frankly, I refuse to be intimidated by a bunch of village bullies! The police will eventually find out what really happened to Posy Burgess, and then I'll expect an apology from a lot of people who were only too ready to believe he had anything to do with it.'

'But Cath . . . !'

Nicolas looked down at her, concern etched on his face. 'I'll absolutely understand it if you'd like to spend a few days with your parents, darling. Just until you recover from your injuries . . .'

Cathryn swiftly placed her fingertips over his lips. 'I want to stay and I shall stay,' she said firmly. 'Nothing will induce me to go.' Then she turned back to Lilian. 'I'm sorry you've had a wasted journey, Mother. Does Daddy know you're here?'

Lilian dabbed her streaming eyes with her handkerchief. 'No, and I do wish you'd change your mind. I'm so worried about you, Cath. Can't you see what you're doing?'

'I know what I'm doing. This is a storm in a teacup, whipped up by some very evil people, but it will blow over and until it does I'm staying here, with Nicolas.'

'But mud sticks, Cath! This disgrace will haunt you until the end of your days.'

Conceptia regarded Lilian with an expression of quiet malice. 'It's too late to try and save the situation now. We are *all* tarred by the same brush. Even you, Lady Brocklehurst, as Nicolas's mother-in-law.'

Lilian flinched, wishing her husband were here to back her up. *Why are men never around when we need them,* she reflected, feeling quite distraught, *but always around when we don't?*

'Nicolas's name will soon be cleared,' Cathryn said confidently.

They all looked at her in silence. Nicolas took her hand and clasped it tightly.

Conceptia shrugged. 'We'd better have luncheon,' she said, leading the way to the dining room.

Downcast, Lilian put her handkerchief into her handbag and followed.

'Wait,' Cathryn said, desperate to avoid hurting her mother more than was necessary. She caught up with her and took her arm. 'Nicolas and I will both come and stay with you and Daddy when this is over. You do understand, don't you? Right now we've got to face the music until the police come up with the answers that will prove Nicolas's innocence.'

'Providing we don't all die of old age in the meantime,' Conceptia remarked, tartly.

Thirteen

WIFE STANDS BY PEER

The young Marchioness of Abingdon is remaining by her husband's side in spite of receiving further poison pen letters referring to his alleged involvement in the disappearance and death of a nine-year-old child. The revelations have shocked her, though. A close family friend who wishes to remain anonymous has told us, 'Cathryn is beginning to feel she doesn't know the man she married. She says it's like living with a stranger . . .'
The Daily Chronicle, February 3rd, 1931

Another spate of anonymous letters had been delivered in the past week, addressed to Conceptia, Cathryn and Hugh Verney, as well as several people in the village. Describing Nicolas Abingdon as a child molester who had grown into a philanderer and adulterer, they went on to contain such phrases as 'Steeped in vice, Abingdon has no morals', 'His lordship is a degenerate man who frequents London brothels', 'Nicolas Abingdon's shameful behaviour must not go unpunished' and 'Corrupt and perverted, he shames the Abingdon family name'.

'This is deeply worrying,' Hugh Verney observed, gathering all the letters together to give to the police. The Abingdons were sitting in the study: Nicolas, Cathryn, Conceptia and Ewan, a family united for once in the face of this anonymous onslaught.

'Look at this one,' Cathryn said, handing him another letter, which had also been made up from individual letters cut from a newspaper and stuck on a plain sheet of paper.

He blanched as he read it aloud.

Cathryn Abingdon!
Check your brakes!
Watch your car!
Watch your back!

He'll get rid of you next!
He only married you to
Get an heir and to
Hide his sins!
Miranda knew what he had done,
Don't be taken for a fool!

'It's definitely from someone who is very, very sick,' Hugh remarked gloomily. 'I'll take these down to the police station right away.'

Cathryn was filled by a deep sense of anxiety. For the first time she felt afraid. There was someone out there who was mentally unhinged and determined to harm them all, not just Nicolas but her, too. Most frightening of all was that they no longer seemed to be 'out there' but right here; in their lives, close to them, reading their thoughts, judging their reactions, determined to crush them to breaking point.

Conceptia's hands were shaking and Cathryn couldn't be sure if it was anger or fear that dominated her thoughts. Suddenly she spoke. 'Whoever it is has gone to a lot of trouble to avoid being caught, travelling all over the countryside to post the letters, which means they must have a car.'

Nicolas looked at his mother impatiently. 'So?'

'Poor people don't have cars,' she shot back acidly. 'It's someone with money. Who do we know who has a car and the time for all this travelling?'

'All our friends, basically,' he retorted drily.

'I don't mean someone who would be one of our friends in our circle, Nicolas. Don't be absurd. I mean a tradesman, perhaps? Who has an axe to grind because he thinks the family has let him down?'

'Maybe Hugh could help there,' Cathryn suggested. 'Hugh, you'll have a record of people the estate has done business with, won't you? A builder? Or a supplier?'

'Yes, I'll go through all our records to see what I can find,' Hugh replied.

'What else can we do?' Cathryn asked. 'The newspapers are still printing all these dreadful stories. Where are they getting them from?'

'These histrionics are getting us nowhere,' Conceptia remarked, getting up and walking towards the door. 'Come along, Ewan. I'm taking the dogs for a walk.'

The others sat looking at each other. They were no nearer to finding out who seemed determined to ruin their reputations.

After luncheon, Cathryn went up to her bedroom to rest. Lack of sleep, no appetite and the constant strain of living under the shadow of suspicion were taking their toll and she felt permanently rundown and exhausted. No longer was her figure curvaceous and the healthy bloom of youth had left her cheeks. She looked ill and gaunt and her beautiful trousseau hung limply on her thin frame.

She couldn't help being aware that whenever Nicolas looked at her now, he felt a deep sense of guilt that she'd been drawn into the nightmare that had befallen him. She even wondered if he now regretted marrying her. But how was he to know that a tragedy that had happened all those years ago when he'd been a mere boy would come back to ruin all their lives?

She dozed off, lying on the *chaise longue* under a cashmere rug by the warm fire. Outside, the darkness of a February afternoon started closing in and still she slept on, oblivious of what was happening downstairs. She didn't even hear the bedroom door being opened and the quiet footsteps of Nicolas walking rapidly towards her.

'Cathryn . . .'

Was she dreaming? Where was she? Confused, she opened her eyes when she heard her name whispered again. Then she saw Nicolas standing over her, his face white, his eyes blazing with unshed tears.

'Nicolas?' Startled, she sat upright, reaching for his hand. 'What is it? What's happened?'

He dropped to his haunches beside her, gripping her tightly by the shoulders. 'I'm so sorry, darling. I have to go . . .'

'Go where?' Her eyes widened with alarm.

'The police are downstairs. I've got to go to the police station for more questioning. I just came to say goodbye.'

She struggled to her feet, desperately afraid now. 'Nicolas, what's happening?'

He took a deep painful breath. 'The forensic department have discovered that the pellets that killed Posy came from my air rifle. They're arresting me on a charge . . .'

'Oh, no!' A dart of ice shot through her heart, splintering into her arteries and sweeping through her body. 'Oh, no!' she repeated, distraught.

'Yes. I'm so dreadfully sorry, darling,' he said wretchedly.

'They can't do this. Someone else must have . . .'

'We'll have to see, but it looks bad. I must go now. They didn't even want to let me see you before I left . . .'

'Nicolas.' She clung to him, shaking with fear and anger. 'Where's your solicitor? You can't go alone.'

'He's on his way down from London and he'll meet me there.' He kissed her quickly. 'Why don't you go and stay with your parents? They're in Berkshire now, aren't they? I'd be much happier if you did, darling. I hate leaving you here, in this terrible atmosphere. It's going to get a lot worse, too.'

'I must stay. I want to know what's happening.'

He stood back, his expression hardening. 'No, Cathryn. You must go. You must get the hell out of here. Things are getting very nasty and this is no place for you. You must go to your family right away. They'll look after you.'

She looked hurt and horrified. 'I can't leave you, Nicolas. I won't.'

'Yes, you will, my darling. I want you to. I'll keep in contact. Just go, darling. Please.'

Then he turned abruptly and charged out of the room, banging the door behind him, leaving her standing there, alone and dazed.

A few minutes later Miss Lewis came hurrying into her room, looking nervous. 'His lordship has given me instructions to pack for you, m'lady. He's already ordered Rogers to drive you to your parents' country house?'

Cathryn nodded, numb with shock. 'I'll only be away a couple of days at the most. I won't need much.' She went over to her dressing table as if she were sleepwalking and sat down and looked at herself in the triple mirror. Who was this young Marchioness of Abingdon who stared back like a complete stranger? A girl still, who'd had the world at her feet until they dug up the remains of a nine-year-old child? A girl with a loving husband, homes in London, Kent and Scotland filled with treasures, a safe containing more jewellery than she would probably ever wear and with more money available than she would ever spend? Where had Cathryn Brocklehurst gone? Where had her dreams of a perfect life gone?

She'd imagined she and Nicolas would always stick together, through thick and thin, but now he'd told her she must leave and that hurt. Surely, if he loved her and knew how much she loved him, he'd want her by his side at this terrible time? She blew her nose and dabbed her wet cheeks, trying to understand. He probably thought he was sparing her feelings. Instead she felt broken-hearted, as if this were the beginning of the end of her marriage.

In the adjoining dressing room her lady's maid was doing her packing and half an hour later two footmen appeared to take the cases to the car, which Rogers had brought round to the front of the house.

By the time Cathryn made her way down to the hall, her make-up was immaculate, and she was wearing a small hat with a veil that hid her swollen eyes. Dressed in her magnificent new mink coat, she pulled on her brown suede gloves. No one was going to have the satisfaction of seeing her creep away like a dispossessed refugee going into exile.

As she crossed the Great Hall, her head held high, she heard Conceptia's voice coming from the study.

'David, please come down right away,' she was saying into the telephone. She sounded fraught. 'Something's happened and I need you desperately.'

Cathryn slowed her pace, straining her ears, wanting to hear more.

Then she heard Conceptia continue, 'No, I can't talk on the telephone, I must see you.' She paused for a moment and then added, 'At least Cathryn is leaving at last which is a great relief . . .'

She didn't wait to hear any more. Averting her gaze, she walked stiffly past Wills and out of the building into the darkness, having no idea when she'd return, or even if she ever would.

As the car drove slowly along the drive to the wrought iron gates where the photographers were grouped, she bent right down so they wouldn't be able to get a picture of her. Then Rogers pressed down hard on the accelerator and they were speeding along the lane that led to the main road, away from Appledore, heading for Maidenhead.

Cathryn sat upright again, settling herself with a rug over her legs for the two hour journey, her mind locked in neutral, refusing to think what the future might hold.

When the car slowed down to a halt, she realized Rogers had stopped at the T-junction, just beyond the village, and was waiting for several cars to pass. Straight ahead of them was the King's Arms, a popular local inn that now stood bathed in the head-lamps of their car. She looked at the cheerful little pub, its windows glowing with light from within, envying the ordinary people inside, leading ordinary lives as they enjoyed a glass of beer and a game of darts.

Suddenly out of the darkness a young man's figure appeared, going up a path that led to a back entrance. At that moment the door opened and another man, silhouetted by the light from the room behind him, came out to greet him. The two men embraced, their arms around each other, and then they kissed passionately.

It was only as Rogers eased off the brakes and the Daimler slid forward that Cathryn realized one of the men was Ewan.

'Why didn't you tell us to expect you?' Lilian Brocklehurst exclaimed, when Cathryn arrived at The Elms. 'Thank God you've seen sense! Come along, my darling. You look worn out.'

'Has Nicolas telephoned?' she asked immediately, shrugging off her coat.

'No, darling. Is he likely to? Doesn't he know you've come home?'

Cathryn was determined to put on a strong front and not let her family know how upset she felt. 'Mother, I haven't come home. Nicolas just wants me to stay away from Buckland for a few days until we see which way the wind is blowing.' She sank exhausted into a deep armchair by the drawing room fire, while her mother fussed around her.

'I'll order tea and you can tell me all about it, darling. Is your chauffeur staying the night? I'll get Burton to help with your cases.' Lilian was in her element, almost clucking like a broody hen at having her daughter back.

'Rogers is driving straight back to Buckland, he's needed there. I don't need all that luggage Miss Lewis packed. Burton needn't take it all upstairs.' she added.

'Very well. You have a little rest, darling. Would you like a boiled egg for your tea? We have some fresh scones and home-made jam and . . .'

Cathryn pressed her hand against her forehead. 'I'm not hungry, mother. I'd just like a cup of tea, please. My head is splitting.'

'My poor darling! Didn't I say it would come to this? Didn't I warn you not to marry that man? Would you like to go up to your room and lie down? I know I have some aspirins . . .'

'I'd rather stay here.' She didn't want to be alone. She'd only start thinking. Wondering. Imagining all sorts of dreadful things happening to Nicolas. A wave of depression swept through her, leaving her feeling shivery and with a sense of deep anxiety, unable to rid herself of the terrible feeling that her life was falling apart and it was all her fault because she'd insisted on marrying Nicolas. To stay sitting by the fire, on the other hand, meant having to listen to her mother's interminable criticism.

'I'm only staying for a night or two,' she insisted, trying to keep her voice steady. 'Just until Nicolas settles everything and then I'll be returning home.'

Sir Roland returned from London shortly afterwards, his kindly calm manner like a balm to Cathryn's troubled spirit, and a welcome barrier between her and her mother.

'I'm sure you have nothing to worry about,' he assured her when she told him of the latest developments. 'Remember what I told you? A child under the age of fifteen can only be convicted of an offence if the prosecution can show the child was *aware* he was doing something seriously wrong. In this case, even if he did shoot that little girl, it would have been by accident. I don't believe anyone would seriously think he'd done it on purpose? Why should he? What would have been his motive? What harm could the child of a washerwoman do to him?'

Cathryn dropped her voice to a whisper, and she kept an eye on the drawing room door in case her mother came back into the room. 'Posy Burgess was actually Nicolas's half-sister. His father had lots of affairs and Posy was illegitimate. Her mother lives in the village and . . .' She watched as her father's smiling face grew grim and his skin bleached white.

'Who else knows this?' he asked sharply.

'Hush!' She put a finger to her lips. 'For goodness sake, don't let mother know. That would be the last straw.'

'So who else knows?'

'Frank Burgess let it slip when I was talking to him, but he told me he loved Posy like she was his own child. Then Nicolas told me about his father's relationships with married women in the village. Conceptia knew all about his affairs and that's why she's so bitter towards Nicolas, because he looks like his father.' Cathryn paused, thinking, before she continued. 'Maybe the staff who worked at Buckland when it happened know Posy was William Abingdon's child, but it won't look good if this ever goes to court, will it? They could accuse Nicolas of wanting to get rid of her in case she claimed her rights as the daughter of the sixth Marquess, when she was older.'

Sir Roland looked doubtful. 'Illegitimate children don't have any rights. They can't inherit titles, property or money unless granted a legacy in the father's will. In this case Nicolas's father would have had to make provision for her, and did he?'

'I don't know.'

He promised me he'd look after her . . . Ida Burgess's words as she sobbed and cursed the Abingdon family came back to Cathryn with frightening clarity.

Her father continued, 'I'll get a copy of the will from Somerset House, but I think it's unlikely he left her anything. It would have caused a scandal when he died if he had and everyone would have known about it.'

'He didn't know he was going to be killed in a car accident though,' Cathryn pointed out. 'Perhaps he planned to provide for her but died before he could.'

'How old was she when he was killed?'

'A year old.' She repeated Ida's remark about him promising to look after Posy.

Sir Roland nodded. 'That would account for it then. Has Nicolas ever mentioned his father's will to you?'

Cathryn shook her head. 'No. I'm sure he'd have honoured it if . . .,' she broke off, frowning. 'Of course he was only six when his father died, so it would have been up to Conceptia and her solicitor to carry out William's wishes . . . and Nicolas would have been too young to know . . .' Her voice trailed away thoughtfully. David Partridge was Conceptia's lawyer. Her confidant. A man who adored her and would do anything for her. Cathryn's mind raced. This opened up a whole new vista of possibilities.

Had they conspired to make sure Posy Burgess inherited nothing? By the time she died she was nine, and by then her mother might have told her who her real father was and that she had prospects when she came of age.

'There's something else I must tell you, Daddy, though I don't think he's connected with all this in any way, but it explains why Conceptia is nervous of the police making all their enquiries and questioning the servants.' Then she told him about Ewan and how she'd seen him meeting another man at a local pub.

Sir Roland raised his eyebrows. 'Not very discreet,' he commented drily.

'Aren't you shocked?'

'I always guessed he was a nancy boy. He ought to be more careful, though. If a passing police car had spotted him in that situation he'd really be for the high jump.'

Cathryn sat in subdued silence. 'I suppose his mother made him the way he is?'

'I don't think people can be "made" that way, Cath. They're either born with the inclination or they're not. Conceptia's possessiveness won't have helped, though. I wouldn't mention this to your mother if I were you,' he added, dropping his voice.

'I'm not sure she'd understand what it was all about, anyway.'

Sir Roland smiled. 'You're right. She's led a very sheltered life.' He stood up, rubbing his hands together. 'Now, my dear, would you like a glass of sherry? Or a cocktail before dinner? I think you need something to cheer you up.'

'I hated the way Nicolas insisted I leave Buckland,' she admitted, ignoring the question. She quickly wiped away a tear. 'I wanted to stay but he wouldn't let me.'

'Nicolas loves you very much, Cath, and I'm certain he just wants to keep you out of harm's way. Those poison pen letters you've been receiving are truly horrible and where will it end? Maybe the sender is intent on driving you over the edge; you may really be in danger from some nut case, in more ways than one.'

She looked at her father gratefully. In spite of not wanting to leave Buckland it was soothing to be back with her parents, being petted and protected like a child once again. Away from the claustrophobic atmosphere, where Conceptia made snide remarks, and David Partridge slyly watched her every move. Where Ewan irritated and Hugh Verney regarded them all with the anxiety of a schoolmaster in charge of a group of delinquents.

She missed Nicolas of course, but most of all she missed the carefree loving man she'd fallen in love with before he became bowed down by the catastrophe that had irrevocably changed their lives.

Sipping the strong White Lady her father had mixed for her, she closed her eyes and leaned her head back against the cushions. Nowadays she and Nicolas only talked of one thing, in tight voices and short sentences. He had aged too, the skin around his eyes dark and his cheeks hollow. She knew she'd changed, as well. She'd seen it in her reflection today, her blue eyes watchful and anxious, her lips pressed tightly together as if to prevent the words of anguish she wanted to utter from escaping. But the biggest change had been within herself. She no longed trusted everyone, nor believed what they said. She'd grown wary and suspicious, no longer the naïve girl Nicolas had married.

Tears spilled from under her closed lids. Nicolas had looked so stricken when he'd woken her up that afternoon and he'd said 'I'm so dreadfully sorry.' Why had he said that? What had he meant?

Cathryn drew in a deep shuddering breath. She wasn't going to even begin to think what he'd meant because only madness lay that way. But then a sudden sense of reality seemed to hit her senses like a sledgehammer.

It was definitely Nicolas's air rifle, which only he used, that had killed Posy. And the forensic findings had proved the pellets fired by that rifle matched the ones found by Posy's remains. That was now a fact, and facts she couldn't refute.

'Oh, no! No!' Sobs broke from her throat as she plunged deeper and deeper into a darkness too terrible to contemplate. Layer upon layer of realization revealed itself with terrible consequences as little things came back to her. The haunted look in Nicolas's eyes when Posy's remains had been discovered, although he'd hidden it under a cloak of compassion for Ida Burgess. Hugh Verney's expression of consternation when he sometimes looked at Nicolas, as if he guessed what had happened. Conceptia's attitude towards her eldest son; she really seemed to hate him. The mysterious person who had made a statement to the police claiming to have seen Nicolas shooting Posy.

Finally all the anonymous letters from someone who obviously knew the truth but was elaborating the facts so they became more damning and more brutal.

Her wild weeping brought Lilian hurrying into the drawing room. Cathryn was alone, standing by the fireplace, hanging on to the mantel shelf with one hand for support, her other hand covering her mouth as if to suppress her sobs.

'Cath darling, what's happened?' she exclaimed in alarm.

Cathryn shook her head, unable to answer.

'Come and sit down. You're overwrought with exhaustion.' Lilian guided her daughter back to the sofa. 'You should go to bed, darling. We'll send up supper on a tray and then you can get a good night's sleep.'

Sir Roland, standing in the doorway, slipped away to his study where he had an extension of the telephone. Reaching for it, he dialled the number of Buckland Place, and when he got through asked to speak to Lord Abingdon.

'I'm afraid his lordship is out,' Wills replied with his usual formality.

'This is Sir Roland Brocklehurst. Am I to understand that Lord Abingdon is still at the police station?'

'I'm afraid I'm unable to answer that question, Sir,' Wills retorted haughtily.

'Don't be ridiculous, man. My daughter, his wife, is staying with us and I merely want to know if he's still being questioned.'

Wills sounded subdued this time. 'I believe he may be, Sir.'

'Very well, please ask him to return my call as soon as he gets back.'

The next call Sir Roland made was to their local family doctor who was also a personal friend. Briefly he explained what had happened. 'Can you be a good fellow and pop over to give Cathryn something to calm her down? Make her sleep, perhaps?'

The next morning, after ten hours of induced sleep, Cathryn sat propped against a mound of pillows, groggily sipping tea. Her mother sat on the end of the bed, while her father stood looking at her anxiously.

'Are you feeling better, dearest?' he asked.

'I'm not sure how I feel.' Her voice was flat, her eyes gazing dully at the rain-sodden countryside through the bedroom window.

Sir Roland cleared his throat and spoke diffidently. 'Do you really think Nicolas had anything to do with that child's death?' He'd been awake most of the previous night, wracked with doubts and worry about what Cathryn had said.

'I suddenly had a terrible feeling soon after I arrived here,' she replied, holding the cup between the palms of her hands for warmth. 'Being away from Buckland changed my perspective and made me realize that *something* terrible is going on. Something too ghastly for words. Nicolas hasn't telephoned here this morning, has he?'

'No, I'm afraid not.'

'I still don't understand why he was so desperate for me to go away. He was adamant I leave, yet in the past he's wanted me to stay with him.' She frowned. 'I feel as if a net is closing in on us and he doesn't want me to be caught up in it.'

'What do you mean?' Lilian asked, alarmed, before promptly answering for her. 'Maybe you were just overtired last night, Cath. It's not surprising that everything got on top of you.'

Sir Roland nodded in agreement. 'It's never before occurred to you that Nicolas had anything to do with that child, has it?'

'No. I've never doubted him for a moment, but now I'm wondering if I haven't been in a state of complete denial. I love him and I'm desperate to believe in him but somehow, I don't know . . . things just aren't adding up.'

Lilian fiddled nervously with her long string of pearls. 'The doctor last night suggested you were getting overwrought, dearest. He said you were to stay in bed resting for several days and he'll come and see you again tomorrow.'

Cathryn didn't answer. Her mind was a whirlpool of turbulent confusion, jumbled thoughts and fragmented memories of recent events. *If only I could think straight*, she thought to herself.

Instead, she demanded aloud, 'How can I rest? How can I have a moment's peace not knowing what's happening?'

Lilian did her best to sound soothing. 'I'm sure he'll ring you as soon as he can, Cath.'

'I think you know in your heart of hearts that Nicolas has done nothing wrong,' her father told her gently. 'Try, for his sake, to stay calm.'

Later that morning Lilian rushed breathlessly into Cathryn's room, saying Nicolas was on the telephone.

'Oh, thank God!' She flew down to the hall, still in her negligee, and grabbed the receiver. 'Nicolas?' she asked shrilly, her nerves in shreds, her head aching with worry. 'What's happening?'

'I'm back at home for the moment, on bail, waiting for my solicitor to return with some papers.' His voice sounded remote, as if he were trying very hard to control his emotions. 'I can't really talk but the situation has changed in the past twenty-four hours.'

Panic swept through her and her brain reeled. She knew immediately it wasn't good news. 'What's changed?'

'I'm afraid there's nothing else for it, darling, I'm going to have to confess. Please stay with your parents and I'll try and get in touch with you later, but I can't promise when.'

'Nicolas, what's happened? What's changed?'

'Sorry, sweetheart. Anthony's just arrived. I've got to go now. Bye.' There was a click and the phone went dead.

A boy came running into the house, his white face blotched red with tears, his eyes terrified, as he flung himself into his mother's arms. She held him close, stroking his silky hair, comforting him with words she didn't believe herself.

'It will be all right, darling. Don't worry.'

'It's w-what you w-wanted . . . isn't it?' he begged, as he trembled and sobbed, beside himself with terror. 'I d-did it f-for you.'

Guilt mingled with horror hit her with the force of an Atlantic roller as she tried to take in what had happened. She'd promised, though. She was strong. Indomitable. She would manage somehow. 'Everything will be all right,' she repeated like a mantra as she continued to hold him close.

Then someone knocked on the door. Her heart leapt and rocked with fear. Had they discovered . . . ?

Giving a little scream she sat bolt upright in bed, the sweat making her satin nightdress cling to her body, her eyes wild with confusion as she glanced around, finding herself alone after all in her bedroom.

'Good morning, m'lady.' The maid entered the room and placed the early morning tea tray on the bedside table. Without another word she moved on silent feet to draw back the curtains, revealing a misty wet February day. Then she left the room and closed the door quietly behind her.

Conceptia sank back against the pillows again and closed her eyes with exhaustion. Was there no escaping the enduring nightmares that plagued her? Was William's original betrayal going to go on echoing down the years, like an eternal damnation of her soul, making her suffer so? There were too many mornings when she wished she'd never woken up. Too many mornings when the pain of recall was unbearable and she committed the sin of wishing the good Lord had taken her in the night so that she could rest in peace. There was no respite though, only raging anger in the depths of her being that William had been the architect of her misery and that she'd been left with the bitter legacy of his infidelity.

Hilary gazed out through the lead-paned glass of their drawing room window, twitching the net curtain when she felt she might be observed, but meanwhile enjoying the sight of the village gossips indulging in chatter. It was obvious what they were all talking about.

'I think he may well be charged this time.' She spoke with satisfaction.

Mrs Pilkington looked up from the breakfast table. 'What, Nicolas? No dear, I'm sure he won't be. What a dreadful thought! And even if he had accidentally shot Posy, he was only a child himself at that time.'

'He's guilty all right,' Hilary blurted out crossly, before she could stop herself.

'What in God's name are you saying?' Her mother put down her teacup and looked at her aghast. 'How can you talk like that? You actually sound as if you hope he'll be found guilty.'

Hilary pushed her lower jaw forward, her expression stubborn. 'Just because he's a marquess with a big house, you think he's perfect. Well, let me tell you something. The man's a rotter and I hope he pays for the pain he's caused.'

'I know it's been terrible for Frank and Ida Burgess; there's nothing in the world worse than losing a child, but even they wouldn't want an innocent man punished for something he hasn't done.'

'What makes you so sure he's innocent?' Hilary challenged, her eyes blazing now. 'You weren't *there*,' she added with sudden passion, her hands tightly clenched, her thick dark eyebrows drawn together as she rejoined her mother at the table.

'Neither were you,' Mrs Pilkington retorted reprovingly. 'No one knows what happened on that dreadful day. That's been the problem from the beginning. Posy went into the garden and vanished and was never seen again.'

'*Someone* saw what happened and they gave a statement to the police a few weeks ago. I just don't know why they're taking so long to charge him with murder.'

'But who gave any such statement?' her mother protested. 'We've never been told who came forward and why they left it over twenty years before saying anything. It's all very fishy if you ask me.' She picked up another piece of toast and reached for the jar of homemade marmalade. 'Why didn't they come forward at the time?'

Hilary rounded on her mother, shouting furiously. 'Because no one would have believed me then! That's why! I was only a child and nobody would have listened to me.'

Her mother's face had turned the colour of putty and her hands started shaking. 'What do you mean, Hilary? Why are you saying these things? You know they're not true.'

'Of course it's true!' All the pent-up years of pain and jealousy she'd suffered rose to the surface and she was beside herself with rage. 'I *saw* Nicolas shoot Posy. He didn't know I was there. He never saw me and I was so frightened I ran all the way home in case he turned his gun in my direction and shot me too. Then I was afraid to tell anyone, in case he came after me! You've no idea how much I suffered . . .' Angry tears sprang to her eyes and she started weeping hysterically. 'I'd like to see the bastard hung,' she shrieked, running from the room. Then the door slammed and Mrs Pilkington could hear her stomping around in her bedroom on the floor above.

She continued sitting at the table, deeply perturbed. What

should she do? Shock had blunted her senses. Who could she turn to for advice? Hilary's remarks confirmed something that had vaguely worried her in recent weeks, but she'd shied away from thinking about it because she had no idea how she would deal with the consequences. Short of money and with only her widow's pension to support them both, she wondered what on earth would happen if her instincts were right.

She made a swift decision. She wrote a hurried shopping list and going into the hall called for Hilary to come downstairs, as if nothing had happened. 'Can you do me a great favour, my dear?' she asked brightly. 'I urgently need to get in some things, and I've nearly run out of navy wool for the cardigan I'm knitting. Could you go to Canterbury and do the shopping for me?'

Sulkily Hilary agreed. 'There's no need to hurry back,' Mrs Pilkington added cheerfully. 'Why don't you treat yourself to luncheon in that nice little café we sometimes go to?'

'What are you going to be doing?'

'I've got some letters to write.'

After Hilary had gone, Mrs Pilkington put on her coat and hat and, bracing herself to face the worst ordeal of her life, she picked up her handbag and a small case she kept for overnight stays. The taxi she'd ordered for nine-thirty arrived, and telling their maid she was going to visit some friends she stepped into the cab and settled herself in the back.

'Where to, Madam?' the driver asked.

'The police station, please.'

He tried to suppress the look of surprise that flashed across his rugged features.

'Would you like me to wait for you and then bring you back here, Madam?'

Mrs Pilkington's mouth tightened and her eyes stared anxiously ahead. 'No thank you. I don't know how long I'll be.'

'I have to get back to Buckland,' Cathryn said, as she flung her belongings into her cases. 'I must find out what's going on.'

Lilian Brocklehurst wrung her hands in agitation. 'Cath, you can't go without having your breakfast. Anyway, Nicolas sent you here to get away from it all. If he did shoot that child then the sooner he confesses the sooner the matter can be cleared up.'

'Mother, I have to talk to him. I also have to talk to his solicitor so we have the best advice. It's madness for him to suddenly confess to shooting Posy. What is he thinking of?' Her tone was desperate as she grabbed skirts and jumpers and crammed them into one of the leather cases that bore her initials under a marquess's coronet.

'But Cath . . .'

'Please Mother, I know what I'm doing. I should never have left Buckland in the first place. I know Nicolas was trying to protect me but my place is by his side and I've got to get back to him. I'm convinced now that he's innocent.'

'You're going to ruin your life chasing after that man!' her mother exclaimed fretfully. 'Can't you see what's happening? You're going to end up a social outcast, and then what will become of you?'

Cathryn straightened up and looked at Lilian steadily. 'Nicolas is my husband and no matter what he's done or not done I'm going to be sticking by him until the bitter end, so there's no point in your trying to persuade me otherwise. I've already phoned the local taxi service so there's no need for me to take your car, and it'll be here in a few minutes. I would be grateful,' she added politely but firmly, 'if you could ask Burton to help me down with my cases. Who unpacked them all, in the first place?' As she spoke she snapped shut the largest one and then started throwing shoes, her sponge bag and her nightclothes into another case. Then she ran her fingers through her dishevelled hair, irritated at having so much luggage.

Without any make-up or jewellery she looked about fifteen again, fresh-faced and full of energy, her blue eyes clear and her manner positive. Lilian's heart broke as she looked at her beautiful daughter, who seemed not to care about her appearance. She grieved at the waste of such loveliness and charm.

'How has it come to this?' Lilian wailed tearfully as she followed Cathryn down the polished oak staircase of The Elms. 'Where is it going to end? The shame of it all is killing me.'

Cathryn turned to look at her mother with an impatient gesture. 'Killing *you*? How do you think Nicolas is feeling? He's got everything to lose.'

'I suppose so.' Her mother pecked her cheek. 'Please take care of yourself, Cath.'

'I'll be fine, Mother. Tell Daddy what's happened when he gets back this evening, and we'll talk on the telephone.' Then she hopped into the waiting taxi, and waved goodbye as it pulled away.

Fourteen

LORD ABINGDON EXPECTED TO CONFESS TO SHOOTING

Lord Abingdon, out on bail, remained at Buckland Place last night to hold crisis talks with his solicitor regarding the murder of nine-year-old Posy Burgess, whose remains were found buried in the woods of his stately home. His second wife left Buckland Place yesterday afternoon to return to her parents' home. It is thought the stress of the past few weeks have caused her to have a break-down. A member of the household said he had no idea when she would be returning . . .

The Daily Herald, February 4th, 1931

The constable on duty behind the desk at the police station smiled benignly at the elderly lady with her small suitcase and large black handbag. No doubt the old dear had lost her way and needed redirecting.

'What can I do for you, Madam?' he asked solicitously.

Her faded eyes betrayed her nervousness as her gaze flickered around the police station lobby. 'May I speak to whoever is in charge of . . .' she hesitated, not knowing how to phrase it. 'Well, it's about the little girl who was found in the woods. You know, little Posy Burgess. The one who was shot,' she added in a whisper, as if the grieving parents were within earshot.

The constable's bushy eyebrows shot up and he blinked. 'That would be Detective Inspector Harding, Madam. I'll see if he's in his office. Can I tell him what it's about?'

'I'd rather speak to him myself,' she said in hushed tones.

'Please take a seat, Madam, and I'll go and have a word with him. What is your name, please?'

'I'm Mrs Pilkington.'

Seated on the wooden bench facing the counter, with the

small suitcase at her feet, she waited patiently, although she was quaking at the shame of her present predicament. She had to tell the police the truth though. She wouldn't be able to live with herself if she kept silent but she tried to shut her mind to the repercussions her revelations were going to cause. *May God forgive me*, she prayed fervently as she struggled for composure.

Down the corridor the constable knocked on the DI's door.

'Yes? What is it?' Harding asked, looking up from his desk.

The young man grinned. 'I think we may have one of those, Sir,' he whispered, 'She's waiting in the lobby, asking to see you.'

Harding frowned. 'What do you mean? What are you talking about?'

'You know, Sir, one of those people who confess to something they haven't done, like that man who saw in the papers that a woman had been strangled, then he comes in here and says he'd done it. She's even brought her things with her as if she expects to be locked up right away.' He chuckled deep in his throat. 'Batty, I'd say she was. What shall I tell her? That you're busy, Sir?'

'What's her name?' He was not amused by his colleague's attempt at humour.

'Pilkington, Sir. Mrs Pilkington.'

'Ahhh…!' Harding raised his eyebrows knowingly, his interest aroused. 'Show her in, Constable. I'd rather like to talk to her.'

Wrong-footed and feeling foolish, the constable hurried back to the lobby to collect Mrs Pilkington.

The DI rose and came forward to shake her hand as she entered his office. 'How nice of you come and see me, Mrs Pilkington,' he said, with old world cordiality. 'Do take a seat.' He indicated the chair facing his desk. 'Now, what can I do for you?'

Mrs Pilkington started trembling and tears sprang to her eyes. 'This is very difficult for me,' she murmured, reaching for her handbag, from which she dug out a neatly folded white handkerchief.

'Take your time, Mrs Pilkington. Would you like a cup of tea or a glass of water?'

She shook her head and with an effort pulled herself together. 'I believe my daughter, Hilary, came to see you some weeks ago and made a statement? Saying she witnessed Lord Abingdon shooting that little girl, Posy Burgess?'

The DI's eyes narrowed. 'What about it?' His voice was sharp now.

'I'm very much afraid she's misled you, Mr . . . ?'

'Detective Inspector Harding, Madam.'

'Mr Harding. I've had private worries about my daughter for some time . . . years really. She has an over-imaginative mind you see and then she gets carried away and says all sorts of things. Some of which aren't true.' Her voice sank so low he could barely hear her.

'I see. Miss Pilkington did give us a signed statement.' He rose again and went to a row of grey metal filing cabinets lining one wall. Taking a key attached to a chain that hung from his belt, he opened the first one, which was labelled A–D. Flicking through the files he extracted a bulky folder and brought it back to his desk, where he opened it and spread some of the papers before him.

Mrs Pilkington leaned forward anxiously. 'Posy Burgess *did* go missing on Thursday 24th November 1909, didn't she?' There was a flat note of dread in her voice, as if she were afraid of his answer.

Harding looked surprised at the question. Then he fumbled amongst the forms and finally picked out a faded-looking sheet of paper and examined it closely. 'Yes, she did,' he confirmed after a few moments. 'November 24th,1909. Why do you ask?'

She let out a long despairing groan. 'That's what I was afraid of but I had hoped I'd got the date wrong.'

'No, she definitely went missing on the 24th. Why? What's wrong?' He watched as she bent down and opened the small suitcase. 'What have you got there, Mrs Pilkington?'

'I had to bring it in a case because it's so heavy,' she explained, as with difficulty she lifted out an old and battered scrapbook. It was four inches thick, bound in dark red and looked as if it weighed as much as a couple of bricks. 'I've had it since I got married in 1896, and it's full of pictures and snapshots and mementos.' As she spoke, she opened it and showed him some faded sepia photographs of a good-looking young man in a morning suit, and a young girlish bride in white with a lace veil, who bore no resemblance whatsoever to the elderly lady sitting before him now.

'This is my wedding,' she said, unnecessarily.

He nodded, wondering where this was leading.

'Here's my daughter Hilary, when she was born, in April of 1900, and then at her christening in June of the same year. Here are the announcements of her birth from *The Times* and *Telegraph*.' She flipped through several pages showing pictures of Hilary playing on a garden swing, blowing out the candles on a birthday cake in a smocked party frock, and then informal snapshots of family picnics, and one of Hilary riding her skewbald pony.

She stopped flipping through the pages when she came to a yellowing newspaper cutting of a young girl holding a puppy in her arms.

From across his desk Harding read the headline above the picture. *PUPPY WINS FIRST PRIZE.*

'This is Hilary when she was twelve, and her puppy won a prize.' She was shaking now, and her voice sounded breathless. 'We were staying with my sister who lives in Ross-on-Wye and we all went to the local fair. This was printed in the local paper, the *Hereford Herald*.' She paused and swallowed with difficulty before reading aloud the caption. 'Twelve-year-old Hilary Pilkington with her puppy, Teaser, who won first prize yesterday in a competition for Best Behaved Puppy at the Ross-on-Wye dog show.'

Harding reached for the heavy volume and took it from her trembling hands. 'May I?' he asked politely. A moment later the shock hit him. The newspaper had been printed on November 25th, 1909. The 'yesterday' it referred to had been November 24th.

'So your daughter wasn't even in Appledore when Posy Burgess went missing?' he asked, stunned.

Mrs Pilkington nodded miserably. 'We were staying in Ross-on-Wye all that week.' She hung her head in shame. 'I'm so sorry. Hilary has only just told me she gave you a signed statement and I can't tell you how terrible I feel. What will Lord Abingdon think of us? We've never been close friends but we've known the family for nearly forty years and Hilary was often invited up to Buckland Place when she and Nicolas were young.'

'This is a very serious matter.' He was enraged now because he'd been made to look a fool. Certain that Hilary Pilkington was telling the truth, he'd spent weeks in the certain belief that all he now had to do was get a confession out of Lord Abingdon, at the same time picking up promotion for himself for having solved a difficult case.

'Have you any idea what induced her to lie like this?' he demanded.

'No.'

'Where is Miss Pilkington now?' He was so furious he got up from his chair and started pacing around the room.

'I sent her into Canterbury to do some shopping.'

'You sent her? Then she doesn't know you were coming here to see me?'

'She has no idea.' Mrs Pilkington's voice was thick and laden with tears now and she dabbed her eyes. 'I hope I've done the right thing, but it's so hard to have to betray one's own flesh and blood. On the other hand . . . Oh, she's going to be so angry with me.'

Harding sat down again, facing her squarely. 'Why did she do this? What possessed her to give a false statement?'

'I've no idea why she did it. Lord Abingdon has always treated her as a friend but I know that Hilary hates his new wife. She didn't like the previous wife either. When she was a young woman I think she may have been disappointed that he didn't care for her more, but I'm not sure.'

'It sounds to me like revenge,' the DI said succinctly. 'A woman scorned is a dangerous creature.'

'I suppose so, but I never thought she'd go to these lengths.'

'She's been sending all these anonymous letters too, hasn't she?'

Mrs Pilkington shook her head in alarm. 'Oh, no. Definitely not.' Genuine shock and indignation dried her tears instantly. 'I'd have known if she had. Living in a small house, I'd have noticed if Hilary had been doing anything like that.'

Harding leaned back in his chair and looked up at the ceiling, thinking aloud as he did so. 'So Posy Burgess's remains are discovered, purely by accident when the woods are being cleared, and your daughter, out of a sense of vengeance perhaps, saw an opportunity to punish Lord Abingdon by swearing she'd seen him shoot the child, thereby providing false witness against him.'

'That seems to be the case,' Mrs Pilkington agreed, her expression wretched. 'What will happen now? Will Hilary be charged?'

He ignored her question. 'Mrs Pilkington, I'll get one of my officers to drive you home now and thank you for coming to see me with this information. I'll require you to leave your album here. The prosecution will need it as evidence.'

She looked panic-stricken. 'Prosecution? Oh my God! Will Hilary have to appear in court? Oh, what have I done? What have I done?'

'The album will be returned to you in due course,' he remarked briskly. Then he strode to the door. 'If you'd like to come this way, Mrs Pilkington, I'll see you into a car to take you back to your house.'

She rose shakily, having gently closed the album that lay on the desk, stroking its leather cover with her hand and giving it a lingering glance of regret as if it were a pet cat that she'd left to be put to sleep. The scrapbook was an irreplaceable record of her life and her moments of glory and she was loath to part with it. Without that precious album to remind her she'd once been a lovely young woman, married to the adoring Everard Pilkington, and a doting mother to her only child, she'd feel as if her life had never happened, and that when she was gone, there would be nothing left behind to say she'd even existed.

As soon as she got back to Ivy Cottage she went straight up to her bedroom, thankful that Hilary hadn't yet returned. Taking off her gloves, hat and coat, she dropped awkwardly to her knees by the side of her bed. Then she started praying, begging God's forgiveness for having betrayed her daughter; surely the most deplorable act she'd ever committed in her whole life. She'd done it for the right reasons but would Hilary see it that way? Probably not, but at least her conscience was clear, because by forcing Hilary to tell the truth, she was also saving her from eternal damnation.

'Please God,' she whispered, 'lead her into the path of righteousness and help her to understand her sins.'

DI Harding returned to his office and put a call through to his Divisional Chief of Police at their HQ in Canterbury. 'Fresh evidence has come up, Sir, on the Posy Burgess case. The signed statement of Miss Hilary Pilkington saying she'd witnessed the shooting and that the perpetrator was Lord Abingdon has proved to be false. On the day in question Miss Pilkington, who was twelve at the time, was in Ross-on-Wye, so could not possibly have seen the incident. I'm proposing, Sir, that as we have no other evidence to go on, we do not proceed with the case against Lord Abingdon.'

'Where is Abingdon now?'

'He is at his home, still on police bail. This new evidence that's just been given to me blows any case we might have had against him right out of the water,' he added bitterly.

'I never thought it would get to court, anyway,' the Chief retorted. 'I think you were rather over keen to bring charges. Abingdon was only fourteen and unless the prosecution could have proved he shot that child with intent to harm her, there never was a case against him. Article 50 of the Children's Act stresses that children can only be convicted if a child, up to the age of fourteen, is aware he is doing something seriously wrong. You should have realized that from the beginning, instead of going at it like a bull in a china shop, Harding. You were far too eager to try and bring down a member of the aristocracy in the first place. Keep your class hatred to yourself in future, Harding,' he added severely.

Crimson-faced, Harding sat chastened at his desk when the call ended. It was true he held a grudge against the upper classes, with their money and position and their patronizing ways, and he held a particularly strong resentment against the Abingdons. That old bitch of a dowager was enough to set anyone's teeth on edge and the way she'd treated his father, kicking him out of his job and his cottage after forty years of working as head gardener, because the poor old boy suffered from arthritis, was criminal.

No matter what his Chief said, he intended letting his lordship and his ravishingly pretty new wife stew for a few more days before telling them he was dropping all charges. Unless, of course, some new evidence came up in the meantime.

Cathryn's taxi rattled and shuddered as they arrived at the gates of Buckland Place shortly after two o'clock. Sitting frozen in the back, realizing how warm and comfortable Nicolas's cars were in comparison, she bowed her head as several rain-soaked Fleet Street photographers surged forward, surrounding them.

The driver braked, startled, and the taxi swerved to a stop.

''Ere, Lidy, wot's this abhat?' he shouted.

'Please keep going,' Cathryn commanded. 'Pay no attention to them.'

By now two of the photographers were standing in front of the taxi, prohibiting it from moving, while three others flashed and snapped through the side windows, shouting to her to look this way and that.

''Ow can I bleedin' keep goin'?' he barked. Then he turned his head to get a better look at Cathryn. His expression changed to astonishment. 'Blimey! You're that Lidy whose 'usband shot that girl, ain't yer?'

'Yes . . . I mean, no. Please get past these photographers. I have to get to my home.' She felt desperate now, imagining how a hunted beast must feel when cornered by predators.

At that moment Jack Stevens, the gatehouse keeper, realizing who was in the taxi, came rushing through the gates accompanied by two of the gardeners.

'Let her ladyship through,' he shouted, and waved his arms at the photographers who reluctantly backed off, whilst grumbling loudly about 'only doing their job'.

'I'm sorry about that, m'lady,' Jack apologized. 'I didn't know you were returning today.'

Cathryn smiled at him, nodding her thanks.

'Cor! Your 'ouse is big, innit?' the driver remarked as they drew up to the portico. 'Get lorst in a plice like that I shouldn't wonder?'

She handed him the fare, a large white five pound note.

'Ta,' he said casually, stuffing it in his pocket, although his eyes widened in delight. A fiver included a most generous tip.

On hearing the unaccustomed sound of a taxi, Wills opened the front door and looked shocked when he saw Cathryn emerge from the ancient vehicle.

'M'lady!' He gazed at her with a perturbed expression. Signalling to two hovering footmen to bring in her luggage, he opened the door wider.

'Good afternoon, Wills. Is my husband at home?'

Wills looked pale and pained. 'His lordship has issued strict instructions that he's not to be disturbed, m'lady.'

'That wouldn't apply to me, I'm his wife.' She started striding in the direction of the library where she was sure she'd find him.

Wills managed to get ahead of her, as if to bar her way. 'He's not alone, m'lady,' he warned.

She stopped abruptly. 'What do you mean?'

'He's . . . having a meeting.'

Tingles of panic swept through her. 'Are the police in there with him?' If she was too late to stop him confessing she'd never forgive herself.

Wills saw her distress and he raised his hands imploringly as if to reassure her. 'Oh, no, m'lady, nothing like that.'

Without waiting, she stepped forward and flung open the library door.

Sitting grouped around the table that stood in the centre of the room and that was usually piled with books and editions of *Country Life*, she saw Nicolas seated with Conceptia, Ewan, David Partridge and a man she'd never seen before.

'Cathryn!' With a bound Nicolas was on his feet, rushing towards her. 'What are you doing here?' he demanded, taking hold of both her hands and gripping them tightly.

'I had to come,' she replied, looking at him steadily. Then she glanced at the others. Conceptia and Ewan were glaring at her angrily, David looked irritated, but the other man's expression was sympathetic. Nicolas intercepted their exchange of looks.

'Come and meet my solicitor, Anthony Warner. He's here to advise me,' he added, leading her towards the table.

They shook hands. Cathryn liked his straightforward manner immediately. He was slightly older than Nicolas, with a kind face and intelligent grey eyes.

'How do you do,' she murmured.

Anthony was on his feet, smiling down at her. 'How do you do, Lady Abingdon. This is indeed a pleasure. Nicolas has told me so much about you.'

She glanced again at the others and then turned back to Nicolas. 'What's going on?'

Conceptia spoke sharply before Nicolas had time to reply. 'This is a family matter.'

Ignoring the snub, Cathryn sank into the chair Nicolas had pulled forward for her.

'Then I'm glad I got back in time for it,' she said. 'So what's happening?'

David decided to take it upon himself to speak on behalf of the family before anyone could stop him. Leaning forward, elbows on the table, his heavy-lidded eyes giving Cathryn a threatening look as if the whole thing was her fault, he spoke pompously.

'It's obvious that the disastrous situation the family is facing has to be brought to an end. That is not going to happen until the case of Posy Burgess has been resolved. In my view the only way to resolve it is for Nicolas to confess once and for all that he accidentally shot that child while he was target practising. He didn't mean to hurt her. It was an accident and . . .'

'*No!*' Cathryn exclaimed, enraged. 'I won't let him do that. Why should he? We all know he wasn't out with his gun that day, so why should he say he was? Let the real culprit come forward.'

Anthony spoke with equal firmness. 'I agree. I'm totally opposed to Nicolas admitting to something he hasn't done.'

She turned to Nicolas with a lost expression. 'Why are you doing this?'

He sighed as if he was utterly weary. 'To bring an end to this mess, that's why. And to save the family from more disgrace. Accidents happen and I can't be charged with murder because of my age at the time and because it was obviously an accident.'

'I know that, Daddy explained it all to me ages ago, but that's not the point.' She spoke impatiently now.

'The good name of the family is at stake here,' Conceptia cut in, her voice like a rapier slashing the air. 'I can't bear to look at another newspaper. The press are dragging our name through the mud as if we were common criminals. The only honourable thing is for Nicolas to speak out like a gentleman, admit his sad mistake, and then we can all get on with our lives.'

'How can you say that?' Cathryn asked with vehement incredulity. She turned to Anthony Warner. 'You can surely stop Nicolas? Why should he be bullied by his family into a confession?'

Anthony gave Nicolas a knowing smile; then he looked at Cathryn and spoke frankly.

'Your husband is far too strong a man to allow himself to be bullied by anyone,' he assured her. 'He knows what my views are but in the end we have to trust him to make a decision he feels is right for him.'

David leaned in, his smile smug. 'Mr Warner is absolutely right. It's understandable, Cathryn, that as a newly married woman you don't want to see your husband in this invidious position, but you're a newcomer to the family, my dear. They must be allowed to make their own decisions, you know. That is why we're having this meeting today.'

Cathryn looked at Nicolas, her eyes filled with hurt. 'Yes, while you thought I was safely out of the way staying with my parents,' she said quietly. 'Don't I have any say in this matter?'

He laid his hand over hers in a firm grip. 'I didn't want to worry you, darling. This is a ghastly time and we're just trying to get through it. By confessing I shot Posy I'll be limiting the damage to this family. Once I'm out of the picture the police will leave us alone, and so will the press. There'll be no story once I've confessed and it will be marked down as just a tragic accident.'

'My God, what a relief it will be when we're left alone again,' Conceptia agreed, her button-bright eyes narrowing as she looked across the table at her daughter-in-law. 'You'll be able to go up to London and shop to your heart's content, Cathryn,' she added in a sweet voice that was edged with venom.

Cathryn jumped to her feet, wrenching her hand away from Nicolas's grasp. Tears of frustration stung her eyes. 'I think you've all gone stark raving mad,' she said shrilly. 'There's a missing link somewhere here. Something you're keeping from me. None of this makes sense and if it's the last thing I do, I'm going to get you to change your mind, Nicolas. Give me one good reason why you should make this terrible sacrifice?'

The silence in the room was almost palpable.

'Well?' she challenged, looking at them all in turn.

'You seem to forget,' David cut in, his manner suddenly cold, 'that the police have a signed statement from a witness saying he was *seen* shooting Posy Burgess. By confessing Nicolas will only be confirming what they already know.'

Conceptia rose to her feet, and there was a look of quiet triumph in her manner. 'Then that's settled. You'll go to the police station this afternoon then, Nicolas?'

He didn't reply but instead gazed tenderly at Cathryn. 'I don't want to hurt you, darling,' he said in a low voice. 'But I have to do this.'

'Why, Nicolas? Why?' She clung to him for a moment, as if she were afraid he was slipping irretrievably away from her.

'Let him go,' Conceptia commanded roughly. 'It has to be done. There's no alternative.'

'Take care of yourself, darling,' Nicolas whispered, giving Cathryn a quick kiss on the cheek before rising and turning abruptly away. A moment later he'd left the library, with Anthony Warner by his side.

'Can I talk to you?' Cathryn enquired, slipping into Hugh's office. He was alone, a stack of estate accounts in front of him. When he looked up and saw her his welcoming smile turned to a look of concern.

'Cathryn! Are you all right? I didn't know you were back.'

She dropped as if exhausted into the chair facing him. 'I suppose you've heard what's happening? I've tried to stop Nicolas going to the police to confess but he won't listen to me. He's just left with his solicitor and I'm so upset and angry I don't know what to do with myself.' Her voice broke as she fought back tears of vexation.

Hugh nodded in understanding. 'I spent hours last night trying to persuade him not to do something as mad as this but he wouldn't listen. His reason was that it's the only thing he could do to put an end to the present situation.'

'But did he say *why*?'

'No, not exactly. He went on about the need to put an end to the police keeping an eye on us all the time.'

'But we've nothing to hide. I'm sure of that now.'

'I believe he's innocent, too,' Hugh said gravely. 'That's why his decision to confess is extraordinary. Unless, of course, all the speculation in the newspapers has got to him.'

Cathryn's eyes widened. 'It's going to be far worse now,' she exclaimed, leaning back in her chair again. 'What's his lawyer thinking of? My God, I wish I could have stopped him.'

Hilary returned to Ivy Cottage shortly after twelve o'clock, and having parked the car neatly in a corner of the drive, carried the shopping into the house, calling out 'Mother? I'm back,' as she headed for the kitchen, where she dumped her basket on the centre table. Taking off her hat and coat she went into the sitting room, where the coal fire had nearly gone out. Tutting with irritation, she picked lumps of coal out of the brass scuttle with the fire tongs and threw them into the dusty ashes, where they quickly started blazing.

A minute later she heard her mother coming very slowly down the stairs and along the passage. As she appeared in the doorway Hilary took one look at her and exclaimed, 'What's wrong with you? You look as if you'd seen a ghost.'

White-faced, her mother almost staggered to an armchair and collapsed into it.

'I had to do it, Hilary. I couldn't let an innocent man suffer a moment longer.' She shook her head and then covered her face with her plump hands.

'What are you talking about?'

Mrs Pilkington gave her daughter a haunted look. 'You were lying, weren't you? When you told the police you'd seen Nicolas in the woods that day, shooting Posy Burgess?'

Hilary flew into a rage. 'I was not lying! I remember exactly what happened! How dare you accuse me of lying? I was going for a walk and I distinctly saw him, about fifty yards away, and he was aiming at something on the other side of the stream. I strained to see what it was . . . and then I saw a movement, and it was Posy Burgess, as large as life, staring at him as if she'd been hypnotized. Then he fired . . . and she dropped to the ground like a stone. It scared the life out of me. I didn't wait. I ran all the way home, terrified in case he'd see me, and then shoot me too.' She raised her chin confidently.

'Then why didn't you tell me at the time?' Mrs Pilkington asked carefully. 'Why didn't you come to me the moment you got home?'

Hilary stared at her, never blinking. 'Because you'd never have believed me! You always doubted everything I said. You've always treated me as if I was a fool. Remember the time when I said I couldn't find my walking shoes? You made me stay indoors because you said I'd ruin my good shoes and I missed going for a walk with our dog.'

Mrs Pilkington looked astounded. 'You were seven years old, Hilary, and you'd deliberately hidden them because you didn't want to go for a walk.'

Hilary didn't flinch. 'That's not true.' She tossed her head pettishly. 'And I did see Nicolas shoot that child. Why do you never believe anything I say?'

'My dear, you know you never saw Nicolas shoot Posy.' Her mother spoke almost pleadingly now, her voice gentle. 'Why did you tell the police that you'd seen what happened?'

Hilary suddenly became incandescent with anger. 'Because it's the bloody truth. Why should I protect Nicolas? He murdered that child and he deserves to be punished.'

'You may have convinced yourself it's the truth but actually it's a fabrication of your imagination. You weren't even in the woods that day. You weren't even *here*. You and I were staying with Aunt Adela in Ross-on-Wye. Don't you remember? It was when Teaser won a prize for being a good puppy. We stayed there for a week. Posy went missing two days before we came back here.'

Hilary turned scarlet and her eyes were like that of a wild animal that has been cornered. 'That's a bloody lie!' she screamed hysterically. 'We were *here*.' She stamped her foot in fury. 'We were here when it happened! We were here when everyone in the village searched for Posy! We were here when the police finally decided the gypsies had abducted her! How can you say we were away when we were *here*!'

Mrs Pilkington started trembling. Hilary was completely out of control now. Wailing and moaning like a banshee, she kept flinging her arms around, and then she kicked the side of her mother's chair. 'You've spoilt it all now!' she shrieked un-reasonably.

'You only think we were here. Maybe you saw him shooting in the woods on another occasion. He was often out target practising, and perhaps you've confused the dates . . .'

'I saw him shoot Posy! I was there! Why don't you believe me?' She bent over, her knees buckling as she grabbed her hair in her fists and tugged at it as if to pull it out.

'Hilary, we were hundreds of miles away on the day that child died,' Mrs Pilkington shouted, shutting her eyes at the unbearable sight of her daughter's madness, coupled with her own feelings of guilt.

'You're lying!' Hilary yelled. With one powerful swing of her arm she swiped all the ornaments and candlesticks off the mantelshelf and they went crashing to the ground, scattering broken glass and smashed figurines.

'I'm not lying.' Mrs Pilkington braced herself, before making a supreme effort to remain calm as she delivered the final and fatal blow to her daughter. 'You should know that I've given the evidence that we were away that week to the police. I'm sorry, Hilary, but I had no other option.'

Hilary suddenly froze, her hands dropping to her sides as she looked at her mother in silence. Mrs Pilkington stared back, shock and disbelief in both their expressions.

'I'm sorry, Hilary,' she whispered at last.

With a wrenching sob, Hilary flung herself into her mother's arms, her face contorted with the agony of a lifetime's disappointment. 'Oh, Mummy! He hurt me and I loved him. I loved him so much. He was my life. He promised to come back to me after the war but he betrayed me. He'd found someone else. He broke my heart. All I've ever wanted in my whole life was to be loved by Nicolas . . .' She broke off, unable to continue, crazed and choking with grief.

'Oh, my darling girl.' Her mother wrapped her arms around her and patted her back. 'I'm so sorry . . . so sorry, my dearest.' There were no other words she could think of to say.

A little while later Hilary rose, calmer now, her manner fatalistic. 'I think I'll go for a walk. I need to get some air. Will the police come to arrest me?'

'They'll only want to question you, dearest,' Mrs Pilkington lied in a soothing voice.

Hilary stood up, nodding. She blew her nose, then tucked her handkerchief into the sleeve of her beige cardigan. 'I shan't be long.'

★　　★　　★

'What the hell do you think you're doing, Anthony?'

Anthony Warner had insisted on driving his Aston Martin. 'Going to the police station in your Rolls would look ridiculous, Nicolas,' he'd said, getting into the driving seat. 'It's quicker in my car, anyway.'

Shrugging, Nicolas climbed into the passenger seat. All he wanted to do was get this ordeal over with. As Anthony swerved swiftly through the gates of Buckland Place, he turned right instead of left, heading for Folkestone. He didn't answer Nicolas at first but gazed impassively through the windscreen, while putting his foot down hard on the accelerator.

'Anthony . . . ?' Nicolas began angrily.

'It's no use, old chap. We're taking the scenic route, and we're not stopping until we get to Perranporth,' he replied evenly.

There was a stunned silence. 'Perranporth? For God's sake, that's in Cornwall.'

'That's right. I have a cottage there. Looking out to sea. Rotten weather in February but never mind. It has a grand view.'

Nicolas turned to him, scowling furiously. 'What the hell are you playing at? Trying to kidnap me or something damn foolish?'

Anthony spoke imperviously, having known Nicolas since they'd been friends at Eton and later Cambridge. 'Something very sensible, actually. We're going to stay at the cottage until I can din some sense into your thick skull. Wanting to make a confession for the sake of your family, who seem to be eager that you should, is about the stupidest thing I've ever heard. What are *you* playing at?'

'But you agreed that I should . . . ?'

'That was only to get you away from Ewan and your mother without too much bloodshed,' Andrew retorted sarcastically. 'As for that Partridge fellow . . . If ever there was a crooked lawyer, that's him. I wouldn't touch him with a barge pole. They want to stitch you up, old chap, and I'm damn well not going to let them. Especially now you're married to such a divine girl, you lucky devil.' He chuckled at the memory of Cathryn standing up to the Abingdons, her blue eyes fiery and her cheeks flushed with anger.

'But you know what will happen if I don't make a confession.'

'I know all right, but actually it's got nothing to do with you. We want to clear *your* name. Not have you make a bloody false confession, to save somebody else's skin, for God's sake.'

They drove on in silence, each of them deep in thought. With unseeing eyes, Nicolas's gaze was fixed on the road ahead, while he struggled to work out what he should do for the best. Anthony was right about one thing. Cathryn was a divine girl and he loved her more than he'd ever loved anyone. If he went ahead and confessed, what would it do to her? And to their marriage? He didn't even dare think what the press would make of it.

On the other hand . . .

Anthony cut into his thoughts. 'If we stop for a bite to eat can I trust you not to go AWOL?'

Nicolas gave his friend a tired smile and nodded his head in agreement. 'Anyway, I've decided what I must do.'

At the police station Hilary Pilkington sat facing DI Harding in his office, as her mother had done two hours before. She'd confessed to making a false statement, but vehemently denied sending numerous anonymous letters to the Abingdon family and various people in the village. After charging her, Harding told her he was going to release her on police bail, pending the date when her case would be heard in court.

Throughout her ordeal she'd sat, hands folded in her lap, her face a study of blank indifference. Harding might have been telling her the price of bread was going up, so devoid was she of all emotion.

'You're free to go home for the time being,' he said slowly and clearly, as if she were retarded. 'I'll get one of my officers to give you a lift.'

Her dark eyes were expressionless. 'Thank you,' she said politely.

It struck him that if her mother had any sense they would get a lawyer who would plead any number of psychological reasons to try and get the charges against her dismissed, ranging from diminished responsibility to downright insanity. It was now just over eleven weeks since the remains of Posy Burgess had been found, Harding reflected bitterly. Eleven weeks of suppositions, interviewing and questioning people and finally drawing conclusions; all wasted.

So who the hell *did* shoot Posy Burgess?

Hilary went up to her bedroom as soon as she got home, managing to avoid seeing her mother who was talking to their maid in the kitchen. She shut her door quietly, and taking off her coat, hung it up in the wardrobe. Then she removed her shoes and padded around in her stocking feet, so no one on the floor below would hear her footfalls.

Dazed with shock, she opened and shut drawers without knowing why and all the time she was telling herself: it's over. All over.

After a while she lay on her bed and closed her eyes, wanting to escape the almost physical pain she felt at this moment. Pain and a terrible sense of loss, like a gaping hole in her heart.

How could it have come to this? Why hadn't he ever fallen in love with her?

Tears slid down her cheeks as she gazed at the magnolia walls of her shabby bedroom, her mind struggling to take in the fact that she'd never have a future with Nicolas. His death would have been easier to bear, because if he didn't belong to her, then he couldn't belong to anyone else either. Gone too were the daydreams when she imagined he'd realize he loved her after all and had always loved her. How happy they would have been. Now there was nothing but the shock of having her future wiped blank, without dreams, without hope, without him. The tears flowed faster as despair swept over her, leaving her trembling. Her heart ached painfully, as if it had been bruised.

Nicolas had been her life, her soul, her beginning and her end, and he'd never known it. The joy of being his lover, his wife, the mother of his children and his lifelong companion were denied to her now and forever. Revenge was supposed to be sweet but this was the bitterest pill and in seeking to punish Nicolas, she'd only ended up destroying herself.

Violent sobs convulsed her thin body and she clamped a pillow over her mouth so her mother wouldn't hear. Nothing was ever going to ease this pain. A sudden sense of panic flowed through her veins, sending her heart racing. She couldn't bear the thought of the empty void that lay ahead. A thousand

million days without him. A thousand million days without
even her dreams of him. A thousand million days of longing
for something she would never have.

She rose shakily, her anguish an illness, her agony too acute to
bear. *It has to stop*, she thought in desperation. *I can't stand it any
longer. It has to stop.*

Fifteen

WITNESS IN CHILD MURDER CASE COMMITS SUICIDE

Miss Hilary Pilkington, thirty-three, who gave a signed statement to the police saying she'd witnessed Lord Abingdon shoot nine-year-old Posy Burgess with his air rifle, has committed suicide, after admitting her statement was false. It is thought she suffered from a broken heart after the marquess, with whom she'd been in love for many years, married for the second time in November. Her distraught mother was unable to comment yesterday, but it's believed Miss Pilkington left two suicide notes.

The Daily Express, February 6th, 1931

The previous afternoon Nicolas had returned to Buckland, to be met by a distressed Cathryn, who was frantic with worry, wondering what had happened to him

'Where have you been? And where is Anthony?' she demanded, the words tumbling agitatedly out of her mouth as she reached for his hand and led him up the grand staircase to their private quarters. A fire burned brightly in their *petit salon*, and as she sank into a sofa facing it, Nicolas sat down beside her.

'I tried to get hold of you in London, but nobody knew what had happened to you. Where in God's name have you been?' she added, almost angrily. 'I've been going out of my mind with worry.'

He put his arm around her and kissed her. 'I'm so sorry, sweetheart. Anthony drove me down to Cornwall where we thrashed out this whole bloody business. He doesn't have a telephone in his cottage and we were miles from civilization and . . .'

She spoke urgently. 'So you didn't make a confession?'

Nicolas shook his head. 'Anthony refused to let me do it. We've been discussing other ways of bringing this business to a conclusion.'

'Then you don't know what's happened? Thank God you didn't confess.' She leaned against him, her head resting on his shoulder, feeling weak with relief.

He looked at her quizzically. 'What do you mean?'

'Mrs Pilkington went to the police station yesterday and she admitted to them that Hilary's statement was false. Hilary wasn't even in Appledore when Posy vanished. She and her mother were staying in Ross-on-Wye.'

He looked stunned. 'Then why in God's name did she . . . ?'

Cathryn looked sombre. 'There's worse, Nicolas. Much worse.'

He looked at her closely. 'What?'

Her voice was very low. 'Hilary has committed suicide.'

Nicolas gave a loud groan of anguish. 'Oh, no.'

'I'm afraid so. Apparently she was arrested and charged with giving false evidence and wasting police time and she was questioned at the police station. Then they released her on bail until her case came up in court. I gather Mrs Pilkington never heard her return home and presumed she was still being questioned. It was only much later when she went into the garden to look for their cat that she found Hilary.' Cathryn paused painfully, taking a deep breath before she continued. 'She'd hung herself from a tree with her dressing gown cord.'

'Oh, my God! I suppose she couldn't face the public humiliation of being taken to court.'

Cathryn shook her head. She kept seeing in her mind's eye the body of a dark-haired young woman whom she'd at first thought could be a friend, alone and in the dark, tying a noose around her neck on the cold winter night. Her voice was wrenched with pity as she spoke again.

'From what I've heard it wasn't the disgrace that made her do it, Nicolas. She left two suicide notes. One of them is for you.'

'Me? Why *me*?' His eyes widened with horror. Then he said reflectively, 'I suppose she felt guilty at having said she'd seen me shoot Posy.'

Cathryn looked at him sympathetically. 'No darling, I don't think that was the reason she ended her life. They're saying in the village that she died of a broken heart. Hugh told me she was devastated when we got married. Maybe, with Miranda gone, she'd hoped she had a chance with you.' Then she saw the anguish in his eyes. 'I feel a little guilty,' she continued, 'because it was me you married and not her. Looking back now I can see how much she loved you. When I first came here she tried to befriend me, but it was obviously just to get to see you.'

'Oh, this is dreadful. I've never even *thought* of her in that way. And her poor mother! I hope she knows I never led Hilary on. She was a nice girl and as children we had a good time but I could never have fallen in love with her. Not in a million years.'

'I know, darling.'

'To take her own life like that! Maybe I should have spotted her infatuation, but I don't recall a single thing that made me feel she was interested in me.' He rubbed his forehead with the heel of his hand. 'God, what a terrible mess. How many more ghastly things are going to happen just because Posy's body was found? If she'd remained buried for another twenty years none of this would have happened.'

'If she'd never been born none of this would have happened either. This has all been caused by the sins of the past coming back, like the ripples from a stone thrown into the water,' Cathryn observed thoughtfully. William Abingdon had a lot to answer for.

At this moment though, her heart ached for the young woman who'd become a casualty of the events spanning from Posy's death. A young woman who would never know Nicolas's love, never be by his side bearing his children, never enjoy all the things in a shared life that she'd taken for granted when she'd married Nicolas.

How many lonely nights must Hilary have lain in bed, wishing Nicolas was beside her?

How many mornings must she have awoken to face yet another day without him?

Nicolas had risen and was walking restlessly up and down the room. 'What can I do for Mrs Pilkington?'

'Write and offer your condolences and send her some flowers?' Cathryn suggested. 'Darling, you can't blame yourself.'

'I still feel dreadful.' He stood looking bleakly out of the window. The greyness of the cold damp day did nothing to lift his spirits. Cathryn went and stood beside him, holding him close in her arms, looking into his face.

'Listen, darling, take comfort in the fact that she admitted she'd made up her story about seeing you shoot Posy before she killed herself. If she'd taken that false allegation to the grave with her, you'd always have had the shadow of doubt hanging over you. Now the police know you're not guilty, they'll start looking elsewhere.'

He spoke grimly and the anxiety returned to his eyes. 'That's exactly what worries me. That was why I was going to confess, but Anthony stopped me.'

She frowned. 'What's behind this desire of yours to confess, for heaven's sake?' she asked intuitively. 'Do you *know* who shot Posy?'

'No, I don't. I've no idea at all.' He looked down at her with a sad little smile as if he wished she understood. 'Anthony and I have talked it through for hours. Don't you realize that it's only a matter of time before the police twig that Ewan is a homosexual? God knows why they haven't found out by now. You do know he'll get up to two years' hard labour if he's caught, don't you? That's what happened to Oscar Wilde in 1895. He was having an affair with the son of the Marquess of Queensberry and it caused the most almighty scandal. He was sent to Reading Gaol and was eventually forced to live abroad for the rest of his life. He never saw his wife and children again and they suffered terribly from the disgrace.'

Cathryn looked at him in amazement. 'So that's why you wanted to confess? To protect Ewan from the police snooping around?'

'To protect the whole family, Cathryn. Not just Ewan. Legally nothing was actually going to happen to me if I'd pleaded guilty; it would have gone down in history as one of those tragic accidents that can happen in any family. But if Ewan's caught it will be terribly serious. My Pa would have been utterly mortified, if he'd still been alive. And I don't want our children to have that sort of disgrace in their background,' he added sadly.

'That's the most unselfish thing I've ever heard,' she said in a low voice. 'You do know that Ewan's . . . er, his friend works at the King's Arms, don't you? At least I think he works there, or he might just be a customer, I suppose.'

Nicolas stepped back from her in alarm. 'Christ! How do you know that? Why didn't you tell me before?'

'There hasn't been time. I was on my way to stay with my parents and I've only seen you briefly since.' Then she described what she'd seen.

'The fool! The bloody fool!' he blurted out. 'I'm going to go over there right now. What did this chap look like?'

'It was dark so I couldn't really see. He seemed taller than Ewan and sort of chunky and I had the feeling he was a bit older. What are you going to do? What can you do?'

Nicolas's jaw hardened. 'I'm probably going to have to pay him off. Damn and blast! Here am I, prepared to do anything to stop him being found out, and there he is, flaunting himself outside a pub. Where's Ewan now?'

'As far as I know he's upstairs with your mother.'

'Do me a favour, will you, darling? Keep an eye out for him, and if it looks as if he's going out, try and stop him.'

'How?' Cathryn looked at him blankly. 'He hates me and we hardly say a word to each other.'

'Oh, make up something! What's his latest craze? Talk to him about that. Pretend you're interested. Just keep him here long enough for me to get to the King's Arms and see if I can find out what's going on.'

Looking doubtful, she went down the stairs with him to the main hall.

'Take care, darling,' she whispered anxiously.

'Don't worry. I'll be as quick as I can.' He kissed her lightly and then turned to hurry through the main door, down the front steps and into his car. It was already dark and she shivered as she made her way to the drawing room. Leaving the door ajar so she could hear if Ewan came downstairs, she asked Wills to bring her some tea and hot anchovy toast. Then she seated herself by the fire and glanced at *The Times* and *Telegraph*, finding it hard to concentrate.

A few minutes later she heard footsteps coming across the hall. Her heart started fluttering with a mixture of trepidation and dread. The steps came nearer and it was almost a relief when Conceptia marched into the room, followed by Ewan. He was unlikely to go out if his mother was around.

'Where's Nicolas? Someone told me he'd returned,' Conceptia asked. Her skeletal face looked even more sinister in the dimly lit room. 'Wills?' she called out shrilly. 'Have some of the lights turned on in here, for goodness' sake! It's pitch dark.'

'Yes, m'lady,' he replied, hurriedly indicating to two of the hovering footmen to switch on the gilt standard and table lamps. A moment later the heavily ornate room sprang to life, bathed in the cheerful glow of a dozen cream silk and heavily tasselled shades.

Conceptia looked at Cathryn accusingly. 'What are you doing?' She glanced suspiciously around as if her daughter-in-law were hiding something.

'Waiting to have tea,' Cathryn replied smoothly.

Her mother-in-law turned to Wills again. 'Lord Ewan and I would like tea, too.' Then she came and sat on the opposite side of the fire to Cathryn and looked at her with narrowed eyes. 'You seem very calm. Have you heard anything? Is Nicolas being held at the police station?' There was the unmistakable hint of hopefulness in her voice.

Cathryn looked at her coldly. 'He hasn't been anywhere near the police station. Thankfully he decided not to make a false confession.'

'What do you mean? Thankfully? What are you talking about? I thought we all agreed that . . .' Her voice rose, more twanging and rasping then usual.

'You haven't heard? Hilary Pilkington has confessed that her statement was false. She never saw Nicolas shoot Posy Burgess.'

'What's she playing at?' Conceptia looked stricken, her bony hand clasping her long ropes of pearls to her chest.

'She's not playing at anything any more,' Cathryn replied sombrely. 'She only made the false statement as an act of vengeance. The tragic truth is she's now committed suicide. Apparently she'd been in love with Nicolas for years and had always hoped he'd marry her one day. The whole village is talking about it.'

Conceptia looked deeply shaken. 'I don't mix with people from the village!' she retorted harshly. 'So where is Nicolas now?'

Cathryn feigned innocence. 'I'm not sure. I think he's seeing to something on the estate with Hugh.'

'Does he know about Hilary?' Ewan asked curiously, standing with his back to the fire.

'Yes. He's obviously very distressed.'

'The girl was mental,' Conceptia snapped. 'How could she have imagined that someone in Nicolas's position would ever have married her? Apart from which she was as plain as a pikestaff and as boring as a block of wood. I for one am certainly not going to her funeral.'

'I'm not sure there will be a proper funeral,' Cathryn pointed out. 'I don't believe one can be buried in consecrated ground, if one has taken one's own life?'

Conceptia shrugged as she continued to fiddle with her pearls. 'None of our business, anyway.'

'But it's terribly sad,' Cathryn protested. 'Nicolas had no idea she'd had a thing about him.'

Conceptia clicked her tongue impatiently. 'Any woman stupid enough to fall for a man is a fool! All men are the same. He probably encouraged her, out of vanity, to think she had a chance.'

'Nicolas would never do anything like that.'

Her mother-in-law's scarlet mouth twisted superciliously. 'How little you know,' she remarked drily, 'but then you're still terribly young and from a rather ordinary background.'

'As were you, until you married Nicolas's father,' Cathryn cut in.

'Don't talk to my mother like that,' Ewan bleated in a whining voice. 'After all she's done for you, making you welcome in her house.'

At that moment the footmen arrived, one with a heavy silver tray on which stood fragile-looking cups and saucers and a silver teapot and milk jug, and the other bearing a tray with a plate of anchovy toast and some lawn table napkins. Conceptia, Ewan and Cathryn automatically stopped talking, and they watched in silence as the tea things were set on a table between them.

The moment the footmen had left the room, Conceptia turned on Cathryn with an ugly scowl. 'You didn't know what fine living even meant until you set your sights on Nicolas,' she sneered. 'You only have to look at your mother and the way she dresses to know she comes from a middle class background.'

Cathryn flushed with indignation. 'At least she's not a snob,' she retaliated.

Ewan, enjoying the spat, grinned broadly as he helped himself to toast. 'That's just as well because she's got nothing to be snobbish about,' he mocked, 'whereas Mama comes from the Calkin family . . .' He stopped dead as Nicolas burst into the room and stood glowering at him and his mother.

Cathryn had never seen Nicolas in such a rage. His eyes seemed bloodshot in his reddened face, and his hands were tight fists.

Conceptia looked at him guardedly. 'What is it, Nicolas?' she asked.

He didn't reply, but took out of his thick overcoat pocket some crumpled sheets of newspaper. Then he strode forward and, unfolding them, spread them on the carpet in front of his mother and brother.

Cathryn instantly drew in her breath sharply. 'Where did you get them from?' she murmured.

Nicolas was staring balefully at Ewan now. 'Go on, Ewan. Tell Cathryn where I found them.'

Ewan had turned a sickly shade and was trembling. 'I-I've no idea,' he whimpered.

'You know exactly where I found them, you little liar!' Nicolas roared. 'Was it you or your boyfriend who cut each of these individual letters out of the newspapers, so you could paste them up as words on a sheet of writing paper? Was it you who composed those filthy poison pen letters that we all received, or was it him?'

'It . . . it was for a l-lark!' Ewan was weeping now, his hands trembling violently as he fumbled for a handkerchief.

Conceptia sat bolt upright, her fury intense. 'How dare you accuse your brother of doing such a thing? How *dare* you! Anyway, they were posted from all around the country so Ewan couldn't possibly have posted them.'

'Oh, he didn't,' Nicolas retorted. 'He got his little friend, whose father owns the King's Arms, and who has a car, to travel all over the place mailing them from as far afield as Wales! You paid him handsomely to do your dirty work too, didn't you, Ewan?'

Cathryn watched in horror as Ewan crumpled like a little boy, sobbing and wailing on his knees before his mother, who reached out to stroke his head in a rare show of physical tenderness. Something about their relationship and his childish distress sickened her so much that she rose, saying quietly, 'This is between you and your family, Nicolas. I'll be upstairs if you need me.'

He nodded in understanding.

She hurried from the room, shutting the door behind her, and almost bumped into Wills and a couple of the footmen who were lurking in the hall, obviously having overheard what was going on. Gaining the sanctuary of their private suite, she dropped on to a chair and covered her face with her hands. The shock of realizing Ewan was behind the anonymous letters had left her stunned, but it was his reaction at being found out that appalled her most. To see a grown man in his thirties sobbing and wailing like a two-year-old at his mother's knee was the most nauseating spectacle she'd ever witnessed.

Nicolas joined her an hour later, his anger spent, his face drawn with exhaustion.

'What's going to happen now?' Cathryn asked anxiously.

'I've given the chap enough money to get on a boat to Calais, then a train to Germany, where he can stay in a cheap hotel in Berlin. He can probably get a job in a bar there. Anyway, he'll not be coming back because I've made sure he knows what will happen if he does.' He went over to a side table, where he helped himself to some whisky from a tray of drinks. 'Want anything, darling?'

'No thank you. What did Ewan say about that?'

'I think he was relieved I wasn't going to report both of them to the police.'

'How did you find the newspapers that had been cut up?'

'Can you believe it? I was walking up the path that leads to the back door of the pub, where you saw Ewan go, past a row of dustbins. One of the lids hadn't been put on properly, and there was this piece of a newspaper hanging out. I noticed that several little squares had been cut out of it. When I lifted the lid, I found several sheets, all with little squares snipped out of them. The chap didn't deny it. Said it was Ewan's idea of a joke. Some joke,' he added sourly.

'What's Ewan going to do now?' she asked curiously.

Nicolas shrugged. 'I've grounded him and stopped his allowance. It's for his own sake. He doesn't seem to realize how close to the wind he was sailing with the law. And as usual, Mother is in total denial. As far as she's concerned, her darling little boy is a saint, who only wants to have friends to talk to.'

'So we needn't worry about the police nosing around any more?'

'I have a feeling they've run out of steam and been made to look foolish by believing Hilary's confession. I doubt if they'll pursue the case any more. It happened so long ago and they've drawn a complete blank up to now. Unless some fresh evidence comes up I think we can get on with the rest of our lives in peace.'

Cathryn suddenly felt herself relax, almost as if a great burden had been lifted. 'Does that mean we can resume our honeymoon?' she asked in a small voice.

Nicolas's face seemed to melt into a warm smile as he reached for her hand. 'Oh, God, I hope so, darling. I really hope so.'

A week later they were to realize that the nightmare was far from over.

Sixteen

UNREQUITED LOVE CAUSED SUICIDE OF FALSE WITNESS

The findings at the inquest into Miss Hilary Pilkington's death concluded that she had taken her own life whilst the balance of her mind was disturbed. The thirty-three-year-old spinster had for years been in love with the Marquess of Abingdon, and his second marriage to debutante Miss Cathryn Brocklehurst at the end of last year was a blow from which Miss Pilkington never recovered. Out of revenge she tried to frame him for murder . . .
The Daily Telegraph, February 14th, 1931

Cathryn watched Nicolas as he read the neatly handwritten letter and saw his mouth quiver and tug down at the corners while his eyelashes grew wet. Then he took a deep breath and pulled himself together.

'It's the saddest thing I've ever read,' he said in a low voice, passing the pale blue sheet of paper to her. 'I'd no idea she felt like this.'

Cathryn skimmed the page, trying not to let it have an impact on her, but after a few lines she too felt overcome with emotion so that the tears streamed down her cheeks. To read the words of a woman who had loved Nicolas as much as she did, but who had been denied his love, was like a painful knife going through her heart. It struck her that she, too, would have felt her life was no longer worth living if he'd shunned her and loved another.

Through her tears she caught fragments of Hilary's heartbreak: *There is no future for me without you in my life . . . I know I'll never find happiness now . . . I can't bear the thought of spending the rest of my life without you . . . Please remember me kindly . . . and if you can't, then don't remember me at all . . . My love, my life, my everything . . .*

'It's too sad for words,' she said at last, handing it back to

Nicolas. 'I know now how she must have suffered. How could she bear to be so nice to me? I'd have wanted to kill me if I'd been her,' she added, blowing her nose.

'How could I not have realized she had these feelings?' Nicolas said in despair. 'She always acted in a perfectly normal way when I saw her.'

'Living alone with her mother in that bleak little house couldn't have helped,' Cathryn said in an effort to comfort him. 'She should have gone to London and met lots of other young people; got interested in charity work, perhaps.'

'They had no money and I think Mrs Pilkington was probably rather possessive,' Nicolas pointed out. 'Perhaps I should have invited Hilary to dinner parties here, and introduced her to some of my friends. I know one or two bachelors who might have quite liked her.'

Cathryn looked at him in disbelief. His masculine naïvety amazed her. 'She wouldn't have been interested in anyone else, Nicolas. She was in love with you and she knew that no other man would ever match up to you. If you'd handed her the Prince of Wales on a plate, she'd have turned him down. I can understand how she felt. When I met you every other man paled into insignificance by comparison. I couldn't even *think* about anyone else.'

He shook his head, not really believing her.

The shadow of Hilary Pilkington's death affected everyone in the ensuing weeks, coming so soon after the discovery of Posy Burgess's remains. All that had happened in the past three months was casting a great sense of unease among the local people, causing them to huddle in corners, whispering ghoulishly about those 'up at the big house' and wondering what would happen next.

Eventually, to the relief of a lot of locals, Mrs Pilkington went to stay with her sister in Ross-on-Wye for an indefinite period and Ivy Cottage was shut up. Whilst she'd remained in Appledore no one had known whether to talk to her and give her their condolences when they met in the street or whether to cross the road quickly and pretend they hadn't seen her.

Although the sensational headlines in the newspapers had ceased as far as Nicolas was concerned, the family as a whole had become fodder for Fleet Street and leading journalists were filling column inches on what was being referred to as 'the curse of the Abingdons', going over the recent family history in great detail. They even harked back to the tragic motoring accident that had killed the sixth Marquess in 1901, obliquely hinting at brake failure.

The gossip writers of Fleet Street hadn't had such a good yarn to spin since the early Roaring Twenties, when the aristocracy forgot their position, dignity and sobriety and let their collective hair down in the manner of Rapunzel.

The only person who enjoyed reading the articles was Ewan. 'It makes us sound such a romantic family!' he drooled, reading and rereading the pieces.

'Think yourself lucky that you're not the main feature,' Nicolas retorted angrily, 'and that they don't know anything about you!'

Ewan flushed deeply and looked away. He hated it when his brother referred to what he called his private life and he deeply resented not being allowed to leave Buckland on his own these days.

'You'd think I was a two-year-old child,' he hissed pettishly. 'If it wasn't for your bloody wife you'd never have known about Alan and me. We were very careful . . .'

'Careful!' Nicolas retorted. 'With all those clipped newspapers sticking out of a dustbin for anyone to see? I shall never know how the police missed spotting them, not to mention your nocturnal activities. You should thank Cathryn for saving you from a long prison sentence.'

Ewan rose, his face contorted with frustration and anger. 'Damn you! And damn your wife! I've got no one now, thanks to your interference.' Then he stormed out of the room, slamming the heavy gilt decorated mahogany door behind him with such force that even the solidness of Buckland shuddered.

Nicolas looked after his brother, his expression troubled. He felt immensely sorry for him, knowing he would never experience the happiness he himself had found with Cathryn, but the younger man had a streak of recklessness that could amount to self-destruction if he wasn't taken care of. And Conceptia, with her blind adoration of him, was the last person who should be indulging him.

As Nicolas made his way to the estate office to discuss spring plans for the home farm with Hugh, Wills intercepted him, saying he had a visitor who wished to speak to him privately and urgently.

'Show him into the study,' Nicolas replied, frowning. He had a strange foreboding that something was wrong.

An hour later he was on the telephone to Anthony Warner.

'Get here as fast as you can,' he instructed him. It had become horrifying clear that not only was Ewan in even greater danger than he'd imagined possible, but so was Conceptia.

'What's happening, darling?' Cathryn asked, seeing him striding grimly back into the study, where she knew he'd been cooped up with 'a visitor', according to the tight-lipped butler, whose beady eyes shone with disapproval.

'The worst has happened,' Nicolas replied distractedly. 'Where's Ewan? Where's my mother?'

She looked bewildered. 'I've no idea. Why?'

He ignored her questions, and ran his hand across the crown of his head in a gesture of desperation. 'Anthony's on his way but he may not be here for an hour or so. Find Ewan and my mother if you can, darling. I've got to talk to them before Anthony arrives, but don't let them come into the study. Tell them to go to the library.' Then he shot forward, opened the study door and disappeared inside, closing the door firmly after him.

Wills emerged from the shadows at the far end of the hall. It was obvious he was bristling with ill contained curiosity. 'Can I get you anything, m'lady?'

'Do you know where the dowager and Lord Ewan are?'

'I believe they've taken the dogs for a walk, m'lady.' His shrewd eyes drilled hers, but she looked away, her expression veiled. 'Can you send someone to find them please, Wills? It is rather important.'

He raised his eyebrows. 'Certainly, m'lady.' He clicked his fingers and several footmen appeared as if from nowhere, making her wonder where they lurked when they weren't wanted. She heard him giving instructions and a minute later three of them hurried down the front steps.

Seating herself in a carved chair facing the study door, she waited as if mounting guard, all the time wondering what on earth was going on. Nicolas had looked more worried than she'd ever seen and she longed to ask Wills who the 'visitor' was, but that would not be the done thing.

In due course she heard Conceptia's querulous voice, complaining that she did not wish to be hurried. A moment later she swept into the hall, in a long coat made of black monkey fur and a close-fitting black velvet hat. Following her, Ewan looked pale, his eyes wide with alarm.

'Whose car is that in the drive?' she asked, the moment she saw Cathryn.

'I've no idea,' Cathryn replied, rising and going forward to meet them. 'Nicolas wants to speak to you both urgently, and he said he'd join us in the library.' She turned to Wills. 'Will you tell my husband that the dowager and Lord Ewan have returned, please?'

Then she started leading the way to the far side of the hall.

Conceptia stood stock still, looking mutinous. 'Wait a minute! Who are you to give orders to me in my own house? I wish to change after my walk, and I will not be hustled like some servant waiting to be interviewed.'

Cathryn looked straight back at her. 'These are not my orders, I'm speaking on behalf of Nicolas. It seems it is a matter of urgency that he talks to both of you.'

'He won't want to see me,' Ewan said nervously, starting to go towards the staircase.

'He does want to see you, Ewan,' Cathryn told him firmly.

Wills had already opened the library door and was standing waiting to usher them in.

'But my shoes are muddy . . .' Ewan grumbled, shuffling unwillingly forward.

The study door burst open and Nicolas came out, tall and purposeful, signalling that they should all follow Cathryn into the library, whilst instructing a footman to see 'that the gentleman in the study remains there and doesn't leave'. Then he turned to Wills. 'Will you make sure we're not disturbed,' he said pointedly as he joined his family.

'Yes, m'lord.' Wills closed the library door with quiet precision and then took his place outside it like a sentry on duty.

'I strongly object . . .' Conceptia rasped, her back rigid with indignation. 'What on earth do you think you're doing, Nicolas, herding us in here like cattle?'

'Be quiet, and listen. This is important.' he said roughly. He looked at his mother and brother as they walked towards the fireplace. 'You've no idea what a serious position you're both in; the two of you and David Partridge.'

Cathryn stared at Nicolas with astonishment, wondering what was going on. Then she glanced at her mother-in-law.

Conceptia had shrunk into her massive shaggy coat as she sank on to a deep leather sofa, her face whiter that ever, her body as limp now as a rag doll. Beside her Ewan was shivering, crouched like a dog who expects to be whipped.

Nicolas walked slowly over to the smouldering log fire, then turned, his feet apart, while his hand stroked the top of his head again thoughtfully.

'I've had a visit this morning from Dougal Russell, the landlord of the King's Arms,' he began in measured tones. 'He's still here.'

'Oh, God!' Ewan groaned, throwing up his hands in apparent despair.

Nicolas continued. 'It seems his son, Alan, told him a great deal about our family before he left for Berlin. So much, in fact, that Mr Russell is now intent on blackmailing us. He has threatened me with the police if I don't comply.'

The silence in the room was so intense that Cathryn could hear the beating of her heart as she tried to take in the seriousness of what Nicolas was saying.

Looking at Ewan, he spoke with profound regret. 'It seems Mr Russell knows every single detail of Posy Burgess's disappearance and of how she came to die. He knows exactly who was involved and why it took twenty years for her remains to be discovered.'

'But how . . . ?' Conceptia gave a protesting cry, her hand flying to her mouth. Then she turned sharply to look at Ewan. She saw his face was crimson and he was shaking violently. At that moment the last dregs of her resolution seemed to drain away.

'Oh, God, Ewan!' she whispered brokenly.

'Alan got me drunk!' Ewan sobbed hysterically. 'I'd kept it secret for so long. It was such a relief to tell someone and Alan understood me. Which you never have,' he added with a burst of spite as he glared through his tears at his brother.

'David and I did all we could to cover up what you'd done,' Conceptia mumbled, brokenly.

'I know! I know!' Ewan sobbed. 'But I did it to please you, Mama. I'd heard you say she was Papa's child and how you wished she'd never been born. That was why I took Nicolas's air rifle that day. That was why I went looking for her, because she often went into the wood. I suddenly saw her right there on the opposite bank! She was bending down and I fired. I didn't think it would be so loud and it hurt my shoulder. I was so frightened but I fired again, and suddenly she went down with a thump.' He sobbed raggedly, the heels of his hands pressed hard into his eye sockets as he rocked backwards and forwards. 'I didn't think I'd killed her . . . I really didn't. But then she didn't get up. She stayed on the ground, not moving. So I ran all the way home. I didn't know what else to do.'

Conceptia closed her eyes. How often had she relived that moment in her nightmares? Ewan tearing into the house, and then running up to her in the study where she was writing letters, and flinging himself into her arms, his little white face blotched red with tears, his trembling body pressed close to hers. She'd tried to comfort him but he was too terrified to listen. 'I did it for you,' he'd said, sobbing repeatedly. Dear God! She recalled now how her blood had flowed like icy particles through her body as she'd half carried him and half dragged him up to her private suite, where he'd been violently sick, choking and spluttering and half out of his mind with fear.

Then she'd put him in her big bed and given him sips of water, all the while telling him everything would be all right. She'd look after him. She'd take care of him.

'Swallow this sweetie,' she'd whispered, slipping one of her strong sleeping pills into his mouth.

It had worked quicker than she'd imagined. As soon as he was unconscious, she turned him on to his side, and gave strict instructions that he was not to be disturbed because he had had a bad bilious attack.

'He's been given far too many eggs recently,' she raged to the housekeeper. 'Tell cook that eggs are to be barred from the kitchen in future.'

Conceptia looked up at Nicolas now. Her voice was muffled. 'It wasn't Ewan's fault.'

Nicolas's expression was a mixture of horror and anxiety.

Cathryn looked up at him. 'You didn't know until now, did you?' she asked intuitively.

Nicolas shook his head slowly. 'I'd half hoped Mr Russell was lying. That he'd made the whole thing up but obviously his son was repeating what Ewan had told him.' He gazed at his brother with stricken eyes.

'Don't look at me like that!' Ewan begged, tears streaking down his face.

Nicolas looked back at him, and at the sight of Ewan's obvious distress, compassion filled his eyes. 'Anthony will advise us what to do, but I think we have to say you were so young, only ten, that you had no idea you were doing anything wrong. What is a real problem is that Mother aided and abetted you in a massive way, so technically she's guilty of perverting the course of justice.'

'Oh, Mama, Mama . . .' This reduced Ewan to a further outburst of hysterics, which Cathryn found both terrible and obscene to witness coming from an adult man.

'What about David Partridge?' she asked. 'Is he involved?'

Nicolas nodded decisively. 'We must get him here at once. I gather he played a big part in covering up what had happened. Is that true, Mother?'

Conceptia stared at the tapestry carpet at her feet, her eyes dull, her expression defeated. 'I couldn't have done it without him,' she replied simply.

As soon as Anthony arrived and Nicolas heard his voice in the hall, he rushed to fetch him. 'We're in the library,' he explained in a low voice. 'All hell has broken loose. David Partridge is on his way. He's involved, as well as my mother. Ewan's in a terrible state.'

Anthony took off his overcoat and straightened his tie. 'Where's this Russell fellow?'

'I've kept him in the library. I didn't know what to do with him until you advised me.'

Anthony bit his bottom lip thoughtfully. 'You can't keep him here against his will. I'll have a word with him and remind him that blackmail is a punishable offence for a start. Then I'll threaten him with arrest if he tries to put the screws on you before we've ascertained all the facts. Do you believe what he told you is true?'

Nicolas nodded. 'I know it is,' he said hollowly. 'Ewan has confessed everything. When Partridge gets here no doubt we'll find out how he helped my mother dispose of the body. God, I never thought it would come to this.'

Wills stepped out of the shadows. 'Luncheon is ready to be served, m'lord. I presume that will be for five for luncheon?'

Nicolas looked questioningly at his solicitor.

'You've all got to eat,' Anthony reasoned in a low voice. 'Why don't we have a quick luncheon and then continue with our business afterwards?'

'Right. Make that six people, Wills. Mr Partridge is on his way and should be here in about half an hour. Show him straight into the dining room as soon as he arrives, will you? Will you also arrange for Mr Russell to have coffee and sandwiches in the study?'

Years of training caused Wills's impassive face to show not a flicker of surprise or curiosity. 'Certainly, m'lord.'

'I'll join you in a few minutes,' Anthony said pointedly, heading for the study. 'I want a word with Mr Russell first. This shouldn't take long.'

It was the strangest and most agonizing luncheon Cathryn had ever sat through, and could only have been held, she reflected, in the grand, highly staffed house of a member of the aristocracy. She'd always known it was not the done thing to talk about anything of a personal nature in front of the servants, as it was not the done thing to bring up the subjects of money, politics or religion at a social gathering, but if it had been her family they'd probably have scrapped a formal meal altogether in light of the seriousness of the situation, and had sandwiches and coffee in the privacy of one of their smaller reception rooms.

Not so with the Abingdon family. At Buckland Place formality had to be observed, so whilst none of them had much appetite, random remarks about the weather and the number of cattle now at the home farm were lobbed to and fro across the table like spent tennis balls, falling flat and sometimes dropping in mid-air, with no one in the mood to catch them. Wills and three footmen hovered, their light footfalls at times the only sounds in the room as they offered the food on silver platters or skilfully removed the dirty plates without so much as a *chink*. More wine was

consumed than usual, Cathryn noted, sticking to water herself,
but it was as if they were all awaiting their destiny with a kind
of shocked despair.

At last the absurd act of pretending to enjoy their luncheon
ended, and as soon as the six of them – for David Partridge had
arrived between the *Filets de Sole à la Mayonnaise* and the *Faisan
en Robe de Chambre* – returned to the library they were all
jabbering at the same time.

'Why did you get me here so urgently?' David kept asking in
agitation.

Anthony suggested everyone should sit around the table in the
centre of the room while he made notes. 'Nicolas, let's start with
you,' he began. 'Tell us exactly what's happened so far.' As he
spoke he drew a yellow legal pad from his briefcase and a fountain pen from the inner breast pocket of his dark suit. 'We can
see where we're going when I have the full picture.'

Nicolas repeated everything Mr Russell had told him. 'Ewan
has confessed to us that it's all true. He did shoot Posy. In his
childish way he thought it was being helpful and what my
mother wanted. You see, Posy Burgess was my late father's love
child.'

Anthony scribbled in silence. When he'd finished he turned to
Ewan, whom he questioned in detail, causing Ewan to whinge
and weep copiously again. Anthony scribbled some more. 'Right.
I'll have to come back to you later for more details. Meanwhile,'
he turned to Conceptia, 'where do you come into all this, Lady
Abingdon? Ewan had come running to you to tell you what he'd
done, admitting he'd shot the child on purpose, so how did you
react?'

Slowly and painfully she told him how she'd put Ewan to bed
with a sleeping pill, before seeking the help of Mr Partridge.

'Ahh!' Anthony looked at David as if he were the much needed
missing link in this tragic saga.

The older man's heavy lidded eyes slid from side to side like
a frog searching for a fly on a very treacherous pond. 'I happen
to be a lawyer and I don't think this is the time or the place to
be cross-examined by a young man of little experience such as
yourself,' he said, arrogantly, licking his thick lips.

Nicolas looked at David irritably. 'For God's sake, we're not in a court of law. Whatever is said today remains, for the moment, between these four walls.'

'Please David . . .' Conceptia quavered. 'We've all had to be honest and this is a terrible ordeal for Ewan.'

'If he'd kept his mouth shut none of this would be happening, Conceptia,' David retorted angrily.

Anthony continued, 'I need all the facts to see if they agree with the version Mr Russell gave Nicolas. This isn't about you, Mr Partridge, it's about finding a way of getting Mr Russell off our backs.'

Looking sulky, David folded his hands on the table in front of him and shrugged. 'Conceptia summoned me urgently, and as soon as I arrived here, she told me what had happened. She was in such a state that for her sake and against my better judgement, I agreed to get a shovel and a sack out of the potting shed, so we could bury the child. Ewan had told us where she lay. Luckily in November the gardeners are mostly working in the glasshouses, so no one saw me. I went the long way round through the woods to reach the spot, where I was unlikely to meet anyone.'

Conceptia leaned forward, wanting to interrupt him. 'David was being so wonderful,' she began earnestly, 'helping me as no one else would have done, and I wanted to help him in this terrible task. I gave orders that Ewan wanted to sleep as he was unwell and I'd promised to stay with him. In fact, as soon as the coast was clear I slipped out of the house through one of the French windows in the drawing room, which I left unlocked so I could re-enter the house the same way.' She paused as if it were too painful to continue, but then she rallied, reaching out to lay her hand on Ewan's wrist. 'When I got to the spot I could see David on the other side of the stream. He was digging . . .' Her voice drifted off and she covered her eyes with her other hand before speaking again.

'I took off my shoes and waded across the stream, which is very shallow and fast running, and the water was icy and the stones hurt my feet . . .' She gulped as her throat tightened. 'It was muddy and difficult to climb out of the stream on the other side but he gave me a hand, and while he dug I pushed the child's body into the sack. Then I collected lots of broken branches. Big ones. Heavy ones. When he'd buried her and filled in the hole, we piled the branches over the spot and dragged some brambles over it too . . . how they tore our clothes and hands. By then it was quite dark.'

Ewan was watching her with haunted eyes, hanging on her every word. Nicolas stared at her too, as if he could hardly believe what he was hearing.

'And then . . . ?' Anthony prompted encouragingly, without looking up from his pad where he was still scratching away with his fountain pen.

'Then,' Conceptia said wearily as she leaned back in her chair, 'while David came back to the house the long way I somehow managed to get back across the stream . . . and I put on my shoes again, picked up the air rifle, and breaking it, carried it home hidden under my long coat. As luck would have it, the servants were having their tea in their quarters by then, and I managed to get back into the drawing room, where I hid the gun under the sofa. No one saw me go up to my room and Ewan was still asleep. I rang for my maid to bring me tea and shortly after there was a hue and cry when the child's mother realized she was missing.'

'What about the rifle?' Anthony asked.

'Later that night, when everyone was out in the grounds searching for the child, I fetched the rifle and hid it in the attic. Where it remained for all these years, until that friend of Cathryn's came to stay.' Conceptia's tone was bitter now and she gave her daughter-in-law a look of glowering vindictiveness.

At last Anthony laid down his pen with a sigh. 'If Mr Russell goes to the police with this information, and his son can verify that the incident was described to him in some detail by Ewan himself, then you are in deep trouble. Although Ewan was only ten, it will be hard to prove he didn't aim and fire at Posy Burgess with intent to harm and injure her. The law will state he knew what he was doing, and he knew why he was doing it. To rid his family of the embarrassment not only of having the illegitimate daughter of the late Lord Abingdon living in the village, but of having her mother, who'd been Lord Abingdon's mistress, still working here, in the presence of the Dowager Marchioness.'

'Can't we plead Ewan's insanity at the time? Surely there must be a way round this?' Nicolas asked grimly.

Anthony spoke frankly. 'That won't stop a judge and jury finding Lady Abingdon and Mr Partridge guilty of perverting the course of justice.'

Conceptia looked as if she no longer cared what happened to her but David's expression was a mixture of anger and fear.

'I did it for you, Conceptia, not the boy!' he muttered accusingly.

'You could have refused,' she retorted.

Anthony rose from the table. 'I'm going to go back to London now to seek the advice of my partners, and I'll have a word with the QC, Sir Oscar Neville. Meanwhile, I suggest you keep Mr Russell sweet by saying you deny the truth of this story and that in any case, you can't lay your hands on the amount of money he wants in five minutes! Bluff him with the threat that if he says a word to the police, you will contact the British Ambassador in Berlin and ask him to inform the German authorities that Alan Russell is a British homosexual who has been forced to leave this country. That should shut the father up.'

'Oh, that's not fair!' Ewan burst out, aghast.

Nicolas ignored him. 'Will do,' he replied to Anthony. 'I'll go and see him right away.'

Seventeen

MURDERED CHILD'S MOTHER COLLAPSES

Mrs Ida Burgess, the fifty-seven-year-old mother of murdered local child Posy Burgess, collapsed at her home in the village of Appledore two days ago. Posy's remains were found buried in the grounds of Lord Abingdon's estate in November, and charges against the marquess were dropped when a statement that led to him being questioned was found to be false. Mrs Burgess is being treated at Canterbury General Hospital . . .

Kent Local Messenger, February 18th, 1931

David Partridge glared glumly out of the morning room window at the grey rain-sodden landscape. 'You should have been firmer with Ewan when he was a child,' he grunted resentfully, 'instead of letting him turn into a namby-pamby mother's boy. What in God's name induced him to tell the fellow at the pub what had happened? Has he no sense of responsibility? Doesn't he realize he's fatally implicated us in his crime?'

Conceptia sat with her elbows on her knees, holding her head in her hands while she gazed with unseeing eyes into her lap. 'A boy of ten can't commit a crime,' she said wearily, as if it were a mantra she was tired of repeating.

David grunted in frustration. 'He's admitted he knew what he was doing, Conceptia. Stop making excuses for him. He deliberately shot that child, intending to kill her, because you didn't want her around as a constant reminder of William's infidelity. That's the long and short of it, whether you like it or not! You colluded in covering up his crime, and you got me to help you. Face facts, woman!' he continued roughly, 'we're up to our necks in it. You've treated me shabbily for years, only seeing me when you wanted something. Now look where it's got me.'

Her head shot up, revealing her scrawny neck devoid of ropes of pearls for once, and her eyes suddenly blazed with fury. 'Don't you dare blame me for everything. How like a man! You call Ewan namby-pamby – you're a weak, lily-livered old fool! You're a lawyer, you're supposed to know how to help people get out of a jam, and all you can do is sit there and feel sorry for yourself. It's Ewan you should feel sorry for. We're old, you and I, but he's got his life ahead of him!'

'And a sordid sort of life if you ask me,' he interrupted. 'You've only yourself to blame for all this, Conceptia. You've turned Ewan into a surrogate husband, someone to love and be loved by, to compensate for the hurt William inflicted on you by only marrying you for your money.'

For a long moment she stared at him in silence as if he'd said something she didn't already know. Then she spoke in a low voice. 'Ewan has always needed me as much as I've needed him.'

David looked out of the window again. 'Perhaps Nicolas will buy Mr Russell's silence.'

'And perhaps he won't.' She rested her head in the palms of her hands again.

'Have you seen the local paper this morning?'

'No,' she replied without looking up.

'Posy Burgess's mother is in hospital. Apparently she collapsed a few days ago. Hardly surprising, with all that's been going on.'

'It's never going to end, is it? The legacy of William's sins. It's like an echo that goes on and on . . . the child's death, Nicolas's divorce, Hilary Pilkington's suicide, and now this.'

'Hilary's death had nothing to do with William.'

'You don't understand.' Her voice quavered, bordering on hysteria. 'This family is cursed and rotten to the core and it's time it stopped.'

'You're overwrought, Conceptia,' David remarked from his armchair. 'You don't know what you're talking about. Buckland is your life and you adore it.'

She stopped and stood dramatically in front of him. 'It will also be the death of me. My dreams have been shattered in this house.'

'Poor Mrs Burgess,' Cathryn exclaimed in concern. 'I must go to the hospital and take some flowers. I hope it's nothing serious. She's had such a hard life.'

She and Nicolas were having morning coffee in the estate office with Hugh, who had just handed them a copy of the *Kent Local Messenger*.

'Do we know what's wrong with her?' Nicolas asked anxiously.

'Apparently she's had a stroke,' Hugh said. 'I've given Frank time off so he can visit her. He was at work when it happened but luckily she collapsed in front of a neighbour who ran into the post office and got them to telephone for an ambulance. I imagine the stroke has been brought on by the terrific strain of the past two months.'

'Is she going to be all right?'

'I gather it's too soon to say,' Hugh replied. 'They seem to be taking very good care of her at the hospital. If it's all right with you, Nicolas, I thought we might give Frank some extra money to get anything she might need. I've already told him to get himself a hot lunch every day at the pub and I've arranged with the landlord to put it on a slate for us.'

'Not at the King's Arms though?'

'Absolutely not,' Hugh replied, who knew what was going on with Mr Russell. 'I've told Frank to go to the Crown and Anchor.'

Cathryn rose to leave the room. 'I'll go and see Mrs Burgess this afternoon.'

'Will you be all right on your own, darling?' Nicolas asked. 'I'm waiting for a call from Anthony so I've got to stay by the telephone, but get Rogers to drive you.'

She bent to kiss him on the cheek. 'With the help of a chauffeur-driven car I think I can just about manage to get to Canterbury and back,' she teased. 'Meanwhile, I'll get some flowers from the glasshouse.'

When she'd gone, Hugh smiled at Nicolas. 'You've certainly chosen the perfect wife this time, haven't you? Everyone adores her: the servants, the outdoor workers, the farmhands. In time she'll make a wonderful chatelaine for this place.'

Nicolas looked sad. 'Yes, if she's given the chance while my mother is around, but I'm afraid she's never going to hand over to Cathryn without a terrible fight.'

'The dowager may have to be elsewhere if . . . er . . . if things don't work out,' he pointed out carefully, not wanting to step over the mark.

'Christ, I can't think that far ahead,' Nicolas admitted. 'I wish Anthony would hurry up and tell me the likely outcome of this disaster, then at least we'd know where we stand.'

'I was wondering if this Russell chap could have told Mrs Burgess what happened? The shock of hearing it was definitely Ewan who shot Posy might have caused the stroke.'

Nicolas's eyes widened with dismay. 'My God, I hadn't thought of that. The police will quickly get wind of what happened if he did.'

'Have you realized something else in the past week?

Nicolas's eyes filled with dread. 'Now what?'

'The newspapers have stopped printing stories about your and Cathryn's every move. Whoever was tipping them off has suddenly stopped.'

'My God, you're right! Everything we did was written about within hours, although we never told anyone of our plans.' Nicolas paused, then said thoughtfully, 'I wonder if Alan Russell was the stringer? Ewan always knew what we were doing, didn't he? He could have told Alan, who could then have phoned the news desks of the various papers with his story. No wonder there were photographers waiting for us when we arrived anywhere.'

Hugh nodded grimly.

Nicolas looked ready to explode. 'The little bastard! How could he have done this to us? Damn it, his own family and he gets some chap at the pub to sell our story?'

'Maybe that was why Ewan thought of becoming a journalist himself at one point? Didn't he say "with our contacts we could get great stories"?'

Nicolas looked appalled. 'I bet they shared the fees they got, too. I never realized we had a Judas in our midst.'

'Would it have been much money?'

'I believe stringers receive between three and five shillings for a tip-off and a guinea for a scoop! Christ, how could he have stooped so low as to sell his family down the river for a few pence?'

'Every man has his price,' Hugh observed quietly, seeing the outrage in Nicolas's eyes.

'And they don't get much lower than my brother.'

★　★　★

Ida Burgess lay so still and looked so pale in the narrow iron hospital bed that for a moment Cathryn feared she was dead. Stepping quietly forward, clutching a large bunch of pink carnations, she peered closer. For once the older woman's wrinkled face was serene and still. At that moment Ida's eyelids fluttered open and then immediately closed again.

'Shall I find you a vase for those, Lady Abingdon?' asked a kindly nurse, indicating the flowers.

'Thank you.' Cathryn sat down on the plain wooden bench provided for visitors.

'How is Mrs Burgess getting on?'

The nurse hesitated. 'It's too soon to say. There's a certain amount of paralysis on her right side but hopefully that will go. Her speech hasn't returned yet so she's unable to tell us how she feels. It will all take time,' she added with a reassuring smile.

'I see.' Cathryn gazed at Ida and realized she looked much younger as she lay unconscious and untroubled. 'She's had such a terrible time and I feel so sorry for her.'

The nurse nodded in agreement. 'Her husband's very devoted, though. He visits her ever so often. We must just hope for the best.'

Cathryn stayed watching over Ida for half an hour. She hardly stirred except for the occasional flutter of her eyelids, and the twitching of the fingers of her reddened right hand. The hand of a washerwoman who had striven all her life to earn a pittance.

'I felt so helpless,' she told Nicolas when she got back to Buckland. 'I wanted to tell her not to worry about anything but how could I?'

'They say people can still hear even when they're unconscious,' he said. 'I believe the new idea is to talk to them, even if they don't respond. It might actually reassure her to know she's not alone.'

'Really?' Cathryn looked surprised. 'I never thought of that. Maybe I could read aloud to her. I wonder what sort of books she likes?'

Nicolas smiled at her naïve sweetness. 'Take something light and maybe jolly to read to her next time. She left school at eleven to go out to work and I doubt if she's picked up a book since then.'

'Eleven? That's terrible.'

'Well, she was the second of thirteen children, so the older ones had to earn money to buy food to feed the younger ones.'

Cathryn looked deeply shocked. 'It's moments like this that make one realize how lucky we are,' she said sombrely. 'I'm already terrified of people thinking I'm some sort of Lady Bountiful. One of the nurses recognized me. She called me "Lady Abingdon" and I felt embarrassed. I was wearing the mink coat you gave me because it's so bitterly cold today but what must they have thought of me? All those poor patients, like Ida, crammed together in a public ward? It would probably have taken the nurse ten years to be able to afford a coat as expensive as mine.'

Nicolas looked at her askance. 'More like fifty years, sweetheart. I only buy the best,' he added drily.

She flushed deeply, her pale neck glowing pink. 'Oh, my God! I feel that next time I ought to go in sackcloth and ashes.'

Nicolas smiled. 'Don't worry about it, sweetheart. That's life. I suspect the nurse you met has had a happier and more trouble-free few months than you've had. You know from experience now that wealth and privilege don't make for happiness or a care-free existence. I can honestly say there have been moments in recent weeks when I'd have given anything to swap places with one of my foresters or gardeners. I bet right now Ewan thinks the same,' he added with feeling.

'You haven't heard from Anthony yet?'

'No, he's been in meetings all day and with the weekend coming up I won't hear from him now until Monday at the earliest.'

On Sunday morning, after they'd been to morning service, Cathryn decided to visit Ida Burgess again. Wearing a plain black woollen coat this time, and a simple beret-style black hat, she arrived just as the majority of patients had finished their bowls of bread and soup.

This time Ida was propped up by pillows and was wide awake. As soon as she saw Cathryn she started jabbering incoherently, and waving the arm had hadn't been affected by the stroke. Cathryn hurried to her side, and clasped the hand with both of hers.

'How are you, Mrs Burgess? You look much better,' she said, smiling warmly.

The urgent jabbering continued and at that moment a nurse who was passing – with a bedpan held at arm's length in both hands – paused next to them.

'Her speech isn't right yet,' she announced cheerfully. 'We can't make out a word she's saying! Otherwise she's ever so much better, aren't you, dearie?'

Ida ignored her, and continued to look at Cathryn, as if trying to convey something.

Cathryn perched herself on the wooden bench, still holding Ida's hand. 'How long will it take before it comes back?'

'There's no knowing,' the nurse replied. 'It might stay like gobbledegook for a long time.' She shrugged before speeding off again in the direction of the hospital sluice.

Cathryn looked into Ida's face, and saw the awareness in her pale blue eyes. 'How are you feeling? Can you hear me?'

Ida nodded vigorously but the mumbo jumbo continued.

'Is there anything I can get you?' she asked the older woman, feeling increasingly helpless.

This time Ida shook her head violently, frowned, and the stream of babble continued. She seemed quite worked up too, and fearing this might bring on a stroke, Cathryn decided to pretend she understood what was being said.

'Really? Is that so?' she murmured soothingly in response to the next stream of gibberish. But Ida was sharp enough to know Cathryn was lying. She pulled her hand roughly away from Cathryn's clasp and gesticulated wildly while still yammering away.

'I know,' Cathryn said suddenly, opening her handbag and groping for a neat little notebook, attached to which was a dainty little pencil. Opening it, she propped it up on Ida's lap. 'Write down what you want to tell me,' she coaxed.

With a frustrated gesture, Ida swiped the notebook away with her good hand so it bounced off the bed and clattered on to the floor.

'Lady Abingdon?' It was the nurse she'd met on her previous visit. With a swift move she picked up the notebook and handed it back to Cathryn, who was flushed with embarrassment.

'I don't think Mrs Burgess can write,' the nurse said quietly with a meaningful look.

Then Cathryn remembered. How stupid she'd been! Nicolas

had told her Ida had left school at eleven. She probably hadn't picked up a pencil since.

'Oh, yes,' she replied, feeling crushed. 'I was so worried because she was getting worked up, trying to tell me something, and I feared it would make her ill again.'

'I know. She was like this last night when her husband came to see her. He couldn't make out what she was trying to tell him either. I think maybe we should leave her for a bit in the hope she calms down.'

'I felt such a fool,' Cathryn confided to Nicolas later that day. 'It was a disastrous visit.'

'Have you any idea what she was trying to tell you?'

'I've no idea except it was something she'd also been trying to tell Frank.'

'I'll have a word with him tomorrow. Maybe, if she gets so worked up, you should stay away until she's got her speech back.'

'Oh, I will,' she replied with feeling. 'I'd never make a good hospital visitor, would I? I either go dressed like royalty, or I do the wrong thing.'

Nicolas stooped to plant a butterfly kiss on her temple. 'Don't be so hard on yourself, sweetheart.'

Anthony Warner contacted Nicolas early the next morning. 'I've got some options for you to think about,' he announced. 'Can you get the family together so I can explain what the partners and I have come up with? I can be with you at three o'clock this afternoon if that's convenient.'

'That's fine and thanks, Anthony. I'm most grateful.'

Bracing himself, and feeling as though he himself were on trial, he told Cathryn first, then his mother and Ewan, who'd hardly left their private quarters in the past week.

At three o'clock exactly they heard the swish of a car on the gravel drive, and a couple of minutes later Wills showed Anthony into the library, where the others were waiting.

'Punctual as usual,' Nicolas greeted him with an outstretched hand. 'Can we get you something to drink? Coffee? Tea?'

'No thanks, I'm fine.' In a business-like way he joined the others at the round table, and opening his briefcase pulled out some papers. 'First of all, have you heard any more from Mr Russell?'

'Not a squeak.'

'Good. Now then.' He cleared his throat before proceeding. 'I can suggest three options which apply to you, Lady Abingdon,' he began by looking at Conceptia, 'and to your son Ewan, and Mr Partridge.'

'You don't hold our future in your hands,' Conceptia cut in haughtily, having regained some of her feistiness. 'I haven't appointed you to represent us, so don't expect me to fall in with your plans, just like that.'

Anthony raised his eyebrows and looked at Nicolas.

'I'm the head of the family,' Nicolas said firmly, ignoring David Partridge's brooding expression. 'Anthony is here to give us the best of his considered advice. If you aren't prepared to hear what he has to say then I wash my hands of the lot of you,' he added angrily.

There was silence. 'Well, get on with it,' snapped Conceptia.

Anthony drew in a deep breath. 'The first option is to give Mr Russell what he wants, and pray he never divulges what happened. The trouble with blackmailers is that they are never satisfied. He'll come back for more. And more. And he'll continue to threaten you with the police until he's bled the family coffers dry. And you still wouldn't have any guarantee he wouldn't eventually spill the beans. To me this is not a viable option and you'd spend the rest of your lives waiting for the other shoe to drop. It wouldn't help to go to the police and report his attempts at blackmail, either. They've already tried to pin the death of Posy Burgess on Nicolas, and they'd love to reopen the case if they could to save face.'

'I agree,' Nicolas said heartily. 'Once you give in to blackmailers you're finished. So what's the next plan of campaign, Anthony?'

'The second is for Ewan to make a confession to the police, pleading that no malice was intended towards Posy Burgess; that he was just messing around with Nicolas's rifle and it accidentally went off, with tragic consequences for which he's eternally sorry.'

'I c-can't! I s-simply can't confess!' Ewan said, bursting into tears, and burying his head in his folded arms on the table. 'Mama, don't make me do it. What will they do to me? I can't go through with it.'

Before Conceptia could say anything, Anthony continued, 'If we could make a strong enough case of it being an accident, and that you never saw Posy and you didn't think you were doing anything wrong, your intention being merely to do some target practice, then you will not be charged because you were only ten at the time.'

'So we're back to Article 50 of The Age of Criminal Responsibility?' Nicolas asked.

'That refers to children under the age of ten so we could use that clause,' Anthony agreed thoughtfully, 'but I was referring to The Children's Act that came out in 1908, which was what we would have put forward if the police had charged you, Nicolas. Our case would rest on the "fact", for want of a better word, that Ewan did not know what he was doing,' he added crisply. 'Now that there are no witnesses to the shooting he will probably get away with it, but it would have been better if he'd come forward the moment the child's remains were found, instead of letting his brother take the blame for the past three months.'

Ewan was sobbing quietly into his folded arms and Conceptia's face was as white and stiff as if she were a marble statue, cold and lifeless.

'So what do you advise Mother and David to do, if Ewan confesses?' Nicolas asked.

Anthony paused and took a deep breath before plunging on. 'If we take the second option and Ewan confesses, it still means that Lady Abingdon and Mr Partridge would be found accessories, in that they not only buried the body and hid the rifle, but lied for twenty years about the whole affair. And again, allowed you, Nicolas, the eldest son, to take the blame when the body was discovered in November. They will be charged, I'm afraid, and are likely to be tried, indicted and punished as principal offenders.' He turned to David Partridge. 'I'm sure you're as aware as I am of the Accessories and Abettors Act of 1861.'

David nodded, his jaws tightly clenched, his hooded eyes glassy.

'And the third option?' Nicolas asked in a strained voice.

'This is a compromise and it's the one I would recommend to any of my clients.' He looked at the group around the table, including Cathryn, who sat tense and pale-faced, and hadn't said a word throughout. 'We do a deal with Mr Russell. Tell him you'll give him half of what he wants and you'll never reveal to anyone about his son, who can return to England if he wants, without fear of his private life being exposed by you.'

The atmosphere in the room brightened. Conceptia's face relaxed, David started to breathe more easily and Ewan stopped crying and wiped his flushed and swollen face.

Only Nicolas and Cathryn knew it wasn't going to be as simple as that as they exchanged covert glances.

'Well, that's all right then, isn't it?' Conceptia remarked, her voice ringing with relief. 'That's what we'll do. Maybe we should give him a bit more than half just to be on the safe side.'

'It's not going to be quite as straightforward as that.' Anthony pointed out.

'I don't understand. You've just said . . . ?'

'I fear, for your own sakes, that this last option is not going to work unless all three of you go and live abroad permanently.'

There were sharp intakes of breath. Conceptia shrieked and Ewan wailed, 'What do you *mean*?'

Anthony looked uncomfortable but he had no option but to explain. 'My suggestion is that you set sail for America as soon as possible. As you're an American, Lady Abingdon, it would not be unnatural for you to want to return to your own country and if it is done quickly and discreetly, before Mr Russell finds out, it will not arouse suspicion. It would also look perfectly natural for you to take Ewan, so you can show him the country of your birth.'

While mother and son tried to digest what was to be their fate, Anthony turned to David. 'It is of course entirely up to you where you go, Mr Partridge. You could accompany your friends to the United States, or you could go to Europe, but if you want to avoid being charged with aiding and abetting, and personally I don't think a jury would bring in a verdict of not guilty, then the sooner you leave the country the better.'

Stunned, Cathryn could hardly take in what was being suggested. Her first thought was how wonderful it would be to be free of them all, forever! Then she looked at Nicolas. How was he going to react?

While the others looked stunned, gazing into space with their mouths open, Nicolas sat, his chin resting on his hand, his brow gathered and his eyes troubled.

'Is there no other way, Anthony?' he asked at last.

Anthony was gathering up his papers. 'You will, of course, need to discuss this amongst yourselves, but when it comes down to it, Nicolas, your mother and brother either leave the country and you do a deal with Mr Russell and his son, or you do nothing and say nothing, always knowing there's someone who can, at any moment, stab you in the back by going to the police whilst blackmailing you until you eventually lose everything. Your money, your possessions and Buckland Place.'

'He's got no proof,' David said loudly as he suddenly came back to life from his trance-like state. 'Who is going to take the word of a couple of young men? They could have made it all up. If we pleaded innocent I'm sure a jury would acquit Lady Abingdon and Ewan because of who they *are*.'

'Mr Russell knows the truth and there's no turning back now,' Anthony retorted. 'Ewan has confessed in front of all of us. Mr Russell admits his son helped Ewan send out poison pen letters. The rifle was found hidden in your attic. What's done is done. Do you plan to sit with your feet tucked under the table, Mr Partridge, enjoying the hospitality of this family, while Nicolas shells out hundreds of thousands of pounds for the rest of his life? Until there's nothing left?'

David flushed puce and ground his teeth. 'I can't afford to go abroad. I only rent my flat in London and I haven't the money to . . .'

Conceptia turned on him with the savage glare of an irritated cat. 'For God's sake stop wittering on!' she hissed. 'You've got to come with us because how am I going to manage on my own?' Then she swung round to Cathryn. 'You're just loving this, aren't you?' she sneered. 'You've wanted to get your hands on this house, my house, ever since you set foot in the place. Well, let me tell you something, I don't regret protecting Ewan and if you were any sort of a decent young woman you'd understand a mother's feelings, instead of sitting there looking judgemental.'

'I'm not being judgemental,' Cathryn retorted spiritedly, 'but I wonder what sort of mother sits back and does nothing to protect her *eldest* son when he's wrongly accused?'

'This is getting us nowhere,' Nicolas intervened gruffly, 'and I don't think there's anything to discuss. We should make travel arrangements for the three of you as soon as possible, and I will cover all your expenses, David, now and in the future. We can ship all your personal goods and chattels to you when you're all settled.'

'If you like I can make the travelling arrangements from my office, as absolute discretion is vital,' Anthony suggested. 'If Mr Russell finds out you're leaving he'll panic and think he's not going to get his money. I'll need your passports but I'll book your passages in false names; otherwise the newspapers will be on to us.'

'Where will we go?' demanded Ewan fretfully.

'I have relatives who still live in Chicago,' Conceptia replied, her voice flat and toneless. 'The name Calkin still stands for something in that city, and I have a cousin who will put us up until I buy a house.'

'But Chicago . . . !' Ewan lamented. 'Can't we get a house in New York? On Fifth Avenue, perhaps? I'm going to be miserable in Chicago.'

David looked as if he'd like to strangle Ewan. 'It's far worse for your mother and me than it is for you,' he snapped. 'We've got to uproot ourselves and at our age that's not easy. You're a relatively young man. You can start a new life over there, Ewan.'

'But this is my home.' Ewan whined, his voice clogged with tears. 'I can't believe this is happening to me. I can't bear the idea of leaving here.'

For once in her life the strain and worry of the situation caused Conceptia to turn on her beloved younger son like a virago. 'Stop being so damned sorry for yourself. I've given everything I've got to keep this place going so how do you think I feel? It breaks my heart to go. Thanks to you I'm having to make the ultimate sacrifice, so just shut up about your feelings.'

No one moved. No one said a word, but out of the corner of her eye Cathryn saw the satisfied smirk on David's face.

'I must be off,' Anthony announced, breaking the silence. He gathered his papers and put them back in his briefcase.

Nicolas and Cathryn went with him to walk him to his car.

'I'm sorry to have brought you such distressing news,' Anthony said almost apologetically. 'I've been going over and over every point with the partners but I'm afraid if your mother and

Mr Partridge stay in this country they will certainly face prosecution. Ewan might get off, but not in a million years if he
admits he shot Posy to please your mother.'

Nicolas stood still, looking down at his feet as he gently
shovelled around the gravel on the drive with the toe of his
brogues. 'I'm very grateful you've gone into the whole business so thoroughly. I know it's the only solution, though the
others may not share my opinion. Let's hope I can keep Mr Russell
at bay until the birds have flown.'

'Until the birds have flown,' Anthony echoed with a wan smile
as he shook hands with both of them and climbed into his car.
Cathryn slipped her hand through Nicolas's arm as they watched
the car drive away.

'This is terrible for you, darling,' she whispered, standing close
to his side. 'Is there anything I can do to help?'

'Not really, sweetheart. My advice is that you should keep out
of the fight. It's not your battle and I don't want you involved
in one of my mother's slanging matches.' He squeezed her hand.
'I'm just so grateful to have you near me, and once it's all over,
which shouldn't be long now, I promise I'll make it up to you
for the misery you've been put through during the past three
months.'

She looked into his eyes with her steady warm gaze. 'I could
never be really miserable as long as I'm married to you,' she
told him.

As they re-entered the house, they could hear the raised voices
of the others coming from the library.

'When thieves fall out,' Nicolas quoted, striding angrily back
into the room. The three of them were grouped by the fireside
and he marched over to where they stood.

'If you want the entire staff to learn of our business then carry
on,' he raged in a low voice. 'It's too late to start tearing each
other to pieces now. You should have thought of the outcome
of your actions twenty-one years ago when the whole thing could
have been passed off as a tragic accident and nothing more
would ever have come of it.'

'He was only ten . . . ! He needed protecting!' Conceptia rasped
throatily.

'Yes, protecting from you,' David whispered viciously.

Nicolas raised both hands in a calming gesture. 'Let's try and be civilized about this.'

His mother spoke accusingly. 'You're just glad to be getting rid of me.'

'Mama, please stop. It's a tragedy for everyone. I don't want you to be forced to leave because I know how much Buckland has always meant to you. It's also always been home to Ewan, and I do appreciate how distressing this is for you, but I will do my best to make it as painless as possible. It also goes without saying that you and Mama can choose to take what you want from here, and I will have it shipped to you. The same goes for you, David.' He took a deep breath before continuing. 'The servants must not know what's happening. I suggest you take your lady's maid and valet as if you were going on a trip to see your cousins in the States. Now, we haven't much time left together, so let's have no more ill feeling and unpleasantness.' He took Conceptia's hand and lifted it to his lips, kissing it lightly. 'Please, Mama?' Then he turned and shook first Ewan and then David by the hand. 'I'm sure I can count on you both to help Mama through this wretched time.'

They had no alternative but to grasp his hand and nod in acquiescence. David in particular was going to be financially in debt to Nicolas for the rest of his life.

Watching, Cathryn felt her eyes well up at the sincerity and genuine regret in Nicolas's voice and it struck her forcibly that she'd married a man of even greater kindness and generosity of spirit than she'd realized, and not a louche boulevardier as her family had at first thought him to be.

As Nicolas had business to discuss with Hugh that afternoon, Cathryn walked over to the home farm. She always enjoyed seeing the animals and being met by Bouncer the sheep dog who, now he'd got to know her, greeted her warmly.

A minute later, Frank emerged from the cow byre, pitchfork in hand.

'Good afternoon, Frank.'

'Good afternoon, m'lady.' He looked more shrunken than ever, a wisp of old man smiling bravely.

'How is Mrs Burgess getting on?'

'She still can't talk.' In his mournful blue eyes she saw a shaft of fear. 'She's frettin' that much 'cos she wants to tell me summat, but it's like listenin' to a baby prattling.'

Cathryn nodded. 'She was like that the last time I went to see her. Have you any idea what she's trying to say?'

'No. All I knows is it's summat important. Very important and she gets that angry with me 'cos I don't understand a word.' He looked so lost and miserable, standing in the middle of the cobbled yard, pitchfork in hand held upright like a pike.

'I think summat happened,' he added knowingly.

'What do you mean?'

'I think summat happened and it gave her such a shock it brought on the stroke.'

Cathryn frowned, racking her brains. 'What makes you think something happened?'

'Mrs Lewis, who's a friend of Ida, dropped in to see 'er. She found Ida throwin' things around the room, wild like! Beatin' the walls of the 'ouse with her fists as if she'd gone mad. She was yellin' and Mrs Lewis thought she was shouting "'ere soon, 'ere soon." Then she went down sudden like on t'floor. Out for the count she was.'

'Here soon?' Cathryn repeated, perplexed. 'Did Mrs Lewis tell you anything else? Had she any idea what had happened?'

'No.' Then he looked pleadingly in Cathryn's eyes. 'I'm fearin' she's lost 'er mind and it'll never come back no more,' he said in a quavering voice.

At that moment Cathryn longed to give him a comforting hug, but knew it would not be seemly and would embarrass him. 'The nurse I saw seemed to think her speech will come back in time,' she said instead in a reassuring voice. 'Try not to worry too much, Frank. These things take time and she is in the best hands. It's very fortunate that her friend dropped in at that moment so she was able to be taken to the hospital straight away.'

He nodded absently. 'Doctor said she'd have bin a gonner if she'd laid there until I comes 'ome at night.'

'Well then! You'll let us know how she gets on, won't you?'

'Aye, I will. It's right lonely without 'er at 'ome. And 'aving no kids I've no one to talk to. Mustn't grumble, though.' He prodded the ground with the end of the pitchfork. 'I'll always be grateful Mrs Lewis found 'er.'

'That's right. The great thing is to stay hopeful,' Cathryn replied robustly. But as she walked back to Buckland her heart was heavy. Something traumatic had obviously happened to give Ida a shock that was so severe she collapsed. Whatever it was, Cathryn couldn't help thinking it concerned Posy's death and might yet prove to be the downfall of them all.

Nicolas strode into the hall, unbuttoning his thick tweed coat and smoothing his ruffled hair with the palm of his hand. 'What a wind!' he observed, as one of the footmen took his coat from him.

'Yes, m'lord.'

'It's practically gale force. I shouldn't wonder if it doesn't bring down some of the old oak trees in the park.'

'Yes, m'lord.'

Wills came bustling self-importantly towards him. 'M'lord, Mr Warner is on the telephone for you.'

'Thanks,' Nicolas said. Striding across the hall he hurried into the study and picked up the receiver. 'Good afternoon, Anthony. How is everything going?'

'I've been finding out about liners going to New York and I've come up with a couple of alternatives. The Cunard White Star has state rooms for three passengers and two cabins on the lower deck for the valet and lady's maid, available on the *Aquitania,* sailing from Southampton on Thursday the 29th —'

'That's in four days' time . . . !'

'I know. There's also accommodation, though nothing like as luxurious as the *Aquitania*, on the Red Star's biggest ship, the SS *Belgenland*, sailing the next day, the 30th.'

'My mother is going to want a big suite of state rooms, and all the luxury she can get,' Nicolas began, but Anthony interrupted him.

'I know, but I think she should sail on the Red Star Line.'

'Why? I want her to have the best.'

'Listen, Nicolas. The press will get wind of your mother and Ewan fleeing to America if they leave from Southampton. Although I'll be booking the cabins in false names, they'll be recognized as they get on board. Photographers will be on the quayside, looking out for any Hollywood film stars or famous people and your family is too well known now for them to go unrecognized . . .'

'Notorious you mean!' Nicolas remarked drily.

'Well, let's get them safely out of the country. That's the main thing . . .'

'So where does this other ship leave from?'

Anthony's tone was flat and matter-of-fact. 'Liverpool, and it'll be full of immigrants setting off to seek their fortune in the States. No one would ever imagine finding the Dowager Marchioness of Abingdon and Lord Ewan Hillier on the *Belgenland*. I've gone into it and they'll have perfectly comfortable state rooms and excellent food. The main thing is they'll be safe from prying eyes both in Liverpool and when they land in New York.'

'I see what you mean,' Nicolas sighed. 'She's going to complain like hell but you're right. Go ahead and confirm their booking on the *Belgenland*. Their luggage should be ordinary, too,' he added thoughtfully.

'Yes, for God's sake don't let them travel with coronets plastered all over the trunks. I also suggest you get a discreet car hire firm to drive them and their luggage up to Liverpool. One look at your Rolls Royces and Bentleys will completely give the game away,' Anthony advised.

'You're right. What about David Partridge?'

'I'll book a state room for him too, but he could go directly by train from London and meet up with them on board. Would you like me to telephone your mother and tell her all this? She's always been accustomed to first class everything, all the way, hasn't she, and she might refuse to go from Liverpool if you tell her?'

'Don't worry, old chap. It's something I have to do. They're going to have to get their skates on, though. They haven't got long for packing up a lifetime, have they?'

After he'd said goodbye and hung up Nicolas remained at his desk, looking sadly out of the window at the beauty of the land-scape he owned, thanks to his mother. Since 1893 it had been farmed and run on professional lines so that it had prospered over the years but he'd never forgotten that it had been Conceptia's money that had saved the family from ruin and he wished profoundly that things had been different between them. By favouring Ewan she'd deprived him of affection, and his letters written from Eton, pleading with her to write to him, had gone unanswered. At Christmas she'd got a servant to go out and buy his present, but she'd gone to Hamleys herself to select the perfect gift for Ewan. Sometimes she'd forgotten Nicolas's birthday altogether, and he once overheard her lady's maid, Miss Maxwell, asking if she ought to go to the village shop to buy him some sweets.

He knew things would have been different if his father had lived, but now he rose from his desk, refusing to let himself wallow in self-pity. He just hoped Conceptia would have the grace to bid him a cordial final farewell.

For the next few days there was a secret but frenzied undercurrent of activity in the house as Miss Maxwell, and Pippin the valet, packed Conceptia's and Ewan's clothes and personal possessions as well as their own things. They'd been told her ladyship needed a rest after the distress of Posy's remains being discovered and she was planning to take Ewan away 'for a holiday' in America. When asked how long they'd be away the answer was given that it would be for 'around six months or so' and she'd need clothes for every possible occasion. The grounds staff at Buckland were kept completely in the dark and knew nothing about the proposed trip, while the indoor staff were sworn to secrecy, in order, they were told, 'to prevent the newspapers finding out and printing more lies about the family'.

'Anyone found gossiping will be dismissed immediately,' Nicolas informed them grimly.

What no one knew, except for Nicolas, Cathryn and Hugh, was that the ship was leaving from the Liverpool docks and that to reach it they'd have to drive through seven counties across England, a journey of well over 500 miles.

Anthony having booked their passages to America, it was left to Hugh to make the final arrangements for their departure.

'They should leave Buckland at five o'clock in the morning in order to get on board and settle down for the night in their state rooms,' he told Nicolas.

'What time does the *Belgenland* set sail?'

'Ten o'clock the next morning. I'll inform Miss Maxwell and

Pippin of the arrangements if you could tell your mother and Ewan.'

Nicolas grimaced, dreading the moment. 'I'd better do it after dinner the night before they leave.'

'That's tomorrow night,' Hugh reminded him.

'My God, so it is.'

'When are you seeing Mr Russell?'

'I'm going to telephone him after they've actually set sail and make an appointment to see him one day next week. That will make him think I'm ready to play it his way. I just hope to God he agrees with my proposal. At least Mother and Ewan will be well out of harm's way by then.'

'I believe ten thousand pounds in cash and arranging for him to get Alan back from Germany should do the trick.'

'The boy had better behave himself if he stays at the King's Arms though. I can promise never to reveal he's a sodomite, but there may be others who will be only too glad to report him to the police.'

'Tell Mr Russell that, Nicolas, so if someone does go to the police he'll know it wasn't you. Personally I think they should move to where no one knows them at all. You'll only feel really safe if they're out of this county.'

Conceptia clasped her hand over her mouth, trying to silence her wrenching sobs. To leave Buckland was the most agonizing thing she'd ever had to do in her whole life. It was worse than facing the death of someone close. She felt as if her heart had been stamped on repeatedly and might at any moment break and stop beating altogether.

As she roamed the large echoing rooms at night when everyone else had gone to bed, she realized there wasn't a square inch that didn't hold memories for her, going back to her first visit, when William's mother had invited her to stay for a ball in 1892. The second time had been when she'd arrived as a bride, a twenty-year-old girl of great beauty and great wealth, with a dazzling future.

She'd made up her mind then that she'd never leave Buckland again and when she did it would be feet first in her coffin. She loved it with a passion as if it were a living, breathing person.

During the early days of her marriage her weekend house parties became legendary and her summer garden parties were the stuff of fairy tales, where guests could sit in rose-covered arbours, listening to a philharmonic orchestra playing Strauss waltzes whilst drinking champagne spouting from fountains. Even after William's death she continued to hold court to Those Who Mattered, which included members of the royal family.

The day it all went wrong was the day Ewan shot Posy Burgess.

The tears streamed down her gaunt cheeks now and her hands shook as she surveyed her collection of jewellery. Each magnificent piece lay in its own velvet-lined leather case. What was she going to do? How could she take it all with her? But how could she bear to leave any of it behind?

Rising, she walked slowly and painfully to one of her *armoires* and took out two large shoe bags made of soft fabric. Then she started casting the leather cases aside as she tipped the contents straight into the bags. Rings, bracelets, brooches and necklaces were mixed up higgledy-piggledy with her ropes of white pearls and black pearls and her gold chains and lockets. With regret she was forced to leave her three magnificent tiaras behind because they were too bulky, so she left them in their cases and wrote a memo to herself to tell Nicolas that she forbade Cathryn to wear them and that they were not to be sold either, but hand delivered to her when she was settled.

Then she placed the two heavy bags in her dressing case, which she would keep with her day and night until she arrived at her cousin's house in Chicago.

Not once during the long days of sorting out what she would take and what she would have to leave behind did it occur to her that she was actually having to leave behind what should have been her most precious thing of all: her eldest son.

Ewan, taking a last nostalgic look around his old nursery, went over to the bookcase, his eyes scanning the stories of his childhood. *The Tale of Peter Rabbit. The Wind in the Willows. The Jungle Book.* His fingers trailed along the familiar spines, remembering his mother reading them to him. A ditty started throbbing through his head. Te-tump, te-tump, te-tumpety tump! Te-tump, te-tump . . . he searched his brain trying to remember the words. How did it go?

If you go down to the woods today/You're sure of a big surprise . . .

He suddenly bent double as a spear of ice plummeted down through his stomach, tearing at his guts, leaving him gasping for air. A moment later he vomited violently onto the floor. You killed someone. You killed someone. You killed someone. His brain fought desperately to stop the voice hammering in his head. You took a life. You took a life. You took a *life!* The voice was screaming now. Murderer! Murderer! *Murderer!*

He staggered down the stairs, clutching the banister for support, and managed to get to his bedroom before he started retching again. Then he slumped down on to the floor into unconsciousness in the foetal position.

'Are you all right, m'lord?' Pippin spoke anxiously, when, an hour later, he found Ewan lying rigidly on his back, staring up at the ceiling.

Ewan didn't answer.

The valet came closer, noting his white face and blank expression. 'Is there anything I can get you, m'lord?'

'No.'

'A glass of water, perhaps? Maybe you've eaten something that has upset you?' he asked carefully, noting the vomit on the floor.

'No.' Ewan continued to stare with apathy at the ceiling.

'I've finished your packing, m'lord. And I've laid out your clothes for dinner tonight.' Pippin tried to hide his panic. How were they going to travel if his lordship didn't buck up? Ewan appeared catatonic and withdrawn, almost as if he were in a waking stupor. Perhaps, Pippin reflected hopefully, his lordship is depressed at the thought of travelling. He himself was looking forward to visiting America. Couldn't wait to set off in the morning. Come to think of it, though, his lordship never went anywhere, so maybe he was just dreading the journey.

'Ewan, where's Mother?' Nicolas asked, as he mixed the cocktails before dinner that night.

Standing stiffly with his back to the fire, Ewan gazed ahead with dull eyes and a blank expression as if he hadn't heard.

'Ewan? Is Mother coming down soon?'

'I don't know. I don't think so,' Ewan replied in a flat voice.

Cathryn felt disappointed for Nicolas's sake. Privately she felt immensely relieved that her in-laws were no longer going to be living at Buckland but she knew this was a very painful moment for him. Their presence had the effect of poisoning the atmosphere and she knew she could never be really happy while they were around, but this last dinner together was nevertheless going to be an emotional occasion.

'Can't you have a word with her, Ewan?' Nicolas asked, looking crestfallen. 'Do try to persuade her to come down. We're having her favourite dishes and some very fine wine and it is the last time we'll all be together.'

Ewan shrugged. 'She doesn't want to see anyone.'

Cathryn looked at him curiously. He seemed so detached and withdrawn tonight. No doubt he was depressed at having to leave Buckland. The magnificent and historic old house had wrapped its magic around even her though she'd been unhappy at times, but for someone who'd been born here it was obviously an appalling wrench to have to leave it for good.

Cathryn could also see Nicolas was struggling to control his emotions. She was very aware that if it hadn't been for Ewan, none of this would be happening. Stepping forward, knowing she was pushing her luck, she nevertheless spoke gently but firmly.

'Ewan, I can understand how unhappy your Mama must be, but Nicolas does so want us all to part on good terms, and as he's ordered this special dinner, just for the four of us, I'm sure you could persuade her to come down? Couldn't you help your brother on this one last occasion by getting your mother to join us?'

'She wouldn't listen,' he retorted stiffly, without looking at her.

With a bound Nicolas strode over and put his arms around his brother in a bear hug. 'It's all right, old chap,' he said quietly.

'No it's not. It's all my fault. I'm sorry . . . I'm so sorry for everything, Nick.'

Nicolas held him firmly by the shoulders and looked into his brother's face with deep compassion. 'You were only ten, for God's sake! Mama and David should have told the truth then and there, and then none of this would have happened.'

'Did I really murder a child?' His eyes were glazed and blank. Te-tump, te-tump. 'I can't get it out of my head.'

Cathryn slipped out of the room. She felt it was important that they should have these final few minutes in private, to lay to rest the ghosts that had haunted the family for so long. Realizing she had nothing to lose now she hurried up the stairs and tapped briskly on Conceptia's door.

A faint voice spoke. 'Come in.'

Cathryn walked into the private sitting room and there was her mother-in-law sitting at her desk, sorting out papers. She was already dressed in a black travelling suit and for once wore no jewellery. She turned sharply to look at Cathryn and spoke coldly. 'Well?'

'I know you don't like me,' Cathryn began in a matter-of-fact voice, 'but I'm asking you to reconsider joining us for dinner, because Ewan is terribly upset. Nicolas has ordered a special dinner in your honour and it would mean the world to him to have you there.'

Conceptia paused before answering. 'You say Ewan is very upset?'

Cathryn nodded. 'I think he's making himself ill because of what's happened.'

'I'm in my travelling clothes because I didn't intend to go to bed tonight. I want to savour every last moment of being here.'

'You look very elegant and it's just a family dinner,' Cathryn persisted carefully. Then she walked slowly to the door and opened it, standing to one side as if waiting for Conceptia to go through first.

Conceptia rose slowly. 'I suppose I'd better come down then. I don't want Ewan getting upset again and blaming himself for everything.'

'Exactly,' Cathryn agreed softly.

A moment later the older woman swept regally ahead of Cathryn, heading for the stairs.

The brothers were sitting close together near the fire when the two women entered the drawing room together a few minutes later. Nicolas looked at Cathryn and the gratitude in his eyes almost made her want to weep.

'Mama! Can I make you your favourite champagne cocktail?' he asked, jumping to his feet.

'Yes, please.' Her manner was brisk but she sounded pleased as

she took a seat next to Ewan, who made no move to acknow-
ledge her late arrival.

The next morning Buckland Place was shrouded in icy mist and
it was still dark when Nicolas and Cathryn went down to wait
in the hall for Conceptia and Ewan's departure. The three hired
cars had arrived a few minutes earlier and already Wills and four
footmen were loading the luggage into the second and third cars;
Miss Maxwell would sit with the chauffeur in one, followed by
Pippin in the other.

Nicolas kept looking at his wristwatch. 'I hope the fog clears,'
he muttered. 'Perhaps they should have gone to Liverpool by
train.'

'I'm sure it will clear as soon as it's daylight,' Cathryn said reassuringly.

At that moment they heard footsteps and looking up saw
Conceptia coming very slowly down the stairs for the last time.
Over her dark suit she wore a magnificent sable coat and a small
black hat with a veil. In one hand she carried her handbag and
in the other her heavy dressing case, refusing to let Miss Maxwell,
who was following, take it from her.

Nicolas stepped forward, arms outstretched. 'Mama,' he said
warmly.

Conceptia walked straight past without looking at him. 'Not
in front of the servants,' she snapped coldly, heading across the
hall to the front door. A moment later she was swallowed up in
the darkness as she disappeared in the direction of the waiting
car where Wills stood ready to see her into it.

Deflated, Nicolas dropped his arms to his side as he looked
out into the darkness after her. She hadn't even said goodbye.

Ewan had reached the bottom of the stairs now and it looked
as if he were sleepwalking.

'Take care of yourself, old chap,' Nicolas said, giving him a
hug. Cathryn reached up to kiss him on the cheek. Not responding
to either of them, Ewan moved as in a trance as he walked towards
the door.

'Goodbye,' they called after him. 'Have a safe journey.'

The three cars had their engines running now, purring in the
misty darkness, blazing headlights spearing the gravel drive and

the grass beyond. Nicolas and Cathryn stood on the front steps watching and waving as the first car drew slowly away. Ewan was looking away but they could see Conceptia's pale profile as she looked straight ahead. Then Miss Maxwell followed in the second car, waving from her seat beside the driver, while in the third car Pippin gave a cheery little salute as the convoy headed off down the drive, having no idea that he'd probably never return to Buckland again.

'Is Ewan all right?' Cathryn asked anxiously, as they turned back into the hall.

'I think his moment of repentance has finally hit him,' Nicolas replied. His expression was grave, as if his face had been carved in granite. 'He has to make reparation for what he did before he can begin to find peace of mind.'

'Yes, I can see that.'

'I'm going to go for a ride.'

'But it's still pitch dark.'

'By the time I've changed and got Septre saddled up it will be dawn.' Then he turned to her and she almost winced when she saw the pain in his eyes. 'You do understand, don't you, darling?'

'Perfectly,' she whispered. 'I'll see you when you get back.'

Lying once again in the warm softness of their four-poster bed, she felt as if a great shadow that had pressed down on her for the past few months had dissolved. The in-laws had gone. Nicolas would sort out Mr Russell. The newspapers would probably never mention them again for the rest of their lives. The nightmare was over and she had a feeling the police would drop the case of Posy Burgess's death now. A great wave of contentment swept over her as she slipped into a deep, relaxed sleep.

It was nearly ten o'clock when Nicolas, windblown and exhausted, clattered into the stable yard. Dismounting, he handed Septre's reins to one of the grooms, and walked round to the front of the house. All his anguish was spent now and with a sense of serenity he hadn't felt for a long time, he strolled in through the front door, ready to order a large breakfast.

At that moment Wills broke away from a group of footmen he'd been talking to, and seeing Nicolas across the hall, came swiftly on his short thick legs, his face scarlet, his eyes popping with a wild but dazed look.

'M'lord,' he gasped as if breathless. 'Someone has called to see you. I told them to wait in the library. I didn't know when you'd be back.'

'Who is it, Wills?'

But the butler had already charged ahead to open the library door. Nicolas paused, clapping his hands to his wind-chilled cheeks. Something was wrong. Terribly wrong. The atmosphere was charged with a fearful tension. Even the clutch of footmen hovering in a corner as if waiting for something to happen looked at him strangely, their eyes agog, their mouths gaping.

Eighteen

NEW TWIST IN TROUBLED ABINGDON FAMILY

It is rumoured there has been a falling out in the troubled family of the Marquess of Abingdon, according to a reliable source in the village of Appledore. It seems his mother, the Dowager Marchioness, is planning to leave Buckland Place in the near future to return to her native America. It is thought that she and her new daughter-in-law, the former debutante Cathryn Brocklehurst, did not agree about the running of the large estate. It is not known if her younger son, Lord Ewan Hillier, will accompany her or not . . .

The Daily Express, February 30th, 1931

The parlour maid tapped on Cathryn's bedroom door with her early morning tea.

Awaking with a start, she sat up in bed, realizing she'd overslept. 'What time is it?' she asked, as the maid set the tray on her bedside table.

'It's just after ten o'clock, m'lady. I didn't want to disturb you earlier, because I know you were up at five o'clock to see her ladyship and Lord Ewan off on their trip.'

'Thank you.' Cathryn lay back against the pillows, reflecting that Conceptia and Ewan would be four and a half hours into their journey and probably somewhere between Berkshire and Oxfordshire. 'Has my husband returned from his ride?'

'I believe he has, m'lady.' The maid paused and blushed with embarrassment as she withdrew from under her arm a folded copy of *The Daily Express*. 'I took the liberty of bringing this up for you. I thought you'd want to see it.'

With dread Cathryn unfolded the paper and looked at the front page. 'New twist in troubled Abingdon family . . . ?' she began reading aloud. 'What is this? What are they talking about?'

'I don't know m'lady, and we've all been ever so careful not to mention that the dowager and Lord Ewan were going on holiday, like his lordship told us.' She looked slightly scared, as if fearing the staff were going to be blamed.

'There's been absolutely no falling out between us,' Cathryn protested, as if she were talking to herself. She put down the paper irritably. 'Fleet Street seem to take pleasure in writing anything they like whether it's true or not, just in order to sell more copies.'

'Yes, m'lady. Would you like me to run your bath for you?'

'Yes, please.' Nicolas, she thought as she climbed out of bed, was going to be furious when he saw this article. The whole point of the departure being kept secret was so that he could negotiate with Mr Russell, whilst Conceptia and Ewan were supposedly still at Buckland. Now the whole of England was being made aware that the dowager and her son were about to leave the country.

Nicolas took a deep breath, bracing himself for whatever lay beyond the open door of the library. Then he hurried forward, his heart pounding uncomfortably. Once inside the room he stopped in his tracks, surprised to see a young woman in her early thirties rising from a chair by the central round table. It was not at all what he'd expected.

She was tall and slender, with dark hair cut fashionably short. Well dressed in a navy blue coat and a white hat with a small brim, she had a pleasant face and she was smiling diffidently at him.

Nicolas looked at her blankly. 'Good morning. Can I help you?' he asked politely.

'I hope I can help you,' she replied. Her well-modulated voice was educated and her dark eyes were searching his face as if she expected some kind of reaction.

He frowned. 'I'm sorry, Wills never gave me your name?'

'I'm Posy. Posy Burgess,' she said quietly.

Nicolas felt his head spin and his legs go suddenly weak. 'What do you mean, you're Posy Burgess?' he demanded almost angrily, his frown deepening. 'How dare you come here, posing as that poor child! What are you after?'

She looked contrite. 'I'm sorry. I didn't mean to give you a shock, but I really am Posy. It wasn't me Ewan shot with your air rifle.'

Cathryn, coming down the stairs with the newspaper in her hand, was met by Wills in the hall.

'His lordship has returned from his ride, m'lady,' he informed her as if he were bursting to say more.

'Yes, I know. Where is he?'

Wills lowered his voice conspiratorially. 'He's in the library, m'lady. When he got back there was someone waiting to see him. They're in there now.'

'Who is it?'

Without answering he signalled for one of the footmen to open the library door for her to enter. Feeling uneasy, she stepped forward to find Nicolas with a smart-looking young woman. They were standing facing each other.

'Oh! Hello.' She looked at Nicolas questioningly.

He put his arm around her shoulders, his expression still stunned.

'You'd better sit down, darling. Let's all sit down,' he suggested in a strained voice.

Cathryn looked at the young woman with suspicion, suddenly fearing this was a female from Nicolas's past. With a feeling of sick dread she seated herself in an upright chair, while Nicolas and the woman sat facing her.

'What is it? What's going on?' she asked sharply.

Nicolas reached out and gripped her hand reassuringly. 'It's all right, darling. There's nothing to worry about. This is Posy Burgess, Cathryn.'

It was as if a shot of adrenalin had been injected straight into her blood stream. She became alert with shock, her mind refusing to accept this new turn of events.

'Posy Burgess?' she repeated incredulously.

The woman clasped her hands in front of her. 'I apologize for giving you both such a shock but I really am Posy Burgess,' she said earnestly. 'I should have written first, but I thought you'd be relieved to find out I wasn't dead after all. And I wanted to apologize to Nicolas in person for the terrible time he's had since that little girl's remains were found.'

'Why have you waited until now to come here?' Cathryn asked, torn between anger and astonishment. 'Whose remains were they if they weren't yours? What about your poor mother and father?' she added in bewilderment. 'They've grieved for you for over twenty years. We had a funeral for you a few weeks ago, and my husband has given them a gravestone, and now Ida's so ill . . .' Her voice broke with indignation and emotion.

'I can explain everything,' Posy said before Nicolas had a chance to speak. 'I suppose I'm not surprised you don't believe me but it is the truth. I'd stupidly hoped my return would be a relief to you all but I should have let you know first. I've just come from Canterbury General Hospital and my mother's better. Her speech is beginning to come back and now I'm here she's assured that I really am alive and well.'

Cathryn frowned, remembering Frank saying all he could make out of Ida's babble were the words 'here soon'. Could she have been trying to tell them that she *expected* Posy?

Nicolas sounded immensely tired as he spoke. 'I think you'd better tell us everything because I have to say we've all been to hell and back since your . . . I mean since the remains of a child were found. It's shattered Ida and Frank, and it's torn my family apart, too.'

'That's right,' Cathryn said, laying *The Daily Express* on the table. 'This article appeared this morning and it's mostly lies, but we've had to put up with this sort of sensationalism for the last three months.'

'Oh, my God!' Nicolas exclaimed, grabbing the newspaper and scanning the piece. 'How the hell did this get out?'

Ignoring what he was saying, Posy continued fervently, 'I promise you I didn't know what was happening here. I've been living in Italy for the past twenty years. I'm married to an Italian man and we live in the depths of the country. We never get English newspapers.'

'You speak Italian?'

'Yes, I do. Fluently now.'

'So how did you find out what was happening?'

'Bartolomeo and I went to Florence for a few days and got talking to some English people who were staying in the same hotel. They were discussing the story and said it had caused a big scandal in England. As I listened I realized . . . Oh!' She covered her face with her hands for a moment. 'It was a terrible shock to hear them discussing how I'd been murdered! I couldn't believe it at first. After all these years everyone was talking about Posy Burgess and how she'd been killed. Bartolomeo also realized it was me they were discussing and I just . . . I just wanted to run away once again. I'd tried to escape my past for twenty years – and here it was – in the headlines!' She shook her head in distress and her bottom lip quivered. 'That's when I decided I must return to England and put things right.'

'When was this? When did you find out about your . . . about the child's murder?' Nicolas asked.

'Two weeks ago.'

Cathryn raised her eyebrows, still not sure that this woman and her motives for coming to see them were genuine. 'Only two weeks ago? When the remains were discovered three months ago? That seems a long time for a scandal of this magnitude to go unnoticed, even if you do live in the country?'

Posy looked pained. 'We're far from the nearest town. All our friends are Italians, so why would I buy an English newspaper? I never wanted to think about England again,' she added passionately, gesticulating with her hands.

Cathryn nodded grudgingly, starting to believe this young woman was genuine. The last few months had stripped her of her girlish innocence and naïvety and these days there were few people she trusted.

'We're going around in circles here,' Nicolas complained. 'Why don't you begin at the beginning, Posy? What happened to you on that fatal day in 1909?'

Posy gazed into the middle distance as she looked out of the window, remembering the day as if it had been yesterday. 'My mother worked in the laundry here and she brought me to work because she didn't want to leave me alone at home.' Then she turned and spoke hesitatingly as she looked at Nicolas. 'You didn't know it but I often went into the garden to watch you and Ewan playing. You never saw me because I always hid when you looked in my direction, but I liked to imagine we were friends. Playmates, having games of hide-and-seek and grandmother's footsteps.' Her voice faltered and she looked down at her hands, suddenly blinking hard. 'I so desperately wanted to be like the two of you and to be friends with you. I longed to sleep in a proper bed and have food on the table so I wouldn't be permanently hungry. I longed to have the sort of toys you had, too, and dogs and ponies. Most of all I wanted to live in a house that didn't smell of damp and had an indoor lavatory.' She paused, remembering lying in a little truckle bed, a coat of her father's laid over her to keep her warm in the winter. 'I made up stories in my head that I'd be a fine lady one day and wear silk dresses and have big hats with flowers on the brim, like your mother.'

The room was silent except for the awkward shuffling of Nicolas's feet as he realized for the first time how luxurious his childhood must have seemed to a deprived child of nine. Cathryn's expression softened, thinking how she'd taken her own happy home life for granted when she'd been small. The thought revived her fear of appearing like a Lady Bountiful now, and looking down she covered her left hand with her other hand to hide her large engagement ring.

'On that day in November,' Posy continued, 'I decided to go into the garden in the hope of seeing you both. I couldn't find you at first so I went further into the woods than I'd intended. Then I suddenly saw Ewan. He was on his own, which was unusual, and he was carrying your rifle. I'd often watched you target practise but never Ewan. I followed him for a few minutes and then he suddenly stopped and raised the rifle. I remember peering to see which tree the target was nailed to and then I saw this little gypsy girl bending down gathering sticks. She was dark-haired like me, and shabbily dressed like me, and now I realize Ewan thought it *was* me.' Posy turned to look out of the window again, her eyes wide as if she could still see what had happened. 'Ewan took aim,' she explained, 'but I never expected him to fire. Then suddenly there was this terribly loud bang! All the birds flew up into the air, squawking and screeching and circling around. I was terrified. Then I saw the child had dropped to the ground. There was a second bang. It seemed louder than the first and I very nearly screamed with fright. When I realized she wasn't going to get up . . . Oh! It was terrible. Ewan seemed to realize at the same moment that he'd killed her and he just threw down the rifle and started running in my direction.'

Posy was breathing heavily now, reliving the moment of blind panic. 'He looked crazed with fear. I dropped down into the bracken so he wouldn't see me. I feared if he knew I'd seen him shoot her, he'd kill me next, to shut me up.'

She clasped her hand over her mouth; her eyes were tightly shut.

'Are you all right?' Cathryn asked in concern.

Nicolas rose to his feet. 'Would you like a glass of water? Or a brandy?'

Posy shook her head, but her face was pale and her eyes had a haunted look, knowing the memory of that awful day would be forever imprinted on her mind.

'My one aim was to get away, as far away as possible,' she said, her hands clasped together once again. 'Once Ewan had disappeared in the direction of the house I started running. I ran and ran, I don't know for how long. I didn't even know where I was.' Her voice was so low they could barely hear her now. 'I was shivering and cold and I'd wet myself. And I was frantic with fear. What was going to happen to me? Would Ewan come after me when he knew it wasn't me he'd shot? I imagined all sorts of terrible things happening to me. I wanted my Ma, but I was much too scared to go home. Anyway I was lost by then.'

'What happened to you?' Cathryn asked, appalled.

'I slept in an empty barn that night and the next morning I was walking along the road when a well-dressed lady in a horse-drawn carriage stopped to talk to me. She asked me who I was, and of course I lied. I said my name was Daisy and my parents were dead and my grandmother had just died and I'd nowhere to go.'

'I wish you'd come home and told us,' Nicolas said sadly. 'We'd have looked after you and kept you safe.'

'I don't think your mother would have approved of that,' Posy observed intuitively.

Cathryn caught Posy's eye and for the first time they exchanged a slight smile of understanding. Posy might only have been nine when she'd run away but she'd obviously been aware, even then, what Conceptia was like.

'So what happened?' Nicolas asked.

'This lady, Mrs Lelia Fitzhammond was her name, was very

elegant and she told me she lived in Italy and was only in England for a few days to collect some things. We talked for a little while and then she suddenly offered to take me back to Italy with her. She promised me a real bed and a room of my own, and all the food I wanted. She said she had no children of her own but that I'd become her daughter and she'd buy me lovely clothes and dolls and she'd turn me into a real lady.'

'And did she?' Cathryn asked, thinking this sounded an unlikely fairy tale.

'Yes.' Posy's face cleared and her eyes shone with enthusiasm. 'She gave me everything I'd ever dreamed of. She loved me and cared for me and made sure I had a good education. Sometimes I felt very bad about having lied to her, but by then I had become Daisy Fitzhammond with what seemed like the world at my feet. I also felt bad at having left my own mum and dad without telling them . . .' she hesitated and looked at Nicolas. 'Frank told me yesterday he wasn't my real dad.'

'I know. You're my half sister,' Nicolas acknowledged quietly.

'Yes.' Her smile was shy. 'But I simply couldn't resist the marvellous chances Mrs Fitzhammond offered me. Somehow, I don't know how, she got me a passport and whisked me to her beautiful villa just outside Rome, and that became my home. I intended to come back when I was grown up but then I fell in love with Bartolomeo Casati when I was eighteen and England and all this . . .' she gestured with her hands again in a continental manner, 'all this seemed so far away. It was another life. One I never really wanted to think about again.'

'Until you met these English people in your hotel in Florence?'

'That's right. I felt very guilty then. I thought about my poor mum and dad and when my own children were born I realized for the first time how dreadfully they must have suffered when I disappeared.'

'It broke their hearts,' Cathryn told her. 'If only you'd gone home after you saw Ewan shooting that child, it would have saved everyone so much pain.'

Posy looked upset. 'I realize that now. When I heard that at one point the police thought Nicolas was guilty of killing me, then I really had to return and put things right. For everyone's sake. So I wrote to Mum to say I was alive and well and to ask for her forgiveness, and to tell her I'd be arriving towards the end of February.'

Nicolas looked at her in surprise. 'Did your mother ever get your letter?'

'Dad told me last night that he'd found it only two days ago. Apparently Mum went sort of mad when she read it. Threw things around the room and had a sort of fit, I think. That's what a friend who'd dropped in to see her said anyway. No one knew she'd had my letter and it had accidentally fallen behind the draining board. He thinks that Ma had read it and it gave her such a shock it brought on a stroke. The doctor says she's going to be all right though. I've told her everything. They've both forgiven me but I so wish things had been different,' she added sadly. 'From now on I'm going to have to make it up to them, for all the years of my life they've missed.'

'So . . . !' Nicolas leaned back in his chair, his head spinning as he tried to take in this extraordinary turn of events. 'Ewan shot a gypsy child thinking it was you? What happens now?'

'Whatever you like,' she said in a small voice. 'I think I should go to the police and admit I'm still alive. They're then going to ask if I know whose body was found, and I can say I don't know, or I can tell them the truth. Dad told me the gypsies had fled the night the little girl went missing and God knows where they'll be now.'

Nicolas nodded regretfully. 'They were no doubt afraid to admit their daughter was missing because the police had ordered them off our land weeks before and they'd been threatened with prison if they didn't go.'

'Who found the remains after all these years?' Posy asked curiously.

'My foresters found them when they were clearing a part of the woods in order to replant some young saplings.'

'So the body had lain there all these years without being discovered?'

'That part had become very overgrown with fallen branches and brambles,' he replied lightly, avoiding Cathryn's gaze. 'Posy, will you tell the police that Ewan was guilty of the shooting?'

She straightened her back, more composed now she'd finished her tale. 'I've been thinking a great deal about that,' she said.

'There isn't much point, is there? After twenty years?' he suggested, trying to keep the anxiety out of his voice.

Cathryn could feel the tension building in the room. She could tell Nicolas wasn't going to take Posy into his confidence, and she could understand why. Was she to be trusted? That was the question. She'd admitted lying to her benefactor to get what she wanted and as 'Daisy, née Fitzhammond' she was still living a lie. How could they be sure she wasn't going to blackmail the Abingdon family, or sell her astounding story to the rags for a large fee?

All this was going through Cathryn's head as she observed Posy considering the question while Nicolas watched her apprehensively.

She paused a moment longer and then said, 'I don't believe anything would be gained by telling the police now. What would be the point? He was only a little boy at the time and he probably didn't know what he was doing.'

Nicolas nodded. 'That's true. Ewan knows he killed a child and he's certainly paying the price right now for what he did.'

'You'll tell the police you're still alive though?' Cathryn asked.

'Yes. I'll admit I ran away and that I've been living abroad ever since. Anyway I'll soon be back in Italy, and I'm taking Mum and Dad with me as soon as she's better. We have a big house surrounded by our vineyard, and I want them to come and live with us.' She looked into Nicolas's eyes, remembering the handsome boy she'd once trailed after in the woods when she'd been a child. 'They've had to do without their only daughter for all these years, but at least they will be with their three grandchildren in future.'

'Does Mrs Fitzhammond know your real identity?'

'No, she died of cancer seven years ago and she never knew. She'd have been very angry if she'd found out and I think she'd have sent me back to my parents. Bartolomeo understood my reasons when I told him who I really was, though. He'd been very poor as a child, too. He's a wonderful man and I'm very lucky to be married to him. I must go now. I promised Mum I'd spend the day with her but can I see Ewan before I go?' she asked, gathering up her gloves and handbag before rising to leave.

'I'm afraid Ewan and my mother are away at the moment.

This newspaper suggests they haven't left yet but I'm afraid they have, though not for the reasons given here,' Nicolas replied, keeping his voice light. 'I'll tell him you're safe and well though, next time I see him.'

The three of them came out of the library together, scattering the gossiping footmen like scared rabbits. Nicolas was thanking Posy for coming to see them while Cathryn tried to gather her confused thoughts together and come to terms with what seemed like a strange dream.

It was inconceivable that after all the weeks of hell they'd been through that Posy Burgess was alive after all.

On the doorstep Nicolas shook her hand, 'Goodbye, Posy, or should I say Daisy? Our father would have been very proud to see you now,' he added warmly. 'He always wanted a daughter and it was very brave of you to come here today.'

'I hope you'll forgive me for all the terrible trouble I've caused you all,' she said earnestly, shaking Cathryn's hand.

'Sometimes circumstances overtake us all and then it's a case of the survival of the fittest,' Cathryn replied, smiling. 'I'm so glad you're well and happy now you have a family of your own.'

Saying goodbye, Posy climbed into her waiting taxi and Cathryn and Nicolas stood on the front steps watching her go. They both knew this wasn't the end of the affair. The newspapers would somehow learn about Posy's existence and it would be blazed in banner headlines the breadth and length of Fleet Street. At least the cloud of suspicion Nicolas had suffered under would be lifted and the others would soon be in America, where Ewan could start a new life. As for Mr Russell, the revelation of today would take the wind out of his sails. Ewan couldn't be accused of murdering a young woman who was still alive and well.

Nicolas clutched Cathryn's hands. 'Let's get going on our own trip,' he said firmly.

She looked up at him in surprise. 'Where to?'

'Where do you think? Tyndrum of course. We haven't had a proper honeymoon yet.'

Nineteen

THE COURT CIRCULAR

The Marquess and Marchioness of Abingdon have announced the birth of a son on March 3rd 1932, at 15, Eaton Square, SW1.
                                            The Times, March 5th, 1932

The six-week-old Lord Philip William Nicolas Hillier lay in Cathryn's arms, resplendent in the satin and lace Abingdon family christening robe, as the congregation grouped themselves around the font at St Peter's Church, Eaton Square. Bursting with pride, Nicolas regarded his sleeping son and heir with a kind of wonder. That he and Cathryn had produced such a beautiful baby made him thank God that they'd come through the worst start any marriage could suffer.

Cathryn turned to smile at him, knowing what he was thinking, knowing also that her parents, standing just behind her, had never thought she'd survive the nightmare of those first three months.

Across the font she looked at Philip's godparents, all friends who had stood by them while the Fleet Street pack had mocked and tried to tear the family apart. Maighread Simmonds, elegant in cream silk and a hat trimmed with bird of paradise feathers; Charles Brocklehurst, a very proud uncle; and Anthony Warner, who now handled all Nicolas's business affairs: friends and family who had supported them, and who were now about to make a solemn vow to protect their son from evil in the years ahead.

After the ceremony they and all their other friends would be going back to their house across the road for a champagne reception, but this was the moment Cathryn would never forget. Standing with Nicolas by her side and Philip in her arms, and thanking God that they all had a future now.